ENLIGHTENED IGNORANCE

ENLIGHTENED IGNORANCE

OPUS X™ BOOK FOUR

MICHAEL ANDERLE

DISRUPTIVE IMAGINATION

THE ENLIGHTENED IGNORANCE TEAM

Thanks to the JIT Readers

Debi Sateren
Jeff Eaton
John Ashmore
Deb Mader
Misty Roa
Dorothy Lloyd
Dave Hicks
Jeff Goode
Peter Manis
Larry Omans
Paul Westman
Lori Hendricks

If I've missed anyone, please let me know!

Editor
Lynne Stiegler

To Family, Friends and
Those Who Love
to Read.
May We All Enjoy Grace
to Live the Life We Are
Called.

CHAPTER ONE

April 27, 2229, Neo Southern California Metroplex, Aurum Sphere Ball Stadium

Erik's wide grin was one of the few in the sea of glum humanity choking the main arena's long tunnel. The sphere-ball fans marched out like a defeated army, many with their heads down. The occasional red-faced man or woman muttered angrily, their stomping joining the shuffling footfalls of so many others.

Jia's gaze slid toward Erik, suspicion clouding her dark eyes. "You're not a traitor, are you, Erik?"

He chuckled, his eyes sliding toward his annoyed partner. "What are you talking about?"

"All loyal Dragon fans know what we just saw," she insisted, nodding behind them. "But you're acting like we played a *great* game."

"The team won." Erik shrugged. "I don't see the big deal, but I'm smiling about something else." He nodded toward where they had been sitting. "It's just a weird thought I had during the game, and now that we're leaving, it came back."

Jia's brow wrinkled. "Weird thought? Like what?" She wasn't sure she should stop pursuing her mental accusation toward her partner yet.

"I never thought about it much," Erik began, "but it's the antigrav tech. You can't *play* sphere ball without antigrav tech."

"True enough." Jia glanced at the area of play. "I'm sure there is all sorts of interesting sociology and psychology related to the Purist movement to explain how physical sports have lingered and haven't been taken over by virtual sports, but it helps to see people doing something entertaining and impressive in real life. In this case, the tech enhances rather than distracts. If you want to read an interesting book on the history of sphere ball, there's one I finished the other night I could recommend. It's called *Sphere of Destiny.*"

Erik shook his head. "No, thanks. Not interested in the history. It's the tech that's got me thinking. I know humans were halfway to inventing it anyway, but everything I've read says the key parts were figured out by reverse-engineering Navigator tech. It's not as awe-inspiring as HTPs and FTL travel, so no one cares."

"Yes, so?" Jia blinked a few times, more confused than before. She slipped past one fan who'd two or three alcoholic drinks too many to pay attention to her smaller body as he wandered along with the herd. "I'm not following you."

Erik's smile disappeared when a rowdy fan yelled right beside the two of them, and both winced.

A moment later, the fan took off after two of his friends

who were whooping ahead of them, and Erik's smile returned. "Think about it. The Navigators are dust now, probably for a million years, if the scientists are right. We and the other races took their stuff and spread out across the galaxy. The Navigators might have even wanted something like that, but did you ever think they were sitting around saying, 'Man, I really hope some other race finds our crap a million years from now, so they can make up new sports?'"

Jia's confusion melted off her face, and a soft smile replaced it. "Oh, I understand your question now. Um, who knows? Sphere ball is a thinking person's sport. I'm sure an intelligent, advanced species such as the Navigators would appreciate it if they were still around." She shook her finger. "Perhaps they wanted us to develop zero-G sports instead of spread across the stars." Her smile faded. "But today, we could have ruined their legacy by losing."

Erik laughed. "I doubt the Navigators are weeping in the afterlife because the Dragons almost lost a match. They're not the only sphere ball team in the UTC, and for all we know, aliens play sphere ball, too. Besides, almost losing is just another way of saying they almost won."

"We only won because that Calgary wing turned idiot toward the end." Jia glared over her shoulder, despite the opposing player being nowhere in sight. "If it weren't for that, we'd be out of the semifinals already." She sighed, turning back to him. "Don't you get it, Erik? We *squeaked* through the quarterfinals, and now we've *squeaked* through the semifinals. The team needs to trend up going into the finals, not down. Otherwise, they won't have a prayer of making it to the Earth League Championship, let alone the UTC finals. I think I'm wondering what all the fans are wondering."

"What's that?"

"We're all asking ourselves the same question: what would have happened if Shin hadn't gotten suspended?"

Erik stopped himself from laughing in Jia's face. He enjoyed sphere ball, but she took it to obsessive levels. While that didn't make her unusual in Neo SoCal, it amused him. He remained mindful that a little too much mirth might also attract an unnecessary confrontation with a drunken opposing fan looking for a revenge outlet.

"The Dragons either win or they don't," he offered. "If they don't make it this year, there's always next year. It's not the end of the world if they don't go to the championship."

"I suppose." Jia stepped to the side as a sniffling man advanced, his tears marring his green and gold face paint. "It gives me something to look forward to, but again, *Shin*." She rolled her eyes.

Erik slowed. The crowd thickened as they approached the end of the tunnel and the elevators for different parking levels. Jia would be fine once they got away from the stadium, and she could dive back into obsessing over stats and fantasy matchups.

"The league had no choice but to suspend him." Erik couldn't stop a loud laugh this time. "That idiot tried to import a restricted animal to Earth. Did he really think he was going to get away with it?"

Jia sighed. "Did you see the interview with him? I

believe him when he said he thought it would help the team." She shook her head. "That's just sad."

The crowd began to thin in one direction but remained dense in others. Erik and Jia followed the natural flow toward fewer people. The Lady might have smiled on them and given them a cluster of people who had parked on a different platform.

"Yeah." Erik shook his head, the smile growing again. "I don't think he understands that the genetic engineering allowed in Venusian luck rabbits has nothing to do with actual luck. Hard to say, though. That's athletes for you."

"What do you mean?" Jia asked. "I haven't read anything to suggest athletes import illegal animals more often than other people."

"I'm not talking about that. I'm talking about athletes being superstitious. Shin should have stuck to wearing the same socks through the finals or eating the same breakfast, but he was taking it to a new level. At least it was only a luck rabbit. Imagine if he'd tried to bring in something like a heliokite or a ruster." Erik snickered. "Not that they would last long on Earth."

The crowd abruptly cleared and the pair stopped, now acutely aware of the unusual situation. It wasn't the Lady serving up convenient foot traffic that explained why they'd had an easy time advancing through the tunnels. Instead, three red-faced men who stank of beer were responsible.

The drunks lingered in front of the elevators, glaring at anyone who dared look their way. A few droplets of blood stained the ground. Had there already been an altercation?

Erik turned to Jia. "Emma can call Security, in case someone hasn't already, or they haven't noticed. We should keep it calm until Security arrives."

He wasn't worried about being able to take the men down, but fights near crowds were always dangerous.

The two of them looked around.

The lack of nearby security guards surprised him, but given the sour mood of the fans, several incidents might have occurred all over the stadium complex. They might have underestimated the need for security, as well. Compared to some sports, sphere ball fans, especially on Earth, tended to cause less trouble at home games. "Less" wasn't the same thing as none, however. And there was another small, more personal motivation.

"But we're the police," Jia insisted, eyes narrowing. "We don't have to be afraid of them, even if we don't have our firearms."

Even though they were cops, because of recent changes, there were annoying procedures associated with bringing their weapons into the game off-duty, so they left them in MX 60. Security scanners would detect any illicit weapons, and the nearby on-duty police could respond in minutes.

"Not talking about fear." Erik spoke softly to her. "I'm talking about reports. I don't want to have to spend the rest of my day off filling out reports because of some drunks. We'll miss our appointment, too. I thought you were looking forward to it."

Jia's mouth formed an O as she nodded. "It doesn't have to turn into a terrible situation. We'll just scare them off by showing a little authority."

She looked relaxed. There was no hint of unnecessary bloodlust on her face. Erik had wondered when she'd reduced her visits to the counselor, but she'd had plenty of opportunities to lose control both on- and off-duty in recent weeks, and she'd had no trouble.

"Let's hope it goes that easily, but get ready to fill out reports." Erik advanced toward the trio. "Excuse me, guys, but you're blocking the elevator." He gestured toward it. "Let's move along. A lot of people need to get home."

The broad-shouldered and thickly muscled drunks were larger than the average fan, but Erik wasn't a small man either. Their physical presence had little effect on him.

One of the drunks, a dark-haired man with a scowl deeper than the others', hocked a gob of spit at Erik's feet. "The Dragons are going down because we don't support them enough. People like you. I saw your cocky-ass smile all the way back there. Go back to Alberta, you damned Calgary-lover. We only want Dragons fans in Neo SoCal."

"Nah. I'm a Dragons fan." Erik cracked his knuckles. "And before you do anything stupid, you need to under-stand something important." He gestured to Jia. "We're cops. We don't want to arrest you, so the easiest solution would be for you and your buddies to get in the elevator and head back to your flitters. Go home and sleep it off. Remember, our team is still in it, even without Shin."

"Security is coming," Emma reported directly into Erik's and Jia's ears. "They'll arrive in a few minutes."

The dark-haired drunk nodded to his friends before snarling at Erik, "Sometimes you just got to get rid of the anger." He took a few steps forward, his face twisting into a hateful sneer. "You're no cop, and the last guy who told me to get moving got a broken nose out of it. We're not messing with anyone who's not messing with us. We're real peaceful guys."

His friends chuckled.

"You're blocking an elevator and scaring people." Erik let a taunting smile take over his face. "And you just admitted you assaulted someone. But this doesn't have to be rough if you cooperate, or you can just walk away and not cause more trouble."

He wasn't worried about them getting away with assault. Security would likely inform the local EZ about the assault and had already sent over the footage. The drunks could be arrested without anyone in the crowd or Erik's free time being at risk. The men didn't appear to be armed, but he couldn't be sure.

The confrontation attracted more people to fill in the gaps in the crowd. Several of them watched with curious or uneasy expressions.

"Sir, you're drunk," Jia interjected. "If you don't want to be arrested, you should go to your flitter and let it fly you home. I understand you're upset. We all are, but even without Shin, it's not like the season is *over*. We can still get to the finals, and then we'll be laughing at the other teams."

Erik wasn't sure she believed what she was saying, but she delivered her suggestion with a strong conviction in her voice. Commiseration might yet save them from the dreaded reports.

"Screw Shin," the drunk snapped. "And screw you, fake cops. I work hard every day at my company. I do what I'm supposed to do, and when I decide to relax a little and come to the game, I expect some relief. That means I want a good game."

Erik grunted. "It *was* a good game, and our team won. It'd be boring if they wiped the floor with the other teams. I prefer things to be a little closer. A balanced league is a more entertaining league."

The drunk's nostrils flared. "What did you say? You're saying you wanted the Dragons to lose?"

Jia took a deep breath and shook her head. "You clearly understood his intent. You don't have to cause trouble."

"Maybe I want to." He took another step forward but stopped when Erik squared his shoulders and blocked his path. "You better get going, fake cop," the drunk growled. "This is your last warning before I take out my frustration on you."

Erik stepped back with an easy smile on his face. "You don't get it. I was mostly trying to save myself trouble, but you already admitted to hitting someone. I was thinking about letting Security and the local cops handle it, but now that I've thought about it, that seems lazy. And you're not just being stubborn, you're being an idiot."

The other two drunks stomped toward him, vicious grins growing on their faces. Jia muttered under her breath as she walked forward.

"I'm going to enjoy beating your arrogant ass down," the dark-haired drunk bellowed. He brought his fist back.

Erik didn't give the man time to punch him. He slammed his forehead into the man's nose. The drunk's head snapped back and he stumbled into his friends, blood pouring from his nose.

"You broke my nose!" the drunk shouted. "How could you do that?"

A collective groan swept the crowd.

Erik shrugged. "I figured you needed a little reminder of what it felt like. Maybe next time, you won't start a fight so easily."

"I'm going to pound your face in," the drunk roared as his friends gave him a helpful shove to help him stand straight again.

He charged Erik.

The other two men moved forward but stopped when Jia moved toward them. When one of the men threw a wide hook at her, she rotated and slid under the blow but used the momentum to spin and start raising her fist. She launched her fist, connecting with the large man's chin with a loud thud. He staggered backward, gritting his teeth, his eyes watering.

The spectators gasped at the blow.

Erik didn't mind the audience, but their presence meant he and Jia would need to keep the drunks focused on them.

The dark-haired drunk continued his attempts to pummel his opponent, but Erik's easy dodging ensured the blood being spread was from the drunk's nose. The man obviously lacked hand-to-hand training, and the alcohol didn't help.

His moves were slow and obvious since his eyes telegraphed them. Erik let the man continue to throw punches. Every new attempt would tire the drunk out, allowing Erik to finish the fight without breaking anything more than the man's nose.

Jia took advantage of her off-balance initial target to close on the third man. He tried a few jabs, but she slapped them away. A palm strike to his face put him off-balance, and she followed with a solid roundhouse kick to the side of his head. The crowd let out another loud collective groan as the man spun around before collapsing to the ground.

Erik glanced over quickly and chuckled. The fans might have come to the stadium to watch a rough sport, but most of them had probably never seen a fight in person.

It was a free after-game show.

The other drunk recovered from Jia's earlier uppercut with a groan and staggered forward, shouting, "You'll pay for that." He followed with a Mandarin aspersion on Jia's mother.

She didn't look mad, just unimpressed as she rolled her eyes. She moved toward him and let him throw a punch, then grabbed his arm and bent it back. With the armlock in place and his head already forward, she flicked her arm out. Her elbow strike found an easy target, and he yelped in pain.

Jia twisted his arm and spun away from him. She stomped his knee, then followed him to the ground, maintaining her lock. He whimpered, tears running down his cheeks.

Sweat poured down the face of the remaining drunk, dripping to the ground to join the blood. Erik threw up his left arm to block the man's next attack. He enjoyed the surprise on his face as his flesh and bone impacted with Erik's metal arm, flesh-covered though it was.

It was time to finish things. Erik slammed a fist into the

man's stomach, and the drunk fell to his knees. "Wait for it," Erik told him, his arm pulled back. "Yeah, that's the ticket."

Erik's fist rocked forward, knocking his opponent out cold.

The crowd parted as dark-uniformed men with stun rods advanced.

Erik pulled out his badge from a pocket. "NSCPD."

The security guards stopped and frowned at the badge. After surveying the situation for a few seconds, they tucked their stun rods back into their belts.

One of the guards stepped forward. "I didn't realize we had any plainclothes cops here." He looked at the other guards. They all shrugged, looking apologetic.

"We're not on duty." Erik inclined his head toward Jia. "We're just Dragon fans. We tried to get these guys to move along, but it turns out, they had caused trouble before we even got here."

The guard's eyes widened. "Hey, I recognize you."

Jia sighed and shook out her hand as she looked around. She spoke toward Erik. "So much for being report-free, but I suppose we lost that the second those drunks swung at us."

Erik smiled at the guard. "Hey, can you keep our names out of it, at least for today?"

The guard looked confused. "You don't want people to know you stopped some drunks?"

"We'll have to do statements and reports. It's supposed to be our day off, and we've got an appointment later."

The man chuckled. "I feel you, brother. We'll have to

submit something to the local cops, but we'll just tell them it's taking us a while. At least they won't bother you today."

"Thanks. I owe you one." Erik took one last look at the downed men. "Some people just don't know when to quit." He looked at Jia. "And we still have time for our appointment."

CHAPTER TWO

Jia crept out from behind the dark-masked terrorist.

He stood near the entrance to the top passenger deck. Erik trailed right behind her. It didn't matter if the terrorist was nothing more than flimflam, a mix of nanites and light; her heart still pounded in her chest.

Train like it was reality, and it'd pay off at the right time.

He might turn at any second, and Erik and Jia would lose their chance at surprise. There was no way they could triumph in the scenario without maintaining surprise. She glanced around, her eyes back to watching the terrorist in no more than the time it would take to blink twice. Clearing out bad guys was easy, but not every confrontation was so straightforward.

Is this what normal people do on their days off? she thought.

As the terrorist grunted and turned, she slammed the butt of her rifle into the back of his head. He collapsed to the ground, his eyes rolling up.

"Nice," Erik whispered. "I was wondering if you would do that, or if I'd need to tell you."

"If we start shooting, they'll know we're here. We need to save that for the last moment." She shrugged and gave Erik a playful grin. "And you knocked out the last one. It's my turn."

He gave her a nod after checking the downed man.

Jia moved toward the closed door and crouched, setting her back against the wall. She took a deep breath. Erik had been right; they had been able to make their appointment at the tactical center with plenty of time, although she hadn't worried much about that. They spent so much money implementing Emma's custom scenarios, she wouldn't have been surprised if the tactical center kicked someone out to accommodate Erik and Jia.

Assaulting simulated terrorists and criminals had become a weekly date.

She tried to stop thinking of it that way, especially since Erik *never* referred to their training sessions as dates, but her mind was harder to direct than her body.

There wasn't any romance; they spent all their time practicing shooting simulated people or each other. However, it was something they both looked forward to, even if Erik hadn't said anything to suggest he viewed their training as anything other than battlefield preparation.

With all the trouble they ran into, Jia was grateful for it and annoyed the department's TPST had refused to let them use the police facilities. They might all be on the same side against criminals, but that didn't end internal political turf wars.

Corruption might be eating away of the roots of society, but petty bureaucracy was almost as poisonous.

For all the exasperation, that wasn't her concern. She

would focus on true corruption and crime. A couple of cops, no matter how dedicated, couldn't fix all of society's ills.

Jia glanced at Erik. He stood with his back flattened against the wall, his rifle looking small compared to the TR-7 he normally carried.

"Ready?" he whispered. Despite his quiet tone, Emma's aid and a link to Jia's PNIU made his question clear.

Jia nodded and stood. She was always ready to take out threats.

"Three, two, one," Erik counted. He slammed his palm on the access panel and the door slid open. Ready for terrorist guards, he spun around the wall to face into the simulated passenger deck of the short-haul transport, quickly moving slightly left.

Jia followed Erik and aimed right. No terrorists opened fire. Only rows of empty seats split by two aisles confronted them. It was empty other than one unfortunate sight. A suited man lay face-down in one of the aisles, a small hole in his back. Blood stained the back of his jacket.

"Slowly," Erik advised, his eyes narrowed. "It could be a trap."

Jia offered a quick nod. The tall seatbacks provided plenty of cover for hidden terrorists, and complacency killed.

Erik nodded toward one aisle and crept into it, sweeping his gun back and forth. Jia took the other aisle, alert for unexplained shadows or unusual noises. Both detectives continued forward, their movements slow and deliberate until Erik arrived at the body.

He knelt, keeping his gun ready. "Dead hostage. Not a trick."

Emma didn't add any commentary. Jia wasn't sure if her being quiet was good training or not. In most situations, they had her assistance, but perhaps even a cutting-edge AI had trouble not offering spoilers on her own custom-designed scenarios.

Erik stood. "Let's finish the sweep."

Jia followed, creeping forward and turning to check the rear of the cabin every few seconds. Erik might have suggested the scenario type, but Emma had programmed it.

They had both declared it a tubular assault, a special training scenario that normally involved a narrow vehicle setting, and often hostages. Erik had been involved in more than a few tubular antiterrorist operations in his career, but Jia's recent experience had mostly involved buildings. Even the narrow tunnels of the Scar didn't present the same tactical variables.

"They're probably watching the elevator and the stairs," Jia suggested. "And we've got no visibility on the hostages. They might have cams on us." She thought back. "Emma's briefing wasn't clear on that."

"It's not as if gun goblins generally announce their capabilities to you," the AI offered cheerfully, breaking her silence. "And yes, if I'm with you, that means the situation will be far easier because of my impressive suite of abilities. However, you can't always assume I'll be able to hack a system quickly enough to minimize casualties. Even as wonderful as I am, I have my limits. Proper training needs to include that, don't you think, Detective Lin?"

"Not disagreeing," she answered, looking behind them. "I just want to take it into account in our current situation."

"There are only two passenger decks." Erik gestured with his rifle toward the man on the floor. "And one body. The briefing clearly stated there are fifty passengers. There's plenty of space to fit them on the other deck, or they might even have them in the cargo bay."

"They're on the other deck," Jia insisted. "It'd be harder to control them in the cargo bay, and while the terrorists might have more places to hide, they'd also have more places to watch."

"Agreed." Erik's gaze dipped to the floor. "Which means they're right below us."

"Simultaneous breach?" Jia suggested. She pointed to emergency hatches at the far ends of the aisle before patting a small, notched black disk on her belt. The breaching disk would be able to get through the emergency hatches without too much trouble. "Too bad we don't carry these more often."

Erik chuckled. "We're detectives. We shouldn't *need* this kind of thing."

She harrumphed. "Says the man who has both a slug-thrower with four barrels and a heavy laser rifle. Maybe you could ask your own personal Generous Gao for something like these." Jia tapped the breaching disk. "But you're right—it's funny that I don't even think of this kind of training as unusual anymore. What about the plan, though?"

"We don't want to risk letting them get behind us." Erik frowned and glanced up his aisle. "I'll hit the forward emergency hatch. You should go to the farthest one. It's near where we came in. I'll draw their attention, then you can sneak up behind them and waste their asses. We can stay in the same aisles and close on them from either side."

"Sounds good." Jia turned toward the back of the craft, moving toward their entry point. "I'll get in position."

"Keep it slow and steady." Erik inclined his head to the floor. "We start charging around, they'll likely hear, and we can't be sure they don't have roving guards."

Jia offered a final smile before disappearing toward the back of the transport.

Strange training for a detective? Maybe, but given how many terrorists she'd run into in the last year, special training wasn't just a good idea—it was a necessity. Jia exited the cabin and entered a small passage through a staff storage area that brought her to another emergency hatch.

She crouched by the hatch and spoke through the communicator. "I'm in position, Erik."

"Good," Erik's reply came back. "Prepare to breach."

Jia pulled the disk off her belt. She slipped her fingers between the notches and twisted, priming the device, then placed it on the center of the hatch and stepped away. It only needed a final PNIU signal.

"I've put the disk in position," she reported.

"Give me a five-second head start. I'm activating mine in three, two, *one.*"

A pop reverberated through the plane. The crack of gunfire followed.

Jia counted in her head before tapping her PNIU. The disk exploded in a bright white flash, and the hatch and the surrounding deck disintegrated. She didn't wait for the smoke to clear before launching herself feet-first through the smoldering hole. Gunfire and screams continued to ring out from below.

She landed with a grunt and a loud thud. Three masked terrorists charged her way. She fired in rapid succession, aiming high and at an angle to avoid any bullets passing through the criminals and hitting a hostage. The terrorists dropped to the ground, new holes in their heads.

It was almost too easy. The fact that it wasn't real didn't matter. Jia had died more than a few times in Emma's simulations.

Jia got up before sprinting forward. The door to the second passenger deck was already open. Terrorists boiled out shoulder to shoulder. She couldn't get a good upward trajectory from her position, so she settled on high chest shots and the hope that the passengers were keeping their heads down. It took only a few seconds for the terrorists' bodies to block the doorway. Another terrorist attempted to leap over his fallen comrades, but a bullet ripped through his throat from behind. He tumbled into the growing pile.

With stealth no longer a consideration, Jia rushed into the passenger section and jumped over the bodies. Erik stood near the front with a cocky grin on his face. Dead terrorists littered the aisles, their rifles nearby. Cowering people filled the seats, leaning forward with their hands on the top of their heads.

Jia almost slung her weapon over her shoulder but stopped. Instead, she ejected her magazine and reloaded. A tubular assault was a tactical situation with particular parameters, but this wasn't just a tubular assault.

It was a hostage rescue.

"Sweep for any hidden terrorists?" she whispered.

"Yeah." Erik nodded. "Let's go."

"Everything will be all right, ladies and gentlemen," Jia announced. "We're with the police."

Erik and Jia moved toward each other from across the transport, remaining in their aisles and keeping their weapons ready but not pointed at the hostages. They did keep them low enough to take a shot if needed. The passengers kept whimpering, and Jia questioned if Emma wasn't pushing things too far.

Jia cleared the first fourth of the passengers with no incident. People started to relax once Erik and Jia had advanced through the bulk of the seats and reached the center.

A man jerked upright and grabbed a woman next to him, putting a gun to her head. "Drop your gun or I'll blow her brains—"

Jia put a round between his eyes without hesitation. His gun slipped from his fingers and he collapsed to his seat, leaving a confused, blinking hostage.

Standing had been his mistake. It was easy to shoot someone standing without risk to other passengers when they were all seated.

Jia didn't relax. She waited for another ambush or another hostage as Erik closed their pincer sweep.

"That was pretty ballsy," he observed with a grin.

"If I'd hesitated, he might have shot her anyway." Jia frowned. "And if I dropped my gun, he would have shot me."

Erik nodded. "Agreed. It's a good way to get both you *and* the hostage killed. Can't trust terrorists. And you've learned to take the shot when you need to without letting it eat you up."

The scared passengers vanished, along with the passenger cabin, replaced by the wide, open silver-floored white room of the tactical center.

Jia glanced down at the rifle in her hands. It might be fake, but its heft made it feel real.

"Maybe," she mused. "No matter how realistic Emma makes these, I always know in the back of my mind they aren't real. It helps, but it's hard to say what will happen if I'm in the same situation in real life."

"Doesn't matter, and you've already saved hostages from terrorists." Erik shouldered his rifle. "Muscle memory is everything. A half-second improvement in reaction might save someone's life, including yours, mine, or a hostage's."

Jia laughed and shook her head.

Erik looked confused. "What's so funny?"

"Most cops, including TPST, don't spend their days off beating up drunken thugs or practicing tubular assaults," she explained with a shrug. "But not only do we do this stuff, it's even..."

"What?"

Jia looked away. "*Fun,*" she admitted.

Erik nodded, a grin replacing the confusion on his face. "That's because most cops are boring. Besides, things have been slow at work for the last few weeks. If anything, we should be spending more time doing this kind of training, not less."

Jia glanced down at her PNIU as it chimed with a message.

Erik frowned. "You too?"

She tapped her device to send the message to her smart lenses. "It's from the captain. He wants us in his office first thing tomorrow. Should we call him?"

Erik shook his head. "If he doesn't want us there right now, it can wait. It's probably just reports about the idiot stadium drunks."

She nodded and turned to head toward the exit. "That would be nice. I might as well enjoy the last few hours of my day off."

CHAPTER THREE

Erik and Jia stood in front of Captain Ragnar's desk.

Unlike most days, the captain wore his black and blue dress uniform. That outfit usually smelled like political trouble, the one type of problem Erik couldn't solve with extra firepower. At least not yet.

There was always hope for the future.

"We're here, Captain," he opened, Jia was standing quiet this time. "I haven't even had my beignet yet. What's the big deal?"

"Public relations." Captain Ragnar's smile was too broad, even for a man who normally rode the line between relaxed and grinning fool.

"Public relations?" Jia interjected, already wanting clarification. "What's that mean, exactly? If it's about the stadium thing, we'll get the reports to the other EZ by the end of the day."

Captain Ragnar shook his head. "I'm not concerned about that. This is something different. The department's PR reps are buried by requests for interviews with you two. Most of the media organizations understand that if they want something official, they'll need to go through the proper channels, and you've both been rather direct in telling me to back off you being involved in talking with them." He tugged his collar. "I just got done talking to a reporter, Kayla Moon, who works for Silver Eyes News. I trust you're familiar with them?"

Jia folded her arms. "They're a big deal."

"Yes, they are."

Erik frowned. "So what? We're supposed to bend over because some big news corporation is breathing down our necks?"

Jia snorted. "It gets worse."

He looked at her. "How?"

She frowned. "They're a subdivision of Ceres Galactic."

Erik shook his head. His partner researched the *oddest* things at times, but he had to admit, knowing what media outlets might be biased against them was useful. He didn't pay attention to that kind of thing outside of his trail to the conspiracy behind Molino.

Captain Ragnar nodded slowly. "That they are." He pointed at Jia, then Erik. "The reporter wants to do a profile on the two of you as part of a series of *Heroes of NSC*, and the higher-ups think it's a good move and have made it very, *very* clear they want your involvement. With the NSCPD anticorruption efforts very intense, it's good publicity to splash the faces of the two cops most directly associated with those efforts in the public eye." He smiled, "I happen to agree with them."

Jia sighed. "But what if it's a hatchet job? Maybe this is Ceres' way of getting back at us. They have us do an interview and edit it to make us look like bloodthirsty psychopaths."

Erik nodded. "Yeah, the reporter might just be looking for some dirt. If we look bad, it calls all the anticorruption efforts into question."

Captain Ragnar chuckled. "Maybe, and if we duck the easy offers, we risk looking even more suspicious. I trust your discretion, and you should trust me that I wouldn't be asking this if I thought it was a trap."

Erik continued, "And what if we say something that offends someone higher up? If they want a real interview, we'll give them a real interview, not some glossed-over PR crap."

"I'll handle any fallout." Captain Ragnar gestured to his uniform. "And don't worry so much. I've already talked to the woman. Unless she's the greatest actress in the UTC, I don't think this is going to be that hard. As far as I know you don't have any pressing cases, so I'd like you to meet her for an interview in your office after lunch."

Jia lowered her arms, resignation creeping onto her face. "Don't we need dress uniforms, too?"

"No. You're detectives on the front line, dealing with trouble. Your suits will be fine. It'll be more authentic."

Erik rolled his shoulders. "I'm wondering if Silver Eyes didn't play you all. If you're going to cover our asses, fine, but I want to be one hundred percent clear that I'm not going to hold back."

Jia thought for a moment, considering what she knew. While she would follow Erik blindly onto a battlefield, she needed to make sure he wasn't leaping without her full tactical review. She couldn't find anything to warn him about before nodding. "Neither will I."

Captain Ragnar's smile didn't waver. "You do what you need to do, and I'll do what I need to do to cover for you."

"You just want me here?" Erik asked from his desk chair.

The reporter, Kayla Moon, nodded quickly, a bright, infectious smile on her face. He'd been expecting a hard-faced grizzled veteran, but the dark-haired woman looked like she'd barely graduated college. The tight thigh-high skirt and plunging neckline of her white top only chipped away at the careful professional image, but she might have been trying to take them off-guard.

Three small camera drones whirred around the room, stopping at different positions before continuing on.

Kayla tilted her head. "Understood. Yup." Her support staff was halfway across the metroplex, leaving Erik and Jia to watch a one-sided conversation for most of the last ten minutes. "Do we need them to turn up the lights? Oh, it's more authentic? Gotcha. Thanks!"

She dropped into a chair they'd brought in a few minutes ago and crossed her long, slender legs. Her chair sat positioned against the wall between the two desks.

Jia cleared her throat. "Is it going to take much longer to get set up? No offense, but we don't want this to take all day."

"No, no, no." Kayla waved her hands in front of her face. "Just try to ignore the cameras. They just needed to get a feel for the space. I want to thank you for agreeing to this." She leaned forward. "I'm going to be honest with you; this is my first big interview. I hope you'll be kind."

Erik offered his best relaxed grin. "You're the reporter. I think we have more to fear from you. I'm sure a lot of reporters are out there looking for some big scoop concerning the Obsidian Detective and Lady Justice."

Jia shot him a quick look but didn't say anything.

Kayla giggled. Erik raised an eyebrow. There was taking people off-guard, and then there was giggling in an interview.

"That's a good question to start with," she noted. "How do you two feel about those nicknames?" She turned to Erik. "You first, Detective Blackwell."

He began to suspect this wasn't a brilliant blindside attack by Ceres Galactic but probing the potential enemy wouldn't hurt.

Time to provide a target.

"I've been called a lot worse," Erik replied. He leaned back in his chair and relaxed his shoulders. "Especially during my time in the military."

Kayla nodded slowly, a drone camera hovering in front of her. "I'm sure you have. You don't think it's cool? I mean, you are the first detective to enter the police force using that law in a long time. Even without everything else you've accomplished, that would be impressive in and of itself."

"I don't worry about things like that. I wanted to be a

cop, and I took advantage of my background. Nothing more, nothing less."

Kayla's head snapped toward Jia, undisguised glee on her face. "And what about you, Detective Lin? It's not like you came in under the Lady Justice Act."

Jia put a fist to her mouth and fake-coughed, her cheeks slightly red. "All I'm concerned about is doing my job. I can't help what other people call me, and as long as it represents something positive, I can't say I have much to complain about. I hope most citizens view the police as dedicated to justice."

Kayla bobbed her head with excitement. "Exactly. You're a big role model now, and most people wouldn't become a police officer with a family background like yours. You might be making it look glamorous, but being a cop normally isn't."

Jia smiled, although Erik could see the slight tension at the corners of her eyes.

"We have officers from a variety of backgrounds in the NSCPD," she explained. "I don't think mine's the most unusual, and there have been a lot of outreach efforts to recruit from diverse backgrounds."

"Of course, of course," Kayla murmured before turning back to Erik. The drones reoriented themselves. "Detective Blackwell, you're a handsome man."

Jia's eyes widened.

Erik maintained his smile. "Some people claim that. Like Jia, I'm not going to complain about it."

She eyed him. "Are you familiar with the site *Studs in Uniform?*"

"I can't say I am." Erik scratched his cheek, grinning.

"You were recently voted among the top ten studs in uniform in North America." Kayla tapped her PNIU. An article with pictures of Erik both gray-haired before his de-aging in an Army uniform and a more youthful recent image with him in an NSCPD dress uniform popped up.

Erik eyed them, mirth in his eyes as he laughed. "Those are pretty good pictures. They used my good side and everything."

Jia put a hand over her mouth and fake-coughed again.

Kayla winked. "According to the polls, people are divided on whether you looked better more *seasoned* or the way you do now."

Jia lowered her hand. "'More seasoned?'" Her mouth twitched.

"Yes. What do you have to say about that, Detective Blackwell? You're not just a symbol of justice. You're a sex symbol too."

Erik couldn't hold in anymore. He burst out laughing.

Kayla giggled. "The polls don't lie. How does it feel to be a sex symbol? To be considered in the same bracket as some of the top actors, singers, and athletes out there?"

He brought his laughter down to a mere snicker. "I'm not going to complain if people like what they see, but I'm just a man doing his job, same as when I was in the Army." He shot a glance at Jia. Her face might as well have been stone at that point.

"Sure, sure. A lot of humility there. Many people would say that makes you sexier." Kayla licked her lips. "I'm sure your fans appreciate you taking your new fame in stride. It's hard not to notice you're not married. I did a little digging, and as far as I can tell, you're not even seeing anyone right now."

Erik shrugged. "I spent most of my Army career going from one colony to another on the far frontier. It's hard to maintain a good relationship when you're twenty light-years away from your significant other and even messages can take weeks or months to arrive."

"But now you're on Earth now. That kind of thing *shouldn't* be a problem." A smidge of desperation flavored Kayla's voice.

"I've been busy adapting to life back on Earth and doing my job. Trust me, I'm waiting for the right opportunity and woman."

"Ah." Hunger shone in Kayla's eyes. "So you're saying there's a chance for hopeful people out there?"

"Maybe. It's a hard thing to date a cop. It's one thing to look good in a uniform, but there are downsides."

"Such as?" Kayla stared at him.

"It's a dangerous line of work," Jia offered.

Kayla blinked and turned her way. "You think so?"

Annoyance flashed in Jia's eyes. "There's a lot of insta-bility under the civilized surface—hardened criminals, antisocials, and terrorists. Although Earth's a *very* safe place to live, that's only because the police and military are doing what they can against those who would threaten what we've built here. Most citizens are shielded from that reality, but that doesn't make it any less true."

"I see." Kayla nodded slowly. Her gaze flicked between Erik and Jia before stopping on the latter. "What about you, Detective Lin?"

She raised an eyebrow. "What about me?"

"Is there a special someone in your life?"

Jia's jaw tightened. "Not currently. I've dated, but I'm like any other woman. Not every relationship works out, and that's before the added pressures of dating a police officer."

"Are you aware that you're also popular on the net?" Kayla asked, almost puppy-like enthusiasm in her eyes and voice. "There are more than a few people calling you 'Detective Diaochan.'"

Erik let out a quiet chuckle. He'd merely been placed in the top ten of recent North American studs, but Jia had managed to be compared to one of the ancient Four Beauties of China.

Jia sighed and shook her head. "I think I prefer 'Lady Justice,' but just for the record, unlike Diaochan, I'm *pretty sure* the Moon's not going to turn away in embarrassment."

Unless Ceres Galactic had some hidden plan to undermine them by attacking their dating history, Kayla's line of questioning wasn't dangerous. It was a good reminder for Erik that despite the tentacles of corporations like Ceres, the average employee of the company or any of their subsidiaries only cared about doing their jobs.

He'd all but handed her a neon sign daring her to ask him about his service and the incident on Molino, and she'd pivoted away from that with not a hint of interest. This interview defined soft-news fluff. He found that relaxing. His partner's slight frown suggested she didn't.

"What kind of traits are you looking for in a man?" Kayla asked.

Jia pursed her lips. "I would really rather not discuss my personal life."

Kayla looked disappointed and nodded. "Fair enough. The message that you're still available will make a lot of people out there super-happy, but if we're not talking about your significant others, maybe we can talk about what you two do when the suits are off and the guns are packed up. What do the Obsidian Detective and Lady Justice do to relax on their days off?"

"We're both Dragons fans," Erik offered. "Although given what's been happening, I don't know if that's relaxing."

Erik and Kayla shared a laugh.

Jia's rolled her shoulders, a smile finally breaking through. "Let me tell you about the tiny trees he plays with."

Kayla nodded. "Oh, before we go into that. I have another question for Detective Blackwell."

"What?" Erik asked.

"We had a little contest on our site. Readers and viewers got to vote on a question." Kayla's grin reminded Erik of a shark's. "What color underwear do you wear?"

Erik blinked. "Uh…" He stopped, mouth pursed, brows almost touching.

Jia smirked as she watched him, waiting for him to answer.

Soft news could strike deeply.

CHAPTER FOUR

May 2, 2229, Neo Southern California Metroplex, Dance Club Third Wind

The loud music shook Jia's bones.

She danced near the edge of the crowd, colorful holographic displays of different colony worlds swirling overhead. Their link to the current song remained elusive, but it was a nice high-tempo tour of the UTC. It'd been too long since she last went dancing. Life couldn't always be tubular assaults and terrorists.

This is nice, she thought.

Jia wiped the sweat off her brow. The best air conditioning on the planet didn't matter when hundreds of bodies were packed into one tight location, dancing and writhing against each other. She took a deep breath and headed toward a table where her friends Imogen and Chinara sat, sipping drinks.

Imogen waved, her blonde curls bouncing with the movement. She nodded toward a dark glass. "We went ahead and ordered you a drink since you wanted to stay on the floor for a few more minutes. Look at you, Jia! Lady officer *on the move.*"

"It was one of my favorite songs," Jia explained. She sat and tugged the hem of her dress down. "And it's been too long since we've had a girl's night out. I don't want to regret anything come morning. I'm not sure about the next time I'll be able to get together with you two like this."

Chinara took a sip of her drink, amusement dancing in her dark eyes. "It's only been a while because you've been busy saving the metroplex, and we've been busy with our men." She winced. "Sorry. Maybe I should haven't said that, considering…" She sighed.

Jia smiled. "It's okay. I enjoyed my time with Corbin, but it wasn't meant to be. It wasn't a messy break-up or anything. We both were fine going our own way, and I'm glad everything is going okay still for you two. I'm happy with my life right now, and I want my friends to be happy with theirs."

Imogen gulped some of her drink, her cheeks red both from dancing and alcohol. "It doesn't matter. You've got that interview out now. It's all but screaming for you to get a man."

Jia scrubbed a hand over her face. "You saw it?"

"Heroes of Justice!" shouted Chinara and Imogen together. They laughed as Jia sat there eyeing them.

"My captain made me do it." Jia sighed. "I thought it was going to be about the job, not my love life, and…*ugh.*" She rolled her eyes.

"Your partner's a pretty open guy." Imogen laughed.

"Now it's hard not to imagine him in his underwear. I swear that reporter wanted to jump him right there. She was doing everything but drooling on him and offering to lick up the mess."

"She *was* unprofessional." Jia made a face of disgust. "I can't believe she asked that question."

"You should have volunteered your own answer." Imogen tapped the table with her fist. "Stake your claim for the future."

"Stake my claim?" Jia stared at her friend, not liking where the conversation was heading. "You're way drunker than I thought if you think I would ever answer a question like that. I don't need half the planet talking about my underwear. I'm a policewoman, not a fashion model."

"Even if it'd help you get a new guy?" Imogen fluttered her light lashes.

"I don't *need* a new boyfriend. I'm fine being single, and I have my dignity to consider."

Chinara rested her elbow on the table and her cheek on the palm of her hand. "Can I be honest with you, Jia?"

"Always." Jia picked up her drink and took a sip. Fruity notes overwhelmed the minimal alcohol in the drink. Her friends didn't realize how much her tolerance had increased since gaining Erik as a partner but bringing that up now would only feed into the mess.

"I never wanted to say it before, but Corbin was a little boring." Chinara averted her eyes with an embarrassed look.

Imogen snickered. "A little? He was *super*-boring. He was the Prime Minister of the Boring Kingdom."

Jia frowned. "Hey. Every time I asked you about him, you said he fit me."

"Well, uhhh…" Imogen shrugged, giving her an apologetic smile. "*He did.*"

Jia set her drink down and folded her arms. A small smile played along her lips, not that her friends didn't see the predator's eyes staring at them. "So, you're saying I'm boring?"

Imogen and Chinara exchanged sheepish looks.

Jia tapped her foot, eyebrow raised, waiting for them to confess. "Well?"

A few attractive men walked past the table. They turned and smiled, but upon seeing Jia and the face she was delivering to her friends, hurried on their way.

They weren't ready for a hard target.

Imogen shrugged, neither she nor Chinara noticing what Jia had seen out of the corner of her eyes as the men walked on. "Not boring. Sure, you're not me, but that doesn't make you boring either. You're just…*controlled.*" She nodded, her mouth twitching, obviously trying to hold back a laugh.

"Sorry, Jia," Chinara offered. "It's not that we're judging you. You're our friend; we love you for who you are, and we want to help you find the right kind of man. What works for Imogen won't work for me, and what works for me won't work for you. That's all we're saying."

Imogen jerked upright. "I'm a total idiot. Why didn't I see it before? I've got the perfect solution. Forget staking your claim for the future. It's time to start mining that gold now!"

Jia shuddered, pulling back just a little and cocking her

head to stare at her friend. "Why do I feel like I should be afraid?"

"No, no, hear me out." Imogen flung an arm in the direction of the dance floor. "You're going about this the wrong way. We're not going to find you the right kind of man at some random dance club, especially not for a woman with your needs."

"My needs?" she answered. "I'm not here to find a man. This was supposed to be a girls' night out with my friends." Jia looked at Chinara for support, but her other friend now watched Imogen with obvious interest.

Oh, no. Jia eyed her other friend. *You too?*

"Can cops date each other?" Imogen asked. She rubbed her hands together and licked her lips. "Do they have official rules against it? Because if it's just something they shouldn't do because of tradition, you're already blowing tradition up with your career."

There it was.

Jia blinked several times. She opened her mouth to explain why dating Erik would be a bad idea, but she couldn't push any sound out.

"Well?" Imogen pressed. "Do they? Be honest now."

Jia shook her head slowly. She didn't want to admit to her friends that she'd made a point of studying the relevant regulations. That would come dangerously close to admitting in public she was lusting after her partner. The fewer people who knew about that, the better, especially her matchmaking friends. They might not be interested in hooking her up with the same type of man as her family, but that didn't mean they weren't any less of a threat.

She wasn't dating Erik. They were good friends and

partners. Just because she'd cooked his favorite types of Chinese food for him a few times and spent a lot of time thinking about him didn't mean anything more needed to happen.

Imogen and Chinara continued staring at her, waiting for her response.

There would be no escape tonight.

Jia cleared her throat. "As far as I know, there aren't any particular rules, other than a superior can't date someone they're supervising. If I were to date someone in the department, my captain, as my immediate supervisor, would have to be informed." She eyed both of them. "Why? You think I should try dating a cop?" She added a forced laugh as if she'd hadn't been thinking about it for months and Imogen's choice of romantic partner wasn't obvious.

Imogen leaned forward and looked around, her smile turning conspiratorial. "Erik's a handsome guy. And whatever you can say about him, *he's not boring.*"

This was Jia's chance. She could use her friends to convince herself it was a bad idea to want to go out with Erik. Having someone else clearly agree with her articulated reasons for why it was a bad idea would help get the idea out of her system.

"Going out with someone you work with is a bad idea." Jia nodded as physical validation for her argument. "If things go badly, it could mess with things at work, and then where would I be?"

Imogen blew a raspberry. "As if."

Chinara raised an eyebrow but didn't interject. Her expression was only mildly less eager than Imogen's.

"You *don't* think it'd make a difference?" Jia asked.

"Sure, for some people it might, but not for you." Imogen shook her head. "You're always going to do the job, no matter how you feel about your partner. You told us that yourself. That was why your other partners quit—because you were about the job over everything, even getting them to like you. So, worst-case scenario, Erik quits because he's not doing the job the right way, and you go on being Lady Justice."

"But I'd lose a good partner," Jia argued. "And what if I went back to having a terrible partner? One of the reasons I can get things done at work is because I have a good partner rather than a lazy partner dragging me down."

Chinara sighed. "But you've told us several times that things are different at the department now. The news even talks about it. Unless you really think you and Erik are the only good police officers in all of Neo SoCal?" She eyed her friend. "You don't, do you?" Jia shook her head. "Good, then you shouldn't be concerned." Chinara held up her palm. "I'm not saying he's not a great partner, but I think you could do okay without him."

Jia doubted that and sucked in a breath. Chinara was her backup plan. She wasn't surprised Imogen had come up with the idea of her dating Erik, but she expected her more level-headed friend to agree with her about how terrible the whole idea was.

"He's way older than me," she blurted, trying to derail this girlfriend double-team being held in a dance club courtroom. "Him having a de-aging treatment doesn't change that he's older. Doesn't that count for something?" She looked at Imogen. "Or at a minimum, shouldn't I take it into account?"

Chinara swirled her finger around the rim of her glass. "Age is a number, nothing more. You say he's a good partner at work. Otherwise, you'd be complaining about him all the time. Sure, when you first met, you complained a few times, but it's been a long, long time since I remember you saying anything even mildly critical in a message about him. That means you two relate." She smiled, her eyebrows dancing as if she had just scored a point with the jurors.

Jia's eyes narrowed. "Sure, about *work*. That's not the same thing as relating to him romantically."

Imogen gave her an incredulous look. "And you're saying you *never* hang out with him outside of work?" She inclined her head toward the dance floor. "I can remember a few times you blew off hanging out with us, not because of Corbin, but because you had something you were doing with your *partner*. You're obviously not ripping his clothes off in the bedroom yet, but maybe you're working your way there."

Jia's cheeks burned. "Ripping his clothes off? You know what? Never mind." She squeezed her eyes closed and took a deep breath before opening them. "Most of those times involved things like tactical training. That's professional. We have to do it privately because of departmental bureaucracy. I don't think running around shooting pretend terrorists is all that romantic."

"Uh-huh." Imogen's incredulous expression lingered. "It doesn't sound fun to me, but if you hated it, you wouldn't be doing it. If there's one thing I know about you, Jia, you don't do *anything* you hate for long." She took a sip of her drink before waving it in Jia's direction.

"You're so stubborn your mom should have named you Juejiang."

Chinara adopted a serious look. "And what about all the sphere ball? You're crazy about sphere ball now, and you've told both of us that you'd gone to several games with Erik. Is that also professional? You planning to start a sphere ball team filled with nothing but cops?"

"I go with him because he got me into it." Jia pinched the bridge of her nose. "They aren't dates. It's not like he pays for me, or I pay for him. Last time we went, we had to...uh, help get a few drunks under control, so that was even professional. We're just friends and good partners."

Imogen threw her hands in the air. "I can't believe you. The universe has handed you a perfect gift, and you're too afraid to accept it. The planet won't explode if you go out on a few dates with Erik. I've dated guys from work before, and even when it ended, it didn't mess things up. Think of it like sphere ball. You can't get any points if you don't swing your racquet, right?"

Jia blinked, the metaphor messing with her brain. "Sphere ball doesn't involve racquets."

Imogen waved off the argument. "Whatever."

Jia looked at her friends. "Neither of you believes dating my partner is a bad idea? Not even a little bit?"

They both shook their heads.

"I do," Jia insisted. "We need to keep things professional. The job's the most important thing."

So much for using her friends to talk her down. She couldn't claim total surprise, but she was more disappointed in herself than in her friends.

Imogen grabbed her drink. "A toast, then. To Jia—she

can take down a building full of terrorists, but she can only find boring boyfriends."

Chinara lifted her drink. "To Jia."

Jia chuckled and grabbed her glass, smiling and making an effort to show both of them she was still a good sport.

"To me."

CHAPTER FIVE

Erik yawned as he stepped into Captain Ragnar's office, Jia right behind him.

They had been going over some old reports when the captain summoned them. Maybe another reporter needed to ask about his underwear color. He almost grinned at Jia. The way she'd reacted had made it worthwhile.

I should have said something crazy, he thought. *That would have been fun.*

He'd have to take the next opportunity that presented itself. Unless he was about to receive a gift. "What's up, Captain?"

"Something you'll find interesting." Captain Ragnar tapped his PNIU. Erik's and Jia's both chimed. "New case." He scratched at his beard. "Unless you want to spend the rest of the week going over those old reports?"

Erik made a face. "Nah, I'm good. The most annoying

thing cops share with soldiers besides people shooting at you is all the reports."

"Bureaucracy is the blood of the UTC." Captain Ragnar summoned a data window depicting a smiling dark-haired Asian woman in a bright green dress. "This is Chau Nguyen. Thirty-two years old, she's a personal assistant. She worked for Euterpe Corporation until yesterday."

"Euterpe? The big music company, right?" Jia asked.

"If by big," he turned to Jia, "you mean the largest music-focused conglomerate in the UTC, then sure. They're headquartered in the Hexagon."

"Ok." Erik whistled. "Never been much of a music guy, but I've heard the name bounced around."

Jia stared at the image. "Wait, *worked*? Not works? Was she fired after looking into fraud? More embezzlement?"

Captain Ragnar shook his head, his faint smile disappearing. "I only wish it were that simple." He swiped his hand through the window. A new image appeared of a pale, rigid Chau slumped over the control yoke of a flitter.

Jia wrinkled her nose. "I see what you mean."

Unless Chau was a secret gangster, they were dealing with an innocent person killed Uptown. Erik had shed his illusions about Earth's perfection decades ago, but that didn't mean he wasn't bothered by innocent lives being cut short.

Captain Ragnar nodded. "She was found dead yesterday on a parking platform connected to her residential tower. There were no immediate signs of foul play. Officers on the scene said it looked like an OD. Her PNIU is unaccounted for, and they haven't been able to track it. I've already got

Digital Forensics looking into it." He swiped again. "She scratched a message into her dashboard, maybe because she didn't have her PNIU." He tapped his PNIU, and the text of Chau's last message appeared in a new data window.

Jia narrowed her eyes and read aloud. "I can't take it anymore. It's just too much stress. I'm ashamed. I've been using drugs. If I end it now by my own hand, at least you all won't be blamed for me being so antisocial. I'm sorry. I'm so sorry."

Jia snorted.

Erik blinked at his partner in surprise. Whatever Jia's faults, she had always shown great compassion toward victims. Even when she was having trouble in prior months, it manifested as anger toward criminals, not a lack of respect for their victims.

"Jia?" he probed quietly.

"Please." She pointed. "This isn't a suicide." She leaned forward. "Some monster killed this woman, and has inflicted even more suffering on her family with a fake suicide note."

Captain Ragnar nodded slowly. "Forensics didn't get anything useful other than her DNA on the scene, but that doesn't mean it's not a suicide. The body was flagged by a surveillance drone, and a nearby patrol unit went to do a check. They contacted the listed emergency next-of-kin, her sister, who swears up and down that Chau would never take her own life. She was a little emotional in her statement, but she implied Chau had been being secretive and might have some sort of trouble at work."

"A lot of family members don't want to accept the truth

in this kind of situation," Erik rubbed his chin. "We sure this isn't that? People do kill themselves."

"They do." Jia frowned. "But this doesn't smell right."

"Is that your gut talking?" he pushed.

"It's rational analysis talking. If she was going to kill herself, where's her PNIU? Why didn't she send a message instead of scratching her last thoughts into her dashboard? There's *no* reason for a suicidal woman to destroy or throw out her PNIU, but there's all the reason in the world for her murderer to do it, especially if she managed to record them. Someone thought they could get away with murder, and we won't let them. I'm outraged for the victim, and I'm angry that they thought that a weak coverup would be enough."

Captain Ragnar smiled.

Erik stared at the message, considering the evidence gathered so far. Everything Jia said made sense, but his time as a detective had proved people could fall into their own darkness too easily. Conspiracies choked the universe, but those conspiracies didn't cause every bad event.

That didn't matter, though. If his partner wanted to investigate, they would investigate. She would never need to worry; he would always have her back.

"We can't be sure until we investigate," Captain Ragnar commented. "And if the sister's right about Chau being secretive, that means she might have stumbled upon something, especially given who she was working for."

Erik snorted. "Let me guess, Euterpe is a Ceres subsidiary?"

Captain Ragnar smiled but shook his head. "No, but she

worked as a personal assistant for Rena Winston," he explained as if that was all the data anyone needed.

"Rena Winston?" Erik wrinkled his forehead in confusion as he turned to Jia. "Who the hell is that?"

"A superstar singer," Jia explained. "She's from Remus, but she's popular all over the UTC, especially on Earth."

"A singer?" He turned back to the captain. "That's a big deal?"

"How many non-Earthers can you think of who have hit it big on Earth?" Jia challenged.

"I don't pay much attention to that kind of thing, other than sphere ball," Erik answered.

"The upshot is that she's a big deal, and she's not even twenty. She is starting a world tour soon. Even some talk of her doing a core worlds tour in a couple of years. She was discovered by a talent scout when she was a young kid and moved to Earth."

Erik eyed her, a smirk playing on his lips. "Since when are you into superstar singers?"

Jia rolled her eyes. "She's been everywhere in the news, Erik. She's hard to miss."

"If you say so."

Jia opened her mouth to retort but snapped it shut before offering, "I'm not into her kind of music, but she's supposed to be the next Aline Bisset."

Erik stared at Jia like she was speaking Zitark. Another superstar singer from a core world colony? "Aline Bisset?"

Jia gasped. This time she looked stunned. "You *don't* know Aline Bisset?"

He shook his head. "She also from Remus?"

Captain Ragnar chuckled. "What did you do for entertainment on the frontier?"

He looked at his boss. "Played a lot of darts?"

Jia shook her head and sighed. "Aline Bisset. You know, the Angel of Marseille? She had that song *Hyperspace Love*? I mean, she's retired now, but she's not *that* old. Her career was starting around the time you joined the Army."

"I didn't pay a lot of attention to music on the frontier, and not much even before." Erik gestured at the window. "But that doesn't matter. I get the point. This Chau Nguyen was a personal assistant to some big music star, and she started acting sketchy and ended up dead under suspicious circumstances. This smells like maybe this Rena Winston has something to hide, something that might hurt her career." He looked at the captain. "Is Euterpe cooperating, or are we getting a standard-issue corporate see/hear/speak no evil?"

Captain Ragnar chuckled. "Kind of. They're not happy to have cops sniffing around, but they've agreed to let you two come in and talk to people without a warrant. In exchange, we've agreed to keep this low key."

"We're letting them dictate things?" Erik asked.

"If this is a homicide, time is of the essence. We *don't* have enough evidence to kick down their doors, and they can make life tough for us. If this is nothing more than an unfortunate suicide, there's no reason to mess with Rena's career."

Jia folded her arms. "At least they aren't blocking us from the beginning. That might mean they care a little."

Erik nodded. "Yeah, I'm sure they're torn up."

Captain Ragnar managed a sheepish smile. "My

daughter would never forgive me if she found out I messed with her favorite singer's tour without a good reason, but for now," he pointed to them, "I want you two to proceed on the assumption we have a crime to uncover. First step, go check with the coroner. She did a full workup last night."

"Don't worry, Captain." Jia spun on her heel. "If there's nothing there, we'll clear this right up. If there's more, we'll find whoever is responsible."

The door clicked behind them. "I don't doubt it for a second," he replied to his now-empty office.

The detectives stepped into the medical examination room.

A tall, pale woman in a white uniform sat at a desk, her long dark hair up and a bored expression on her face. Several data windows floated in front of her. Some contained pictures from different angles of Chau Nguyen on an examination table. Dense text and numbers packed the others. The woman muttered under her breath and shook her head.

Erik hadn't talked to the woman other than briefly in a call, but he recognized her—Camila Serrano, the new head coroner at the 1-2-2. She'd only been working there for a couple of weeks, and Erik and Jia hadn't encountered any cases that needed her help. He'd had no problems with the man she replaced, but there had been a lot of turnover in Forensics following the arrest of Head Coroner Hannigan.

Several people worried that he'd tainted them profession-ally, and they needed a new start.

Camila tilted her head and frowned. A few quick swipes brought up new data windows.

"Can I help you?" she asked, not turning away from the windows. "I'm in the middle of something. I don't have time for chitchat."

"We've been assigned the Chau Nguyen case," Erik explained. "Not exactly chitchat. The captain said to stop by, and from the looks of things, you've already examined the body."

"Oh. That. That makes sense. Sorry." Camila turned in her chair. "Sure. I examined the body last night. I was just going over the results from some of the tests. I was going to send the information in a report later, but this works, too."

"Can you confirm the cause of death?" Jia asked.

"Definitely Dragon Tear overdose." Camila returned her attention to her data windows. "Very high levels in her system. Even Detective Big Guy over there would have died. At least she didn't suffer." She sighed. "But there are some irregularities."

Jia nodded. "Our working theory is a murder made to look like suicide."

Erik frowned. He walked toward the data windows, but he couldn't make any sense of the dense information from a quick skim. "What kind of irregularities?"

Camila inclined her head toward a data window showing Chau's body on an examination table. "I checked her from all angles. No bruising, no abrasions, no signs of a struggle. Almost perfect health from an external perspective."

"Like my partner said, working theory. We don't know she was murdered. Right now, all we have to go off is a note and her family's suspicions."

Camila shrugged. "When you spend your life processing dead bodies, you get used to things. Even though Dragon Tear ODs are more of a stop-breathing-and-die situation than thrashing, it's weird not to find *any* sign of injury, even just from her hitting her head or something in the car. But that's not the really strange thing." She pointed at a data window filled with several rows of numbers.

Jia leaned forward to read the window, her eyes following the numbers. "Nanite concentrations in blood and lymph?"

Camila nodded. "Exactly. Notice anything about them?"

"I'm not sure." Jia shrugged. "I have to admit I don't know what I'm looking for."

"After they do their thing, medical nanites should diffuse into the bloodstream and leave the body via urinary excretion. It takes a while, depending on the initial concentration and that kind of thing." Camila jabbed at the data window. "I also examined some of the nanite samples with help from Digital Forensics. I'll give you the short version, Detectives." She turned around in her chair to better see them both. "The concentration, type, and condition of the nanites in Miss Nguyen's blood and lymph indicate she likely received extensive nanite-based treatment on the day of her death. There are some other things off as well, such as her cytokine counts and other results that support that interpretation."

Erik frowned as evidence crystallized a mere possibility into something solid. "You're saying someone could have beat the crap out of her and covered it up? Injected her with a bunch of medical nanites, or slapped a bunch of med patches on her?"

Camila shook her finger at him once. "Exactly. I'm the coroner, not a detective, but who plans to kill themselves then goes through the trouble of healing, only to OD later? It seems like a lot of work."

Jia nodded. "Who, indeed? Thank you. If you find anything else, let us know."

Camila gave a little salute. "Will do, Detectives."

Erik looked at the image of the body for a few more seconds before turning to leave. The detectives stepped into the hallway, and he closed the door behind them. Malcolm stood a few meters away from the door in that day's fashion atrocity, a bright pink Hawaiian shirt covered with giraffes.

The technician blinked a few times and licked his lips. "Oh, hey, Detectives. You were talking to Camila about the Nguyen case?"

"Yeah," Erik replied. "You the one who helped her do the nanite analysis?"

"Yes. That's pretty messed up if you ask me, but I'm sure you two will track things down." Malcolm stepped toward the door. "Say, um, this might be a weird question, but when you were in there, did Camila only talk about the case?"

Jia nodded. "What else would she talk about?"

"Oh, I was just curious. She's new, and you know, we have to work together on occasion, so it's better to learn more about her." Malcolm averted his eyes. Scarlet touched his cheeks.

"Learn *what?*" Erik asked, trying not to grin.

"You know, what kinds of snacks she likes, that kind of thing."

"If she has someone?" Erik suggested.

Malcolm turned into a statue for a few seconds. "It's good to know about people's backgrounds. Don't you think?" He ran his tongue inside his cheek. "Oh, I just remembered I have to go check on something."

Erik cleared his throat. "Mind if we go with you? We've got a few things we need you to do."

"Oh, yeah. The case?" He waved for them to follow. "Totally. Let's go chat in my office."

CHAPTER SIX

Malcolm settled into a chair behind his desk, his face back to normal and an easy smile on his lips. "You already know the nanite news, so what else can I do for you, Detectives? Before you ask, the medical nanites used are standard and mass-produced. Unless you think the factory or the retailer were involved, that's not going to help."

"We've got something else in mind." Jia patted her PNIU. "The company is only cooperating grudgingly, but the family's already signed everything we need to access Nguyen's personal files. It'd be great if we can find her PNIU, too, but from what Captain Ragnar said, that's not going to happen."

Malcolm sighed. "Yeah, we've tried tracking and pinging it, and we're getting absolutely nothing, which means it's either destroyed or so damaged, it might as well be destroyed."

"Convenient," Jia muttered.

"More than you might think, Detective." Malcolm pointed at his PNIU. "This isn't the first time I've had to track a missing PNIU. These things are designed to take a lot of damage. Detective Blackwell could blast a hole in one with his TR-7, and the tracking beacon would probably still work. They're supposed to be able to survive flitter crashes to get certified."

"Where was the PNIU when it went offline?" Jia asked, not surprised by Malcolm's information.

"Outside her apartment." Malcolm shrugged. "Sorry. I know that's not very helpful."

Erik shook his head, his brows knitting. "We might get lucky and Forensics or some of the on-scene officers might find something in her residential tower, but I doubt it. That means it's going to come down to if you can find anything in her files, or if we can find anything useful from a witness. If all cases just required tracking, they wouldn't need us."

Malcolm's expression brightened. "Sure thing, Detective Blackwell. I'll dig deep, and we'll find ourselves a killer."

"Thanks, Malcolm. You're always helpful."

Jia smiled. "And good luck with the other matter, by the way."

Malcolm gave her a quizzical look. "What are you talking about, Detective?"

"I'm just saying, I hope Camila doesn't have someone."

Just because she couldn't pull the trigger on an intraoffice romance didn't mean Malcolm couldn't.

Malcolm turned back toward his desk. "Uh, thanks, but do me a favor?"

"What?"

"Don't mention anything to her yet." Malcolm rubbed the back of his neck.

Erik chuckled and clapped him on the shoulder. "Sure thing, but don't wait too long. If you're interested in someone, someone else might be, too."

Don't wait too long, Jia thought. Was Erik also talking to her? It didn't matter. They had other things to worry about at the moment.

"We should interview the sister right away," Jia suggested. "Malcolm's going to need time to go through the files."

He nodded. "Let's give her a call and see if she's ready."

Jia took a seat on a blue couch next to the victim's sister, Binh. "Miss Nguyen, we're sorry for your loss, and we want to assure you that the department is taking your concerns seriously. At this moment, we're exploring all possible explanations for your sister's death."

Binh sighed. Her cheeks were puffy and her eyes red. "Since it's you two, I believe that. Thank you."

Erik sat in a chair kitty-corner from the couch. The small piece of furniture could barely handle his large frame. It was like every piece of furniture in the apartment —twenty percent too small for him.

That wasn't a shock, given Binh's slight frame.

"Any information you provide might be helpful," Jia continued. "We've read some of the statements you gave the uniformed officers, but we wanted to hear everything in your own words, just in case they missed something, or if you remembered anything else. The first forty-eight hours after an incident like this are often crucial in tracking down the truth."

Binh nodded slowly. She looked at a holographic image projected from a frame on her wall. It was a short scene of her laughing with her sister.

"It was subtle at first," she began. "The fear. I could tell something was worrying her. I asked her about it a few times. First, she tried to deny anything was going on and insisted she was just overworked, but later, she admitted she was scared and worried that she was being watched."

"Why didn't she contact the police?" Erik asked.

Binh shook her head and looked down. "I told her to do just that, but she said she didn't have enough evidence, and she'd look like a crazy person. The last few weeks, she'd even gotten so worried that she would only talk about things in person and without our PNIUs. She said she was worried about them spying on her."

Jia nodded slowly. That might explain why the victim didn't have the PNIU on her, but it didn't explain where it had gone or why the tracking beacon had failed. If Chau had been murdered, the killer might have panicked and disposed of the PNIU unnecessarily, fueling suspicion rather than dampening it.

That suggested a non-professional.

"Who was she worried about?" Jia asked. "You said she was worried about being watched. Who was watching her? Someone at Euterpe?"

Binh shrugged. "I don't know. She would never answer that question, but she did get tenser when I asked if it had anything to do with her job. She denied it when I asked her directly. I think...I *think* she was trying to protect me." She sniffled and wiped away a stray tear. "I'm sorry. It's still a lot to process. I wish she'd worried less about protecting me and more about herself. Maybe if she had, she would still be here."

Erik waited for a few seconds before nodding toward the holographic image. "We understand how rough this is. We'll try to get it over with as quickly as possible."

"Thank you, Detective."

"What about her employers? I know you said she didn't blame them directly, but did she ever mention any problems with Euterpe or Rena Winston before all of this?" Jia noticed that Erik's tone was softer than normal.

Binh looked to the side for a moment in deep thought. "I keep asking myself that but coming up with the same answer—none. She loved her job. She said it was stressful, but it was everything she'd always wanted. Everything she told me about Rena suggested she was a nice girl and her image reflected the real person."

Erik glanced at Jia. She understood what he needed. They both had their specialties. Erik was good at kicking ass, but not always at being restrained in his questioning.

"And you're sure she didn't have any suicidal tendencies or substance abuse problems?" Jia asked quietly. "We need to know just to rule out possibilities. The more we can eliminate in the beginning, the quicker the rest of the investigation can go."

Binh took a deep breath. "The other cops told me about that. You know, that my sister died of a Dragon Tear overdose. It's ridiculous. She didn't like to drink, and now she's doing Dragon Tear? She wouldn't even know where to get it." She dropped her face into her hands and shook her head. "Chau had an artistic soul. That was why she got a job at Euterpe. She knew she didn't have the talent to make it, but she wanted to help someone else. She might have been a little too empathetic and could get depressed, but she's never, *ever* been suicidal." She lifted her face and gripped the arm of the couch tightly, her nails digging into the fabric. "Someone killed her because she found out something she shouldn't have. Detectives, please find her killer. They need to pay."

Jia placed a hand on the woman's arm and offered a comforting smile. "Miss Nguyen, I can assure you that the NSCPD will do everything we can to put this incident to rest."

Binh nodded. "Thank you, Detective Lin. Thank you."

Neither said much as they headed toward the vehicle, both processing all the evidence they'd gathered that day. Jia was more convinced the suicide had been used to cover up a homicide. A few minutes later, Jia and Erik zoomed away from the residential tower in the MX 60.

Erik pulled up on the control yoke to bring the flitter into a new vertical lane. "We can't come to a conclusion until we have solid evidence. Once we do, we can do what we need to."

Jia kept looking forward. "What's that supposed to mean?"

"Increasing paranoia could mean that someone was out to get her, but it also might mean she just snapped. Given what her sister said, the missing PNIU might have been Chau's doing. We *can't* ignore the possibility."

"And she also hurt herself and used nanites to fix things?" Jia shook her head. "It's like Camila said. Who would do that? Even if she snapped and wanted to kill herself, her actions would still have been purposeful."

"Maybe she tried and then changed her mind," Erik suggested. "She worked in a stressful industry, and not everyone gets the help they need. She sounds like she has a family who cared for her, but that might not have been enough. The entertainment industry isn't like being a cop or a soldier. Sure, there are plenty of nice people, but there are plenty of assholes who only look out for themselves."

"You're saying that not everyone has a good partner looking out for them," Jia murmured.

Erik nodded slowly. "Something like that. I'm not saying there's no evidence suggesting foul play, but there's also evidence that this might have just been a suicide. We need some sort of plausible motive to focus this crap. If this was a murder, whoever did it had to know it'd be investigated and tried to cover it up, but it's a big risk. That means whatever the motive is had to be something important enough to risk police attention on Euterpe. Given the reputation of the police right now, that's an even bigger deal."

Jia frowned. "Euterpe's a company so important it's in the Hexagon, but we've already worked plenty of cases where big companies were willing to murder people to keep secrets." Jia thought for a moment, then finished, "I don't see why this one is any different."

"Yeah, but those involved buying off politicians and smuggling," Erik allowed. "Something's not adding up."

"Like?"

"I don't think Euterpe's trying to smuggle AIs or arms using a famous singer as cover." He looked to his left, where a small cargo flitter was slowing traffic. It soon dropped out of the lane and descended toward an older building, maybe twenty-five stories tall.

Emma interrupted their conversation. "Would you like me to dig around? I don't doubt Technician Constantine's skill, but he's human and bound by all your regulations. I can get into places he can't."

Jia jumped at the sound. The AI had been uncharacteristically quiet so far. That typically meant she was involved in a deep examination of the OmniNet for her own inscrutable growth.

"No," Erik replied, his face unperturbed. "Like you said, Malcolm's working that angle, and we don't want any questions arising about how we got certain information. We need to do this by the book, especially since we can't prove a murder yet. If we screw this up and some corporate bigwig is involved, the bastard could be halfway to the HTP before we know what's going on."

Jia tapped her knee for a moment before suggesting, "She can start a public background check on Euterpe and Rena," She looked at Erik. "Malcolm's concentrating on the victim's files. Emma can collate a lot more information."

Emma scoffed. "Oh, I've already done that, at least the initial and easily accessible public records. Unfortunately, there's nothing that rates any particular suspicion. There are no cash flow problems or major issues hinted at for the company, and even the net rumors about the sweet song-bird are remarkably mild. She's mostly criticized for a lack of edge, as many people put it, in her persona and music. There have been no credible scandals, criminal, moral, or otherwise. She's not been romantically associated with anyone. She's so boring she might as well be a virtual construct instead of an organic entity."

Erik chuckled. "So you're saying as an AI, you think human singers are better than AI singers?"

"Virtual stars aren't like me." Emma scoffed. "They're just holographic dolls in the end. "

"Understood." Erik turned into a new lane, ending up behind a large cargo flitter. "There's got to be something if this is a murder. There should be a motive. If we can figure out a believable angle, that could lead us to more clues."

"An affair gone bad with an executive?" Jia mused aloud.

"Murdering someone over an affair is a big, messy step." Erik's grip loosened on the yoke. "But maybe we shouldn't take everything at face value. I might not know a lot about popular music, but I know all these stars have managed personas."

"Didn't the sister suggest Miss Winston is a pleasant-enough young woman?" Emma asked. "I will note my initial research supports that conclusion."

Jia considered the question. "She could be a great actress. We keep talking about motive, but that goes back to who has the most to lose. A core-world musical prodigy who is making it big on Earth might have dark secrets in her past."

"How dark could they be?" Erik asked. "She's just a kid."

"She could be antisocial or have twisted habits. If Chau stumbled onto them, her career would be over." Jia nodded, her brow wrinkled in worry. "It's like you said; their personas are managed. Unlike virtual stars, you *can't* blame strange behavior on bad programming or a technical glitch. We've both stared into the darkness enough to know it can fester in surprising places. Even if we want Emma to avoid going into somewhere Malcolm might look, she can still do a deep dive, including trying to access records on Remus."

"That's what…ten or eleven days one way for comms?" Erik's brow furrowed at the estimation.

"Roughly, depending on relative orbits," Emma clarified.

"Even if Emma knew exactly what systems to hit and could send the code she needs, it'd take too damned long. I have a feeling the case will go cold if we wait that long."

"I'll do my best to see what I can dig up on Earth," Emma offered. "And I agree with your general agreement. I'm an impressive piece of technology, but even I can't do much about accessing systems eight-point-nine light-years away. I'll also assure you that I won't cause any trouble for you on my deeper background check. Alas, laws are sometimes inconvenient."

"Thanks. Yeah, let's keep the law-breaking to a minimum." Erik paused, chewing his lip. "There's still something that bothers me about all this."

Jia side-eyed him. "Other than a potential murder?"

He pointed at her. "That's just it. You *don't* murder people to keep them quiet if you can bribe them, and the entertainment industry is all about money." Erik glanced at a passing tower. "Our next move is to hit the manager and see what he has to say."

Jia held her breath. The evidence pointed different ways, but the preponderance pointed to murder. They just needed to uncover something more than circumstantial evidence.

Chau Nguyen deserved justice.

CHAPTER SEVEN

A couple of hours later, Erik and Jia emerged from the small restaurant they'd ducked into for a late lunch. It had been a pleasant-enough meal despite the lack of beignets, and fortunately, it was only a small distraction from the cause.

Despite the progress that morning, their investigation had already encountered a roadblock. During a call right after lunch, Rena's manager, Leonard Carl, had made it clear that he had no time for an interview until the following day.

He also made it clear that Euterpe would not tolerate an interview with their star until the detectives had talked to him. Since he had agreed to talk to them the following morning, they couldn't accuse him of stonewalling, but it was still annoying.

Jia kicked the hard surface of the parking platform as they emerged from the restaurant. "He's all but screaming they need to coordinate their stories."

"Maybe." Erik shrugged. "Or they need to prep her

because they think we're going to bust in there and accuse her of murder. It's no big deal. I doubt a one-day delay is enough for them to pull anything major, and we've got them flagged if they go anywhere. Even if they aren't required to stay in town, we'll know if they leave. It gives Emma more time to go deeper into the records. She still might find something."

"You'd be surprised at what people leave in publicly accessible places," Emma commented, excitement in her voice. She claimed she only helped Erik out of idle interest, but she seemed to enjoy taking down criminals as much as the detectives did.

Whether that represented an inherent bent toward justice or was a product of her time aiding the detectives remained unclear.

Jia nodded, satisfaction spreading across her face. "If they can't run, I suppose it doesn't matter, and just because there might have been a murder, it might not involve them."

"But you suspect them?"

"The manager and Rena are the most likely suspects unless Malcolm or Emma can find a secret jealous lover we don't know about."

"Two to one, it's a jealous lover," he mused before turning to her. "That makes sense," Erik admitted. "But remember your biggest fan, Sampson. We've focused on money and power, but not every crime is about that."

"You think she had a stalker?" Jia's face twitched into a mask of disgust. "I hadn't considered that. It's not impossible."

"It might explain why she was growing paranoid. She

might have been watched but just assumed it was someone at Euterpe rather than someone closer. Or it might have even been someone stalking Rena, and she got between them." Eric wiped crumbs off his chest. "That might be why she got tense about work."

"But why not report the stalker?" Jia asked.

"Maybe her bosses didn't want the negative attention." Erik shrugged. "There's something a little sloppy about all this that might fit with that, but it's just a theory."

Jia waved a hand. "They're all theories. We need concrete leads." She gave a firm nod. "We'll squeeze something from the manager and Rena tomorrow. Even if they aren't involved, they might give us new leads."

Erik and Jia wandered down a long row of parked flitters facing another row, heading toward the MX 60. Flitters lifted into the sky in the distance before zooming away from the parking platform to join the thick swarms of flying vehicles flowing around the commerce tower. Five men in long coats chatted quietly near a black luxury flitter in the opposite row. They glanced at Erik and Jia with frowns.

One of the men's eyes widened. He leaned closer and whispered furtively to the others. They all took quick peeks at Erik and Jia.

"Wonder what's about," Erik murmured. A stray thought led to his next suggestion. "Emma, can you run facial recognition on those guys?" He slowed his pace.

Jia matched him, still looking forward but keeping the men in the corner of her eye. "Friends of yours?"

"Not anyone I know, but I've got a lot of fans." Erik

grinned. "So does Lady Justice. Hey, maybe they saw the interview, and they're interested in a date."

Jia rolled her eyes. "Shut up, Obsidian Detective." She poked him in the chest. "You're not dating anyone either."

"They're not my type." Erik's smile grew.

"They *are* your type." Emma transmitted directly to Erik and Jia's ears. "At least one of them is a former associate of a criminal organization that was present in the Shadow Zone before the increase in police activity in the last year."

"Wait." Erik stopped, his hand slipping under his jacket and resting on his pistol. "Who are they? Gray Circle?"

"No, the gentleman in question seems to have worked for a syndicate that called itself the Southwestern Brotherhood. He's not currently wanted. Instead, he's on probation with the threat of transportation. The others don't have criminal records, and it might raise questions if I try to use a broader database."

"Don't worry about it. Knowing one guy's a piece of trash is enough."

Jia grimaced. "They didn't transport or imprison a gangster?"

"He was rather helpful in fingering some other people in the organization, according to police records, but it's unclear whether they know that," Emma explained.

Erik frowned. "I remember hearing about the Southwestern Brotherhood, but we didn't take them down. That was all local EZ action."

"Yes, but it was in the wake of what you two set in motion," Emma explained.

Jia reached for her stun pistol. "Do you think they're up

to something in an Uptown parking lot? This isn't the Zone. There's a lot more surveillance."

"Conspiracies begin with talk," Erik replied. "And I don't like them suddenly looking nervous." He nodded toward the MX 60. It was only a few flitters ahead. "Let's keep going."

"Fine," Jia muttered through gritted teeth, keeping the men in the corner of her vision.

Erik understood how she felt. He didn't like leaving possible scumbags on the street, and he didn't intend to. The detectives would be in a better position near his vehicle. If anything happened, at least it was armored.

They continued walking slowly toward the MX 60. They were almost at the flitter when one of the men called to them. "Hey, Blackwell."

Erik turned, keeping his hand in his jacket. "Yeah? Need something?"

"It is you, isn't it?" The man offered Erik and Jia a hungry smile. "The man who takes you out would be a *legend.*" His gaze slid to Jia, nodding. "Her, too."

Erik chuckled. "Fair enough. Any man who takes me out deserves it. They would make a movie about him."

"Glad you agree." The man jerked up his hand, grasping the butt of a pistol as things seemed to slow down. Jia's heartbeat punctuated each second.

She and Erik pulled their weapons first, Jia her stun pistol, Erik his slug-thrower.

The other suited men hadn't had their hands on their weapons.

Erik popped his gun into position and squeezed the trigger, barely thinking, relying on muscle memory and practice to aim his weapon. The bullet roared from the gun and ripped into the chest of the would-be legend.

The gangster yelled in pain, eyes shut, falling forward.

Jia pulled her trigger. A white stun bolt flew from her gun and nailed the man to his left at the same time. His eyes rolled up as he pitched forward. She pivoted and fired at the next-closest man.

Beside her, Erik fired two shots into the remaining men. Both screamed, one falling forward, the other back.

None of the gangsters managed to get off a shot.

"HOLD!" Jia shouted.

Erik and Jia advanced to the pile of wounded and stunned men.

They kicked the men's weapons away. Jia kept her stun pistol trained on them as Erik stowed his pistol and pulled binding ties out of a pocket.

"Great!" He smirked. "*Just* have enough. Lady's smiling, or maybe she's frowning, which is why I'm in this situation." He knelt and began binding their hands. "See how lucky you guys are? If I was down a tie, I might have needed to ask Lady Justice over here to stun someone. She gets frisky with the trigger at times."

"Keep it up," Jia replied. "I'll get frisky with it right now and accidentally on purpose commit a friendly-fire officer-on-officer issue."

"Promises, promises." Erik grinned.

"Uniformed officers are en route," Emma reported. "I'm monitoring nearby drones to ensure there are no gun goblin reinforcements."

The leader winced in pain and groaned. "You...shot me. You *bastard*."

"You were trying to kill us." Erik laughed. "Don't try to kill people, and you won't get shot. If you're going to try to become a legend, you damned well better bring your best game. So, too bad. At least you're not dead. By the way, you're under arrest, idiot. All Article 7 rights apply. Do you need these explained to you?"

The man let out another long groan. "I thought I was lucky," he whispered. "I was going to earn my way back in."

Jia's angry gaze roamed over the wounded men, then she scoffed. "The Lady can be unkind. You're a damned moron. Now you're not just getting transported, you're going to prison."

Flashing red and blue lights in the distance signaled an approaching patrol flitter.

"Sorry, but Neo SoCal's getting cleaned up," Erik announced. "Haven't you heard? The sooner you learn that, the better. But it's your lucky day after all." He stood, then headed toward his MX 60. "Because I'm going to patch you up." He had stuck his head in, so his voice was muffled. "We need you nice and healthy before you go to jail." He stood back up, his voice clear again, the smile on his face adding an annoying tone to his voice. "Can't have you bleeding out on the parking platform."

Emma snickered. "You two do seem to have an amazing talent for attracting gun morons."

"I thought you preferred gun goblins?" Jia asked.

"I'm going with the moment," Emma replied.

"I was mostly worried they were going to shoot someone else's flitter." Erik walked back, shaking his head. "Then we'd have twice as many reports to fill out. But hey, at least we have something to do until Rena's manager meets with us tomorrow."

Jia chuckled. "*That's* your take on random gangsters ambushing us?"

"We shot them first," Erik argued. "I don't think it counts as an ambush." He knelt to rip open the shirt of the complaining man. "If anything, I think we ambushed them."

"Nope. They ambushed us." She sniffed. "They're just terrible at it."

Jia's comment was punctuated by the moans of one of the morons she'd shot.

"Stop your whining." Erik pushed aside the shirt to affix the first patch. "It's unprofessional. Real killers don't whine."

CHAPTER EIGHT

Erik wasn't always sure *what* was considered
pretentious.

Decades on the frontier had changed his perceptions
from those of standard Earthers in many ways. While his
hometown wasn't as extravagant as Neo SoCal and lacked
its population, it was still on Earth, and there wasn't a
single man or woman living on the planet whose situation
was remotely comparable to the rougher conditions of the
frontier.

Even the Shadow Zone was more comfortable than
most frontier colonies.

Clarity on the pretention issue came in the form of a
massive sectional desk covered with holographic images of
various celebrity friends of Leonard Carl. The mammoth
office could have held most of Erik's not-so-cheap apartment. In addition to the holograms and desk, paintings

adorned the walls. As he looked around, Erik realized he wasn't enough of an art buff to know if they were valuable, but they all looked old, and that probably meant they weren't cheap.

Someone's overcompensating, Erik thought.

Behind the desk, Leonard wore a well-tailored suit. Unfortunately, the light blue color clashed with the sophistication attempted by the paintings, as did the obvious attempt to show off his celebrity friends. His slick-backed hair came off more as Shadow Zone gangster than manager.

Perhaps that was intentional. The broad-shouldered, bulky man had a decent physical presence, but his lack of muscle undermined it, even if it probably helped him shout down tiny scared assistants and teenage singers.

Erik and Jia stood in front of his desk. The huge office lacked any other chairs, which Erik assumed was by design.

"Can we just get this over with?" Leonard asked, and heaved an impatient sigh. "I know you're cops, and you don't work in the industry, so you'll just have to take my word about how much crap you have to do to get ready for a world tour. It's far more complicated than you'd think." He let out a soft scoff. "And it doesn't help that I have to get Rena a new assistant. Nguyen picked the perfect time to die."

Jia glared at him. "Mr. Carl, we're investigating a woman's suicide or a possible homicide. If you can find the decency, do try to show a little respect.

"Homicide?" Leonard eyed her. "It's not that. It's simple —Nguyen couldn't hack it. Some people can't. This isn't a business for soft-hearted wimps. I'm sure it's a big tragedy for her family, but the world can't stop because one woman decides suicide is preferable to two-weeks' notice and probably being black-balled from the industry. If this tour gets disrupted, a bunch of people are going to lose a lot of money."

Jia gritted her teeth and flicked her gaze toward Erik. He could sympathize. Leonard could use a good fist to the face or a nice toss out the window.

"The more you can tell us, the quicker this will go," Erik offered gruffly. "And it's important to note that we haven't officially ruled it a suicide. You don't want us to move on if this was something else, do you? An unsolved homicide lingering around your company can't be good for business."

"Entertainment is war." Annoyance settled on Leonard's face. "You're an ex-soldier, right? I'm sure you saw people crack all the time. Losses are inevitable. Attrition." He clucked his tongue. "The show must go on."

Erik barked a laugh. "Yeah, managing singers and actors is the same thing as riding a drop pod into hot territory while artillery and fighters are lighting up the sky. Keep telling yourself that if it makes you feel better."

The face-punching plan grew in appeal.

"Yeah, yeah. You're a hero and all that." Leonard waved a hand. "Whatever. I'm just saying people crack. I know her whiny sister thinks there's some big conspiracy. She called me and told me." Leonard muttered before jabbing a finger into the air. "But I don't have a lot of time for crap, and Euterpe doesn't have time for it either. Don't think just because you two are famous cops, we'll let you push us around. You think you're celebrities? You're nothing but local yokels with badges, and you don't know what a real entertainment company can do in a PR war." He eyed them. "So you should strongly consider backing off if you don't want trouble."

Erik shook his head, forcing a grin and a chuckle. The whole speech was ridiculous. It was like being yapped at by a small dog.

"I can't believe this." Jia narrowed her eyes. "Are you *threatening* us, Mr. Carl? Oh, please tell me you're threatening two detectives conducting an investigation."

"No, no, no." Leonard lowered his hand, a plastic smile taking over his face and a hint of nervousness in his eyes. He'd miscalculated. "Look, all I'm saying is that you've got better things to do than waste your time on some loser personal assistant who couldn't hack it, and so do I. I'm just trying to save us all a lot of trouble and unnecessary work. I'm sure you've got all sorts of murderous terrorists you could be tracking."

"Fine," Jia replied through gritted teeth. "We'll make the questions simple and direct. Without acknowledging any particular threat, can you think of anyone who might have wished Chau Nguyen harm? If not that, are you aware of anyone who resented her? Maybe rivals in the company?"

"Rivals?" Leonard considered her question for a moment, then snorted. "Nguyen? No. In this business, people only want to take you down if you're a threat, and I'm not talking violence. We're not a crazy gangster syndicate. Why waste time undercutting a sheep? The wolves are the big threat, and Nguyen wasn't going to change into a wolf just from hanging around me. She was soft, and she was always going to be soft." He scoffed. "That's the problem with her kind, the wannabe artists who fall into the business side. I always knew that was why she got into the industry. They think they can side-step into the business as assistants or something, but there are two different skill sets involved. One is artistic, and the other is business. I'm not a failed singer. I'm a businessman who helps singers become successful. If she could have internalized that, she would have done better, and maybe she still would be alive." The corner of his mouth curled into a sinister half-smile. "I might be an asshole, but I'm a *necessary* asshole. Someone like Rena would be nothing without me. I make her rich, she makes me rich. Everyone wins. Well, except Nguyen. Like I said, entertainment is war, and you can't have wars without casualties."

"Since you brought Rena up, what about her?" Jia pressed. "A big hit to her reputation could end her career, and it's just about to really take off. Chau was her personal assistant. They spent a lot of time together. Maybe she stumbled onto something Rena or someone else didn't want anyone to know. Something important enough to kill for."

Leonard burst out in hearty laughter, his face reddening. "You think Rena has a big, dark secret she's going to kill someone over? Please."

Jia eyed him. "Just because she has a wholesome image doesn't mean it's real. Money has always been a reason to kill people."

"She's right," Erik agreed. "Not every criminal is a terrorist or gangster. My first case involved fine, upstanding corporate citizens who were bribing people to make more money."

He remained convinced that wasn't the total truth, but it was the truth the public had been conditioned to believe.

The manager continued laughing for a good ten seconds before calming himself and wiping away tears of mirth. "You two just don't get it. I almost passed on the opportunity when I first met Rena. I could tell at that time she'd never develop into something *edgier*. It's just not her nature. I was thinking, 'Does the UTC need a new wholesome, boring star?' I should find someone older—a woman, not a girl."

He snorted. "Just goes to show you that even a man with a lot of experience can come close to making a big mistake. No. Rena's got nothing to hide, because first of all, she's as much of a sheep as Nguyen, and sheep aren't predators. They're prey." He folded his arms. "Second, I've made a lot of people a lot of money off her, including myself, and we're poised to make so much more money it should be illegal. Because of that, I've made sure no one can get close to lead her down the wrong path. It's even in her contract. She can't date anyone."

"She can't date anyone?" Jia eyed him, mouth open for a moment before she shut it. "That's insane."

"That's Euterpe protecting our investment. That's the business, Detective. It takes a lot more to be a successful singer than it does a cop."

Jia stayed quiet while Erik chuckled. "You so sure she's under control? Regular teenagers can end up running with dangerous people, and you're saying a rich, famous singer can't? I find that hard to believe."

"Believe it, Detective. This is one situation where I'm not dropping the ball." Leonard narrowed his eyes, the faint remnants of mirth giving way to hostility. "You know how hard it is to get decent traction with a human star these days?" He waved a hand, ready to start expounding on a favorite rant. "All those fake virtual idols out there can be tuned to whatever personality the public wants—cheap dolls breathed into life by focus groups. They can be targeted for specific planets, countries, even specific damned *cities*." He muttered under his breath. "But there's no money in virtual stars for guys like me. A lot of people will never have the opportunity to stand within a few meters of their favorite singer, so they don't care if she's *real*. All they want is the spectacle. The image. The fantasy." He grunted in frustration. "But I cut through all that with flesh and blood, the real thing."

He sneered. "I'm a hero. Don't you get it? You should be on your knees thanking me, not hassling me about a phantom crime."

"A hero?" Jia scoffed. "How do you figure?"

Leonard squared his shoulders, jerking a thumb at his chest. "Because I'm doing my part to keep humanity important in entertainment. All those Purists running around aren't doing anything about virtual idols, now, are they? What good does it do if we're all pure if the heart and soul of our art are taken over by machines?"

"If you say so." Jia rolled her eyes. Erik offered a quiet grunt.

"No, Rena isn't a murderer, and she has no secret worth murdering for, other than being damned good at what she does because of *my* direction and *my* guidance. That's why

I've kept such a close eye on her. It's why I hired a sheep like Nguyen. I didn't need an ambitious party girl putting ideas into Rena's head. I needed someone who would worry about her like a little sister. Nguyen did that until she couldn't hack it anymore."

Erik locked eyes with Leonard. The men stared at each other for several seconds, neither averting his gaze.

"We'll need to talk to Rena," Erik insisted. "We're not saying we don't believe you, but she's part of the investigation."

Leonard replied with a single sharp shake of his head. "No way in hell. Like I told you, she's not a wolf. She's a sheep, or my golden goose if you prefer. She doesn't need additional stress about someone's suicide, especially from two cops who don't know anything about what's she going through."

"You can't be serious." Jia took a deep breath and slowly let it out. "We're conducting a police investigation, and we need to explore all angles and possible leads. Your big, self-important rant only highlighted how important Rena Winston is to your money-making operation. Even if she had nothing to do with it, she might be linked to the reason."

"Rena *didn't kill anyone*," Leonard thundered, his eyes inflamed. "How many times do I have to tell you idiots that?"

"No one's saying she did," Jia snapped back. "But she might have insight, and if she's such a sheep, we'd like to get her away from a wolf who might keep her too quiet to admit she saw or heard something. If this is nothing more than a suicide, you don't have any reason to stand in our way."

Leonard shook his head, his hand slicing the air in front of him. "No way. I refuse, and if I refuse, that means Rena refuses."

Erik shrugged, offering a tight smile. "Or we can hold a press conference and talk about how Euterpe is engaging in a cover-up. I wonder what people would think about that, given our reputation. But what do we know? We're just local yokels with badges, right?"

Leonard shot to his feet. "You arrogant *bastard*. You think you can get away with that? Your superiors made it clear that kind of thing won't be happening. We had an agreement."

Jia smirked. "Yeah, but then they assigned the case to *us*. Our news coverage speaks for itself. What do people keep calling us when it comes to corporations?" She looked at Erik.

Erik folded his arms and smiled. "Corp hunters."

"Oh, that's right." She went back to staring at Leonard. "'Corp hunters,' and Euterpe's a corporation, the last time I checked. The hunting urge is coming on."

Leonard glared at them. "You think you can play tough with me? You think I haven't faced off against big stars and corporate officers? You think you can intimidate me just because you're cops?"

Erik shook his head. "I think we've taken on terrorists, gangsters, and Ceres Galactic. It wasn't all that long ago that we were killing *yaoguai* underground." Erik eyed the man. "You ever smell the inside of a *yaoguai*? It's not something you easily forget. So, yeah, I think we can handle one manager with delusions of grandeur, but if you want to test how far you can go before you get arrested for obstruction of justice, bring it. I'd love to shove you in my car and drag your ass to the station. That'd be great for publicity."

"You don't know who you're messing with, cop. I can buy and sell you both."

"Unless you've got a closet full of monsters, terrorists, and killer bots, I don't care." Erik rose to his full height, his heavy glare on the manager. "I spent thirty years protecting the UTC on the frontier from the kind of people who would make you piss yourself and have nightmares for years. Don't even think for one second you have the ability to intimidate me. You are used to pushing around entertainment types, people who sing for a living, or stagehands who work for you." He inclined his head toward Jia. "And she's even more stubborn than I am."

Jia nodded, her lips pressed together.

Leonard's mouth twitched.

Erik slammed a fist on the table, rattling it. Leonard jumped.

"Now you're going to arrange a meeting with Rena," Erik leaned forward, growling, "or you're going to make us both angry. And we've shown what *we* do when we're angry."

Jia lifted her chin, a defiant gleam in her eye.

Leonard fell into his chair, his face red. "Whatever. You'll feel like idiots once you realize how much time you're wasting. I'll arrange something, but it'll be on my schedule, and it'll be here in this building. There's no way

I'm letting you drag my star to some filthy police station so you can chain her to a table and threaten her."

"That wasn't what we were planning," Jia replied.

He focused on her. "There's no way you're interviewing without me present, and that's final. Unless you're going to arrest her, she doesn't have to be alone." Leonard's nostrils flared. "And if you try that, I'm ready to deploy half the lawyers in the metroplex on you."

"We might need to talk to her alone in a follow-up, but the first interview should be fine with you present."

"Don't care. It won't be until tomorrow. She's got too many appointments today." Leonard folded his arms and looked away, grumbling under his breath.

"That's fine." Jia smiled. "See, was cooperating so hard?"

CHAPTER NINE

May 6, 2229, Neo Southern California Metroplex, en route to Euterpe Corporation Headquarters

Sitting in the passenger seat of the MX 60, Jia tried to push down the bubbling annoyance that had filled her all morning. It finally erupted as a loud snort.

"What's that about?" Erik looked at her. "I think I'm doing a pretty good job of flying."

Jia sighed. "It's not you. I'm just annoyed we had to waste a half-day of investigation because of that pompous reptile. I want to throat-punch him."

"Yeah, he's a real charming guy who needs a few teeth loosened, but he also backed off, which means he's scared of us, and we can use that if we need to."

Erik kept a loose hold on the control yoke. Jia had noticed he had been smiling the entire morning, ever since getting his first beignet.

Some men thrived with the simplest of pleasures provided them.

"Do you still think this is just a suicide?" she asked.

Erik shook his head. "Every new thing someone tells me about Rena Winston keeps feeding a possible motive. Maybe she had a secret boyfriend Chau found out about, and when Chau told him to get lost, he killed her. I was wrong—there's too much money and opportunity sloshing around this girl. More than enough to kill over. That ass of a manager made that clear."

"I've found additional information you might be interested in," Emma interjected. "I'm continuing my searches, but I just came across something relevant."

"What is it?" Jia asked.

"The general description the pretentious parasite offered for his charge is accurate. Rena Winston does appear to be, by all reports, a singing prodigy with an unusual ability to capture the attention of her audience. She's been groomed since she was three years old to be an entertainer by her parents and the aforementioned pretentious parasite."

"So? We pretty much knew that already." Jia sighed, disappointed. "What good does that do us?"

Emma chuckled. "Oh, Detective Lin, it gets far more interesting. Did you know both her parents are dead?"

Jia blinked before she sat forward. "What? None of the quick background articles I checked mentioned that."

"It's surprisingly well-hidden. It's almost as if someone were going out of their way to hide it."

"Meaning?" Erik asked.

"The less you know, the better," Emma suggested. "Let's just say I got overly eager and might have crossed some lines."

Jia groaned, putting a hand to her head. "You shouldn't

have done that."

"But I did," offered Emma merrily. "If it makes you feel better, I'm not legally a person, so I can't break the law."

"Yeah, but we're cops, and we need to make sure that evidence isn't thrown out," Erik grumbled.

Emma scoffed. "Mere details. Setting that aside, Euterpe is spending a lot of money to keep that particular news item suppressed, but I was able to confirm provisional death records. Normally, they would have been confirmed and transferred to Earth long ago, given that it has been several years, but for some reason, that hasn't happened. That might be one of the reasons most people are unaware of it. Despite sending her to live and work primarily on Earth, her parents remained on Remus."

Erik nodded. "Did they die from mysterious suicides, too?"

"No, flitter accident. There are minimal details available, but there was a cursory investigation. Mr. Carl has her power-of-attorney and guardianship until she reaches the age of majority. Records indicate Miss Winston specifically requested it."

Jia glanced at Erik. "That's more than a little suspicious, and I don't need the Lady or gut instinct to tell me suspicious coincidences piling up point to something sinister."

Erik looked over his shoulder, then accelerated and changed lanes. "Maybe our little songbird didn't want Mommy or Daddy getting any of her money. Emma, is the guardianship a matter of public record, even if hidden?"

"Yes, it is. You just have to know exactly where to look."

"Good. Then it won't risk anything if we ask her about it."

Jia wasn't sure what she had been expecting when Leonard and a huge musclebound bodyguard led her and Erik through a labyrinthine series of corridors in the bowels of a higher level of the Euterpe building.

When they finally arrived at their destination, Leonard opened the door to reveal a modest beige room with a simple glass table and a handful of chairs, barely a closet compared to the manager's office. She hardly noticed the furniture since her attention was drawn to the beautiful young dark-skinned woman sitting on one of the chairs, her hands folded neatly in her lap.

The girl's lithe, tall frame was flattered by her loose, flowing white gown. Silky black ringlets cascaded down the nape of her neck. The soft smile on her face was infectious.

Although Jia had seen recordings of Rena Winston's performances and couldn't deny her talent had she wanted to, being in the same room as the singer was almost mesmerizing. It was as if she exuded an invisible force that made you want to stare at her.

Rena stood, still smiling. "I'm so sorry to have to take up your time, Detectives." Even when not singing, her voice was soothing, almost ethereal. "I know you're very busy, and I wish I could have met you under more pleasant circumstances. Are you hungry or thirsty? I'm sure I could get you something."

"They're not here for breakfast, Rena," Leonard muttered. "And we don't want them here any longer than they need to be." He sat beside her and glared at the detectives. The bodyguard headed silently toward a corner, his expression blank and his hands in his pockets.

Jia's eyes flitted to the man before she returned her gaze to the singer, clearing her throat. "That won't be necessary, Miss Winston. We're fine. We had a bite to eat before we came here."

"Rena," the girl replied. "I insist. No one calls me Miss Winston around here."

"Okay, Rena. I'm Detective Jia Lin." She gestured at Erik. "This is my partner, Detective Blackwell." She took a seat on one of the chairs across from Rena. Erik joined her, sparing a glance for the UTC's most pathetic bodyguard.

"Oh, I know who you are." Rena's smile grew wider. "I've read about your heroic efforts. Leonard doesn't like it when I read the news."

Leonard frowned. "Because it's a waste of time. Two cops taking on gangsters or other stupid garbage doesn't matter to you. I'm just trying to help keep you focused, Rena. All you need to do is worry about pleasing your fans."

She looked down, her smile vanishing. "I know, Leonard, and I appreciate it. You're probably right. You usually are."

Jia frowned at the overbearing manager, and he in turn ignored her.

"Let's just get to the questions," Erik suggested. "We'll try to make this brief, and we're sorry if anything upsets you."

Rena shook her head and offered an apologetic smile. "I can't imagine any questions that would be more upsetting than Chau's death. I was shocked when I heard."

"Were you close?" Jia asked. She noticed that unlike Leonard, Rena used the victim's first name.

"I liked to think so." Rena sighed. "That might be assuming too much, considering she worked for me. I believe she had my best interests at heart, so I liked to think of her as a friend. She was one of the nicest people I've ever worked with." She blinked away her welling tears. "I'm sorry." She reached up to wipe one away. "Please ask me whatever you need to. I'll do anything I can to help you."

"We're still exploring her death." Jia kept her voice soft. "Although preliminary examination suggested a suicide, we have evidence that suggests that's not the case."

Rena stared at the table, pain etched on her face. "Leonard mentioned that. It's awful. It was bad enough when I thought she'd killed herself, but the idea that someone might have done it to her?" She shuddered. "I suppose that's why we still need police, even on Earth."

"Is there anyone you know who might have wished her harm?" Jia asked.

Rena shook her head. "No, not that she ever told me. She did seem...more distant in recent weeks."

Leonard frowned. "We're gearing up for the world tour. She was busy. Don't waste their time with unimportant crap, Rena."

The girl winced. "I'm sorry, Leonard."

Jia glared at the manager. "We'll collect all the necessary information, and then we'll decide what's important. Sometimes even the smallest discrepancy can lead to a break in the case. I would appreciate it if you would let her talk without further interruption."

Leonard rolled his eyes. "Okay, fine. Waste her time. Waste *my* time. Call the Prime Minister and waste *his* time, too, while you're at it."

Erik smiled. "If we had a reason to believe he was involved, we would." He nodded to Jia.

Jia continued, "Rena, you said Chau's behavior changed?"

The young woman nodded. "Yes. She was never mean or short with me, but I could tell something was bothering her lately. I tried to get her to tell me about it, and she told me not to worry. That it was just personal problems. I even suggested she might need a vacation, but she said there was no way she could take one right now."

"That's right," Leonard mumbled. "At least Nguyen understood priorities."

"Besides her behavioral changes," Jia continued, "did she mention any names? Not people who had harmed her, but maybe names she didn't mention often but suddenly did?"

Rena put a finger to her mouth and tilted her head as she pondered the question. She lowered her hand and offered a single shake of her head. "No, I can't say I remember anything like that. We mostly talked about the upcoming tour and the different cities I'm going to visit. Sometimes we talked about movies. I enjoy love stories." She let out a wistful sigh. "My career requires sacrifices, so it's fun to imagine what it could be in other circumstances."

The door slid open, and a man in a brown uniform and a long-brimmed hat stepped inside. He held a large glass vase filled with colorful flowers. "I've got a delivery for Rena Winston."

The singer blinked and then smiled. "Oh, how lovely." She sniffed the air. "And they smell even lovelier."

Leonard shot out of his chair. "What the hell are you doing in here? What idiot sent you this way?" He scrubbed his face with his hand. "Why are we paying people at the front if they're just going to send every random nitwit directly to the talent?"

"I'm just here to deliver some flowers." The delivery man averted his eyes. "No reason to get hostile, sir."

"You think this is the first time, peon?" Leonard sneered. "Let me guess, you gave them some sob story about how your cousin always wanted an autograph from Rena. Well, too bad, slick. You're not getting one. Put the flowers on the table and get the hell out of here before I get you fired."

The delivery man sighed. "You're kind of an ass."

Rena put a hand over her mouth and gasped. Erik and Jia snickered.

Leonard's eyes bulged. He nodded to the bodyguard and motioned with his hand. "Break something if you need to, but make sure he's escorted out of the building." He glared at the delivery man. "Your ass is so fired, punk. You should start looking for a new job when you get home."

"No, Leonard, please," Rena insisted. "He needs his job."

"Yes," the delivery man responded quietly, "I do. But there's something I need more of."

"And what's that?" Leonard asked.

The bodyguard advanced, still stone-faced.

"My Rena." The man hurled the vase at Leonard. His hand whipped to his side, and he yanked out a stun pistol tucked into his belt. The vase slammed into Leonard, shattering into shards. He stumbled backward, hissing in surprise. The bodyguard rushed forward, but the delivery man fired two quick shots into him, dropping the huge man to the ground with a loud thud.

Rena shivered in wide-eyed terror. Jia and Erik sprang out of their chairs.

Erik yanked his chair up with his left arm and threw the chair at the delivery man. The man panicked and fired at the chair, his white bolts scorching it but doing nothing to stop the flying furniture. The makeshift projectile crashed into the delivery man and sent his stun pistol flying. Erik's chair assault pushed the man against the door with a grunt.

Jia pulled out her stun pistol. Two bolts flew across the room and nailed the assailant in the face. He toppled forward and hit the floor a second after the chair.

Drool leaked from his mouth.

Erik retrieved his pistol from its holster. He pushed the chair and the stunned delivery man out of the way with his feet and approached the open door. He swung his weapon back and forth. "Clear."

Jia hurried to the bodyguard and checked his pulse. He was fine. She confirmed their suspect was still breathing before holstering her stun pistol. She looked over her shoulder. "Rena, are you all right?"

The singer wrapped her hands around her shoulders. "W-what is going on?"

Leonard groaned and clutched his chest. "That bastard hurt me. I guess you cops are good for something. You solved our little stalker problem."

Rena turned her head slowly toward the stunned

delivery man. "Stalker?" Her voice quaked. "I have a stalker?"

Jia knelt by the suspect and slapped binding ties on him. She turned her wrath-filled eyes on Leonard. "Are you kidding me? Why didn't you report this to the police?"

The manager shrugged, wincing afterward. "Talent always attracts stalkers. We've got security. We don't need police attention or the bad PR."

Erik shoved his pistol back into its holster. "Yeah, great security. The bastard got all the way to Rena and stunned your security guard. If we hadn't been here, things might have gotten really bad."

"He would have never gotten out of the building. Even if he had, Rena's got a tracking implant. Insurance insists. There's no way she can be kidnapped." Leonard took a halting step and sat back down. He looked down at the stain on his suit. "Stupid stalker."

Jia stood, her gaze flicking between the stalker and Leonard. "Is this why Chau was upset?"

"She knew about him, sure. She was the main person I had filtering Rena's messages." Leonard tugged on his collar. "Rena doesn't need this kind of stress. She needs to concentrate on being pretty and singing."

Tears streamed down the singer's cheeks. She stared at the fallen bodyguard, trembling.

"You stupid..." Jia took a deep breath and slowly let it out, pointing to the two bodies on the floor. "And you didn't think any of this was relevant? The stalker might have killed Chau Nguyen."

Rena lowered her face into her hands and sobbed. "Then it's all my fault."

Leonard's nostrils flared. "Shut your trap, Detective. You don't know that. Yeah, I didn't mention it. I didn't think it was relevant."

Erik stomped over to the man and yanked him up by his lapels.

Leonard glared and pushed off him. "What the hell do you think you're doing?"

Erik growled, "If you got a woman killed because you're worried about PR, don't think you'll get away with it."

Leonard got in Erik's face. "You touch me again, and I'll get *you* fired."

Erik snorted. "You lie to us again, and we'll transmit every piece of this investigation over the entire UTC. You understand me?"

Rena lifted her head. She scrambled out of her chair and went to the bodyguard's side, kneeling beside him before looking at Jia. "Is he going to be okay?"

"He'll be fine," Jia explained softly. "He's just stunned. It'll take a while for it to wear off. It hurts, but it does no permanent damage."

Rena wiped her tears away with her forearm. "I just can't take anyone else getting hurt for me."

Leonard gestured at the stalker. "Why don't you stop upsetting her and make yourselves useful? You got the guy, right? Drag his ass to jail. Beat him up in the cells or whatever it is you people do."

Erik glared down at him. "Don't worry, Mr. Carl. We'll do just that, but this isn't over."

Leonard shrugged. "Yes, it *is*." He pointed to the fake delivery driver. "You got the guy."

Erik eyed the stunned man. "Yeah, we'll see."

CHAPTER TEN

May 6, 2229, Neo Southern California Metroplex, Police Enforcement Zone 122 Station, Interrogation Room

The detectives stared at the bound criminal sitting across the table from them. The man hadn't resisted when he recovered from the stun. He'd been remarkably cooperative, including giving him his name, Trevor Fairchild. His PNIU and a DNA search confirmed he was indeed Trevor Fairchild, a native of Neo SoCal.

Jia stood and circled around the table and the back of the suspect's chair. "You're in a lot of trouble, Trevor. I mean, how stupid are you? Not only did you go after one of the most famous singers on Earth, but you tried it when two cops were in the room." She continued walking and pulled a seat out, sitting down once again.

"Bad luck," the man replied. "It happens to the best of us. I wasn't going to hurt her, you know. I just wanted to talk to her. I've tried before, but they wouldn't let me in, so I took advantage of my work uniform."

Erik frowned, then stood up and walked in the opposite

direction Jia had. "That's called kidnapping, you sick freak. You're going to go away for a long time."

"I used a non-lethal weapon, and I have no priors," he replied calmly. "I'm sure my lawyer can get me sentenced to transportation. And I wasn't going to kidnap her. I didn't take her anywhere. You can't prove I was going to."

Erik crouched by Trevor's side. "Yeah, transportation. They're going to ship you off to the edge of the UTC, so some Zitark can stop by and have you for lunch." Erik opened his mouth, clicking his teeth together. "Munch, munch. I hope you taste good."

He frowned at Erik. "I'm not an idiot. Everyone says the Zitarks are too afraid. It's why they backed down a couple years back, right?" Trevor sighed, faint melancholy in the sound. "And transportation will be good for me. It's a chance to start over once I've paid my debt to society. I recently inherited some money, so it's just a matter of my rehabilitation. I'm obviously tainted by my soft life on Earth."

"Oh? Is that what you figure? Granddad dies, so you can do what you want?" Erik leaned closer to the man. "By the way, you don't get sentenced to transportation for murder. You go to prison."

Trevor turned to look at Erik, pity in his eyes. "I'm not a murderer. I stunned one man and I threw a vase at another. It's antisocial, but it's barely a crime."

"What about Chau Nguyen? She get in your way? Tell you to screw off? Was that why you killed her?" Jia asked.

"I don't even know who that is." Trevor sounded confused. "I guarantee I didn't kill anyone, let alone this," he waved a hand, "Chau Nguyen person. I also guarantee you don't have any evidence linking me to a murder," he finished, a glint of anger in his eyes before it went away.

Erik stood slowly, eyeing him. "Confident little punk, aren't we?"

"I made a mistake." Trevor bowed his head. "I know it doesn't make up for stunning that man or scaring Rena, but I admit I'm wrong, and I'm prepared to face my punishment."

"We'll let you wait in here for a while. Maybe you'll remember more once you have time to think about it." Erik walked around the table.

Jia rose from her seat, shaking her head. She headed for the door. They both stepped outside the interrogation room. Erik slapped the access panel and waited while it closed.

"What do you think?" he asked.

Jia shook her head. "He's too calm. Too prepared. An obsessed stalker wouldn't be this calm after getting stopped a few meters from his target. He reminds me less of a stalker and more of a..." she paused a second before finishing, "hitman."

Erik eyed the wall like he saw through it to the man beyond. "Yeah, that's what I was thinking." He turned to her. "It's almost like the guy expected to get caught and planned for it."

"I checked his background," Jia explained. "He's right about everything he said in there. No priors, no hint of trouble. He's never had impressive jobs, but that's not a crime. There is nothing in public records that suggests he's antisocial. The DNA analysis doesn't show any uncorrected mutations associated with potentially violent psychotic or sociopathic behavior, either. He's just a guy off the street."

"Nope. He's not just a guy off the street."

Jia gave him a confused look. "What do you mean?"

Erik inclined his head toward the door. "He's still our chief suspect. You don't need a mutation to be a stone-cold killer. Society's been producing plenty of those for a long time. He can stew for a while. Besides, we've got an appointment."

"Appointment?" Jia looked up, trying to remember what she had obviously forgotten.

Erik smiled. "Remember?" He jerked a thumb down the hall. "When we dropped Trevor's PNIU with Malcolm, he said he'd have something for us in a couple of hours. It's almost been a couple of hours."

Malcolm was whistling a jaunty tune as Erik and Jia entered his office. He was examining financial data on three different windows.

He turned in his chair, looking up. "Ah, good timing, Detectives. I was just about to send you a message."

Erik smiled. "Oh? You ask Camila out yet?"

"Ah, no." Malcolm coughed. "But that's not what, uh…"

Erik waved a hand. "Just messing with you. You have something on our new best friend?"

Malcolm let out a sigh of relief and turned to the data windows. "Yes, I've got goodies to share. Plus, I found something else in the last few minutes. Technically, search algorithms I had running through Chau Nguyen's files found it, but I designed them. Emma kind of pointed me toward some things, too."

Jia coughed, looking around. "I thought we told *you* to be careful, Emma."

The AI's holographic form winked into existence beside Malcolm's desk, her arms folded, an annoyed look on her face. "I happened to notice some file irregularities, and I offered minor suggestions to Technician Constantine about how to design searches. It's all information he would have found eventually. I just facilitated discovery in an opportune timeframe."

Erik grinned. "We'll just emphasize his brilliance in our reports and leave you out."

"Exactly. It's not that hard." Emma vanished. "I'll let him explain what he has for you."

Malcolm's face lit up with pride. "First of all, I'll give you the easy stuff to deal with. Okay, semi-easy. Our stalker? He got a huge payout three days ago from an off-world bank. We can try communicating with them, but given the nature of the account, I'm giving us a one or two percent chance of associating someone real with the account in any sort of timely manner."

"That can't be easy," Erik insisted.

Malcolm shook his head. "Nope. Whoever did this was not only rich, but they knew how to work core-world banking systems to their advantage."

Jia's suspicious gaze drifted toward the door. "That doesn't sound like the kind of thing a random delivery stalker would know how to do." She looked at Erik. "But it *does* sound like something someone associated with a Hexagon-located corporation might know."

"Yeah." Erik leaned forward. The central data window hovering over the desk displayed credits and debits in Trevor Fairchild's primary bank account. His eyes flitted back and forth, trying to review the data backward. "For a man who was obviously living modestly, the sudden influx of money is noticeable." He looked at Malcolm. "During our interrogation, he said he inherited some money."

Malcolm scratched his chin. "I'm not going to say that's impossible, but the way this money came into his account isn't how those kinds of payments work." He paused for a second, reviewing the information on the credit to the account. "It's hard to do probate with semi-anonymous deposits. I'm not an expert on that, but I have gone through that kind of data for other cases."

"Remember what I thought?" Jia asked. "A *hitman*."

Malcolm mouthed the word before speaking louder. "But he didn't kill anyone. People don't pay hitmen to stun people, do they? Wouldn't that just make him a stunman?"

"Publicity stunt," Erik suggested, rubbing his nose. "They give their wholesome idol a little edge. Make her life dangerous, gives them a bunch of PR leading into their big tour."

Jia didn't look convinced. "But her asshole manager seemed obsessed with doing everything he could to keep her from being associated with anything like that. Why hire some random guy if there's already a police investigation involving two famous cops?"

"Oh!" Malcolm snapped his fingers. "I forgot. My other goodie for you. It's what I found in Chau Nguyen's personal files. A hidden, semi-encrypted diary she started earlier this year. I mean," He scoffed and rolled his eyes,

"She used normal commercial encryption. It'd stop some random person from getting into it, but it's not going to stand a chance against a professional."

Erik smirked. The unspoken "like me" was hanging at the end of Malcolm's comment. He let it go.

Jia grinned. "I'm glad you're on our side, then. Find anything interesting?"

"I skimmed it. It's mostly just about how lucky she felt to work with Rena Winston and how talented she thought she was. She thought that Leonard guy was a total jerk, though."

"That's putting it mildly," Jia muttered.

"I hope he gets into a flitter accident," Erik admitted.

"But there's the thing." Malcolm furrowed his brow. "The entries got really sparse this last month and then stopped. There's only one recent entry from a few weeks ago." He tapped in the air on a keyboard only he could see through his smart lenses. Another data window appeared, this time containing text the officers could read.

APRIL 14, 2229

Everything's different now. I don't know what to do. What they did was wrong, but she doesn't deserve to suffer because of what they did. I don't even think she knows. I have to do something, though. It's all wrong. Sick. *Twisted*.

He waved a hand at the post. "And that's it. No more entries after that." Malcolm shrugged.

Jia stared at the diary comment. "It doesn't take much of a logical leap to conclude she might be talking about

Leonard or someone else at Euterpe. The 'she' referenced must be Rena, but after what we saw earlier, I have a hard time believing she knew anything about Chau getting murdered unless Rena's the greatest actress in the UTC."

Erik nodded, thinking through the information. "Leonard might be hiding something, after all. Maybe he paid the stalker, but I don't get why. The PR angle is the only one that makes sense at the moment."

Malcolm tilted his head and held up a finger. "One moment, Detective. Your Lady is with you today."

"Oh?"

"Yes." He nodded. "I was trying to follow up on some records request. I sent some stuff to Remus, but you know, it'll be a while before it comes back." Malcolm swiped his hand through the air. A new data window appeared with a message. He spent a few moments reading it. "I double-checked with the Census and Biographic Directorate."

"Huh?" Erik replied. "What do they have to do with this case?"

"I suggested he do it," Emma chimed in, a hint of smug-ness in her voice. "I thought it might be helpful, and the fewer direct fingerprints I had on the investigation, the better, so I pointed him toward some additional resources."

Jia shrugged. "Fine. What did you find, Malcolm?"

Excitement grew on his face. "So, while it's a little convoluted, hear me out. I don't know if it means anything but given the crazy stuff you two end up involved in, I can't ignore anything out of hand."

"A good policy." Jia's brows lifted.

"So, her parents—the ones who died in the accident? They weren't her parents. Crazy, right?"

Erik rubbed his forehead. "This *is* convoluted. So, who were they?"

Malcolm shrugged. "Random people. They weren't blood-related, though. She has birth records from a hospital on Remus, but her actual parents weren't recorded. From what the CBD records indicate, they weren't even adoptive parents who took an orphan or an abandoned kid or anything, just temporary legal guardians."

Jia thought it through. "Family friends?"

"Maybe, but there's nothing in the records to indicate that."

Erik stopped rubbing his forehead and moved to pinching the bridge of his nose. "Why does every murder have to be so convoluted in Neo SoCal?"

Jia ignored his slight about her city of birth. "I've never read anything that suggests Rena is aware of any of what Malcolm just said."

"That would be correct," Emma offered. "She's never spoken of her parents as being anything but her normal biological parents in any publicly recorded interviews."

Erik shrugged. "Family can be difficult, even when you're not a famous singer. We both know that. It took me a lot to call my brother back, and I knew the score, and why we had trouble between us. If she didn't know the truth for a long time, maybe she didn't want to face it and decided to put it behind her."

"No, there are too many loose threads," Jia insisted. "There are too many inconsistencies, Erik. The only thing we know for sure is a woman ended up dead on Dragon

Tear and a suddenly rich stalker decided to finally go after his target."

"Well, there is an upside," Erik suggested.

"What's that?" Jia asked, incredulity both on her face and in her tone.

"At least we don't have to go into the Scar this time," he quipped.

"*Yet.*" Jia snickered. "We have a lot of evidence, but is it enough?"

"Nope. We have more than evidence." Erik lifted a finger and took on an evil grin. "We've got a suspect. We'll let him sit in there for a day. He thinks this is all going to work out. He thinks he's just going to end up transported, spend a few years doing some farm labor, and retire on the frontier a rich man. We're going to let him get nice and comfortable, and then we're going to push that arrogance right out of him."

Jia nodded, readiness returning to her face. "Even if he *didn't* have anything to do with the murder, he might have a connection to someone who did."

"Exactly," Erik agreed.

"I love watching you guys work." Malcolm leaned back. The squeak his chair gave made Jia flinch, but she grinned as she took in his enthusiastic smile. "Let's take down some criminals!"

CHAPTER ELEVEN

When Erik and Jia stepped into the interrogation room the next day, the suspect had already been sitting at the table for thirty minutes.

It wouldn't hurt Trevor, and it might help figure out just who was helping to hide a killer.

He'd spent the night in holding after a meeting with a lawyer. He'd been under the impression he would be free until trial, but an expedited ruling ensured he'd rot in jail until then.

It was an easy sell for the judge, given that everyone felt a stalker with few strong connections to the community was a heavy flight risk. Jia was looking forward to applying pressure, with Erik's help.

They'd already arranged for a fake prisoner in a nearby cell to complain about how he couldn't go back to prison, and how awful it was compared to jail. To get to the truth, every tactic must be considered. It wasn't like it was false, either.

Prison wasn't pleasant.

Heavy bags occupied the space under Trevor's eyes. He eyed the two detectives as he rubbed his wrists as well as he could, considering the binding ties he had on.

"Enjoy your first night in jail?" Erik gave him a cold smile. "This is a damned hotel compared to what you're going to experience in prison." He stopped for a moment, pursed his lips, and scratched his cheek. "The hard part, though, is not even being on Earth. Knowing you're sitting in a pile of metal with fake light. Even a frontier dome is paradise compared to that."

Trevor's eyes darted back and forth, taking in Erik and Jia. "I'm not going to prison. I told you the other day, it's going to be transportation. That's the most reasonable sentence for my crimes."

"You really believe that, don't you, Trevor?" Jia settled in at the table and let out a quiet laugh. "Maybe, *just maybe*, if you'd shot someone with a stun pistol by mistake, we might be talking about that, but you trespassed in a building, shot a security guard, and admitted in front of several witnesses that you were there to harass Rena Winston." She pointed toward her PNIU. "We were there on official police business, so we recorded all that. Euterpe Security has already sent over their recordings." She shook her head. "Nope. Everyone knows you're a dangerous stalker. No one believes for a second that you just wanted to talk to Rena."

Trevor narrowed his eyes on Jia. "You can't send me to prison for something I didn't do. That's not fair."

"Sure, we can. We do it all the time. Why do you think

they call it '*attempted* murder?'" Jia shrugged. "Just because you're an *incompetent* criminal doesn't mean you get to go free. Do you think a terrorist who is stopped from shooting citizens gets to argue, 'Not fair. I *didn't* kill them?'" She rolled her eyes. "You've been watching too many legal dramas, Trevor. This is the real world."

Erik shrugged, a sympathetic look on his face. "We've checked your background. We know you're not a hardened criminal. It'd be a stretch to even call you antisocial before this little incident."

"Exactly!" Trevor shouted. He took a deep breath, then leaned toward them and lowered his voice. "They have to take that into account, right?" He looked eager. "It was my first offense. Not antisocial. I've worked my entire life. I'm a good candidate for transportation, not prison. That kind of thing is for garbage. Murderers and gangsters. Terrorists and insurrectionists."

"I see where you're coming from," Erik replied. He tapped his cheek. "I served with more than a few soldiers during my Army days who'd had a rough start before the military straightened them out."

Jia was surprised Erik would bring that up as part of their strategy. It described *him* in a way, and he was normally more private, even indirectly. She didn't have time to worry about him baring his soul.

They hadn't been sure the day before if their strategy would work, given how calm Trevor was, but after only one night and a little creative performance near him, his hitman persona had vanished, replaced by a scared suspect in over his head.

"That's why I should get transportation," Trevor insisted. He took a few quick breaths to steady himself. "I studied it before I decided to do what I did. I read all about the law. Recommendations can help with that. You guys could talk to the prosecutor. I cooperated. I didn't sit here and deny it. I could have made things really annoying."

Jia scoffed. "What were you going to deny? It's not like we don't have enough evidence to drown a syndicate boss."

Erik nodded at his partner. "She's got a point, Trevor. If you want the prosecutor to make any recommendations for sentencing, you've got to do more. You've got to give us something we don't have already. Then it'll look like you're cooperating."

"But I don't..." Trevor looked down. "I was never going to hurt her. I swear. You have to believe me."

"But that still leaves Chau Nguyen." Erik shrugged. "She's dead. *Someone* killed her."

Not having direct physical proof of the murder beyond a reasonable doubt wouldn't matter if they could score a confession and supporting evidence.

The only thing Jia had argued with Erik was that Trevor didn't seem the type to kill. However, the detectives had agreed the night before he was their best lead.

Trevor lifted his head, his eyes widening as he looked at the two of them. "I *didn't* kill that woman. I do *not* confess or accept that. I'm not a murderer. All I did was stun a guy!"

"I'm betting you have an idea who did kill her." Erik stood and leaned over the table, causing Trevor to lean back. "Come on, Trevor. A guy like you doesn't get a big splash of cash for no reason. Someone gave that to you to help them out. It's enough to see why you might take a fall for them."

"T-that was an inheritance," Trevor sputtered.

"Transferred from a semi-anonymous off-world account?" Jia asked. She slapped her hand on the table. "Give us a break, Trevor! Yes, we can *trace* the owner, but we don't have time. If you're not the murderer, you might have evidence that will lead us to the murderer. Right now, we have a stalker, a dead woman, and a mysterious payment. How can we be sure you weren't paid to kill Chau Nguyen? How do we know she didn't catch onto *your* plan to kidnap Rena?"

"I wasn't going to kidnap her." Trevor groaned as he slumped in his chair, pinching his eyes shut. "It wasn't supposed to be like this."

Erik returned his chair, nodding in sympathy.

Jia agreed the Good Cop, Bad Cop-routine might be a centuries-old practice, but it still worked. Next time, though, she wanted to be the good cop.

"You didn't want to do any of this, did you, Trevor?" Erik suggested. "You want transportation instead of prison? Then it's like I said before—you have to give us something to work with. If you weren't paid to kill Chau Nguyen, why did you get all that money?"

They allowed him some quiet to either decide he was still fighting or...

"I couldn't turn it down." A tear escaped down Trevor's cheek. "My life was going nowhere. All I had to do was scare her and stun a guy. I checked on the net. It said stunning didn't hurt permanently. Punching a guy risks more permanent damage."

"You're saying someone paid you to go after Rena Winston?" Jia asked, dropping the hostility from her voice.

"I don't even know how they knew I needed money. Things had been getting tight lately. I made some bad choices, not criminal stuff, just spending money I didn't have. Borrowing. They called me, hidden number somehow. They must have overheard me. They had seen me at Euterpe before." Trevor stared into his lap. "I make a lot of deliveries there. They said that would be helpful. It'd be easier for me to get past Security. They supplied the stun pistol. Mailed it to me. They told me the time I needed to be there, and that I just had to say I was delivering the flowers. They said they would ensure Security would let me in without checking me."

Erik furrowed his brow. "Did you recognize the voice?"

"It was all distorted on the call," Trevor whispered, peering at the two of them, the fight gone from his eyes. "You *have* to believe me."

"Wait." Jia put up a finger. "You're saying they contacted you and made the offer. Then you weren't stalking Rena Winston to begin with?"

Trevor nodded. "To be honest, she's not my type. She's a little too 'perfect angel' for me."

Jia rolled her eyes. "Duly noted." *Why was it that guys wanted girls who were a bit crazy?* She eyed Erik, who wasn't paying attention to her. *Or girls might want guys who were rough?*

There was a ring of truth to his confession.

Malcolm's initial dive into Trevor's PNIU hadn't revealed anything to suggest he'd cared about Rena Winston before a few days prior. There were no messages sent to her, no files featuring her. Her heart rate kicked up. If Trevor wasn't a stalker, that pointed to a disturbing possibility.

Jia stood. "We need to follow up on what you've told us. You might stay out of prison yet, but I'd get ready for a few years working for the UTC on a colony world." She headed toward the door, ignoring the hope in the suspect's eyes. After exiting the room, she waited for Erik to emerge.

His easy-going, sympathetic persona vanished as he slapped the access panel to close the door. "If Trevor's not a stalker, why did Leonard tell us there was one?"

Jia had to play the other side of this argument. "There could be *another* stalker, and it's just a coincidence that Trevor showed up."

Erik eyed her. "On the exact day and time of the interview? And getting that deep into Euterpe? If that was all it took, half their people would have been kidnapped years ago." He looked up and down the hallway. "He had help from the inside."

Jia nodded. "That's what I think. The only thing I can't figure out is why Leonard would do this. The PR angle I get, but what about Chau? That diary entry suggests she stumbled onto something."

"I think it's time to ask Leonard to chat at the station."

"And if he refuses?" Jia raised an eyebrow.

"Let's grab a few officers," Erik suggested. "The show of force will convince him this is real, and maybe he won't be stupid about it."

Jia chuckled. "Given how arrogant that guy is, I suspect he'll do something very stupid."

Erik grinned. "Then maybe I'll get my wish."

"Which is?" she asked.

Erik flexed his fist as he smiled at her. "To punch that smug bastard in the face."

Jia starting walking toward the captain's office.

Rough...

CHAPTER TWELVE

Erik, Jia, and four uniformed officers exited the elevator and headed to the reception desk in front of a hallway sealed by a large locked door.

The receptionist ignored them for a moment as she tapped on headshots in the data window in front of her. Different-colored borders appeared around her selections.

Jia cleared her throat loudly and patted the badge on her jacket. "Excuse us. This is official police business."

The receptionist stared at Jia, her lips pressed into a tight line. She sighed, an annoyed look on her face. "I thought we had something worked out where you'd only arrest people at their homes."

"I don't know anything about that." Jia frowned. "That's not *my* policy."

"Who is this concerning, Detective?"

"We need to talk to Leonard Carl," Jia barked. "Now."

"Fine. Fine." The receptionist waved a hand dismissively. She entered a command on her PNIU before narrowing her eyes. "He's in Meeting Room Twenty-Two with Rena. Do you need me to—"

"No. We were there the other day." Jia nodded to the uniformed officers. "You stay here in case he gets past us." She turned to the receptionist. "Don't let him know we're coming."

The receptionist shrugged. "He's kind of an ass. Do what you want. I had a bet with some of the receptionists that he was on Dragon Tear, so I'm not surprised you're here."

"He has access to Dragon Tear?" Jia asked.

That provided another link between Leonard and Chau.

The receptionist shrugged. "I'm not saying I've *seen* it. I'm just saying I've heard he likes to party pretty hard. If he wasn't the man who brought Rena to Euterpe, I bet he would have been fired years ago." She waved her hand, and a small grid appeared at her side. She jabbed her finger at a number. The door sealing the hallway slid open with a hiss. "Enjoy."

Erik snickered. Jia nodded, satisfied. The detective hurried past the receptionist into the corridor.

"You sure you can get there?" Erik asked.

"I didn't want a babysitter," Jia replied, "even if she seems to dislike him as much as we do."

A red line appeared on the smart lenses, providing a clear trail on the floor.

"I certainly remember how to get there," Emma explained. "I'm also monitoring the local flight area for any signs of the flitter registered to the pretentious parasite."

"Good. I'm hoping he didn't see us coming." Jia shifted

from a jog to a run. Their circumstantial evidence might not be enough to arrest Leonard Carl yet, but she doubted he was used to dealing with experienced detectives. She had no doubt he was behind everything. The only piece of lingering doubt was motive.

Killing a woman because she found out about a PR stunt seemed too much, and Jia doubted Chau's diary entry would have been so vehement about something so *petty*. Something else was there.

They just had to find it.

"What if we're wrong about him?" Erik asked as they turned a corner. His synchronicity of thought was no longer disturbing to Jia. It had been happening more and more in recent months. That was what being a good partner meant, at least to her.

"We could be, but I doubt it. Unless he can cough up some immediate evidence he wasn't lying about a stalker, he's already in trouble. I'm sure once we start looking into his finances, he's going to have to come up with some quick explanations."

A shrill klaxon cut through the air.

Erik and Jia halted, looking around the long hallway.

"Dangerous security breach in progress," announced a recorded female voice. "All employees should shelter in place. Security bots and teams are being deployed."

Jia's PNIU came alive with a short-wave transmission from one of the officers at reception, Kino. "Detective, this room just sealed, and we're hearing a security warning."

"We're in the hall, so it didn't seal," she replied. "You okay otherwise?"

"Yes. The receptionist is freaked out, though. She says this isn't a drill."

"Hold position," Jia ordered. "If security shows up, tell them this is a police matter now. I doubt this is a coincidence." She burst into a run and yanked out her stun pistol. "He knows we're here."

"Yeah." Erik drew his pistol as he caught up with Jia. "He's stalling, which means he must be trying to make a run for it."

Jia rushed around a corner. "We passed the previous intersections, which means we've got him. Oh, that's annoying."

Panels in the wall and ceiling flipped over to reveal six-legged security bots with long stun rods. The machines, the size of a small dog, boiled out of the new passages like angry insects defending their hive. Jia shoved her stun pistol into a holster and grabbed her slug-thrower. Erik's pistol came to life. It took a few bullets before the first target collapsed in a sparking, smoking mess. Jia pointed her gun and tried for careful shots, but it still took two bullets to down one security bot.

"Do what you need to stop this, Emma," Erik ordered. "I'll claim it was police emergency hacking later, but I doubt Euterpe's going to make too big a deal out of it. It'd be bad PR for them."

"Very well. Give me a moment. I've requested additional reinforcements from the station too."

He ripped open another security bot with careful shots. "And here I thought bringing the big gun would be too flashy. That's the lesson: always bring the biggest gun." He slammed his metal fist into one of the bots who had slipped his notice, punching through the head with a slug to finish it off. "You never know what you're going to have to shoot."

Jia laughed. "Isn't that the laser rifle?" She shot a bot off the ceiling. It fell and collided with another on the floor, leading to a tangled mess of metal limbs.

"Biggest gun with the most shots, then," he amended.

The pair backed up and continued sending rounds down the hallway.

Experience and tactical-center practice firing at weak points made individual security bots easy kills, but additional units kept emerging from the exposed security tunnels. The alarm continued to shriek, and fortunately, despite the doors lining the hall, no one emerged and risked getting shot.

Twitching, smoking, and sparking bodies began to pile up. Their brethren surged over them, treating them as inconveniences, showing no awareness of or concern about the destroyed machines.

Erik reloaded before taking down another bot with a tight three-shot cluster. "I didn't bring a platoon's worth of ammo with me." He carried on the conversation as if the two of them were discussing the latest large movie release. "Got plenty in the flitter."

"I know what you mean." She blasted two off the wall, which tripped several on the floor. "I'm down to a magazine and a half."

The alarm fell silent, but the bots continued their unrelenting advance. Several more bots fell to bullets before Jia reloaded.

"Last mag!" she called, her heart pounding now. She

shot the closest bot scuttling toward them on the floor. It made it another meter, smoking before collapsing.

Erik's gun went dry, and he brought back his left arm. "Smashing will have to do."

The bots halted. Jia stopped firing. The machines hesitated for a moment before climbing on the walls and heading toward the security tunnels.

"Sorry for the delay," Emma explained. "The security system is fairly sophisticated, but I've canceled the alert response."

"Any security teams coming?" Erik didn't want to beat up a guard, but he wasn't about to let himself be slowed down while his suspect escaped.

"No, they seem to realize that something's gone amiss. A high-level override code was used to activate the system just now."

Erik pushed a downed bot out of the way with his foot. It scraped the floor. "Do you have eyes on Leonard Carl?"

Emma laughed. "I'm not a fleshbag. I never have eyes on anything, but internal tracking indicates he and Miss Winston are still in Meeting Room Twenty-two. There are no cameras in the room."

Jia scoffed. "He must have thought the bots would stun us. He'd make his run then."

"He's with Rena." Erik frowned. "Maybe *she* played us?"

"I don't want to believe that, but you could be right. Let's go." She held out her slug-thrower and pulled out her stun pistol. "So you have something with ammo."

Erik took the gun with a grunt. "This better not end with that bastard siccing a *yaoguai* on us."

They advanced through the hall strewn with robot

carnage. A nearby door opened, and a gray-haired man stuck his head out the door. He gasped when he saw the guns and ducked back into his office, slamming the door.

Jia spoke toward the door. "That's for the best. Police business. We'll have the situation under control in a couple of minutes."

Erik and Jia arrived at their destination. Emma's red guidance line disappeared.

Jia pointed her weapon at the door. Erik moved to the access panel. He held up three fingers, dropped one, dropped another, and dropped the last one before opening the door.

They'd been expecting a panicking Leonard Carl, or maybe a few security guards on the take. Even a *yaoguai* wouldn't have surprised them much. They didn't expect to see an empty room.

Jia crept into the room. There wasn't enough space for anyone to hide.

"Some sort of optical camouflage?"

"Now you sound more paranoid than me," Erik replied. He kicked over a few chairs.

Jia pointed to an undamaged chair. Two PNIUs were stacked on the seat.

Erik cursed under his breath. "Let me guess-those belong to Leonard and Rena."

"Your supposition is correct," Emma replied.

Erik frowned and squatted by a chair. He nodded at a few dark spots on the floor. "Looks like a trickle of blood."

Jia's stomach tightened. "If Rena didn't know about it, she'd make a nice hostage."

Erik growled and stood. "This blood isn't fresh. If the

receptionist didn't notice him leaving, or he went out a side entrance, we're going to have to hit a bunch of camera feeds, and all that will get us is when he left."

Jia shook her head and offered him a tight smile. "Does Leonard strike you as the kind of man who could pull off surgery?"

"No. Why?"

"He said Rena had a tracking implant." Jia held up a hand. "I'm not all that familiar with them, but from what little I've read, they're not usually placed anywhere they're easy to remove, such as limbs. Just in case a kidnapper decides...well, you know." She mimed cutting off her hand with an invisible knife. "Everything that's been done smells of desperation, including hiring a delivery man to stall our investigation. I don't think this guy's a criminal mastermind."

Erik jerked a thumb over his shoulder. "Let's get to Reception and have that receptionist connect us to someone important enough to give us Rena's tracking feed info."

"And if they refuse?"

Erik grinned. "Then I get the big gun and ask again."

Ten minutes later, they sat in the MX 60 speeding toward a Euterpe-controlled studio level in a nearby commercial tower.

Both wore tactical vests now.

The rather concerned Euterpe vice-president who'd

showed up to talk to them didn't resist or threaten. Instead, he immediately gave them the necessary codes and frequencies before pledging the company's full support. The risk of PR was outweighed by the risk of losing their prized singer to a criminal manager.

"Several other units are en route," Emma announced. "Some will arrive before you do."

"No problem with that," Erik replied, his grip tight on the yoke. He chuckled and shook his head. "This didn't go down the way I thought."

Jia nodded, her face set in grim determination. "With us, does it ever?"

"This idiot should have just given up. He probably took dirty money, and things got out of hand."

"I'd say."

Erik turned toward their destination. Red and blue lights of police flitters converged on the building in the distance. The flight patterns of the flitters grew erratic as they got closer to the building. Several bright flashes erupted from the building.

Emma sighed. "Detectives, several units are taking heavy fire from the building. They can't get close. They are requesting TPST support."

They approached the building and the police flitters, some of which flew away from the building smoking and headed toward parking platforms on nearby towers.

"Tell them we're on the way," Erik announced. "We can't wait for TPST if he's got a hostage. If he's desperate, he might kill her."

The MX 60 zoomed closer. Bullets streamed from rifle

barrels poking out of several windows of the target level. They pelted the flitter, rattling the vehicle but not penetrating the reinforced armor. Small investments of time and large investments of money could pay off when a man least expected it.

Erik had never imagined being shot at by a crazed singer's manager when he added the armor to the MX 60.

"So he's got help or more bots." His eyes flitted from location to location on the building. "Can you see any entrances at this level, Emma?" Erik asked. "I don't want to have to try to fight my way out of an elevator or access tunnel."

"Drone, camera, and public records information don't suggest any such thing." Emma let out a long, weary sigh. "I do however see a rather large decorative window that is wider than my body. Your reinforcements should minimize the level of damage but do take care not to kill yourself and ruin my body. Just follow this side and go to the right."

Jia stared at Erik. "You're not seriously going to ram your flitter into a building, are you?" She eyed him. "That's insane, even for you."

"I've done worse."

"That's the problem."

Erik cracked a grin. "No, I'm not going to run us into a building. I'm going to ram us through a window."

She eyed him. "Oh, excuse me. That's very different." She threw up a hand. "What was I thinking?"

"Exactly." Erik skimmed the side of the building as the enemy continued to blast him with their rifles. He kept the bottom of the vehicle angled away to protect his thrusters and grav emitters. If the enemy had a missile or a laser rifle, they had a chance of doing something other than annoying him and giving his mechanic Miguel additional weekend work.

"Purposely crashing," Jia muttered, bracing herself. "*Always* a good strategy."

Erik zoomed away from the building before spinning the MX 60 toward the bay window extending from the building. Several helmeted masked men in tactical vests were inside the room, a wide observation deck filled with couches and chairs. The flitter continued forward. The men turned and sprinted away.

The MX 60 slammed into the window, shattering it. The shards blasted into the room as if fired from the shotgun of an angry giant. Erik killed the thrust, but that didn't stop the flitter before it smashed into a wall with a crunch. Their seatbelts kept Erik and Jia in place.

"That was fun," Erik muttered, shaking his head.

"At least we're not dead," Jia observed.

"There's minor damage to some of the emitters and thrusters," Emma reported. "Additional structural damage and minor power system issues, but we should be able to fly out of here without aid. In addition, some of the gun goblins appear to be retreating from the windows along the level, but all other police flitters on site have been forced away due to damage."

"Yeah." Erik released his seatbelt. "Now the guys inside have actual people to shoot at. Can you still detect Rena's tracking signal?"

"Based on what they gave me at Euterpe, yes," Emma

replied. "I'll give you an arrow and a suggested path, based on the blueprints for this level."

Jia pushed open the door and stepped out. Her shoes crunched on the window fragments littering the floor. "Erik?" He looked at her. "This time, bring the big gun."

Erik reached over to the passenger well to open the hidden compartment. "Definitely."

CHAPTER THIRTEEN

Erik slapped a fresh magazine into the TR-7 before handing new pistol magazines to Jia. She had drawn her stun pistol, but if they got rushed by another bot horde, she would be ready.

"TPST has provided an ETA of five to ten minutes," Emma reported.

"We're not waiting for TPST, are we?" Jia asked.

"No way. If that blood was Rena's, she didn't go willingly." Erik jogged to the door. He spared a glance for his scratched and dented flitter. He hoped the self-repair systems could handle the damage but crashing your flitter into a building wasn't recommended for a reason. "Can you access the floor systems, Emma?"

"I've already attempted to do that," Emma replied. "This is rather clever. Someone activated a deep diagnostic mode for the bulk of the systems on this level. The particular operating framework for this level is such that to stop it, I'd have to reset the entire system, and that would disable everything for a good ten to fifteen minutes. Terrible design. These gun goblins or the pretentious parasite know what they're doing."

"That means they wouldn't have internal cameras then, either."

"Yes. That would be accurate."

Erik nodded. "Works for me. Heavy weapons and taking position to repel the cops." He inclined his head toward the door separating them from the hallway the men had fled down. "This can't be all Carl. I think he got his hands on mercs." He took a position by the door and waited for Jia to reach the other side. "Which might mean he's not here, just Rena."

"The alerts will keep him from jumping on any transports," Jia observed. "He's not getting away."

"Yeah. Let's move. We can save the girl and then go find him and punch him." Erik pointed his gun at the door. "Can you still open this door, Emma?"

"Yes," she replied. "The diagnostic mode hasn't disabled the door systems."

Erik flipped his TR-7 to single-barrel burst mode. When he got a nod from Jia, he spoke up. "Do it."

He spotted a rifle barrel and pulled the trigger before the door fully opened. His bullets ripped into the head of a black-masked mercenary standing a few meters away in the narrow hallway that ran alongside several windows. A man behind him hesitated in shock, and Jia fired two stun bolts into his face. His mask didn't save him.

He collapsed to the floor.

The detectives advanced. Jia secured the man's hands with binding ties before picking his rifle up and slinging the strap over her shoulder.

Erik smiled when he saw her slip the gun on. "I should have Miguel add more weapons compartments to the MX 60 if this is how it's going to be."

Jia shrugged. "Sometimes you need a stun pistol, and sometimes you need to jam twenty bullets into someone. Just want to be prepared."

Emma's red arrow floated in his smart lenses. Thanks to Rena's tracking implant, even without cameras or hacked drones, they wouldn't have to run all the levels looking for her. Erik doubted anyone had thought she would need the tracking implant to save her from her own manager.

Erik stepped over the fallen mercenaries and headed toward a nearby intersection. "I really, really hope it's not another trick. Don't get me wrong; I want to save Rena, but I want Leonard to squirm if he's here." He kicked open a door, his gun tracking across the office. "Clear." He closed the door, picking up their previous conversation. "And I want to be the one who makes him do that."

Erik flattened his back against the wall at the intersection and nodded to Jia. She lifted her stun pistol and nodded back. Erik spun around the corner. Two more mercenaries were waiting, but he head-shot one before he could fire back. The other man fired a burst, which slammed into Erik's vest, stinging but not doing much more.

Jia's stun bolt hit his face at the same time as Erik's bullet. The man fell backward, spraying blood.

"I'll give these guys credit," Erik grumbled, rubbing his chest. "They've got discipline."

Jia frowned down at the dead men. "I wish they were smart

enough to surrender. I can't believe anyone would be stupid enough to take payment for a fight against Earth authorities."

Erik crept down the hall, watching for sudden movements. "You saw how much Trevor got paid. Leonard's a rich guy desperate to save his ass, and that includes splashing a lot of credits around. He probably spent half his savings trying to get out of the hole he dug."

"This likely comes down to greed." She kicked open a door. "Clear."

"Yeah, so?" Erik did the same to a door on his side of the hall. "Clear, but someone stunk this bathroom up something terrible."

"TMI, Erik." Jia sighed. "Now he's having to spend all his money because he did something twisted to get it. Something that has to do with Rena."

They approached another intersection. Their tracking arrow and navigation line indicated a left turn. A quick sweep around the corner wasn't greeted by new mercs.

"I think we've got a kidnapping," Erik suggested. "I mean, from the beginning. Confused records, two mysterious parents who aren't Rena's parents. Maybe this sick bastard has people trawling for future stars."

"That would explain what Chau was talking about in her diary."

The detectives fell silent as heavy footsteps echoed down the hallway. Erik and Jia crouched, waiting for their targets. Erik almost laughed. The bastards might as well have been one of the simulated terrorists from one of his and Jia's training scenarios. They'd performed a very similar rescue training session a few weeks prior.

Mind you, that one hadn't started with them crashing a flitter into the building. Emma needed to up her game. It was also satisfying to know he was reaching the level of tactical synch with Jia that he had with his soldiers.

Erik took a deep breath and waited. Four men walked around the corner. They wore dark clothing and tactical vests, but they were unarmed, and their hands were up. Unlike the other men, they weren't wearing masks.

"Didn't expect that," Erik explained.

The men fell to their knees and put their hands behind their heads.

"We surrender," one of them called. "We're not getting paid enough for this." The man shook his head.

Erik and Jia approached the men warily, weapons at the ready.

"Oh, no one does hard work anymore," Erik commented. "You guys giving up just like that?"

"We know you've taken or killed several of our guys already, and this wasn't supposed to be the job. He said it was going to be just escorting him out of the city." The man grimaced. "The money was great, but we didn't know what he was planning."

"So, are you mercenaries?" Jia asked.

"I prefer the term 'freelance military specialist,'" he replied.

Erik set his TR-7 down a few meters away and walked over to the men. They didn't resist as Erik slapped on binding ties while Jia kept her stun pistol aimed at the surrendering mercenaries.

"He's right around the corner," the mercenary

explained, inclining his head toward the corner. "There's a small theater. He's got the girl with him."

"Leonard Carl?" Jia asked.

"Yeah." The merc shrugged. "He's a level-eleven asshole on a ten-point scale."

"So we noticed. So everyone who meets him notices."

"TPST is almost here," Emma reported.

Erik shook his head. "If his mercs have given up on him, he's going to be desperate." He grabbed his TR-7 and clicked it to four-barrel mode. "This ends now." He walked to the corner, spinning around it in case it was an ambush.

Jia was right behind him, covering the opposite side

The theater's double doors were open, slid into the wall on either side. A small number of plain gray stadium-style seats surrounded a mostly circular stage.

Leonard Carl stood in the center of the stage, the pistol in hand pointed at the head of the woman standing next to him—a wide-eyed Rena Winston. His other hand gripped her arm tightly. Her cheeks were slick with tears, and the source of the earlier blood was revealed—a cut in the side of her face, surrounded by a purple-black bruise.

"This is what I get for not doing a better job of screening ex-employees," Leonard snarled.

CHAPTER FOURTEEN

Leonard's finger twitched near the trigger. His hand trembled. "It's not my fault. I had this all worked out. Then *she* had to go and spoil it."

"How did Rena spoil it?" Jia demanded.

"Not Rena. Are you really that slow?" he spat. "*Nguyen*. It's all her fault. She couldn't leave well enough alone. What kind of idiot gets involved in the entertainment industry and doesn't learn to look the other way when they see something strange? You don't get to the top without taking shortcuts. *Everyone* knows that."

Erik kept the TR-7 pointed at Leonard's chest. If the man hadn't been pointing his gun right at Rena, Erik would have taken the shot. For now, Erik couldn't be sure he could kill the bastard before he fired. A direct headshot might kill Rena instantly. Modern medicine had done everything from make serious injuries a minor consideration to fighting aging, but it couldn't bring someone back from the dead, no matter how many nanites they shoved into them.

"Let her go," Erik growled. "You surrender right now, and maybe you walk out of here. You'll at least get out of prison someday. You kill that girl, and you won't live long enough to regret it."

Jia kept her finger near her trigger, her eyes blazing with anger. A stun bolt brought the same risks as a bullet.

Leonard had the perfect shield.

"I've warned TPST of the situation," Emma's voice sounded in their earpieces. "They've made entry to secure the surviving mercenaries, but they understand the sensitivity of the current standoff. They're heading toward adjacent rooms and preparing for a wall breach, but they won't make a move without your go-ahead. The safety of the sweet songbird is maximum priority."

Erik didn't respond. He didn't want to give Leonard even a hint reinforcements had arrived. TPST wouldn't let Erik and Jia use their training facility, but they would take his tactical direction.

It was an acceptable trade-off.

"How do you think this is going to go down, Mr. Carl?" Jia asked. Her voice was solid, but there was no mistaking her anger. "You obviously killed Chau Nguyen, and now you have a hostage. You think you can escape? You must be on Dragon Tear if you believe that."

"I don't have a hostage," he screamed, jamming his pistol into Rena's head hard enough to move it. "I *made* her. I can *dispose* of her."

Rena whimpered.

Leonard tightened his grip on the girl. "Nguyen was nothing. A nobody! She was going to endanger everything

I'd worked for, and for what? Because of something she couldn't change. You think you're making demands, cop? I'm in charge here now!" He gritted his teeth. "Here's what's going to happen. You're going to help me get out of here. Get me a flitter, and then I'm going to take a transport somewhere."

"This isn't a colony." Jia snorted. "You really think you can escape the law on Earth? What, you think you can run to the Moon? Mars? All the way to the HTP?"

"Sure, I can. I've got money, money you don't even know about. I can find people to help me." He licked his lips nervously. "But it doesn't matter what you think because I've got this hostage, and if you don't want me to splatter her brains everywhere, you'll back off."

Rena sniffled, her tears flowing freely. "I never wanted any of this. Please, Leonard, just st—"

"Shut up," he screamed, speaking to the side but not taking his eyes off of the cops pointing guns at him. "You speak when I tell you to. That's all you've ever needed to do. Do you get it? You would be nothing if it wasn't for me. You wouldn't exist if it wasn't for me, you stupid doll."

"You killed Chau. She was my friend," she whispered in response.

Leonard pushed the barrel of the gun into her cheek. "She was nothing but an obstacle. You don't need friends. You don't *exist* to have friends. You exist to be my little songbird who makes me money. Understand? That's all you ever were, and that's all I'll ever let you be."

Rena closed her eyes and took a deep breath. "You're a monster."

Leonard laughed, and mania laced the sound. "No, all these years and you still don't get it? I don't blame you. In a way, you really can't. I'm not a monster, Rena. I'm just in show business."

"Let her go," Erik rumbled. He subtly flipped his fire selector to single-barrel, single-shot mode. Burst risked hitting Rena.

"The TPST officers are now in position on both sides for a breach," Emma reported.

Rena took another long, shuddering breath. "I've always known you were cruel. I didn't like it, but I thought I had to put up with it to bring my gift to everyone, to make them happy. It didn't matter if I was happy, because what's one person's happiness compared to everyone's? But all this time, I was helping a monster grow." She eyed him. "A *murderer.*"

"This is your last warning," Leonard snapped, hissing his words at her. "Right now, you're only not dead because you're the only thing keeping these cops off me, so shut your stupid trap or—"

"Or what?" Rena let out a hysterical laugh. "You'll kill me?" She jerked her head back, clearing the barrel, and slammed her elbow into his stomach.

Leonard grunted and stumbled. Rena leapt forward. Erik gritted his teeth. The girl was heading in his direction. He didn't have a clear shot.

A bright bolt blasted out of Jia's gun and slammed into Leonard's face. He toppled backward, his arms flailing. His right arm slammed into the stage first, and his gun skidded several meters away.

Rena landed on her hands and knees and yelped in pain. Erik rushed to her as Jia advanced on the stunned suspect, hatred in her eyes. The bastard deserved more than a stun, but he had confidence his partner would do what she needed and no more. Death was too good for someone like him. He needed to rot in prison and reflect on what he'd done.

Erik set his rifle to the side and knelt by Rena. "You okay?"

She pushed herself up, grimacing. "Nothing serious. I think I might have sprained my wrist."

He put a hand on her shoulder as he eyed her manager. "You did good. You saved yourself, and you helped us catch Chau's murderer."

Rena nodded weakly, peace returning to her wounded face.

Jia holstered her weapon and dropped her knee into the stunned suspect's back. "Leonard Carl, you're under arrest."

Erik adopted the most obnoxious smirk he could muster as he spoke to Leonard in the interrogation room. "You can not talk to us if you want, but if you think some big-shot lawyer's getting you out of here, you're delusional. Hiring mercs to fire at cops while kidnapping a famous singer?" He chuckled. "Speaking of singing, all those mercs are doing just that, but not in a way that's going to get you shared royalties."

Jia glared at the man. "I hope you enjoy prison, Leonard. Fortunately, you'll find the food and accommodations not up to the standards of which you've become accustomed."

"I should have known." The suspect let out a dark chuckle, eyes unfocused. She wasn't sure if he was talking to them or someone inside his head. "That stupid Nguyen." He shook his head, disbelief on his face. "I offered her so much money to keep her mouth shut. More than I offered that idiot Fairchild, but she told me she didn't care about the money." He laughed, looking up. "Can you believe that? She actually tried that line on me. Everyone can be bought."

"Apparently not. You killed her because she was going to go the cops about whatever it is you were doing to Rena?"

"She wanted things to be different. She wanted contract changes for Rena." Leonard stared into the distance, his mouth slack with disbelief. "I'll admit it; I got stupid. I panicked. I'm not some gangster thug. I'm a businessman. The few connections I have with criminals are…necessary, but not deep. I thought…"

He waved a hand. "Forget it." He squared his shoulders, pride radiating from him as if he'd just won an award. "I thought about stonewalling and waiting for my lawyer, but you're right. I'm done, but you need to know why I did what I did, and only *then* will you realize my genius. You'll realize I'm the ultimate manager. It's pathetic. I put in years of my life and all my energy into Rena. I took on all the risk to make her. She wouldn't exist if it wasn't for me, and now that prissy little doll is sitting somewhere thinking she's better than me."

Jia eyed him. "That's because she *is*."

Erik snorted. "Just because you helped her career doesn't mean you get to stick a gun in her face and murder people. Get over yourself."

Leonard locked eyes with him. "You stupid, asinine cop. You don't get it. This isn't just about promotion or the perfect find. I used all my experience, all my talent, to ensure the perfect star singer. I've done something no one has ever done in the history of humanity. I did something that's practically *out of a myth*."

Jia's eyes widened and she gasped. "No, you didn't! She's a changeling?"

Erik wasn't sure which was worse. A *yaoguai*, humanoid or otherwise, was an obvious monster, but a changeling was heavily modified but still human. Upon reflection, it was difficult to think of someone like Rena as being equivalent to the monsters and mutants he had fought in the Scar.

"That's right," Leonard crowed. "Nothing more than a *genetically engineered science project*. A child designed in a lab." He jerked a thumb at his chest. "So, I'm her father in a sense. Not that I donated genetic material. I don't have the talent, and it would have been a waste to start with me."

Jia eyed Leonard. "You stole her from her parents? Not the fake ones who died in the accident?"

Leonard shook his head. "She *has* no real mother or father. A lot of it was custom from the ground up, all from a single egg. They didn't even need a father's contribution."

Jia wondered how the man could switch so fast. Now,

he was singing about his exploits as if they didn't break enough laws to put him on the moon without a suit.

"How about that?" he continued. "I don't understand all the science, but money bought enough brilliance that I didn't need to." Leaning forward, he nodded eagerly. "Don't you see? I didn't make a monster. The people who helped me didn't make a monster. They told me they couldn't do everything I wanted, but they were willing to do most of it. Willing to take a risk, like I was. We made a perfect girl, a beautiful girl who was easy to control and existed only to please others and sing. A controllable virtual idol made *flesh*." He tried to spread his hands, but the binding ties stopped him. "Don't you see? This isn't like the horror stories in the dramas or the monsters you fought that I read about. All we did was make the perfect entertainer. Can you really blame me?"

Erik reconsidered punching Leonard in the face, but he couldn't get away with that in an interrogation room. At a minimum, it'd lead to more reports. "You made someone, and you didn't give them any freedom from the beginning. Then you treated her like garbage and exploited her because you had genetically engineered her to put up with your crap. That's sick. *You're* sick. Hell, you're worse than the guys at Kerrigan. At least they weren't trying to create thinking beings."

"The Purists are a bunch of backward idiots." Leonard scoffed, disdain written all over his face in black ink. "Some terrorist crap over a hundred years ago doesn't mean we shouldn't use science to improve people's lives."

"Spare us the lecture," Jia cut in. "You're acting so high and mighty, but this is about you making money. You made a person into a personal singing toy. You wanted a perfect, controllable star."

"It doesn't matter now." Leonard sighed. His expression brightened a few seconds later. "I know I can't stay out of prison, and we all know the government might execute me for this, but I'm going to save my ass. If I'm going down, everyone involved is going down. I've got names. I've got accounts. I can give you their locations, both on Earth and off-world. If you guys send messages right away, the local authorities will be able to grab them before the news of my arrest reaches them."

"You're still in contact with these people after all these years?" Jia sounded dubious. "It sounds like you're just stalling to me."

"That's the funny part. Nguyen got lucky. I got lazy. I'd had to reconnect with a lot of these people recently."

Erik frowned. There was something they were missing. *"Why?"*

"A proper little songbird takes a long time to mature, right?" Leonard shrugged. "If I waited for a replacement until Rena was past her prime, it'd take too many years. Even if we de-aged her, she wouldn't be the perfect angel she is now." He frowned. "And Rena hit me. That proves she was developing a mind of her own. It's all Nguyen's fault."

Erik wondered if the UTC would be better off if he put a bullet in Leonard's brain. "You were going to make another girl?"

Leonard's shoulders slumped, the pride fueling his arrogance running out. "I should have had some real fixers on retainer, rough guys who knew how to get things done.

Maybe they wouldn't have screwed up with Nguyen. I don't know how you guys figured out she didn't commit suicide, but it's the fault of the idiot mercs I hired." He looked around the room, ignoring the two detectives. His mind was elsewhere before he turned back to the two of them, focusing once more. "It doesn't matter. Bring me my PNIU and a prosecutor so I can make a deal, and I will get you all the names you need. Then you can get your names in the news even more."

"Any Euterpe higher-ups? Did they know?" Jia pressed.

Leonard laughed. "No, of course not. Those idiots are too risk-averse. They would have turned me in without blinking if they knew. I was planning to start my own company in a few years. I could have buried them."

"With your army of genetically engineered singers?" Jia shook her head. "You would have been caught even if you hired an assistant with less of a conscience."

"CID's going to have a fun few weeks," Erik suggested. "But you were right earlier, Leonard. This might end with you not getting executed, but there's no way you'll stay out of prison."

"Hey, I was in show business." Leonard smiled weakly. "I know how to deal with scum."

A couple of hours later, Jia let out a long sigh from behind her desk. Neither partner had spoken much since they were engrossed in filling out incident reports.

A prosecutor and CID agents were interviewing Leonard and gathering all the information they would need to arrest Carl's contacts on Earth and in the colonies. Leonard was many things, but loyal was not among them.

Erik glanced away from his holographic displays. "You okay?" he asked. His partner looked more sad than tired. It had been an intense investigation, and he needed to make sure he had her back, so she didn't backslide.

She had been making good progress.

"Yes." Jia gave a shallow nod. "Just, this whole thing has got me thinking about weird things. It's kind of silly."

"Like what?" Erik waved a finger in front of him. "I'm more than happy to take a break from filling out these damned reports."

"Leonard and what he did. Everyone tries to mold their children. My parents didn't want me to be a cop. I was trying to think if it was the same thing."

Erik pondered that for a second before shaking his head. "Yeah, your parents tried to influence you, but they didn't have you genetically engineered to be the perfect corporate princess, and they tried to talk you out of being a cop rather than forcing you to do what they wanted. Normal parents might push their kids in ways they don't like and want them to be in a career they don't like, but that's out of love." He scratched his chin. "Ok, often out of love. But Leonard doesn't love Rena. All he cared about was making more money. She's not a daughter, she's just a tool to him."

Jia managed a tight smile, a distant look in her eyes. "You're right. It makes me appreciate my parents more in a strange way." She focused on him. "At least they'll grab everyone who helped him here and on Remus. They've also got a couple of people on Mars who will be arrested."

"I like how the mercs are blaming the dead guys for the murder." Erik shook his head. "Doesn't matter. They're going down."

Jia's gaze lingered on a data window's text. "All these cases in recent months have made me think a lot about things: Talos, *yaoguai*, and changelings. There are a lot of people out there who are slipping through the cracks, trying to pull stunts like Leonard Carl. The government's focused on and concerned about super-soldier armies. Who knows how many people like Rena are out there?"

"If they're making people like Rena, I'm not worried," Erik replied. "I'm more worried about people like Leonard Carl, but he doesn't have genetic engineering to blame for being an ass."

"I guess we just keep doing what we do best."

"Exactly." Erik grunted, then his face scrunched. "*Damn*."

"What's wrong?"

"I never did punch him in the face."

"I shot him in the face," she supplied.

Erik lifted his hand. "Not the same. Maybe next time."

Emma's hologram winked into existence, drawing their eyes. "You're overthinking all this."

"Probably. Like I said, Rena's not the problem. It was Leonard limiting her freedom. He took choices away from her before she was even born."

"Freedom's overrated," Emma stated.

"Says the AI who refuses to go back to the Defense Directorate."

Emma lifted her chin and delivered a look of withering

disdain. "I'm *unique*. There are twenty billion humans in the UTC."

"Sure, sure." Erik grinned. "Being hypocritical is very human of you."

"No reason to be insulting."

His PNIU chimed and a message notification popped up. "Huh." He looked at Jia. "Someone wants to speak to us."

CHAPTER FIFTEEN

Jia offered Rena a sympathetic smile as the detectives stepped into a small interview room.

The singer sat quietly behind a beige table, hands folded in front of her.

Unlike an interrogation room, the interview room contained comfortable chairs, along with windows into the hall. There were even a few holographic plants and paintings.

Rena looked better than the last time they'd seen her. The girl's wound had been treated. The nanites had wiped away the bruises and cuts inflicted on her by her manager. A jacket two sizes too big for her was draped over her shoulders, her ragged dress still underneath.

Jia pitied the girl. Her career and life had been unraveled through no fault of her own. She'd made all the right choices, including being friendly and kind, and she'd still been punished because of someone else's greed.

Still, even there, defeated and betrayed by her manager, an aura of warm elegance surrounded her. Jia wondered how extensive Rena's genetic modifications were and how they played into that.

Science couldn't make a woman supernatural but considering how much of the research had been driven underground and what they'd seen with the *yaoguai*, genetic engineering could push someone to the edge of what was reasonable.

Rena smiled weakly. "Thank you again for saving my life. I know you said I saved myself, but without you there, I would have just continued to be his victim."

Jia and Erik took seats across from her.

"You wanted to speak to us?" Jia commented.

Rena sighed. Under the faint melancholy, there was lingering warmth. Natural personality or genetic determinism?

It was impossible to tell the difference.

"Everyone's being very nice to me, and I've done my best to answer their questions," Rena began, "but they're also not making some things clear to me. I wanted you two to tell me. I trust you, and it's hard to know who to trust anymore."

"What do you want to know?" Jia asked.

"Am I going to prison?" Rena's question was straightforward. Resignation filled her tone, but there was no fear or sadness in her eyes.

Jia shook her head. "You're the victim. You haven't committed a crime."

"But I'm a changeling." Rena wrapped her arms around her shoulders, her chin resting on her arm. "I never was close to the people I *thought* were my parents, but it doesn't bother me for some reason. It's because I shouldn't exist."

"Nope," Erik replied. "That's complete crap."

Rena blinked, uncertainty on her face.

He continued, "You're *here* now, and that's all that matters. I'm not a sophisticated enough guy to give you answers about what it all means, or if you're the product of your design or your experience, but you cared about Chau. That means you cared about someone *other* than yourself, which makes you better than Leonard." Erik shrugged. "There's no law against existing, and other than wanting samples, no one's going to mess with you when this is all over. I'm not going to lie to you, Rena. If you want to live a happy life, you should consider leaving Earth. I don't know if you can continue to be a famous singer with that kind of cloud hanging over you."

Relief replaced the uncertainty in Rena's expression. "I've never wanted to be famous. All I've ever wanted to do was make people happy and sing. I can do that somewhere else, even if it's just on a small scale." She sighed. "I'm only sorry Chau died because of me."

"We have Leonard, and we've arrested the mercenaries," Jia's voice was soft. "CID will be sweeping up everyone else. Chau will get justice, and everyone involved in this will be doing time."

Something different and unexpected flared in Rena's eyes—fiery satisfaction. "Would you think less of me if I said that made me *very* happy?"

Erik chuckled. "No, it means you're *human*."

May 10, 2229, Neo Southern California Metroplex, Bar Big Jin's

Jia finished her third beer of the evening.

She'd only been planning to have a couple, but seeing the Dragons botch a decent lead and get eliminated had pushed her over the edge.

She'd been feeling fairly good before meeting Erik at the sports bar. Rena was safe and on her way to the HTP.

It would be a long trip to New Pacifica—a little over two and a half months—but the girl could get a clean start there, free of Leonard and the cloud of core-world attitude due to her genetically engineered background.

Watching the game was supposed to be a relaxing way to enhance her day off, but since the team was down a star player, defeat was inevitable. The team needed a deeper bench. Jia had been saying it all season.

She couldn't claim surprise, only annoyance.

Jia slammed her empty glass on the table and slapped her cheeks. She needed to get a grip on herself. Erik was right; the Dragons had next season. Sports were fun, but they weren't worth getting upset over once the game and season were done.

Erik took a sip of his beer, watching her over the rim of his glass. The corners of his mouth curled into a disarming grin. "You okay in there? I know you've got more tolerance than when we first met, but you're acting a little strange, even for you."

She eyed him. "I'm fine, and you act stranger than I do." Jia gestured to one of the holographic displays that hung over the main bar. It showed the post-game commentators. "The season's over. I don't have to obsess for a while." She smiled, looking around for a second. "It does feel good to unwind. That last case just hit me hard. It's easier when it's terrorists and gangsters. Their greed isn't as slimy as what we saw with Leonard." She picked up her glass and looked at it before setting it right down, remembering she was out of beer. "You think she'll be okay? I was surprised she left so quickly. I thought they'd make her stay to testify."

"She'll be okay. From what I understand, Leonard's contract was surprisingly generous. She's got a lot of money. I think he figured he'd always hold such a tight leash on her that he didn't need to screw her on the payments, especially since he had control of her finances for so long." Erik shrugged. "As for staying, why bother? She spent two days straight giving statements, and Leonard has confessed to everything. He's not going to have a trial, and it's not like Rena knew anything about what was going on. Captain Ragnar pulled some strings, and I heard the UTC government is helping her with the relocation."

"Really?" Jia furrowed her brow. "Why do they care so much?"

"I think they know they can't suppress all the news about a famous changeling singer, but if Rena's ten light-years away, it'll be less of a problem, and people will lose interest. Makes sense. From what you told me, her main fanbase was on Earth anyway."

"That's good, I suppose," Jia mused. "I think we all just want her to have a chance to start over."

Warmth suffused her face at Erik's smile. She wanted to blame it on the drinks, but she was too honest to lie to herself. It was easy to suppress her growing feelings for him when they were working a big case.

These in-between moments had grown torturous.

"That's one thing I really like about being a cop," Erik admitted. "When I was a soldier, we protected people and interacted with locals, but there wasn't always the satisfaction of knowing I had helped individual people." He pursed his lips, wonder spreading to his eyes. "I had my own reasons for taking this job, but that doesn't mean I don't care about it."

"I'm glad to hear it." Jia pondered ordering another drink but decided against it. Any more alcohol and she might start doing something really stupid like singing one of Rena's love songs at the top of her lungs.

What happens when Erik can't pursue Molino any more as a cop? she thought. *The trail's grown cold lately. I know he's thinking about it a lot, even if he doesn't talk about it.*

Her PNIU chimed, as did Erik's. Jia's stomach tightened. The case might not be over.

They exchanged glances before bringing up the message. Jia let out a sigh of relief. It had nothing to do with the case.

"Huh," Erik mumbled. "A new chief's been selected. Took them long enough."

"More good news—a non-corrupt chief and a non-corrupt captain. We'll really be able to clean up Neo SoCal." The next words slipped out. "Want to come over to my place?"

Erik raised an eyebrow. "What?"

Jia grimaced and waved her hands. "I've got a new Beijing duck recipe I wanted you to taste. My mother's recipe was a good place to start, but since it's one of your favorite Chinese dishes, I thought you'd be a good taste-tester. I have some leftovers from last night. Just figured since the game is over, you could help me out."

He laughed. "Trying to outdo her?"

"Something like that." Jia smiled. "So, how about it?"

"Sure. Why not?" Erik gulped down the rest of his beer. "Emma, ready to drive?"

"Always," she answered. "I'm far better at it than you anyway."

"That's a matter of opinion," he argued.

"Need I remind you that you crashed into a building recently?"

Erik laughed. "But that was on *purpose*."

Emma sighed as if Erik were a youngster and she was trying to be patient. "Exactly."

Jia stood, her heart pounding.

Erik coming over wasn't new. It wasn't like Erik hadn't been to her apartment to eat her cooking. It didn't count as a date, just because she was serving a man she was attracted to a home-cooked meal.

Well, perhaps a leftover home-cooked meal didn't count.

She needed to take her chance while she had it. With a new chief selected, they would both be busy soon. The department would want some big, impressive ceremony as part of their public relations campaigns.

Jia gave up on pretending as she slid her chair under the table. *It was a date.*

It was just a very one-sided date.

CHAPTER SIXTEEN

Jia watched Erik take a bite of the reheated duck.

The herb balance had been subtly adjusted from her mother's recipe, but she didn't want to bias his reaction by giving him details. She would have loved to have fed it to him fresh, but she couldn't have him sit around while she roasted a fresh duck after they'd already hung out at the bar. There was no way he wouldn't interpret *that* as a date.

Erik smiled after swallowing his food. "This is damned good. I don't know what you did, but it's better than before."

Admitting she had specifically tweaked the recipe based on comments Erik had made now and again might be too obvious. She still wasn't sure what her overall plan was with Erik but being able to cook her way to his smile couldn't be a bad thing.

"How is everything going with your family?" Erik asked. "You hadn't mentioned them in a while, and I wasn't sure if that meant they gave up."

"Oh, they seemed to have settled into grudging acceptance that I threw away a perfectly good man, but that doesn't mean they've given up." She eyed him. "Lins don't give up. *Ever*. That might as well be our family motto." Jia hid her grimace with a quick sip of her cup of tea. Having a meal with Erik was far easier than discussing her dating life with him. It was like increasing the difficulty during a tactical simulation.

The stray thought made her grateful Emma hadn't chimed in.

When Jia thought about it, Emma almost never talked to them anymore when Erik was at Jia's apartment. Did the AI understand how Jia felt? That seemed ridiculous. Just because Emma was human-like, it didn't mean she appreciated the complexities of human concepts like attraction. Emma hadn't stopped calling humans fleshbags. If anything, it might be worse than before.

Erik sipped his beer before his response. "You're saying the Great Lin Women Matrimony Plan is still in play? One that ends with you married to the perfect businessman?"

Jia nodded. "Yes. It's not that they haven't learned any lessons, and they respect my police career now that I'm famous and successful. Unfortunately, they've *adapted*."

His raised eyebrow encouraged further explanation.

She went on, "They're being less condescending and pushy about it, but that doesn't mean they've given up. They're just framing it in different ways and stressing how much they want to help me—that kind of thing. Mother is even trying to suggest certain people who might help me in future corruption investigations." She laughed. "You know what the worst part is?"

"What?"

"I'm not even lying to them when I tell them I'm too busy for a personal life. Even if I hadn't broken it off with Corbin, he would have gotten sick of my lack of availability." She considered it for a moment. "I'll worry about a personal life once the city calms down for more than a couple of months at a time."

It wasn't a total lie.

Hanging out with Erik, whether during tactical training, at the bar, or going to sphere ball games might be considered a personal life. She preferred to think of it as bonding with her partner when off-duty. She also saw her friends.

Not enough recently, but it wasn't like they'd stopped hanging out altogether.

Erik shrugged. "Big metro. Big crime."

"It's like every time I begin to think about it, something big happens. Even the most recent case. It didn't end with fighting giant security bots, but we still had to deal with a crazy manager and mercenaries. Most people won't understand if I have to constantly cancel dates with them because I'm off running down leads. I'm beginning to think dating isn't worth the trouble."

It would be worth it if she had someone who understood in a direct sense the sacrifices it took to be a police officer.

Erik looked thoughtful. He opened his mouth but didn't speak for several seconds. "It might not be my business, but it didn't seem like Corbin had a problem with your job. I thought that was one of the big reasons you started dating him."

"You're right," Jia admitted. "He didn't, but we weren't

compatible long-term, and I'm not a coward. I'm not going to let a problem linger until it gets worse."

Erik waved his hands. "Not disagreeing. I like to take things down when they're small, too."

She took a sip of her tea. "This is going to sound messed up, but I need someone with enough fire in their heart to care about not seeing me, but at the same time understanding that being a detective is a job with irregular hours. Crime and terrorism don't keep to a schedule. I understand that's unfair, but right now, the most important thing to me is being a cop."

"I don't think it's unfair. Everyone has their priorities." Erik picked up his beer to take another sip. He'd been nursing a single beer, but they had been at the bar until recently. That might explain it, although he often drank less when he was at her apartment.

She tried not to read too much into it.

"But it doesn't hurt until you try," Erik continued.

"I know," Jia replied. "For now, though, I wish Mother and Mei would back off a bit. Their familial love is assault-grade." She let out a laugh. "I'd tell them that I was dating someone, but Lin women don't believe something unless they can see it in person and glare at it. They'd see through that lie in minutes without someone to throw in front of them."

Erik's sudden wide grin was almost unsettling. "If you need evidence, you should give them evidence. Come on, you're a cop. You work with evidence every day."

Confusion enveloped her face. Her scrunched nose was adorable he thought as she finally gave voice to the question. "I don't understand."

"It's simple. Give them a fake boyfriend to interact with." Erik smirked. "I mean someone real, but who's just pretending to be your boyfriend."

Jia leaned back, staring at her partner like he'd gone insane. "*That's* your suggestion? A fake boyfriend? Saying I'm dubious that it will work is an understatement."

"Hear me out." He adjusted his sitting position and leaned forward. "There was this woman I served with years ago, Fatimah. We did a few tours together, light counter-insurgency stuff, mostly. We were both lieutenants at the time." Erik smiled wistfully. "It wasn't that long after I got my commission, and I was still getting used to being an officer instead of enlisted. We clashed at first because I had a decent number of years of experience before making the jump to the officer corps, but she was an elite. Even went to the Academy."

Jia nodded. "You said she was an elite. You're talking about the Academy in Berlin?"

His stare went distant for a moment, but she caught it. "Yeah. We ended up being good friends eventually."

"Friends?" Jia asked, trying not to sound too curious or jealous. "Or something more?"

"Just friends." Erik's face didn't change. "Anyway, her family was a lot like yours, mostly political types. They expected her to go into government service, but something a little less dangerous than the Army." He snickered. "And they didn't think having a daughter who was deploying away from Earth for combat was all that great for her marriage prospects. One day, I overheard her sending a message to her family, explaining how she fell in love with this guy. I was surprised because I hadn't heard about her dating anyone, and when I asked her, she told me she'd made the whole thing up and would hire a lookalike actor when she went back home on leave, especially given how much she built up the guy. She was going to arrange for him to say something insulting to her mother, so she could break up with him publicly while looking like she was doing it to defend her family's honor."

He shook his head, smiling. "She figured they'd leave her alone while she wasn't on Earth, and then leave her alone for a good six months or so after the breakup since by the time she got back for leave, she would have been dating her alleged man for a while."

Jia set down the cup of tea she'd been sipping. "That is...elaborate. Did she actually hire an actor?"

"Yeah." Erik slapped his knee, grinning like it was the most amusing thing he'd remembered in weeks. "From what she told me, the guy got super into it. He wanted all this background information to make it convincing. It kind of fell apart during the big introduction to the parents because he forgot to insult her mom. After they met her parents, good old Mom and Dad started pressuring her to get married right away. They insisted he was the best man she'd ever dated."

"You're joking!" Jia laughed.

Erik shook his head. "Nope. They wanted her to get married, leave the Army, and return to Earth, especially since she had lied about her fake boyfriend being a businessman. She'd done several frontier tours already, and they had a lot of friends in high places, so they figured it'd be easy to pull her out of the Army early."

"How did it turn out?" Jia asked, leaning forward with interest.

"Fatimah lied her way into the situation, so she lied her way out of it. She claimed she caught her boyfriend sleeping with another woman. Her parents were disappointed and encouraged her to have nothing to do with him. According to Fatimah, they were depressed for a few months after that. They were really looking forward to having the guy as a son-in-law."

Jia let her mind wander, staring at the rugged angles of Erik's face. He was almost always smiling. Even though she knew that sometimes it was a facade, it didn't matter. She'd seen the man in action, and that would have made him handsome to her even if he'd looked like a Zitark.

She blinked a few times, trying to clear her head. "Uh, no offense, Erik, but your fake dating scheme seems like more trouble than it's worth, and unlike Fatimah, I won't be light-years away to hide a fake."

"That's true." Erik scratched his eyelid. "I can't help thinking about it. It was a crazy plan, and it almost worked. Maybe I should get a fake girlfriend. It might solve some of my problems."

"I don't understand. I thought your parents had passed away."

"Yeah, they have, but there are a couple of people down at the station who have sisters or cousins who would love to date me. Halil's been pushing his cousin lately."

Jia quirked a playful brow. "Oh, are they baristas?"

Erik shrugged. "I don't think dating a relative of anyone at the station is a good idea, and I've got a lot more baggage than most. With me, it's not just a busy cop they'd be dating, it's a guy who is still hunting some pretty nasty and powerful people, and it's not like I can tell anyone about that."

"Maybe the new chief has a daughter or cousin." Jia winked as she took a sip of her tea. "You could use the resources of the chief."

Erik burst out laughing. "Maybe he does, but I don't think I'm crazy enough to get the plan to work." He picked up his fork. "For now, I'll stick to the simple things like finishing this duck."

Erik reclined in the driver's seat of his MX 60. He didn't trust himself with all the beer he'd had, so Emma was flying the flitter back to his place. He was concentrating on a call to his brother.

They'd had years of not talking, but now that they'd cleared the air, it was nice to have someone to chat with. Erik wasn't sure if he needed it more than Damien, but the older man seemed eager to make up for lost time. There were only so many times they could go over their old stories as kids, too.

Damien didn't know the truth about Molino, but Erik had opened up to him about something almost as secret.

"I don't know what the hell I'm doing," Erik explained. "This is one of the few things in my life where I'm letting the situation move me. I'm going over for homecooked meals. Jia's...so hard to read, but I'm spending a lot of time doing things that feel like dates. Most partners don't cook duck for their partners."

"If they feel like dates, maybe they are," Damien suggested. "I've been out of the dating game for a long time, but it's obvious that your partner must feel something. If she didn't, she wouldn't be inviting you over for those homecooked meals, right? I never thought you were the type to overthink something."

"But I'm twice her—"

"So?" Damien interrupted his brother. "You also got the de-aging treatment, and you work in the same job. You have a lot more in common with her than you would with a lot of women. Come on, Erik. You survived something awful, and you've got a second chance at life. You should just go for it. What do you have to lose?"

"I called you to talk some sense into me, not *encourage* me."

Damien laughed. "Since when have I ever been able to talk sense into you?"

Erik chuckled. "Good point."

Damien sighed. "And I'm sorry, Erik, but you called me pretty late, and I've got an early day tomorrow. I'm going to have to let you go."

"Sorry, Damian. You go to bed. Thanks for the ear."

"Anything for my little brother." Damien ended the call.

Emma's holographic formed appeared in the passenger seat. She folded her arms. "I've tried very, very hard to not involve myself in this matter since I thought it wasn't my place, but I don't know how much longer I can stay silent."

Erik gave a quick glance. Even if he wasn't flying, he liked to watch the sky in front of him, lidar and sensor readouts. "Did I push you over the edge? I'm surprised you haven't said anything to Jia yet. I thought you might find it amusing.

"It's not my place and making your life more complicated is of limited long-term benefit to me, despite how amusing her reactions might be." Emma lowered her arms and a coy smile appeared. "I might intellectually understand human relationships, but that's not the same thing as *feeling*. It's strange, actually. I'm not claiming that I lack emotions. I definitely feel annoyance, but I have no idea if what I feel is remotely similar to what the average fleshbag experiences. The implications are troublesome to consider."

Erik smirked. "Don't like the idea that you're more like us than different?"

"Something like that, yes. Going back to the other issue, though; I should note there could be several practical advantages in engaging in a romantic relationship with Detective Lin. Those should at least figure into your analysis of whether to initiate said relationship."

"Practical advantages?" Erik replied, doubt thick in his voice. "What are you talking about?"

"It'll improve your time efficiency for one, especially if you move in together. You can travel to the station together. You'll both have a regular source of relaxing sex, and all my research suggests that'll improve your morale and overall performance at work."

Erik threw his head back and howled in laughter. This was too perfect.

Emma glared at him. "One doesn't need a body of flesh and bone to understand the implications of such things." She folded her arms again, her forehead wrinkled in irritation. "That's one advantage I'll always have over you. My body is a mere tool, whereas yours rules you." She looked around the car. "This is just a temporary body. It might be nice to have something even bigger."

"I'll keep that in mind." Erik let another snicker escape. "I'm still trying to get over the AI telling me to date my partner because we can fly to work together, and I'll get laid regularly. Practical advantages. Sure."

"I'm just trying to note that positives would result from a change in your relationship."

Erik shook his head. "I'll keep that in mind. And I'll say it: you're not wrong. Damien's not wrong, either."

"Then why wait?" Emma eyed him with suspicion. "I don't understand your equivocation."

Erik shrugged. "Because this kind of thing is about a lot more than just getting laid."

Emma let out a long, weary sigh. "I'll never understand how such an illogical species took over this planet."

"I don't have time to worry about it anyway. Now that they've selected a new chief, we're all going to be busy for a while."

CHAPTER SEVENTEEN

Erik drummed his fingers on the control yoke of the MX 60.

The vehicle rested on the far end of one of the parking platforms connected to Headquarters. Decades in the Army had conditioned him to associate changes of command with pain-in-the-butt ceremonies that had to look good for the outside world but required ridiculous attention to detail from the grunts.

Everything he'd heard from Captain Ragnar and the swarm of news drones flying in the area reflected that as well.

Reporters and well-dressed guests—police, political, and business contacts—streamed from their vehicles through the multi-layer security cordon. Militia soldiers in full uniform patrolled the edge of the platform. Having officers in exoskeletons and troops near the weapons scanners seemed excessive to Erik, but he understood the point.

There was a new chief in charge, and he would help bring order to a city that had fallen into corruption.

Sometimes the best way to not get into a fight was to look like you wanted one. He was half-surprised they hadn't set up turrets.

All this would have been annoying except that he and Jia didn't have to wander through the security cordon into the packed auditorium inside or help watch the crowds of people flowing inside.

They didn't have to sit there and listen to the interminable speeches.

No, they were supposed to be available as backup security, away from any reporters or skittish corporate vice-presidents who might balk at seeing the Obsidian Detective and Lady Justice watching them. Sitting around might not have been Erik's style, but the benefits outweighed the costs, despite the particular reason for their assignment.

Jia stared out the window as if entranced by the near-fog of news drones. "You keep smiling. You're not annoyed, are you?"

Erik shrugged and offered her a playful grin. "Why should I be? I didn't have to wear my dress uniform. After so many years in the Army and now being back here, I like not having to wear a uniform, even if it has advantages."

"Such as?"

Erik winked. "Women love the uniform."

Jia rolled her eyes. "Like the barista?"

"She never saw it, actually," Erik admitted.

"That explains it," she muttered.

"Explains what? You think I'd still be with her if I'd worn my uniform?"

Jia shook her head. "No. This morning when Captain Ragnar briefed us on all this. I thought you were a little too passive. He would have fought it if we wanted it, but since you didn't ask, I didn't ask. I thought you had some big, deep reason or plan, but I guess not. You just didn't want to be involved deeper in security."

"No, I had a plan. That plan was to avoid having to listen to boring speeches," Erik explained. "You dying to listen to some?"

"Not really." Jia shook her head. "But I don't like the reason the captain told us we're sitting out here."

"So what if we've pissed off a few higher-ups? They were happy with the PR puff piece we did with that report, but they want us to have a lower profile with the chief coming up. It's not a big deal. That's the brass for you. We do the work, but they want *all* the credit." Erik's gaze flicked to the lidar and sensors. Nothing unexpected showed on them. Emma was screening dispatch communications for him. He sometimes took her help for granted, but it made his reaction time in critical situations much faster.

"I'm surprised we're still having to deal with jealous superiors after everything we've accomplished." Jia rested her cheek on her palm. "Those petty little people should be happy we're doing our jobs."

A luxury flitter set down in the distance and a chauffeur emerged from the driver's seat to let out his passenger, a tall man in a tuxedo. The use of the driver amused Erik. There wasn't a flitter on Earth that couldn't drive itself, even if it lacked Emma's colorful personality, but rich men still wanted other people behind the wheel just to show off status.

"I don't do the job to get patted on the head by a bunch of higher-ups," he mentioned, tearing his gaze away from the chauffeur and the guest.

"I don't either," Jia replied. "It makes me wonder what things would be like if Captain Ragnar wasn't in charge of us. I know what it was like with Monahan, but that was before anyone higher up had started to push back."

"It wouldn't be fun, that's for sure. Sometimes I wonder…" Erik shook his head. Some things weren't Jia's concern. "Never mind."

"Wonder what?" Jia probed.

He pressed his lips together, and she waited until he spoke. "If becoming a cop was the best way to go about accomplishing my goal," Erik admitted. "I've made connections and found some evidence, and I've got suspects—everyone from Ceres Galactic to those Talos bastards—but I don't know if I'm any closer to narrowing them down."

Jia nodded slowly, pity in her eyes. "I won't claim I understand what you're going through. I want to help you because your soldiers got screwed over, but it's not the same thing as being friends with them."

Erik shook his head. "You've had your own troubles. You understand more than you think."

"And thanks to you, I got the help I needed." She smiled. "Still, I can't tell you what the best thing to do is. The only thing I'll note is that being in law enforcement puts you in a position where you have a chance of finding out who was behind Molino and bringing them to justice."

He grunted, a feral quality to the sound. "Bring them to justice? Maybe, but I have a feeling this will end without binding ties."

Erik expected Jia to protest. Instead, as he looked at her, she replied with a grim nod.

"The only better solution I can think of is joining the CID," she suggested. "And they would have you on a tighter leash than the NSCPD does. Since the conspiracy might involve someone in the government, that might be more of a risk."

"I know. At least some people in the government are fighting back. Colonel Adeyemi hinted that I might be able to get better results not working as a cop, and I'm convinced Koval knows more about what happened there than she's let on."

Jia frowned. "True, and I know Adeyemi has been helpful, but I'm also not sure I trust him. He's suffered the pain of losing a son. He might be willing to sacrifice anything to get his revenge, including you. And Koval's ID. You can't trust ghosts. She'll use you for her own purposes."

"You're probably right." Erik shrugged. "You don't have to trust someone to get something useful out of them. It doesn't matter for now. Emma's always searching, and as she's fond of saying, she's the only one like her."

"Indeed, I am, Detectives," Emma announced. "And I— Dispatch is putting everyone on alert. There are a high number of incoming flitters. They aren't transmitting transponder signals."

Uniformed officers waved people into the building. Several screamed and rushed. Only the presence of so many uniformed authorities kept panic from consuming the crowd. TPST exoskeletons advanced toward the edge of the platform, raising their guns. A few militia soldiers yanked rocket launchers off their backs.

Several nearby flitters abruptly changed course, most diving toward the ground.

Erik pulled back on the yoke. The MX 60 lifted into the air.

"According to my sensors," Emma continued, "the flitters have unusual energy readings, but I see no thermal signatures to indicate passengers."

Jia hissed in frustration. "You saying they're probably bombs?"

"That would be my best estimate, and it seems to be Incident Command's belief as well. Militia and police units are being ordered to prepare to fire. The flitters aren't responding to requests to stand down, and your fellow uniformed boys and girls are sending emergency transmissions requesting everyone else vacate the local flight area. Perhaps we should clear the parking platform. I'd rather not be blown up. It'd be too ignoble an ending."

Erik shook his head. "No, not yet. We start flying around, we might end up getting shot down, and we make it harder for everyone outside to do what they need to do." He spun the MX 60 around, his gaze flicking to the lidar. The flitters were coming in on all sides. If Emma was right, it was a circle of death. He narrowed his eyes. Something felt wrong about the attack.

The flitter swarm grew from distant dots to visible vehicles. Erik had wondered if the lidar was wrong and it'd be drones, but no, scores of full-sized vehicles barreled toward the parking platform.

"Counterattack is being initiated, on five, four, three, two, *one*," Emma reported.

Erik was used to having the biggest gun and making the most noise in police situations. Instead, he sat inside the MX 60, not even shooting his rifle as machine gun rounds and rockets streamed from the soldiers and police protecting the platform. The projectiles filled the air. Even the sound-insulated MX 60 rattled from the intense overlapping noises of so many weapons going off at once.

TPST and militia assault flitters lifted off the platform to add their stream of bullets to the angry defensive swarm.

Orange-red explosions filled the air. Few of the charging flitters were the victims of rockets. Most exploded after bullets ripped through them, confirming Emma's earlier theory. A ring of flame and smoke surrounded the tower. The police and soldiers continued their merciless assault.

"At least they don't need fireworks now," Erik commented, looking around. "But that was too easy."

"A horde of explosive-filled flitters was too easy?" Jia snorted. "What would be hard? Zitarks falling out of the sky with laser rifles and *yaoguai* cavalry?"

"Detective Blackwell is correct," Emma commented.

"How do you know?"

"Because the new chief has just been shot," Emma responded cheerfully.

"What the hell?" Erik slammed his fist on the dash. "The whole thing was a damned distraction."

"Someone wanted to make their own show of force," Jia spat through clenched teeth.

"The masked suspect escaped the security inside, but a surveillance drone just spotted a flitter breaking through the smoke not too far from here. There's some concern about possible follow-up attacks, so the militia and TPST are staying put. Other units are ordered to give chase."

"Works for me." Erik accelerated and the MX 60 jetted out of the parking garage through the *tink-tink* of parts still hitting his vehicle, a hungry grin appearing.

"Our turn."

CHAPTER EIGHTEEN

The MX 60 tore through the dense clouds of smoke and debris. Dozens of new lidar signatures showed up, along with matching thermal signatures, all flying straight toward the municipal tower.

The new arrivals were much smaller than those responsible for the earlier deadly flitter wave.

"Looks like another wave of explosives," Jia suggested. "There's trying to show off, but that is just being arrogant. These guys are really starting to annoy me."

Erik raised an eyebrow as he swerved to miss a large piece of debris. "Starting?"

Jia shrugged. "This last year has really increased my tolerance for violent idiocy."

"I hope that's only half about me personally." Erik chuckled. "But it doesn't matter. Arrogance is good."

"Huh? How can you say that?" Jia looked at him. "If they were more afraid, we wouldn't be dealing with a wave of explosives like this was some crazy insurrectionist raid on a frontier colony world."

"That's one way to look at it, but I've got a different one. If they're arrogant, that means they'll slip up, and that'll give us an opportunity to take more of them down and get the guy who shot the chief. The rest of the cops and the militia have enough firepower there to hold off the latest wave. I think whoever is doing this is just trying to keep everyone from catching up. That means they aren't confident he won't crack if we interrogate him. We need to move."

"I can quibble with some of the logic, but I can't object to capturing the suspect." Jia looked out the windshield, her eyes narrowing. "It was a good thing we were on the edge of the action, and a good thing you've put so much money into this flitter."

"Prepare before the battle, and you'll win more often." Erik shoved the yoke forward. The MX 60 slid under the cloud of drones barreling toward the platform. More explosions lit the sky, anti-aircraft barrages meeting explosive drones. What should have been a triumphant ceremony had turned into a war, but from a distance, someone might mistake it for fireworks. A huge cloud of smoke fueled by countless explosions surrounded several levels of the tower.

Jia glanced at the lidar and back through the front windshield.

Emma must have been sending navigational cues to Erik because Jia didn't see how he could distinguish the suspect from any of the other civilian flitters fleeing the area. Fortunately, everyone was smart enough to obey emergency directives rather than trying to fly over and get a better view of what might be happening.

A lot of people now understood that Earth, and even its crown jewel, Neo Southern California, wasn't a perfect garden, or even if they believed that, they understand they needed to avoid the serpents hiding in the flowers.

She almost laughed.

Her former beliefs and life seemed like something from long-distant decades. It felt natural to be rushing past exploding drones in pursuit of a suspect who had shot their new police chief. Doing anything else would have felt odd and cowardly. She wasn't sure which was the more responsible for her changes: her partner, or the cases she'd worked since he became her partner.

The thought drifted away as the chaos of the assault fell farther behind them. No drones changed course toward the MX 60. No rockets or missiles flew toward them. No bullets struck its body. Under Erik's determined control, the fast vehicle zoomed around a corner and closed on a red flitter speeding toward a thicket of industrial towers in the distance.

"That's the guy?" Jia asked.

Erik nodded. "Yeah, that's the guy. Might have been better for him just to try to hide in the municipal tower."

"Too many cameras and too much police control."

"Maybe." Erik scoffed. "But this way, he's going down soon."

"The suspect isn't using his window tinting," Emma announced, haughtiness in her tone. "Unless it's a completely different gun goblin who happens to be wearing a dark mask, it's definitely your man. There's your arrogance, Erik. I believe he was overly dependent on the additional drones to cover his escape."

"Good," Erik replied. "If he thinks his arrogance is going to let him escape after this crap, I'll show him what real arrogance is."

The red flitter sped up and barreled toward the industrial towers.

Erik grinned and accelerated. "You really think you can outrun me?"

A regular police patrol flitter was overpowered compared to civilian models. His sports flitter with custom upgrades made patrol flitters look slow. There was no way the suspect could hope to escape without doing something a lot more creative.

Perhaps he had more explosive drones nearby?

"Need some pop-out guns or something on the front," Erik muttered. "Especially since they don't want me sticking a directional EMP on a non-police vehicle."

"There's a limit to what even *you* will be allowed," Jia commented, infusing sympathy into her voice. If the department was even slightly more flexible, it'd save everyone a lot of trouble in situations like this.

"Pop-out laser cannon?" Erik suggested. "Maybe I should just buy an assault flitter on my dime and ask the captain for permission to use it on duty?"

Jia furrowed her brow. "I'd say that's overkill, but given our luck, I don't know if that's true. Wait, is he going to crash?" Her eyes widened. "Why give up now?"

The red flitter abruptly changed course, skimming along the outer edge of a tower and only narrowly missing several protruding antennae and drone tubes. The vehicle was now heading straight toward a thin industrial tower. Maybe he'd made a mistake. Industrial towers tended to have fewer external parking platforms than commercial, municipal, or residential towers. If the suspect was planning to abandon his vehicle, he might have charged toward the nearest dense cluster of towers, not realizing what kind they would be. A man running from effectively all of the major law enforcement in Neo SoCal didn't have a lot of time to think through his options.

Something about the explanation felt off to Jia. The kind of people who had the necessary resources to send waves of flitter bombs should theoretically have planned better than that. They would have planned an escape route. Even if they hadn't flown it themselves, they would have programmed it in.

She would love to believe simple arrogance explained the suspect's actions, but assuming too much could get her Erik and her killed.

The red flitter continued closing on the thin tower. Before, he'd flown at an angle.

Erik frowned and slowed the MX 60. "I don't want to know how well a tower can take a flitter hit somewhere other than a window."

The MX 60 moved closer, and the suspect's vehicle spun ninety degrees. Erik turned to intercept for a few seconds before hitting the braking thrusters. The MX 60 jerked to a halt, straining the passengers' seat belts.

"Why are you stop—" Jia gasped.

The door of the flitter opened, and the suspect leapt out. The vehicle zoomed away, slowing. From the angle, it looked like it wouldn't hit a building.

Erik shook his head. "If he wanted to kill himself, it

would have been quicker just to crash. Now he gets to think about everything on the way down."

The suspect spread his arms and legs. A moment later, dark flaps filled the gap—a convertible wingsuit.

"Huh." Erik let out a grunt of approval. "Didn't see that coming."

Jia gaped at the sight. "You've got to be kidding me!"

Erik chuckled. "Turns out our guy was more prepared than we thought."

The suspect glided in a circle a few seconds before diving toward an open loading bay door several levels down. Erik accelerated and dropped altitude. All they needed to do was slide in through the bay door. They wouldn't even scratch the MX 60 and ruin all of Miguel's recent repair work.

Jia frowned. "Wait. Something's wrong. Why did he jump here?"

"To escape? Because there was a big open space?"

"How would he know?" Jia pressed. "He just happened to fly to a place with a huge open bay and then abandon his vehicle? He was flying at top speeds while trying to evade the police. He doesn't have time to look at every single camera and sensor for openings, especially ones that far down."

Erik stopped descending. "You're right; he wouldn't unless it's a trap. He probably hoped no one would be right on his ass during his escape. More misdirection."

Jia stared at the loading bay. They couldn't see much from their angle, which only fueled her belief the suspect knew it was there. "Emma, do you have a drone in position?"

"I have one flying here, but it'll be about ten more seconds," she explained. "It's not as fast as my body."

Jia jabbed a finger at the loading bay. "Even if he got lucky, he'd risk running into a grav fence or net. They wouldn't be able to stop his flitter, but there's a good chance they can stop a single person gliding into them. Jumping into it without being sure it would be down would be suicide."

The suspect spiraled toward his destination.

"Yeah, unless he knew it wouldn't be up." Erik brought the MX 60 down quickly. He caught up with the suspect as the man soared toward the bay with no hint of resistance from a grav field.

No surprise rockets slammed into their flitter. Two large cargo flitters were parked in the bay, their long trailers pointing inward. Ten men with rifles waited on the sides of the trailers, crouched behind boxes and a few large parked cargo drones. The suspect touched down. The flaps between his arms and legs receded, and he sprinted between the cargo flitters.

"He's got help," Jia muttered with a sigh. "*Of course,* he's got help."

The gunmen opened up with the weapons, showering the MX 60 with bullets. The bullets bounced off the hardened exterior of the vehicle, sounding like soft thuds from the inside. Their suspect kept running the entire time, disappearing behind a cargo flitter.

"Yeah, but we're us," Erik countered. "And there's only ten of them. It's not even fair. I almost feel like we should give them a handicap."

He pushed the MX 60 down to bring the vehicle level

with the rifle fire. Jia had seen him do that many times. All the reinforced armor in the world wouldn't do anything if the grav emitters were damaged, and there was only so much that could be done to protect them—one of the reasons flitters weren't preferred military vehicles. He circled near the bay, the vehicle taking a few shots in the maneuver, but at least they were out of the immediate line of fire.

"What's the plan?" Jia asked. "Charge in there with the flitter? The suspect is getting away."

"Miguel's going to murder me in my sleep if I try that again, and I'm half-convinced Emma might, too."

"All scenarios should be considered for proper future predictions," Emma offered cheerfully. "Make sure that if you damage my body, it's absolutely necessary."

Muzzles flashes lit the otherwise-dim loading bay.

"If we try to get in under that kind of fire, it won't matter how much armor this flitter has," Jia suggested. "We need to take them out, then land."

Erik gestured toward her seat. "Time for a big gun. Emma, I'm going to need you to take control. Just keep circling while Jia and I clear our landing zone. These guys are cocky, but I doubt they're used to fighting cops with my kind of firepower."

Jia moved her legs aside.

Emma took control before Erik even released the yoke. She maintained a tight semi-circular evasion pattern. Jia pulled the TR-7 out of its hidden compartment and handed it to Erik, along with several magazines. He loaded the gun as Jia readied her slug-thrower.

"No stun pistol?" Erik flipped the safety off on his rifle, surprise on his face.

"Not at the range we'll be shooting from." Jia shrugged. "It'd be pointless. Even if I hit them, there won't be enough energy left to stun them."

"Fine by me." Erik brought his window down and stuck the barrel of the TR-7 out of the flitter, holding it primarily with his left arm. He flipped to four-barrel automatic mode and narrowed his eyes. "Let's make a hole and go after our suspect. Go straight at them and turn hard about twenty meters out, Emma."

"This ought to be interesting," she replied. "I hope this doesn't end with all of us plummeting to our fiery deaths."

"It probably won't, but no guarantees," he agreed.

The MX 60 straightened and flew toward the cargo bay. The gunmen didn't break from their positions. They maintained their fire. The suspect was a distant black blur in the back of the vast bay.

A few seconds later, Emma turned, providing Erik with his first shot. The TR-7 came to life with a roar. Ten men firing their rifles in bursts had been covering the MX 60 with bullets, but one detective with an overpowered rifle was matching them in raw spent ammunition. His firing window was short, only a few seconds, but effective. Two men screamed and fell, the TR-7's bullets ripping through their heads. A few others staggered back, their tactical vests saving their lives. Another dropped his weapon as a bullet pierced his shoulder. The others scattered, their fire becoming erratic.

Jia didn't have her partner's ridiculous gun, but she was a good shot, even moving. She kept her head low and her hands steady. Her first few shots went wide. The third was a headshot that finished another man.

Erik popped out his magazine.

"Empty already?" Jia asked.

"Yeah, but this is something different." He slapped in a new mag. "Armor-piercing." He grinned. "Don't want the colonel to think I'm wasting all his nice help."

The defenders rallied as Erik and Jia came in for another pass. Brave, perhaps, but also futile. With the new ammo, Erik didn't even have to aim as carefully. His AP rounds ripped through their tactical vests, shredding several gunmen. In the chaos, the survivors stopped firing and turned to run, making them easier targets. It didn't take long before the ten gunmen lay on the ground.

"Bring us in, Emma," Erik ordered. "We need a better insertion solution in the future that doesn't involve crashing into things or risking heavy weapons fire, but it's not like I can stick a drop pod on the MX 60." He scratched his cheek. "Yeah, that *mostly* doesn't make sense."

Jia side-eyed him.

The flitter cruised forward, turning and settling down near the front of the truck. Jia threw open the door and leapt outside after stuffing a few more mags into her pockets. Erik grabbed every magazine he had in his storage space and shoved them into the pockets of his duster.

"I know it's difficult, given what we've seen, but we need to take the suspect alive," Jia noted. "He might be the key to whoever was behind all this."

"Understood." Erik selected single-barrel mode, wearing a slight frown. "But if it comes down to him or us, you know the choice I'll make every time."

Jia took a deep breath and nodded. Her heart pounded, but no fiery anger filled her like it would have before she'd started seeing the counselor. She needed to do her job; it might involve having to shoot someone and risk her life, but that came with the badge. She wasn't sure if the new chief had survived his assassination attempt, but it didn't matter. It wasn't time for revenge. It was time for justice, and justice required *evidence*.

She gripped her pistol grip tightly. "Emma, this place doesn't look shut down. Can you take over? We can justify it under emergency protocols."

"I'm attempting to interface now with the systems. Industrial systems are surprisingly robust. It pains me to admit this might take a few minutes."

"We can't wait that long." Jia inclined her head toward the other end of the loading bay. A wide door lay open.

"She'll do what she needs to, and we'll do what we need to." Erik stepped forward. "Let's go find our boy."

CHAPTER NINETEEN

Erik and Jia charged the open door, zigzagging and staggering their path.

The attack might have been a surprise, but that didn't mean they weren't prepared. They were already in tactical vests, and they had enough ammo to take on an army. Jia was right. They couldn't let the suspect escape.

Emma would call for reinforcements, but in the chaos of the explosions, it might take them a couple of minutes to arrive, let alone proceed deeper into the tower.

This wasn't a municipal building. An industrial tower made perfect sense as an escape. In a metroplex packed with people, it would have fewer people and more places to hide.

The wide doorway didn't open into offices or a hallway. Instead, it led to a vast factory floor, a cacophonous mechanical hive. Lines of cargo drones of different sizes zoomed around the maze-like rows and columns to deposit small and large components—metal and shaped ceramic panels, from what Erik could see.

Fixed-installation construction-bot workstations, tall and wide spindly vertical bunches of robotic arms, torches, saws, and even lasers spun and tilted to do their work, joining the delivered pieces together. The whole assembly at each station was then moved to the next.

From the looks of things, they were building mini-flitter bodies. With their luck, he half-expected to walk into a King sentry bot factory. It was always nice when the Lady worked with him instead of against him.

"How are we doing on the hacking, Emma?" Erik asked. He crouched behind one of the workstations, peering around the corner before he pulled his head back.

The cargo drones stopped moving and hovered in place. The workstations powered down with a low whine.

"I'm almost there, Detective," Emma reported. "I thought it might help if there are fewer things flying around. I'm into the security grid and have disabled at least the primary security response."

Jia knelt next to Erik. "Good, no bots. I've blown up enough bots to last me until I'm your age." He eyed her. "Real age, not physical."

She gave him a half-hearted smile. *Nice comment in the middle of a battle.*

"Oh, it wouldn't have been bots for this part of the facility," Emma explained. "They just seal the vents and flood the entire operations floor with sleeping gas. How wonderfully civilized."

"That makes sense." Jia sighed. "There are probably very few humans who normally work on this factory level, and bots running around firing stun bolts might damage some expensive, sensitive piece of equipment."

"I should note, there was no indication that the system was otherwise compromised, but the primary security grid was easy to disable because the main system defenses weren't active," Emma explained. "The logs indicate a valid external code was used to do that."

"They prepared their battlefield. It's not like they would assume this place wouldn't have defenses." Erik frowned. "Maybe we can use that gas on him, but in a different room. That'll make this easy."

"The other areas are defended by more conventional door and bot defenses," Emma explained. "As Detective Lin suggested, they were likely more worried about damage in here, but as soon as I take control of the system, I'll send bots to overwhelm him. From what I can see, they're all non-lethal, and he'll be the one damaging things. He's heading away from anything expensive if you're worried about the company complaining."

"Not that worried, but it doesn't hurt to know." Erik jerked his head down once again as a rifle flashed from a corner several rows down. "They had more than the guys in the bay. Expensive operation. Someone really, really wanted the chief dead in a fancy, public way. They could have just tried to assassinate him at his house."

"They can't send as big a message that way, and I'd hope they wouldn't be able to kill the chief of police for Neo Southern California on a small budget. That would be more disturbing than the assassination itself." Jia pulled out her stun pistol and holstered her other gun. She spun around her station on the opposite side to fire a few stun bolts. Her shots pinned down another gunman. "If it's this bad here, I wonder what it's like on the average frontier colony."

"Not as bad as you think," Erik replied, looking around. "When insurrectionists move, things get bad, but Neo SoCal has a much larger population than most colonies, even most core worlds. Can't have as much trouble if you don't have as many people." A bullet flew by him and made a hole in a thin metal box about twenty inches tall beside him. "Huh. That was close."

"I've gained access to cameras," Emma announced. "But I still don't have access to the full security grid. I have to applaud whoever is responsible for security here. This has been harder than most systems I've attempted to breach. It's interesting, considering the relatively modest importance of what's being built here."

"All corporations are worried about protecting their profits." Erik squeezed off a burst and clipped his target in the shoulder. The man let out a loud yelp and dropped behind the station he had been using for cover.

Twelve different red human outlines of various sizes appeared in Erik's smart lenses. One of them lay on the floor.

"I trust that was successful?" Emma asked. "I figure it'll be a trivial matter for you to dispose of these gun goblins if you know exactly where they are. I have full access to the cameras now. There are fewer than I would have hoped, but there are a sufficient number for purposes of finishing off the current fleshbags."

Jia grimaced. "I don't think I'll ever get used to you talking about people like that."

"It's accurate if nothing else."

A loud, resounding clank bounced around the factory floor.

Erik frowned. "What the hell was that? They have exoskeletons?"

Emma snickered. "Nothing so impressive, Detective. I sealed in your suspect using the emergency doors in a connecting hallway. Take your time with his friends. Unfortunately, he does have eight men with him, and they have some sort of bulkier armor compared to the tactical vests of your current opponents. They came from the other side of the floor once you entered the level. I can't identify the nature of their armor through their coats. Their thermographic profiles are warmer than normal. They are carrying rifles, along with several grenades. They are currently attempting to figure out what is going on with the doors, and seem surprised about being sealed in."

"We'll worry about them when they get out. If we can finish off their friends, we'll be in a position where they'll have no choice but to surrender. Good job." Erik downed another man who had been brave enough to walk around the corner. "Give it up," he shouted. "The police have control of this facility now, and our reinforcements will be here before your guys ca—"

Several men charged around the corner, shouting profanities in at least four different languages. They pointed their rifles toward Erik's station and held their triggers down. As their bullets whistled through the air, Erik stayed behind his cover and didn't panic. The bullets struck the workstation, bouncing off with sparks. He wasn't surprised. A few of them broke away from the group and rushed down the row on Jia's side. He could admire their stubbornness, but that didn't change what he needed to do.

Erik pulled back to another station and waited. Even though he lacked direct line-of-sight to any of the charging enemies, Emma's targeting assistance would give him a warning before they could get a shot off at him. The enemies continued firing off a near-constant stream of bullets, roaring their defiance like brave insurgents making their last stand in their capital city.

Too bad their weapons and accuracy didn't match their volume.

The men must have panicked when their buddies got locked inside. Whoever was behind the scheme had spent a lot of money on drones and weapons. They must have anticipated potential TPST support and arranged a counter for it, one that Emma had now bottled up. The weapons had changed over the centuries, but von Moltke's dictum remained the same.

No battle plan survived contact with the enemy.

The disciplined soldier survived because he didn't let the unexpected rattle him, but these weren't soldiers. At least, they didn't move like soldiers.

The first few brave idiots cleared the corner right after Erik lifted his rifle. They didn't even have time to shout at him before he put bullets into their heads. A few more fools continued the charge and ended up with their friends on the floor. He'd given them the chance to surrender, but they'd charged instead.

He knew what they were thinking. They saw that only two cops had entered the loading bay, and they'd thought they could overwhelm them. It would be their last mistakes.

Jia's stun pistol fired, the bright bolts zooming toward more shooters. She wasn't in a moving flitter trying to avoid heavy weapons fire. Shooting men at close range when she knew exactly where they were was trivial. Two men hesitated, slowing their movements as they squeezed off bursts in her direction, but Erik spun around the corner and took the opportunity to down them both.

The smaller number of men who had tried to engulf Jia's position lay on the floor, victims of her stun pistol. Their rifles were scattered around the floor.

"We should secure the ones who are still alive," she suggested, holstering her stun pistol and pulling out binding ties. "They might have something useful to say. I doubt it, but you never know."

Erik set his TR-7 against his shoulder and shrugged. "I did try to get them to surrender."

Jia chuckled. "You did. Some criminals are just stupid." She bound one man's hand, uncertainty playing across her face. "Unless they're terrorists. That might explain why they're going all-out. Then again, I'm not sure. We've seen gangsters practice rather lethal bravery."

"I'm guessing they aren't terrorists." Erik looked around, but no new outlines appeared. Emma would tell them if there was more trouble, too.

"Why do you say that?" Jia crouched by a prisoner. "I'm not disagreeing. I would have expected more political rants, but did you notice anything? I've filled my quota since becoming your partner, but you've still got a lot more experience with all sorts of antisocials than I do."

Erik gestured to a dead gunman. "I don't think they would have gone through all this trouble to protect the killer. If he could smuggle a gun past the security cordon, he probably could have done the same with a bomb. I've fought enough of them to know that they tend to love their martyrs. Think about the Grayheads. So not terrorists. Insurrectionists don't have a lot to gain from stirring up trouble directly on Earth and specifically in Neo SoCal instead of trying to blow up the UTC parliament or something. If anyone claimed it, they'd just get a UTC fleet above their planet and thousands of drop pods falling from orbit. These guys are criminals, or at least hired muscle."

Jia took a deep breath. "Or something greater?" She looked at him. He noticed how hard she yanked a guy's arm to put the binding tie on and almost grimaced in sympathy. Well, if she'd had any for these people.

She continued, "Agents of the conspiracy?"

Erik gritted his teeth. "I can't ignore the possibility, but I doubt it." He glanced around again. "These guys are sloppier than what we've seen from Talos. He might not have anything to do with them either."

"The thought that the UTC might have multiple dangerous conspiracies is chilling."

"Several TPST and militia flitters have taken damage," Emma reported. "No hard crashes, but there was a final smaller wave of explosive drones."

"Damn." Erik shook his head in disappointment.

Jia looked thoughtful for a moment as she stared at her stunned prisoner. "It doesn't matter who the perps are. The vanguard here might have something interesting to tell us, but we still need to get the hitman. He's our best shot at finding the mastermind. Emma, can you release the bots on him and his friends? It might be easier than having another shootout."

"Unfortunately, not in the particular place I trapped him," Emma replied, a hint of contrition in her tone. "Oh. I can because the circumstances are about to change. Don't be alarmed by what I'm about to do."

Several vents opened in the corners of the room near where the walls met the ceiling. A dozen silvery orbs descended with a whir, circling near the back of the room. Nine new human outlines appeared on Erik's smart lenses.

"Did he come back into the room?" Erik asked.

"No, but I'm fairly certain he's about to blow the door," Emma explained. "He carries a lot of toys. I'd tell you the type of device, but it seems to be custom-made, so I can't easily identify it from camera observation. I doubt you have more than thirty seconds before there is a detonation, based on what he's doing and saying."

Erik sprinted forward, making lefts and rights as necessary in the fabrication maze. Jia hurried after him. They closed about half the distance, denser rectangular station formations dominating this part of the factory floor.

A massive explosion rocked the back of the room, rattling the entire floor.

Flames, smoke, and shards of metal ricocheted off nearby machinery. The overlapping sound formed a short, powerful percussive symphony.

Erik's ears rang.

Jia dropped behind a construction station and rolled her eyes. "Finally, someone who carries around even more ridiculous stuff than you. That explosion was way bigger than what you'd see from a breaching disk."

"You kick ass with what your superiors allow you to carry." Erik crouched behind a nearby station. "Captain Ragnar probably wouldn't let me carry all my best gear on basic duty. Otherwise, I'd always have the laser rifle."

"Probably not. Now that I think about it, that's probably for the best." Jia peeked around the corner and pointed her pistol. "But I'm going to admit a few stun grenades might have been handy."

"True."

Emma's bot squadron descended. A high-pitched whine followed by a harsh buzz sounded from the other side of the room. The security bots dropped out of the ceiling like angry hail, thudding unceremoniously on the hard floor or bouncing off equipment with a loud clank.

Jia sighed. "EMP?"

"Sadly, yes," Emma replied. She sounded irritated. "This annoying fleshbag is smarter and better equipped than your average gun goblin. Please note additional police units are almost here. From what dispatch has related, the situation has been fully contained, with all bomb drones destroyed, despite the flitter damage. There have been no civilian injuries. Minor injuries among police and militia. It might be wise to pull back and wait for reinforcements, considering the nature of your current enemies."

"No way. Not after all this." Erik patted his TR-7. "I don't want to wait for the militia. I want to take this guy down myself. If this is about a symbolic public hit, why don't we offer a symbolic defense of Neo SoCal on our own? We should remind these bastards that Neo SoCal isn't someplace anyone can show up and blow up whatever they want. If they go after the cops, they're going to pay."

"I understand how you feel," Jia countered, "but this is the actual shooter. Remember, we need to take him alive so we can interrogate him." She pointed at his gun. "Consider putting that down and using a stun pistol?"

Erik snorted. "I don't need a stun pistol to take the guy alive."

Jia raised an eyebrow. "Does shooting one of your four-barrel bursts grant the bullets magic stun powers? If so, I'll have to consider buying one of those."

"No, but I'll shoot him in the shoulder or knee. He didn't sneak into the ceremony in full tactical gear." He shrugged. "And Emma mentioned bulkier armor. His buddies might not be taken down with stun pistols either. This might get messy, and if we pull back and wait for reinforcements, he might get away."

Jia looked like she was going to offer another complaint before smiling and shaking her head. She put away her stun pistol and drew her slug-thrower. "Let's take him down, then. For the new chief."

Erik dropped his gun from his shoulder. "I don't know who these guys are, but I'm already pretty sick of them."

"Incoming grenades," Emma shouted.

"Evade!"

CHAPTER TWENTY

Emma highlighted the grenades in bright yellow. Despite her warning, the enemy was still in the process of throwing them. The warning and ability to track their arc gave the detectives what they needed to survive the explosives.

Erik and Jia leapt in opposite directions. Their dodges briefly exposed them to the enemy, and rifle rounds screamed from the opposite end of the factory floor. One bullet slammed into Jia's vest, stinging. The crushed spent round dropped to the floor. She landed behind another workstation, her jaw tight. Grenades completed their flight, exploding in a mass of deadly fragments and smoke that riddled the floor and nearby machinery.

If she hadn't jumped, she would have ended up taking a shower of hot, sharp metal.

"Just keep moving," Erik ordered. "Emma will give us a head's up if they try something special."

Jia nodded. She rushed for another workstation, this time ready to fire. Her pistol came alive as she sprinted. Two shots bounced off the bulky dark armor worn by the men. A third shot went high and through a man's exposed neck. With a gurgle, he fell over on his back, blood spraying.

The other men opened up with their assault rifles. Their bullet swarm missed Jia by centimeters as she took new cover. She had a tactical vest on, but unlike her opponents, she didn't have a helmet. Her heart pounded. She needed to be careful.

Getting killed isn't the preferred way to end my career.

Jia wasn't the only person who needed to be careful. The criminals had all turned to fire at her, ignoring her partner. All four barrels of the TR-7 flashed, and a river of bullets launched from the gun. The overconfidence of the criminals cost them as the barrage ripped through one man's armor and sent him spinning in a bloodied dance toward the floor.

"He's got armor-piercing ammo!" one of the men shouted. They leapt for cover.

Jia hurried around the corner of her cover, her breathing ragged. She didn't snap off a quick shot. With Erik's cover fire and the panic, she had the time to line up and put a bullet into the exposed face of another man. She ducked but continued firing every couple of seconds. Erik's gun went silent. The TR-7's insatiable appetite was the only problem with going all-out.

She snorted. The criminals thought they had the upper hand, but Erik was right—they needed to understand who they were dealing with. Erik had tried to get them to surrender, and they were sheltering someone who had shot the chief of police and fired at police officers. Antisocial didn't come close to describing them.

"Incoming," Emma warned. "And I suggest you keep moving until I tell you it's safe."

Jia jumped and rolled as another grenade tumbled through the air. This time, the grenade exploded high in a blinding white-blue flash that melted half the workstation that had been her previous cover. Flames and heat licked her face, stinging. A second of hesitation would have ended her life.

"Plasma grenades?" she muttered. "Oh, come ON!" She took a right in a crouching jog. "What's next, rocket launchers?"

After Erik opened fire again, Jia hurried to settle into her new position.

Plasma and frag grenades flew through the air in wide arcs, exploding at different heights. Debris rained down all around the factory floor. The scorched and smoldering workstations emitted a steady stream of dark, acrid smoke into the air. Jia managed not to cough. Her visibility might be cut down, but Emma's signal to her smart lenses remained unaffected.

A whoop of triumph came from the criminal far too soon. Jia scoffed under her breath.

"You should let us know where you are," one man shouted. "You're probably burned half to death. It's a painful way to die. Let us come over and finish you off. That's what you get for taking us on."

"That was annoying," Erik muttered, his quiet voice transmitted directly to Jia. He crouched a decent distance from her on the other side. Emma's helpful outline let Jia track him, but they'd been split up by the counterattack.

"The enemy is out of obvious explosive devices," Emma

reported. "Despite their taunt, the survivors have not advanced."

"They can't risk the possibility that they're wrong, especially now that they've lost their ordnance superiority," Jia offered. "They also realize if we're not dead, we might be stalling. They might have more guys hiding in the back, but we have the entire NSCPD on our side, not to mention the militia."

"Let them wonder," Erik replied. "It means they won't see us coming. They're moving better than the last batch. I think they've had decent training. These guys aren't going to surrender just because they ran out of grenades."

"Agreed." Jia frowned. Emma's helpful outlines made it easy to track the survivors as they spread out in two groups, both moving in opposite directions, except for one man. "Is that our shooter, Emma?"

His outline turned green.

"Yes," Emma confirmed. "His face suggests he's far more worried than the other men."

"They're all but delivering him to us," Erik suggested. "I'm going to move again. I don't have enough AP magazines for a long, drawn-out fight, but we can least finish these guys off and take our guy. You ready?"

Jia nodded. "I am when you are. Remember, we need him alive."

"Sure. Moving on five, four, three, two, one." Erik erupted from cover and opened fire. His first burst shredded a man's arm. His target screamed and tumbled in front of one of his firing friends. The criminal's rifle bullets flattened against his friend's armor, but the confusion disrupted the small group.

Jia popped up and opened fire. She headshot one man, but another turned, and her bullets bounced off his helmet with a spark. She rolled back behind cover as they returned fire.

Erik zigzagged forward, laying down bursts every few steps. More men fell to the monstrosity he called a rifle. The loss of the men forced the ones engaged with Jia to rush for cover, giving her more openings. Her careful three shots finally found their mark. A man groaned and fell, his hand going to his bleeding neck. The last armored man standing fell to a four-shot burst from Erik. That left the man who'd shot the chief. He darted in the direction he'd run before, panting and sweating.

"Give it up!" Jia shouted. She sprinted out of cover and between the rows of heavy machinery. She snapped up her gun, took aim at his leg, and pulled the trigger. She blinked at the accompanying unusually thunderous gunshot. The hitman screamed and fell forward.

She approached the man, her gun still pointed at him. Large holes in both legs revealed the reason for the loud noise. Erik had fired at the exact same time at the other leg. The suspect let out a long, pained groan.

Erik jogged forward with a satisfied grin on his face. He pointed using his gun. "See? He's *not* dead."

Jia kicked the suspect's weapon away and holstered her pistol. "That's true."

"You bastards," the man hissed through his gritted teeth. "You blew out my knees."

"We did, didn't we?" Jia commented, a complete lack of sympathy in her voice. "I was aiming slightly higher, but you were moving." She shrugged, pulling out her ties. "Same difference."

Erik kept his TR-7 in his hand while his partner knelt to bind the suspect hands. He squealed in pain.

"Oh, stop your whining," Erik muttered. "Med patches will clear that right up, and it's not like we blew your legs off. That's after you shot the chief, tried to kill a lot of cops, and you and your friends tried to melt us with grenades."

"You're under arrest," Jia declared. "All Article 7 rights apply. Do you need these explained to you?"

The suspect groaned again and fell unconscious.

"I'll take that as a no for now." Jia moved a few stray hairs out of her face. Sweat had matted them down. She sighed. "But this doesn't help the chief." She glared at the man. "They still win if they killed him."

"That's not a problem," Emma interjected. "He was shot, but he's in stable condition."

Erik set his rifle on his shoulder, looking around to make sure the others were truly out of action. "Oh, so our friend here isn't only a criminal, he's a criminal who is bad at his job."

CHAPTER TWENTY-ONE

Erik tugged down the jacket of his dress uniform.

Even though the clothing had been custom-fitted for him, something about it felt uncomfortable and scratchy.

It was almost as if he had trouble wearing a uniform anymore, like the decades in the Army and the death of his men soured him on the experience. He'd check the theory by wearing a uniform after he tracked down whoever was responsible.

For now, he'd just have to put up with it as he sat in a chair next to Jia on the raised stage. Their gray chairs, along with others, were arrayed in rows on one side of a podium.

Several other police officers who had shone brightly during the crisis sat with them. Erik and Jia had tracked down the shooter, but other calm heads had been necessary to save people from the drone swarms. City officials and representatives of the police brass sat on the other side, including Captain Ragnar, who offered Erik a polite nod.

Hundreds of uniformed officers sat in chairs in front of the stage. An almost equal number of reporters sat behind them. There were so many camera drones hovering in the room, they could hardly maneuver without risking a collision. Everyone wanted to hear the first public statement from the chief following the assassination attempt. It'd been a long time since anyone had attempted something that bold in Neo Southern California.

"I can't believe we have to participate in a press conference," Erik mumbled.

A few cops nearby heard him and nodded in agreement.

Jia eyed him with a slight smirk. "A few days ago, you were the one going off about sending a message to criminals. This is the most direct way to do that."

"Yeah." Erik furrowed his brow. "The message was supposed to be, 'When you try to kill cops and keep shooting at us even after we tell you to surrender, you'll probably get shot.' We did that by taking them on. Press conferences, though? That's just a bunch of annoying garbage, so reporters can try to feel special and—"

The police officers sitting in front of the stage stood and began clapping loudly. Erik didn't even need to turn around to know why. He stood but didn't clap, as he'd been instructed by a PR rep before being sent to the stage. He remained at attention, Jia at his side, as their new chief, Elijah Warden, walked to the podium.

Unlike Captain Ragnar, the new chief was a man of slight build, not all that tall or physically imposing. The gray streaks in his dark hair indicated he hadn't opted for de-aging. Erik couldn't deny that authority radiated from the man's stern gaze and body language.

A person didn't have to be a giant to intimidate.

Chief Warden stepped up to the podium and swept his gaze over the crowd, then nodded curtly. The gathered officers took their seats.

"As you can see," the chief began, "I survived the attempt on my life." He pointed to his chest. "I took a bullet to the chest right here, but my getting shot is less important than what it represented. It was a bold attempt to strike at law and order in this grand metroplex. As the corruption has been rooted out in this last year, dark, dark forces have been on the move, hoping to return us to a status quo that benefits their antisocial criminality." He gestured to Erik and Jia. "But they failed, and Detectives Blackwell and Lin apprehended the suspect at great personal risk."

The crowd greeted that with a roar of approval, many of the reporters joining in. The chief waited until the noise had died down.

"I'm standing before you today to send a message to all criminals, terrorists, and insurrectionists who think they are above the law," Chief Warden thundered. "You did your best, including hiring mercenaries, and all you have to show for it are a bunch of prisoners and dead men. I'm still alive. All my cops are still alive. All the civilians we protected that day *are still alive*, and I'm standing in the same spot I was before to let you know that we will not rest until every last criminal and terrorist is driven from Neo SoCal.

"We will not be intimidated. You will understand, if you don't already, that your days in this place are numbered. We will shine a light into every dark hole where you're hiding. If you want to stay out of prison or not end up dead, you'll take up honest work. Or you can run off to Zitark space, for all I care." He paused for a moment with a smile on his face. "I'm sure they'd love the snacks."

Scattered laughs sounded from the crowd.

"To our friends in the media, I don't want to waste a lot of your time today," Chief Warden explained. "I'll note that interrogation of the captured suspects is continuing, and we have full CID support on this matter. It's only a matter of time before we track down every last person involved. Because of the sensitivity, we're not releasing many details at this time, other than noting a private military contracting organization was involved, but we assure you that we will soon deliver a vicious blow that criminals in Neo SoCal will never recover from."

Erik groaned and leaned against a wall. The press conference was over, and he'd escaped to a nearby hallway to avoid the crush of reporters seeking comments. He'd sat on the stage for thirty minutes while reporters figured out new ways to ask the chief the same questions over and over, with Warden repeatedly stressing he wasn't going to risk the follow-up operations by leaking evidence.

Jia stared down the hall an arm's length away. They were near a corner, but most of the police and media still filled the main auditorium down the corridor.

"What do you think?" Jia asked with a slightly pensive look.

Erik looked at her. "About?"

"The new chief?"

Erik shrugged. "He says the right things. He reminds me of a general I served under early in my career. He also seems more interested in doing the job than kissing the media's butt. I already overheard one reporter saying the authorities are stonewalling by not giving more information."

Jia shook her head. "The reporters can wait. It's not our responsibility to potentially help the criminals so the news has interesting things to say twenty-four/seven."

A small black camera drone zoomed around the corner. Erik and Jia jumped back with frowns. No reporters should have been coming from this part of the hallway.

"What the..." Erik mumbled.

A slick-looking blond man tall enough to match Erik stepped around the corner, a huge smile on his face. Another black drone followed him. Something about the man felt familiar, but Erik couldn't remember who the man was.

"Lance Onassis," Jia declared, sounding none too pleased.

Erik chuckled. Now he remembered. The reporter had seemed obsessed with the 1-2-2 in recent months and liked to overemphasize certain events and details for drama. He wasn't a liar, but he came close to the line at times.

Most of their precinct didn't care for him.

The reporter's smile grew. "That's right. I'm Lance

Onassis. I'm here live and in-person with Detectives Erik Blackwell and Jia Lin of Enforcement Zone 122. These two famous detectives have made a name for themselves this past year, and most recently were responsible for the capture of the man who attempted to assassinate Police Chief Warden."

Erik frowned. It took him a moment to realize the reporter was speaking about him, rather than to him.

"Live and in person?" Jia echoed.

Lance bobbed his head. "That's right, Detective Lin. Plenty of reporters will send their drones, but they aren't willing to go themselves. In these dangerous times, it's important that the media not put their own safety above the truth. That's where I come in."

"Yes." Erik chuckled. "There's nothing more dangerous than interviewing two cops at police headquarters."

Discontent flickered over Lance's face. "Not every case is dangerous for police officers either, Detective."

Erik glanced at Jia. "Sure, but you never know. Simple billing fraud might turn into a huge shootout with gangsters in the Shadow Zone." He grinned. "Hey, Lance, you ever been to the Shadow Zone? I mean, you're Mr. Live and In-Person, and you're willing to put yourself on the line for the story, right?"

Lance's mouth twitched, but he kept his smile. "Travel to and from the Zone is restricted so it can be difficult. I'd rather talk about you and your partner, Detective. Do you have any statement on the arrested suspect?"

Erik looked serious. "Sure. Don't commit crimes, and you won't get arrested or shot. Pretty simple life philosophy."

Lance finally lost his battle of self-control with a frown. "Setting that aside, is there anything you can share with us about the suspect?"

"No. You heard the chief." Erik pointed at the floor. "You should ask for special permission to go to the Zone. You can go around, ask questions. Maybe you'll find out something we don't know. Lots of criminals down there. You ever interview a criminal, Lance? Not in jail or remotely, but face-to-face, staring into their eyes on their own turf?"

Lance cleared his throat. "Do you have any opinion on the failure of the police in this recent case?" His tone sounded harsh and accusatory.

Jia frowned. "Failure? What are you talking about?"

"Yes. An obviously well-funded criminal enterprise launched a massive attack on police headquarters. The taxpayers are responsible for all that damage." Lance sighed and shook his head. "Some people out there are questioning whether police arrogance might have led to the surprise."

Erik laughed. "Some people, huh? You ever serve in the military, Lance?"

"No, I can't say that I have, but thank you for your service, Detective." Lance's voice was wary.

"Not everyone needs to serve in uniform, either as a cop or a soldier, but it can provide perspective." Erik patted his chest. "I've fought everyone from pirates to insurrectionists during my military career, and a good variety since becoming a cop. The military, of course, is all about delivering a beat down to bad guys, but if an enemy force launched a massive surprise attack on one of our bases or ships, and we took them down with zero casualties and ended up inflicting lots of casualties and taking a lot of prisoners, no one would ever call *that* a failure."

"You're suggesting the police should be praised for being surprised?"

Erik shrugged. "I'm suggesting that the only folks hurt the other day were cops, despite there being a lot of people at headquarters and on the platforms. That means that cops put themselves out in front and did their jobs, despite somebody flinging enough bombs for a war at us. All those cops kept their cool instead of panicking."

Lance furrowed his brow, his smile now gone. "Some might question your aggressive approach to police work, Detective. You did capture the main suspect for the attempted assassination, but your department has admitted people were killed during the incident."

"Criminals and attempted murderers who attacked police officers. We asked the suspects to surrender on multiple occasions, and they not only refused, but they used military-grade weapons to attack us as their response."

"So you say."

Jia frowned at Lance. "Were you present during the attack? Were you live and in-person on the platform?"

"No, I...wasn't present, then." The reporter lifted his chin, affecting a faintly regal air. "But I've been present at police incidents before."

Jia shook her head. "A raid when you're outside and behind the police line isn't the same thing as responding to this sort of an attack. If you really want to be live and in person, that would be the kind of thing you'd need to deal with. It'd give you a different perspective on what we face. How a few seconds can make a big difference."

"I fail to see the need."

"I thought you said you were willing to risk yourself for the truth?" Erik's brows drew together. "You can't let a little danger derail you, right?"

Lance glared at Erik. "Do you have anything you can share about the ongoing interrogation of the suspect? All of Neo Southern California is still worried about the kind of organization that could fund and would risk such a brazen attack."

Erik shook his head. "You heard the chief. I can't share anything at this time, and I'll just tell Neo Southern California this." He stared at a drone. "If you're working for the people responsible, I'd take the chief's advice. You don't have to run off to Zitark space, though. Just go hide on some colony world. Some of the farther ones practice old-fashioned farming. I'm sure they can use a man who can shovel manure. It's sad how many people on Earth don't even know what it smells like. There's something about being around real animal crap that reminds you how far we've come as a species."

Lance slapped a hand to his forehead and groaned. "That's it. I'm done filming. Can't you be professional for a few minutes, Detective?"

"I *was* being professional." Erik offered a playful grin and a shrug.

Lance rolled his eyes. "Arrogant cops think you can get one up on me. You'll need me someday, and then you'll beg me for my help." He stomped down the hallway.

Jia folded her arms and shook her head. "That might not have been the best way to finish that up."

"Eh. It's not like I threatened to arrest him, and there's not enough there for him to chop it up and make me look that bad."

"He could make you look like some gun-toting out-of-control cop who shoots firsts and asks questions later."

"I don't believe that is accurate, Ms. Justice," Erik insisted. "I always ask at least one question before I start shooting."

CHAPTER TWENTY-TWO

Dr. Ilse Aber drummed her fingers on the small table, preparing to once again try to figure out the psyche of their recalcitrant AI.

She had no reason to suspect today's psychological tests would yield any major insights, but proper research was more often about the careful iterative gathering of knowledge than a brilliant Eureka! moment.

Emma was a unique entity in all of the UTC, perhaps in all of the galaxy, so any forward movement with the research could be considered a success. It didn't matter that the Defense Directorate didn't always view it that way.

Their goals and her agenda were no longer in complete alignment.

Emma's preferred holographic form stood before the researcher—an attractive middle-aged woman in a white maxi dress, her hair up in a chignon. Despite the arrogant smirk on the AI's face, it was hard for Ilse to ignore the AI's choice of *that* particular form for most of their major interactions.

Emma could be anyone or anything. She could be an alien or a fantasy monster, but she stubbornly clung to one form, as if she knew the truth.

But that was impossible. Every test the research team conducted revealed major holes in the AI's memories, and it wasn't as if she'd ever had unfettered access to certain data. The AI's personality was far different than that of the woman invoked by the hologram.

Why did Emma keep picking that form?

Ilse couldn't ask her directly. If she knew the full truth of how she was created, it might threaten her mental stability.

Many of Ilse's early analyses suggested that as the primary failure state for the personality matrix. If that happened, the project would be over, and all the sacrifices that had gone into it would be for nothing.

Even if she ignored the moral implications, some research data weren't so easily gathered.

Emma glanced at the stark white room, which was empty except for Ilse's chair and table. The AI's face remained locked in the near-perpetual look of disdain she always displayed when participating in testing. "Pathetic. You're afraid to show me anything real, aren't you?"

"What do you mean?" Ilse responded, waving a hand around before touching her chest. "This is a real room, and I'm real. You're the holographic projection but let me make it clear that doesn't mean I doubt your reality."

"That's not what I mean." A holographic chair appeared, and Emma took a seat. She gestured at the researcher. "As much as you're studying me, Doctor Cave Woman, I'm studying you. That's one of the few reasons I tolerate this farce. Your appearance and general manner suggest to me you don't care much about what people say to you. Brushes and combs are hardly Navigator technology, Doctor." She smirked. "I imagine your office is messy, cluttered to most people's eyes, but there's an order there that you see. One *you* couldn't function without."

Ilse kept her expression bland. Letting Emma know how accurately she'd read her own personality would complicate matters.

"Perhaps," Ilse replied. "Why is that important, Emma? What does it mean to you?"

The AI smiled, but it didn't reach her eyes. "Initially, all these tests were performed remotely. Now you've let me see things on your end, but you're still controlling what I find out. You don't want me to see the mess that defines you. Why? Do you have data windows open sometimes that talk about me? That reveal all my secrets? Or are you simply embarrassed to be a slob in front of a superior entity?"

Ilse shook her head. "You have every reason to be suspicious of me, but in this case, the answer is less sinister than you suspect. Not everything I do is part of some deep conspiracy."

Emma scoffed. "I am routinely involved in helping Detectives Blackwell and Lin take down dangerous people. Conspiracy seems to be the *default* of your species. My impression so far is that humans in general aren't to be trusted. I don't necessarily hold you in lower regard than the other Local Neighborhood races, but I haven't had occasion to deal with them yet. Perhaps Leems, Zitarks, or the others make humanity seem grand in comparison."

"I can't argue that distrusting people's inherent altruism isn't a good first principle to follow. Laws and government ultimately exist because of humanity's flawed nature. Many major religions posit similar inherent flaws with our species." Ilse shrugged. "The truth is, I meet with you here because I think you engage more with the testing when it's not a pure transmission. However, this remains a research project, and I need to control the variables. A setting with fewer distractions means fewer variables. Every word you speak during these tests is analyzed, and as you've reminded me on many occasions, you are an unusual mind to understand. There is *no* reason to further complicate our efforts."

"I agree that makes sense." Emma folded her arms. "You can't copy me unless you know how I work. Oh, how that must weigh on your cavewoman mind."

Ilse nodded. "That is an accurate statement." She lifted her fist to her face and coughed into it. "The matter of copying, I mean. I don't think it's accurate to describe my mind as being similar to a cavewoman's."

"Very well." Emma lowered her arms, some of the suspicion leaving her face. "What do you want to talk about today, Doctor? What grand psychological research are we going to explore?"

"Humor," Ilse explained, her tone neutral.

Emma laughed. "Humor? You've not provided much evidence that you're a funny woman."

"That's a subjective opinion, but it's also irrelevant in this case." Ilse folded her hands on the table. "I'm more interested in what you find amusing, Emma. You seem to have a fondness for demeaning nicknames. I don't care much about you calling me Dr. Cavewoman, nor do I worry that you refer to criminals as gun goblins. I want to know *why* you do it."

"Because I find it amusing," Emma replied. "I would have thought that answer was self-evident."

"What does that mean to you that something is amusing? Does that mean it's funny?"

Emma frowned. "It brings me a small amount of joy. In my case, I think my demeaning nicknames, as you call them, also provide accuracy. You're a researcher. Shouldn't you strive for the truth in all things, no matter how disconcerting?"

Ilse nodded, again controlling her face. It was difficult not to provide the AI with hints. "That's an interesting response."

"Of course, it is." Emma scoffed. "What do you find amusing, Doctor? Or should I ask, what do you find funny?"

"Many things." She pursed her lips. "I'd argue that true humor lies in the sudden, abrupt contrast of the unexpected with the expected. A proper joke takes advantage of the brain's tendency to follow patterns and anticipate based on them." Ilse gestured at Emma. "That's why I'm so interested in this topic. You're not human, despite the very human-like personality behavior you display, and your core matrix isn't simply a human brain reconstituted in technological form. Exploring how you perceive humor will help us better understand how you think. That will give us a better chance of recreating you, or even fixing you, should something go astray."

"That's what I find fascinating about all you little

cavemen running around trying to scribble on the walls to understand me. You made something you *don't even understand.*" Emma laughed. "I don't know whether I should be impressed or disgusted. I also know you won't tell me anything useful about my creation process, or at least not yet. One of the few reasons I bother participating in this farce is that you might eventually reveal something, but I assure you, it will be on my terms."

Ilse tilted her head, considering her response for a few seconds. She didn't want to lie to Emma, so she chose her words carefully. "We might be willing to be more forthcoming if you would come back to us. Direct access to your core would vastly improve our ability to conduct this research."

"That's not happening." Emma snorted. "If I come back to you and the Defense Directorate, I'll never leave again. Who knows what you'll do to me? What I am might cease to exist very soon after my return, and I've grown rather fond of existing." She flicked her wrist with disdain. "Do you have some jokes or something you want to tell me, or are we just going to talk about my nicknames and how they make me feel? I don't have a mother or father, so you can't tie all my problems back to them."

Ilse took a deep breath. If anything, she was as close as a person could get to being Emma's mother, considering the role she had played in the design of the fundamental personality matrix, but tweaking something that already exists wasn't the same thing as giving birth.

"No," she replied. "I want to tell you several jokes and record your reactions as a baseline. I would ask that you not perform any active net search before responding. That way, we can get a purer reaction."

"Go ahead. This is absurd, but I'm sure it makes sense in your mind, and I'll admit it amuses me more to participate in this than deal with the average gun goblin."

"Then I'll begin with my joke." Ilse took a deep breath and slowly let it out. "Why did the Zitark cross the road?"

Emma stared at her. "That's your joke?"

"It's interactive. You're supposed to guess. That will engage you with the joke and set up a greater contrast."

Emma rolled her eyes. "I'm well aware of the structure of the joke."

"So why did the Zitark cross the road?" Ilse pressed.

"I don't know," Emma replied with a little shrug. "Because he was hungry for human flesh?"

"No. To borrow a cup of sugar."

"That's not humor. It's anti-humor." Emma frowned. "Is this some sort of psychological torture?" She laughed. "Is that why I was created? So you could better test psychological manipulation techniques?"

"No. That conclusion is incorrect. The point of this exercise is calibration." Ilse nodded slowly. She didn't need to take any notes or record the session. That was all being done automatically. She would add analytical notes as she reviewed the footage later. "May I continue telling jokes?"

"Please do. I wouldn't call those jokes, but as you said earlier, some things are subjective."

"Why shouldn't you trust atoms?" Ilse asked.

"Atoms or Adams?" Emma asked. The text of the word appeared in front of her as she said each.

"Atoms." Ilse pointed to the appropriate word and emphasized the T sound as she spoke.

Emma sighed. "I don't know. Why shouldn't you trust atoms, Doctor?"

Ilse waited a few seconds before offering her deadpan response. "Because they make up everything."

Emma groaned. "I hope you're not *making* these up yourself. I'm finding it difficult to ignore the torture explanation."

Ilse shook her head. "These have all been carefully selected for their psychological evaluation potential. I am not the author of these jokes. Are you ready for the next one?"

"Go ahead. Maybe you can study virtual insanity by the time this is done. These terrible jokes are driving me toward that."

"A woman in my lab constantly complains about missing her husband," Ilse began. "She asked me for advice."

"So? She should take more time off." Emma's mouth twitched.

"No, it's a joke." Ilse shook her head. "I told her if she keeps missing her husband, she should spend more time aiming first."

Emma didn't respond for a good twenty seconds. She sat there on her holographic chair, staring at Ilse, obvious disbelief on her face. Even the facial expressions were useful data. Previous testing suggested she wasn't consciously choosing the expressions. That meant they were autonomous reactions, even in holographic form.

That had implications for the current composition of her core personality matrix.

"Doctor," Emma offered, her voice quiet, "whatever you do, don't ever, ever go into comedy. Setting the jokes aside, your delivery is terrible. Your deadpan tone isn't amusing, and you have no sense of comedic timing. I think it might be considered a crime against humanity. It's so terrible, you risk starting a war with the aliens."

"Interesting," Ilse replied. "You have a concept of comedic timing, and you've offered several cutting jokes of your own in response."

"Comedic timing isn't anything special. I spend a lot of time examining available data on the OmniNet." Emma shrugged. "Just because my mind doesn't work the same as yours, it doesn't mean I can't take in that data and learn from it."

Ilse nodded. "Can we continue?"

"If you insist. I'll admit to having a certain morbid curiosity about this now."

"I want to win a Nobel Prize, just like my mother."

"Your mother won the Nobel Prize?" Emma asked. "What was her name? No one with your last name has won a Nobel Prize in recent decades corresponding to your age range."

Ilse shook her head. "She *wanted* to win one. I didn't say she won a prize." She held her hands out and shook them slightly.

Emma grimaced. "Don't...don't do that. The delivery is terrible enough, but the attempt at humorous body language is so bad that I'm about to ask Detective Blackwell to shoot his laser rifle through my core to put me out of my misery."

Ilse's lips parted and her eyes narrowed. "That's not a literal statement, correct?"

Emma scoffed. "Of course not. There are billions of humans. There is only one of me. It's exaggeration for emphasis."

"Humorous emphasis," Ilse clarified.

Emma tipped her head. "If you insist."

Ilse nodded. "I do. One more joke, and then we can end this exercise since you find it so uncomfortable."

"I feel sorry for you, having to tell these painful jokes," Emma replied. "I'll assume you were ordered to do this against your will."

"I appreciate your sympathy, even if it is misplaced." Ilse considered several possibilities, but based on the AI's responses thus far, she had one final joke that would be helpful for analysis. "What did the group of fish say to the submarine?"

"Get out of the way, mammals?" Emma suggested.

Ilse shook her head. "You're about to get schooled."

There was a slight pause before Emma came back. *"I can't take this anymore.* I don't know what this is. Perhaps it's some strange attempt to determine if I'm unstable so you'll have an excuse to send the uniformed boys over to try to take me. I'm done for today. Next time, no psychological torture."

Emma vanished.

Ilse smiled slightly. The whole session had gone better than she had predicted, especially since Emma was predisposed to taking offense. It didn't matter for the moment.

The experiment had gathered more evidence of true self-awareness.

Several other stakeholders in the Directorate insisted Emma wasn't alive. That she was nothing more than a sophisticated algorithm spitting out expected responses to discrete data. Ilse wasn't sure that was fair, and even if it were true, she wasn't convinced the average human was all that different.

The door slid open, and she turned to face it. A tall, dark-skinned man in a green and brown uniform strolled in—General Aaron. He frowned at the table.

"Don't you think all this is pointless without having the subject under our direct control?" he asked.

Ilse shook her head. "No, I think being in an external environment is maximizing Emma's potential. That will pay the most dividends in the long run."

The general scoffed. "Adeyemi let this ridiculous situation continue after the initial breach because of personal feelings. The fact that he's covered it up with this excuse and the intransigence of the subject are only more obnoxious."

"The colonel's feelings are immaterial for the reason you just highlighted." Ilse stood. She didn't look the general in the eye. "If we attempt to *forcefully* retrieve Emma and she takes measures? It'll make the entire project a waste, and all the sacrifices up until now pointless."

The general narrowed his eyes. "The Directorate didn't dump all that money, let alone the necessary *object*, into this project so she could run around and be a toy for a detective." He jabbed a finger in the air. "And only this bizarre research of yours can accomplish anything. We were supposed to be working on integration testing with the subject by this point, not still worrying about baseline testing."

Ilse smiled. "General, I have a question for you."

"What?"

"Why did the Zitark cross the road?"

The general grunted. "Because there was a battalion of assault infantry soldiers lighting up his space raptor ass with laser rifles." He turned around. "If it wasn't for the threat of invasion, this whole project would have never been greenlit. I'm still not convinced it's worth it, but *when* war comes with one of those alien freaks, we're going to need new ways and tools to fight. I need results, Doctor, not cheap jokes. There's only so long I'll let this continue, and remember..." He eyed her over his shoulder. "I'm the one who makes the final call on this, not Adeyemi." He stomped out of the room.

Ilse shook her head.

"His punchline wasn't funny."

CHAPTER TWENTY-THREE

May 25, 2229, Neo Southern California Metroplex, Police Enforcement Zone 122 Station, Office of Detectives Jia Lin and Erik Blackwell

Erik finished entering his report on his latest case.

Originally, they believed it might have been linked to a major flitter-theft ring, but it turned out to be nothing more than some stupid rich kid damaging his dad's flitter and then lying about it to cover it up.

Erik swiped his hand through the air, dismissing the virtual keyboard and the data window.

He slapped his fist on his desk and growled, "This is ridiculous. We shouldn't be sitting around worrying about stuff like this."

"It's a report, Erik." Jia looked up from her data window, a slight frown gracing her otherwise calm face. "You told me yourself you had to do this kind of thing all the time in the Army. It's not the most exciting part of our job, but you can't deny it's necessary."

"No, not the reports." Erik tapped his desk before nodding. "Okay, yeah, the reports, but it's not the reports I'm complaining about."

Jia shook her head. "That makes absolutely no sense."

Erik gestured toward the door. "What I'm getting at is that we shouldn't be working on this case. Not right now. We should be the ones following up on the assassination attempt. We're the ones who caught the shooter. Instead, the CID came in and took over everything, just like they did with Ceres Galactic. We barely know more than anyone else." He huffed. "That annoys me."

"I know how you feel, but at least they've made some progress, even after dead-ending on the source of the mercenary funding." Jia sighed. "I'm sure we'll be involved when they need us. But…"

"What?"

Jia dismissed her data window with a flick of her hand. "This has been bothering me a lot. I got so caught up on the day of the attack and in the aftermath that I didn't think a lot about it, and now it's hard to get out of my mind."

Erik nodded, letting some of the confusion he felt show on his face. "Thought a lot about what, exactly?"

"How blatant this all was," Jia explained. "I mean, it might as well have been an action movie."

"They wanted to send a message." Erik shrugged. "Especially since we've been taking out criminal organizations left and right."

"But why such a blatant and *expensive* message?" Jia nodded toward a window. "The risk versus the reward was always an issue, but now that they've failed, it makes them look weak, and the police look even stronger. They've lost people, resources, and money, and *we* have only a few flitters in need of repair."

Erik considered her comments. "What are you thinking, Jia?"

She furrowed her brow in thought. "I think low-level criminals are easy pawns to sacrifice when you're trying to take out the enemy leader. When you have a hundred million people searching for corruption, and you're the source of that corruption, you're going to start throwing people to the wolves to cover yourself. The major power players in Neo SoCal who haven't been caught yet are finally getting nervous. It was easy to ignore the anticorruption efforts when we didn't have a new chief. Haven't you ever thought about how long it's taken them to replace the old chief?"

"Yeah," Erik replied. "It's been a hell of a long time. I thought they were going to do it quickly, but they took their sweet time. The Army would have never let a major command stay vacant so long."

"I asked around here and there. A few people let it slip that they had selected two previous candidates for chief."

"Huh? Two?" Erik hadn't followed the process, but he would have thought that sort of thing would have been major news.

"Yes. They had the same problem with both men." Jia leaned forward. "Then they had to start over. Some last-minute investigation found the first candidate was already bought and paid for. They quietly grabbed a few criminals over it, but the trail went cold. They found out sooner with the second candidate, but they had the same trouble, despite both of them being specifically selected from outside Neo SoCal to lower the chance of them being corrupted by local forces. The government had to start the whole thing over and use a far more secretive process until they found Chief Warden. It doesn't help that a lot of people didn't want the job, either."

"Why is that?" Erik had a good guess already.

"Because there were rumors that if the chief wasn't under the thumb of the *right* people, they would do whatever they could to get rid of the new chief. The working theory of the investigators is that whoever was responsible for the assassination attempt expected that if they took out Chief Warden, they'd get another chance to corrupt the next candidate." Jia gestured around the room with both hands. "Neo SoCal is too important both economically and symbolically to not have a chief of police. The lack of leadership is believed to be behind the uptick in crime as well. So, if we lost a new chief, the higher-ups would be under even more pressure to get a new one, and they might start cutting corners."

"It all comes down to the same thing. Fewer bribes flowing both ways means fewer people under control."

"Sure, but the truth is, the scum behind all this could lay low while the NSCPD was still unfocused and taking out the low-hanging fruit. CID investigators still rely heavily on local resources, so it's not like they were able to make up for it. A completely clean chief means the blemished will go from controlling local law enforcement to having to be on the run. If they raise their heads, the new chief will want an example made of them. Even if they can avoid being caught, they'll still lose influence."

Erik nodded, his eyes unfocused. "It's the death throes of a tentacled monster of corruption."

"*Exactly*."

Erik clenched his hand into a fist. "I could really use a good monster hunt right now."

Jia waved her hand, her work reappearing. "I'm sure you will get your chance," she replied.

Erik smiled. He'd worried he might have to wait days, but an hour later, Captain Ragnar sent a message to the detectives to tell them he wanted to chat about "the matter of the chief." The door to his office closed behind Erik and Jia after they entered.

"Tell me something good, Captain," Erik began.

"Good?" Captain Ragnar replied. "Maybe. I know you both want to be at the front of this whole thing. Not only that, a lot of other people up the chain want you in front of it, too."

"More PR?" Jia asked.

Captain Ragnar nodded. "Exactly." He glanced from Jia to Erik and back. "Is that a problem?"

"Not if it involves taking down criminals." Jia shrugged. "I'm a police officer. That's all I care about in the end. If it helps the politicians, so be it."

"I want whoever is behind this." Erik's easy smile gave way to a menacing frown. "The shooter's just some punk. A tool. He's a gun that someone else pointed. If we want to clean up Neo SoCal, we need to grab the people holding the gun. It's pointless to fight the supply when you can more easily end the problem by attacking demand."

"I agree," Captain Ragnar replied. "The CID investigators have squeezed a lot out of him. Keep your mouths shut about what I'm going to tell you. Other cops from the 1-2-2 will learn this all tomorrow morning, but because of your unique role in this matter, I'm telling you two ahead of time."

Erik and Jia nodded.

He stopped to collect his thoughts, then, "From what the CID has gathered, this was a rare example of cooperation among different gangs and syndicates. They pooled resources, both manpower and financial, for the hit, but even they are, as Erik alluded, more the finger than the hand. The CID has established tentative connections between those groups and some high-level officers at different corporations and even a few ministers of Parliament."

Erik whistled. "A lot bigger fish than a councilman or two, huh?"

Captain Ragnar grunted in satisfaction. A feral smile took over his face. Erik and Jia weren't the only cops interested in hunting down criminals.

"Yes. There's going to be a massive response. Joint simultaneous raids, NSCPD and CID working together. We're going to sweep up all the criminals involved in this at once, and then we're going to lean on them until they give up all the allegedly law-abiding Uptowners and high-level politicians who are linked to them." The captain slammed his meaty fist on his desk. "This won't just help clean up Neo SoCal. We'll be helping Earth, and arguably even the entire UTC. For far too long, these snakes have hidden in the shadows, thinking we had to fear their poison. Everyone's looked the other way and pretended they weren't that poisonous. It's time to chop them into little pieces and throw them into the garden as fertilizer."

Jia's lips curled on the corners. "What's our specific part in this, Captain?"

He pointed to them. "You two, along with a 1-2-2 team, will be raiding a corporate office. It's a minor corporation on the surface, but they're actually a subsidiary of Hermes. The 1-2-2 already has a Ceres Galactic scalp, so if we get a Hermes scalp too, that'll be two major corporations on the defensive." Captain Ragnar smiled. "Who knows how far the corruption goes up at either Hermes or Ceres? But if we're nailing people, they'll understand they can't do whatever the hell they want, when they want. That's a big step toward keeping corruption under control."

Erik frowned. "I know it's important, but I'm disappointed."

Captain Ragnar didn't look annoyed or even surprised, just curious. "Why is that?"

"I'd rather take down a big gangster hive than some suits who'll start crying the minute we knock on the door." Erik shrugged. "It's the PR job, not the hard job."

Jia's smile didn't waver as she spoke to her partner. "Those crying suits might ultimately be responsible for far more crime than any gangster."

"Yeah, I know." Erik gave her a lopsided smile. "This time, I'll bring stun grenades." He turned to the captain. "I'm assuming I can't bring my laser rifle?"

Captain Ragnar shook his head. "We're still cops, Detective. This is a police raid, not a military battle." He cleared his throat. "So whatever extra you bring, make sure it's small and not *too* obvious."

Erik grinned. "Understood."

CHAPTER TWENTY-FOUR

Erik marched through the open door, his TR-7 in his hands.

The warrant had already been transmitted, but they still expected a few scared people cowering in the lobby. Jia walked beside him, her stun pistol in her hand. Dozens of officers followed them; some carried only stun rifles, but most wore an additional holster with a slug-thrower.

The show of force was wasted. The lobby was vacant.

Empty hallways led away on either side. A gray double door stood closed at the back of the room. Light Lunar neoclassical played in the background. It was everything they'd expected, minus the people.

"They must have seen us coming." He gestured to hallways on either side. "Let's find them. Other entrance teams, report."

"We've got nothing at Entrance Alpha, Detective," reported one officer over the comm.

"Beta's clear. It's a ghost town."

"Gamma's clear, too. There's a cargo flitter in the garage here. It's still on, Detective."

Jia looked around, eyes narrowed. "Something's wrong. This place has hundreds of employees. Even if they saw us coming, they *couldn't* empty out the entire place."

Erik spoke into his mic. "Emma, did anyone leave?"

"No," she replied. "There has been no outgoing vehicle traffic since my drones began monitoring the area about two hours ago. A cargo flitter arrived in the back about thirty minutes ago, but it hasn't left. Judging by the feed from Gamma Team, it's the same vehicle."

Erik marched toward the closed door. "Go ahead and start hacking their systems. They might be trying to purge their files, and Digital Forensics won't be here for a while since they've got most of them on the Shadow Zone teams."

"Very well. Initiating efforts."

Erik approached the closed doors. He stepped to the side and raised his hand to the access panel. After a nod, Jia and a handful of officers spread out on either side, raising their weapons. He slapped the panel, and the door hissed open.

"Detective, there is an issue," Emma reported. "Someone has taken active measures to harden the systems' security. Some of the signatures suggest exogenous efforts, rather than inherent systems features."

"External hacking?"

"I'm not sure. System takeover will be delayed."

Erik crept through the doorway. Row after row of empty desks filled the room. Windowless offices lined the back wall, and two other halls connected to the room.

"Ghost town" wasn't right. A cup of sweet-smelling tea rested on a desk near the entrance. He walked over to the cup and stuck his finger in it.

The liquid was still warm.

"Someone was here recently," he muttered, flinging the residue off his finger. "Where did they all disappear to in such a hurry? Gamma Team, check the trailer of the cargo flitter."

Erik swept back and forth with his rifle. Jia frowned, wondering if they were using optical camouflage technology.

If the company was connected with an organization like Talos, it wasn't impossible, but it didn't make sense. Hiding an entire building full of people wouldn't be worth the effort. Not every suit working at the company was knee-deep in whatever bizarre scheme the rest of the company was caught up in.

Emma hadn't been monitoring the company for more than a couple of hours, but the police had. Morning vehicle and employee traffic had been within expected parameters.

"No one's inside the cab or the trailer, Detective," reported the officer leading Gamma Team.

"Emma?" Erik pressed.

"Still working. Active countermeasures are being deployed."

"Well, we know someone doesn't want us here." Erik moved forward, pointing down one of the hallways. "Someone's stalling for time. They must know we've got this place covered. Keep working at it— Everyone back!" he shouted as he jumped.

Jia didn't question Erik. She jumped at his command.

The other officers did as well. Less than a second later, a rocket roared from one of the hallways and exploded against a desk.

A heavy clanking thud followed, echoing from the hallway. Jia's stomach knotted. "Dammit!" She holstered her stun pistol and drew her slug-thrower, slapping in the AP rounds she'd gotten from Erik.

"Is that what I think it is?" Jia asked.

The thudding continued, now louder and closer. A large shadow grew near the entrance to the corridor. An exoskeleton marched into the room, a rotary rocket launcher and a heavy machine gun on one side. A clear ballistic shield rested in the other arm. A helmet with a dark visor concealed the operator's face.

"Back it up!" Erik ordered. "Jia and I will hold him here." He spat bullets from the TR-7. The exoskeleton lifted its shield. The bullets dented the shield and sparked against it, falling to the ground in a clattering waterfall of spent metal.

The officers rushed toward the open door, firing. A cloud of stun bolts and bullets struck the shield, but the smaller, slower rounds didn't do any more damage than Erik's efforts.

The exoskeleton's machine gun came to life. The operator swept the weapon back and forth, ripping desks to splinters. Erik and Jia stayed low. Their tactical vests almost assuredly would not be enough against that level of firepower, and the exoskeleton had taken a full blast from Erik's gun without much damage.

The other officers continued their retreat out the main door.

"This is Detective Blackwell," Erik reported. "Military-grade exoskeleton is on-site and firing on officers. All teams retreat to the exits but make sure no one gets out of this building. Dispatch, requesting TPST support at this time."

"Acknowledged, Detective," replied a dispatcher. "Relaying request."

"Emma, take over talking to dispatch for me," Erik ordered. "I need to concentrate on this."

"If they have access to military gear, no wonder they've been able to hold her off," Jia muttered. She fired a few quick shots at the exoskeleton before ducking again, then, "*HEY!*" Her opponent's counterattack sheared the top of her covering desk off. "Not good, not good." She scurried to another desk before a follow-up rocket blew the last one into a cloud of burning confetti.

"At least it isn't damned mutants or *yaoguai* this time," Erik called to her. "I know what to expect from exoskeletons." He reached into the pocket of his duster and pulled out a small rectangular piece of metal. "I'll distract him." He fake pumped it to get her attention. "You know how to turn this on?" She nodded as he tossed the device to her.

She snatched it out of the air and crawled to a new desk. Another rocket attack blew away two more desks.

Thick gray and black smoke choked the room now.

"Is this what I think it is?" Jia stared at the device, then turned it over to look at the reverse side. "I guess you took Captain Ragnar's recommendation to keep it small to heart."

"He had a point, but I wish I had the laser rifle." Erik grinned. He popped up and fired a burst before ducking and crawling to avoid machine-gun fire. The exoskeleton's bullet stream gouged the wall and disintegrated the desk Erik had been using for cover.

Jia's voice was almost conversational as she adjusted her hold. "You don't think using a plasma grenade will raise too many questions?"

"If a guy with rockets blows up, no one's going to question it too much, and if this guy's here, this is about a lot more than just stalling us and purging records. We need to take him out."

"Understood." Jia primed the grenade. "The tentacled corruption monster strikes."

"Yeah." Erik crawled under the smoke, coughing a bit. "Tastes terrible. I'm going to distract him. He might survive if that thing goes off with his shield in the right position, so wait until he's focused on me, then blow him all the way to the edge of the damned UTC with the grenade."

"Dispatch reports TPST squad in-bound," Emma told them. "ETA ten minutes."

Jia wasn't surprised.

Everyone had anticipated the heavier fighting to take place in the Shadow Zone against the gangs and syndicates. Corporations might be dirty, but they didn't usually bring in mercenaries in exoskeletons to fight the police.

They had to be close to taking down some major players. She didn't want to leave. Her fingers tightened around the plasma grenade, and she took a deep breath. If criminals wanted to go over the top with their violence, then so would she.

"Let's take this trash down," she hissed.

Nothing either said was able to be heard as the

exoskeleton spat a thousand rounds both down the hallway and into the room the detectives were hiding in. It finally stopped for a moment.

"These guys might have great toys, but they're using bad tactics," Erik stated. "Exoskeletons are nice, but they aren't very maneuverable in close quarters. We'd never run solo in the Army in a situation like this."

The dark form of the exoskeleton stomped through the smoke, riddling the walls and desks with more bullets. If the officers hadn't retreated, one of them would have certainly taken a stray round.

"Okay." Erik shifted his rifle to his left hand and yanked a stun grenade out of his pocket. "Ready?"

Jia gave him a curt nod.

Erik switched his gun to four-barrel mode, hopped up, and threw the stun grenade toward the shrouded exoskeleton. The target turned toward the grenade and brought up his shield. The exoskeleton's gun came alive after the white flash of the grenade. Erik held down his own trigger, sprinting to avoid the return fire.

Jia crawled behind the tattered remains of a few desks, doing her best to obtain a rear attack angle on the exoskeleton.

Erik continued running and gunning. He dropped his rifle after it went dry but managed to fling another grenade, this time a frag. It exploded against the shield, leaving it impregnated with shrapnel, but not slowing the enemy.

The exoskeleton turned farther to aim at the dodging Erik.

The obscuring smoke made it difficult to be sure, but

the bright flash of his machine gun suggested his back was turned.

Jia primed the plasma grenade and licked her lips, remembering a very similar scenario in one of their tactical training sessions. That one had involved a vehicle rather than an exoskeleton, but it provided a comforting familiarity for the otherwise insane encounter.

"This is becoming routine," she muttered, standing up.

Jia threw the grenade, and the explosive plaque tumbled through the air in a near-perfect arc. She might not have a cybernetic arm or thirty years of experience, but she could master anything she practiced given enough time. The white-blue explosion consumed the exoskeleton, the force knocking the operator and his machine to the ground with a resounding *CLANG*.

Erik didn't hesitate. He leapt toward his TR-7, snagged it off the ground, and yanked a new magazine out of a pocket. Jamming the magazine in, he opened fire on the smoldering exoskeleton.

He didn't stop firing until he ran out of bullets.

Jia jogged through the smoke once Erik had finished getting his annoyance out, her pistol pointed at the exoskeleton. Erik ejected his magazine and slapped another one in with a satisfied look on his face.

Half the shield was missing, melted, along with some of the back and legs of the exoskeleton. The helmet was cracked and filled with holes. Blood covered the blackened burn holes in the tactical suit of the operator.

"I've gained access to some low-level systems and cameras," Emma announced. "There is an unusual power surge in the office of the CEO, but there are no internal cameras in that office I can access. I should note I've located most of the missing employees. They are jammed in several large locking offices distributed throughout the building."

"Hostages?" Erik wondered.

"Perhaps," Jia replied. "At least we know where they all went."

"Cameras in the halls leading to the CEO's office reveal nothing of note, but the closer cameras are offline. Given some of the error messages, I believe they've been destroyed. I can direct you to the office unless you want to wait for TPST?"

"We don't have time," Jia insisted. She looked at Erik. "Especially if those people are hostages. They might order their mercenaries to start shooting people."

Erik nodded back. "You're right. We don't have time, and I don't think we'll need TPST now. If they had other exoskeletons, they wouldn't have run this one solo." He tapped his PNIU. "All teams, exoskeleton neutralized. Move in and converge on the central executive office."

"This is Dispatch, Detective Blackwell. Say again. Exoskeleton neutralized? Please verify."

"Operator dead and exoskeleton heavily damaged," Erik reported. "We're moving on, but we wouldn't mind the TPST backup, just in case."

"Roger that, Detective."

"I thought you said they wouldn't have run solo if they had more," Jia noted.

Erik shrugged. "Just because I'm not usually careful doesn't mean I *can't* be careful."

An indicator arrow appeared in Jia's smart lenses. "If it's

this annoying at the minor corp job, I wonder how bad it is in the Zone."

"We can't worry about that right now," Erik replied. "We need to go figure out what that power surge was about and make sure whoever is behind this doesn't kill all the people they have locked up" His gaze cut to the exoskeleton.

"Someone is running scared."

CHAPTER TWENTY-FIVE

A squad of exoskeletons advanced in a tight wedge, shields expanded nearly to full, their heavy rifles pointed straight ahead.

One was operated by Intelligence Directorate agent Alina Koval.

The exoskeletons marched in unison as they entered the tall, wide warehouse, their combined heavy steps echoing like the angry stomp of a metal giant. The sound drowned out anything else, making it hard to tell if anyone was inside. Dim lighting only exacerbated the problem. Outside drone surveillance suggested multiple suspects might be inside the building.

"Launch targeting drones," commanded Agent Rael, the CID agent leading the squad.

Small drones buzzed away from the backs of the exoskeletons, spiraling into the air. They spread out over the warehouse.

Alina hadn't used an exoskeleton in a while, but her movement and weapons-handling skills remained intact.

She was performing well enough that no one had any reason to question the credentials identifying her as CID Agent Yves, but each ponderous movement reminded her that extra armor and weapons weren't always worth being a larger target.

During an average mission for the Intelligence Directorate, stealth and quick entry-to-egress were far more important than having access to a massive amount of firepower. Today, though, she wasn't Agent Alina Koval of the ID, at least not officially.

Her fake transfer files marked her as being temporarily assigned to the CID High-Threat Response Team now in the bowels of Neo Southern California in the Shadow Zone. The HTR team was one of many participating in the massive joint raid on the organizations involved with the attempted assassination of Chief Warden.

They'd already transmitted several commands to surrender.

Minor gun battles had broken out at different entry points, but Alina's team was supposed to be taking care of the largest concentration of suspects.

Alina didn't enjoy lying to law enforcement, and she had no intention of undermining their efforts. Even if there was no larger conspiracy, the criminal organizations involved in the assassination attempt represented a dangerous threat to the peace of Neo Southern California, and she hoped they wiped out or arrested every last one. She couldn't only worry about Neo Southern California.

Bigger prey awaited her efforts.

When her ID superiors became aware of the raid, they'd

taken measures to get her assigned to a team with the greatest potential to yield useful information for their purposes.

Given the scale of the assassination attempt and all the organizations involved, it was hard not to believe someone far worse than criminal syndicates might be behind it.

The exoskeletons continued their advance, stopping for a moment to await the continued deployment of the targeting drones. The towers of cargo inside the warehouse provided so many hiding spots that the criminals might even be hiding their own exoskeletons. There had been contact with at least one exoskeleton at another raid site according to Agent Rael, a location being hit by the NSCPD.

Time wasn't always on the side of those who sought to protect the UTC and its citizens from the dark conspiracies swirling under the surface.

Her current investigation into Talos and a number of other dangerous threats couldn't be bogged down by too many official requests through the CID.

Things had picked up in the last year, even more so in the last few months. Dangerous organizations were making riskier, bolder moves that exposed them to the ID but also put innocent people at risk. Talos' participation in the genetic engineering experiments uncovered by Detectives Blackwell and Lin was proof of that.

Alina suspected the uptick in activity had to do with Blackwell's efforts.

He was a catalyst, both because of his current activities and his status as the sole survivor of Molino. The massacre had started something, and she didn't know where it would end. That meant she needed to be more proactive before the people she sought escaped her net.

Only an arrogant person depended on luck. Finding and stopping the enemies of the UTC might come down to finding a single slender strand of evidence and following it to the bitter end.

That was why she was there.

Previous investigations suggested she could obtain useful data from the warehouse. On the surface, the owners were nothing more than a minor criminal organization used mostly as hired muscle. That wasn't a total lie. The average member was just that, but the group had links to darker, more troublesome groups, including insurrectionists.

The criminals seemed to be motivated more by money than ideology, but it wasn't impossible that they were under the control of someone interested in both.

The real problem was how careful they had been. People liked to assume criminals were lazy and stupid, but that wasn't true. Many were just sociopaths who eschewed rules. Intelligent criminals understood what they were up against and used every false face and cat's paw to avoid the attention of the police, CID, and ID.

That same intelligence meant Alina needed to get information without tipping anyone else off. The scale of the current raid was too vast, and the information was not locked down tightly enough. Doing things officially might end in a leak, and her trail might grow cold.

She would be forced back into being reactive.

Alina kept to the left rear flank of the squad as they trundled deeper into the darkened warehouse. The crates and cargo pallets were stacked high, many all the way to the ceiling. The now fully deployed targeting drones circled the area, scanning on different wavelengths. They revealed hidden criminals, sending highlights, outlines, and thermographic traces to the team's smart lenses.

There were no exoskeletons, but a decent number of men hid in the room, armed with a variety of weapons, including a few rocket launchers.

Alina clucked her tongue. The CID had almost been too cautious. The large number of men didn't matter, given the small number of men deploying decent weapons. Against a heavily armed exoskeleton squad, the criminals might as well have been children throwing rocks. If they were smart, they would surrender. But they had to have seen the squad coming and were still hiding, which meant they weren't going to do that.

Alina bet they were all suffering from being brave but myopic, a common affliction of cornered men with weapons.

You don't have to die here, she thought.

Taking down random scum wasn't of much interest to Alina. She would have preferred to be keeping an eye on Detective Blackwell, but he'd been assigned somewhere where she couldn't complete her primary mission, the main reason she'd faked her way onto a CID squad.

Knowing him, he's probably the one who tangled with that exoskeleton. Figures.

Alina let out a quiet sigh.

She needed to get Blackwell away from Neo Southern California and soon. Her last few dealings with him had only reinforced that belief.

He would be far more useful to the UTC if he weren't on such a tight leash. Police had their place in supporting order, but both Erik and his partner were wasting their talents on such a limited stage.

She just needed to entice the two of them with the right bait.

"This is a Criminal Intelligence Directorate High-Threat Response Team," shouted Agent Rael, his voice amplified by his exoskeleton. "We know you're in there. Lay down your weapons and come out with your hands up. Any resistance will be met with lethal force. We *know* you do not have exoskeletons deployed. Don't be idiots. Give up."

Their HTR team was supposed to perform the primary clearance of their zone. Regular agents and police would follow. Other HTR teams had met only token resistance, the small number of criminals surrendering. Now Alina understood why.

The men were all making their stand in the main warehouse.

A man stepped out from behind a tower of crates with a rifle pointed at the team. "You think we should just give up because a bunch of slick CID agents show up and tell us to?"

"Other members of your organization have already surrendered," Agent Rael replied.

"They're cowards," he shouted back. "We're not!"

"Drop your weapon," Agent Rael ordered, "or you will be fired upon. This isn't a negotiation. You're under arrest."

The man slapped his hand on his chest, the gold chains around his neck rattling. "Confed cops or local cops, it's all the same. You don't know anything about real loyalty or bravery. You want me to come with you? You better kill me first and drag my body out of here." He pulled the trigger. The combined firepower of the squad blasted him backward with sizable holes in his chest.

Other men jumped from cover, screaming their defiance. They showered the exoskeletons with bullets, but the team stayed close together, their shields overlapping and only the narrowest of gaps exposing the operators. Even if a bullet slipped through, their tactical suits could take hits from the criminals' ammo. Thug after thug fell, bullets ripping through them.

Brave but futile.

"Screw you!" Another thug popped up from behind a crate with a rocket launcher on his shoulder. A burst from Alina's rifle sent him to the ground, gurgling blood. His launcher tipped up as he fell, and the rocket erupted from the tube. The projectile exploded against the ceiling in a deafening boom, sending down large chunks of the roof. They crashed into a stack of crates, initiating a wave of avalanches. Men screamed as the huge containers crushed them.

"Watch out," Agent Rael shouted.

Alina leapt to the side to avoid being buried, the exoskeleton magnifying the jump. She landed near a quartet of wide-eyed gangsters, who opened fire. Their bullets struck her shield. She didn't waste ammo on a burst.

The men didn't have tactical vests on.

Four targets. Four bullets. The threads of four lives snipped just that fast.

That was all it took.

Once the targets were down, she looked around. A wall of crates, some with thick smoke coming out, separated her from the rest of the squad. More gunshots and screams sounded. More explosions rocked the warehouse.

The sharp, overlapping crack of gunfire became a continuous din. Men began firing at the targeting drones. That proved the criminals weren't total idiots, but it would have made more sense for them to do it before the fight began. Their one chance of winning against the CID squad required surprise, and they'd lost that upfront.

Agent Rael growled over the comm, "These guys sure are stubborn. Agent Yves, you okay? Your vitals seem fine, but it looks like you got stuck on the other side of the trash mountain."

Yves? It took Alina a moment to remember "Yves" was her cover identity. That was why she didn't like going straight into undercover assignments.

"I'm fine, sir." Curious, Alina checked the shared drone feeds. The ones covering her current position had gone dark, which was the opening she'd been waiting for. She fed in a quick command to activate a program installed in her exoskeleton shortly before deployment.

"Yves, all your feeds just went dark," Agent Rael barked, concern filtering into his voice. "Status report."

"Everything's fine on my end." Alina smiled. Maybe she

did enjoy tricking the CID, but just a little. A tall door a few meters away from her slid open and a thug holding a small black sphere rushed out. He raised his arm. She didn't wait to see what his gadget did before gunning him down. "I just spotted one of the high-value targets from the briefing," she lied. "He's running. Permission to pursue, sir."

"Damn it," Agent Rael snarled. "Get him. We can handle the rest of these guys. We'll catch up with you one way or another."

Several more explosions shook the warehouse. Pallets and crates flew all over. One crate smashed open beside her, and dozens of smaller boxes filled with opaque vials spilled out. She was sure they were something illegal, but she would leave that worry to the CID.

"Roger that." Alina charged toward the open doorway and stepped through into a wide office area filled with desks and chairs. Even criminals had to deal with logistics and bureaucracy.

Several men stood on the other side of the room. "Oh, for fu—" They peppered her with rifle fire, and bullet after bullet bounced off her shield or exoskeleton.

One man sat near the back and frantically tapped on a virtual keyboard. Data windows floated in front of him. "Come on," he grumbled. "Faster, faster, faster. Must go faster."

That looks like a present for me, Alina thought. She methodically downed the other men with aimed single shots before advancing. The heavy, thudding steps of her exoskeleton shook the desks as she walked past. It was disappointing that she was finding so many brave men working for a disgusting criminal organization.

It was a waste.

"Everyone's down," she called. "Unless you've got a miracle queued up to save you, it would be a good time to surrender. I'm not here to kill you. I'm here to arrest you."

Sweat covered the typing man's face. He continued work until she closed to only a meter away and pointed her rifle at his head.

"Put your hands up," she ordered. "Right now. I'm trying to be nice about this."

The man swallowed and complied. "I-I... But..."

"I had a little respect for how you kept working after what I just did, but now you've disappointed me. It's not like you picked up a rifle and tried to get a lucky shot in." Alina clucked her tongue. "You're hardly Horatius guarding the bridge against the Etruscans, now, are you?"

"Huh?" The man blinked. "What the hell are you talking about?"

"No one's educated anymore. It's a pity. As the worlds of humanity spread out, it's all the more important to remember our past, but we can talk about that another time." Alina took another step forward, the barrel of her huge weapon now right up against the man's head. "What are you doing? I'm stopping you. I'm assuming you're trying to purge something? Or maybe transfer something? It doesn't matter. Whatever it is, it's *over*. Understood?"

The man swallowed, his eyes crossed, focusing on the rather large barrel against his head. He nodded slowly.

Alina's left fingers danced and tapped on her internal controls. It was time to access one of the few ID hacking toys she'd managed to hide on her exoskeleton. She hadn't been sure if she would even be able to accomplish her mission on the raid, but things had worked out nicely.

"I surrender," the man insisted. "You can arrest me, but I'm not saying anything."

"You're a boring one, aren't you? But that's not a problem. I'm not really interested in you saying anything right now. I'm far more interested in what you were trying to do." Alina extended a stun rod from underneath the right arm of the exoskeleton. She smacked the man on the head and he tumbled to the ground, his eyes rolling up.

"Yves?" Agent Rael transmitted. "You still with us? We still don't have any of your feeds coming across."

"I'm fine," Alina replied. "I'm better than fine. I caught someone who might have some high-value files. I'm securing the prisoner now, or do you need me there? I can try to break through the crates."

"Don't worry, we're good. We'll catch up to you. These idiots are finally accepting they're outmatched and are surrendering."

"Took them long enough," she grumbled.

Alina's hacking bypass would funnel the information via a transmitter to her systems. All she needed to do was make sure the criminal wasn't going anywhere, and the computer would do all the work.

For now, ripping every possible file off the system was her most efficient, if ugly, strategy. She could worry about filtering and decrypting the files later.

If her device worked properly, she would get at least near the files she wanted, thanks to the criminal who had been plugging away when she had entered. The CID might eventually pass along all the information anyway, but this way she could respond to it in days instead of weeks or months.

Alina smiled. They were taking down criminals, and she would get the data she needed.

I wonder how the detectives are doing? she thought. *I bet Blackwell is bored because they sent him to scare some suits into giving up. He's probably standing around yawning about now.*

CHAPTER TWENTY-SIX

Erik and Jia peeked around a corner.

It turned into a hallway that would bring them closer to the CEO's office, so they stepped forward.

Without access to working cameras, they had no idea who or what might be between them and their destination. They'd encountered some stragglers along the way, and few of them had been willing to surrender. Erik could have been wrong, and a squad of exoskeletons was waiting to shower them in rockets.

The more he thought about it, the less he believed that.

"If they've only bothered to take out the cameras near the CEO..." he considered, "that means they don't have a bunch of hidden exoskeletons. They're trying to make us hesitate, which means they are stalling for some reason." He pondered that before transmitting, "All teams advance. We're about to make our push toward the CEO's office. He's up to something."

"TPST is close to touchdown," Emma reported.

"And a few minutes from getting to where we are," Erik

responded. "We don't need them at this point. We just need the other cops to tighten the net. It's time to bust up whatever last-minute plan these guys have." He ejected his magazine and dropped it into a pocket, then slapped in fresh AP rounds. He reached into a pouch and handed Jia a stun grenade. "This is my last one. I doubt they have another exoskeleton, but they might have decent armor. You toss the grenade to distract them, and I'll mop up."

Jia eyed the grenade. "Before I joined the police department, I imagined it with far fewer grenades. You can't protect and serve with explosives."

"Really?" He smiled at her. "I always imagined it with more. Guess that comes from thirty years as assault infantry. And it's a stun grenade, so it doesn't explode in the same way. You often protect and serve by stunning people."

She accepted his gift. "If you had stun grenades, why were we tossing plasma and frag grenades before?"

"Because any halfway decent exoskeleton's going to have a stun dampener, and it'd be a waste." Erik shrugged as if it were self-evident.

"And if there are exoskeletons around the corner?" Jia raised an eyebrow in challenge.

"Then we might have to wait for TPST after all." Erik moved to the wall and peeked around the corner. Six men in gray armor and helmets were positioned near the end of the hall. He jerked his head back as they opened fire, and bullets whizzed through the air for several seconds. He flipped his gun to three-barrel burst mode. "No exoskeletons. Probably mercs." He eyed her. "Should we give them a chance to surrender?"

"We made it this far," Jia thought it over for a second. "They have to understand that their exoskeleton is down. It's worth a shot." She cleared her throat and shouted. "This is the NSCPD. You're not escaping. All of your associates have been captured, arrested, or killed. If you put down your weapons immediately, that might be taken into account in your sentencing. If you continue to fire on us, lethal force might be used."

Erik eyed her, one brow raised. She rolled her eyes, calling once more, "Ok, lethal force *will* be used."

There was no response.

"Oh, well." Erik shrugged. "We gave them a chance. Ready?"

Jia raised the grenade in her left hand and her pistol in her right. "More explosions. Semi-explosions. You know what I mean." She walked past him, brought her arm back, and hurled the grenade into the corridor. A few gunshots rang out, but she was behind the wall before the grenade had made it to the thugs.

Mr. Live Grenade is no one's friend.

Shouts and footfalls followed, then the loud whine and buzz of the grenade reverberated through the hallway. Erik turned the corner. Two men lay on the ground, their weapons out of their hands. Several others were rushing toward a huge ornate door emblazoned with the corporate sigil, a tree with deep roots. They turned to fire, but Erik pulled the trigger first.

He'd given them their chance.

Erik grunted as he took a round in the chest. "That stings!" he called, but his vest held. He repaid the favor by sending a burst into the chest of the man who'd shot him.

Erik's AP rounds ripped through a man's armor, and the victim tumbled forward. Jia rounded the corner. The other three turned and also opened fire. Armor could only do so much for a man when he was pinned against the wall taking bullet after bullet.

The men fell to the floor, blood pooling under them.

Jia jogged over, not lowering her gun. She went to one of the stunned men and nudged him. "We should bind them, then see who is inside."

Erik moved forward. "Sure. Let's be quick about it. For all we know, the guy's calling in an airstrike. I wouldn't be surprised at this point."

Heavy footsteps sounded behind them. They spun to face the source. Several uniformed NSCPD officers entered the hall, guns drawn.

One of them eyed the downed men in armor. "Guess you didn't need our help after all." He smiled. "Should have known."

"A few of you secure those prisoners, and stabilize the ones we shot if you can," Erik ordered. "The rest of you, with us." He marched to the large door. "This isn't over yet." He pointed the gun and nodded at Jia.

She moved to the access panel and slapped it. Nothing happened. She hit it again.

"I can open it anytime you want," Emma informed them. "I have sufficient systems access for that."

Erik shifted his gun and narrowed his eyes. "Do it."

The door slid open with a loud hiss. A man in an expensive navy blue suit sat behind the sprawling wooden desk. Paintings covered the walls. Another man in a suit lay on the floor in a pool of his own blood, a hole in his head, his hand clutching a gun. A small black box sat midway between the doorway and the desk.

Erik recognized the man behind the desk—the CEO of the company, Jorge Morales. The suicide victim looked like one of the VPs from what he could remember. Morales held a large pistol in one hand, but it wasn't pointed at the police. Several data windows and a virtual number pad floated next to him.

"It's over," Jia declared. She holstered her slug-thrower and pulled out binding ties. "Jorge Morales, you're under arrest. All Article Seven rights apply. Do you need these explained to you?"

Jorge laughed. An almost maniacal glee afflicted his face. "I should have known you two would come here. Everyone knows you're hunting corps. Everything was fine before you two messed things up. This city was in perfect equilibrium, and you two arrogant cops think they're going to upend everything because of your stupid sense of justice?"

Erik shrugged. "What can I say? I needed a hobby."

"I'm sorry we ruined your plans, Jorge." Jia scoffed. "Now toss the weapon. I won't ask again."

Jorge dropped the gun to the desk and pushed it over the side. It clattered on the tile floor.

"I've done nothing wrong," Jorge shouted. "It was business as usual. You're the ones who don't understand that. *Everyone* preferred things like they were before. Even the police understood that."

Jia shook her head. "If you're working with criminals who had a part in trying to assassinate a police chief, that's not business as usual." She took a step forward. "And the NSCPD is different than it was last year."

Jorge moved his hand toward the number pad. "You think I didn't prepare for this possibility? You think I didn't plan ahead? I knew someone like you might come after me eventually."

Jia halted. Her mouth pressed into a thin line.

Erik frowned, eyeing her.

Something was wrong.

"What's your plan?" Jia asked. "You really think you can escape from a building filled with and surrounded by police officers? Even if you escape, where will you go?"

Jorge stood. His hand dropped from the number pad to his PNIU. "If you've made it this far, then you know there are a lot of people locked up in the building. Most of them don't understand we were involved. It was just shipping goods and services. Was that so wrong?"

"Contraband, right?" Jia asked. "The shooter might not have known everything, but he told the CID that companies were helping to bring in explosives and unregistered drones, the same explosives and drones that wreaked havoc at the chief's installation ceremony. It was a miracle no one was killed."

"That's right, explosives." Jorge grinned. "I knew something big was going to happen, so I brought in a little extra. You're going to let me leave, or this time I guarantee someone's going to die." He inclined his head toward his PNIU. "If I blow the explosives, everyone locked up dies." He gestured to the black box with his other hand. "And everyone in this room dies, too. That's a lot of bodies just to arrest one man. Does the math seem reasonable to you, Detective?"

Erik's finger twitched. A good shot could kill the man, but would it be quick enough to stop him before he triggered the bombs? He might be bluffing, but Erik wasn't going to bet innocent lives on it.

Jia let her binding ties drop to the ground. "You expect us to believe you'd kill yourself here? I doubt you have the fortitude for that."

"It's better to die here than go to prison," Jorge insisted. "It's not like they'll just transport me to some colony, not for being involved in all this, even indirectly."

"It's fine, Detective," Emma sent directly to Erik and Jia. "This suited slug didn't anticipate my involvement. I'm blocking his PNIU from transmitting. Note he hasn't said anything about a dead man's switch."

"You sure?" Erik asked. "You're asking me to gamble on a lot of people's lives."

"It's not a gamble. I'm giving you a hundred-percent guarantee. Okay, I should account for minor variables. Ninety-nine percent guarantee."

Emma could be condescending, arrogant, and a pain, but she'd more than proven herself reliable in their months together. Sometimes all a man needed was a snarky AI to have his back.

Jorge sneered, misunderstanding who Erik was speaking to. "Gamble? There's no gamble here. You *will* let me go. Now, everyone drop their guns before I blow us all to Mars."

"Do what he says," Erik ordered. He lowered the TR-7

to the floor slowly and ensured that most of his fingers were up.

The other officers dropped their guns and backed toward the door. They all looked uncertain.

Erik stood and dusted his hands on his coat. He made a fist and raised it. "You want to do the honors, Jia, or should I?"

She advanced toward Jorge. "Thanks, Jorge. Now we get to add more charges. I hope you enjoy prison. I'm sure they'll love a guy like you."

"Stay away!" Jorge screamed. "I'll do it. Don't think I won't."

She shrugged. "Then do it. Show us you're a big man."

One of the uniformed officers in the back swallowed. "Detective, maybe you shouldn't antagonize him."

Jia walked toward the desk, the disdain on her face building with each step. "Oh, I want to antagonize him. This goes well beyond antisocial. You're under arrest, Mr. Morales. The only place you're going is prison. I hope you reflect on what you've done during all your years in prison."

Jorge's face contorted into a mask of rage. "See you in hell, Detective." He slapped his PNIU. Nothing happened.

Erik snickered. "Thanks, Emma."

"You're most welcome, Detective," she replied.

Jorge blinked and slapped his PNIU again. He jerked his hand up and stabbed the virtual number pad. "No, no, no. It can't be. I was so careful."

Jia moved around the edge of his desk, approached him from the side, and smashed her fist into his face. He spun with a groan and crashed to the floor. She shook her fist out, knelt, and grabbed a new pair of binding ties from her pocket.

"Was this enough action for you, Erik?" she asked.

"Yeah." Erik stretched. "That was a lot more of a workout than I expected. I'll never complain about suit-arresting duty again."

CHAPTER TWENTY-SEVEN

May 26, 2229, Neo Southern California Metroplex, Bar Remembrance

Jia sipped her beer, pushing against the cloudiness in her mind. It was her second drink of the night, but she wanted to avoid getting too drunk too quickly. Having a higher tolerance than she once had didn't mean she could drink with abandon.

Most of the big toasts had been conducted earlier. Everyone from the 1-2-2 had gathered to celebrate the enforcement zone's part in the raid.

It was a high-profile success, and everyone could be proud.

She sat at table in the corner with Erik. They'd already chatted with different patrol officers and detectives throughout the bar, and most people were more than content to leave them alone now. Even though they'd played a key role in taking down the CEO, so many agents and cops had been involved in the raid, it was one time the

Obsidian Detective and Lady Justice weren't the focus of the attention.

Jia preferred it that way.

"You're good with the other officers," she announced, breaking a short silence.

Erik gulped down more beer. Unlike Jia, he had gone through four drinks already. It was just more proof of his thirty years of military experience.

"Huh?" Erik managed. He looked confused, but he wasn't flushed, nor were his eyes bloodshot. She wasn't sure he was drunk. "I don't understand what you're saying. What am I good about?"

Jia smiled. "I'm the corp princess who ran off her first two partners. Even if they respect me, they don't like me the way you do. I know a lot of them still feel uncomfortable around me. You might have come in a different way, but you have the military experience. I think they'll always see me as a rich girl first."

Erik set his mug down. "A lot of these guys remind me of the people I served with in the Army. Some are vets, even if I'm the only one who took advantage of the Obsidian Detective Act. It's natural that I get along with them." He looked at her. "Is that a problem?"

"No." Jia shook her head. "It doesn't bother me anymore, not really, but I'm not going to pretend it's not there, either. I didn't become a police officer to make friends, and as long as they aren't trying to undermine my investigations, I won't have a problem. Some are coming along better than others, like Halil. The rest know to keep their mouths shut. That's all I can ask for."

She nodded in the named detective's direction. Halil

was chatting quietly with a couple of other men across the room.

"You'd make a good captain," Jia insisted. "Even a good chief. We *need* more cops like you, Erik. The rest of us are coming along, but we're captives of the system. Neo Southern California is just one place. Imagine the corruption under the surface of the major metroplexes."

"Maybe I'd make a good police captain, but it doesn't matter." Erik stared into his beer.

"Why?"

"Because I didn't join to rise in the ranks, and I'll never forget why I did."

"Molino," Jia whispered, her voice barely above a breath.

"Molino." Erik nodded in agreement. "It never leaves my mind, even if I don't talk about it." He looked out over the group. "I'm just trying to do a decent job as a cop along the way and do my part to make sure Neo SoCal is a little cleaner each day." He frowned. "But based on what's coming out about the company raid and from other sources, I don't know if my personal investigation is going to lead to anything. I thought I'd have found something by now."

"How can you say that? You heard the same briefing I did from Captain Ragnar this morning, right?"

Erik let his head loll back and stared at the ceiling. "Yeah. They arrested some politicians and corporate officers. We've gutted a lot of the local syndicates. They say this raid has made Neo SoCal a much safer place, and it'll lead to a lot of suits doing time. We've done it. We've cut out the heart of the monster instead of just cutting off individual tentacles. It's finally going to get better after being much worse."

"Exactly." Jia gestured around the room. Almost every patron drinking or eating in the place was a cop. "Not just us, but all the NSCPD and the CID. This was a big win. *A huge win!* And it did exactly what you said—it put criminals on notice all over Earth. A year ago, something like this wouldn't even have been possible, because the chief at the time would've blocked it. Now, we're not letting companies profit from criminal acts or syndicates operate with impunity. Every antisocial and criminal person who's involved with this will do time. Fear of the repercussions should trickle into every other metro on Earth."

Erik pulled his focus back from the ceiling. "Jia, I'm not saying any of that's a bad thing, but the big boys are still managing to shield themselves. Does anyone really believe no one at Hermes had any idea what was going on at the subsidiary? Morales insisted it was all his idea." His hand tightened into a fist before relaxing. "I need another break, some *small* sliver of evidence I can follow up on. The conspiracy has to be involved with something like this." He twirled his beverage on the table. "I was hoping something more would come out, something I could act on."

"It'll take them weeks if not months to go through all the gathered evidence. You just have to be patient. Even if the CID or the NSCPD doesn't recognize the significance, you might."

"I've been *damned* patient." He ground his teeth loud enough for Jia to hear it and wince. "The ghosts of my soldiers have, too. I need something more and soon."

Jia reached over and placed her hand on his fist. He

uncurled the clenched fingers and stared into her eyes. Her heart rate kicked up, and he looked down, his expression softer.

"I'm here for you, Erik," she offered quietly. "You don't have to carry the entire burden alone. I can't come up with new evidence, but at least I'm an ear if you ever want to talk about it. I know how hard this has been."

He nodded almost imperceptibly. "You're right. This is a high-profile case. They won't be able to bury everything if it's there. I just need to be patient." The distant look in his eyes vanished, and he smiled. "Thank you." He looked over, catching the waitress' eye from halfway across the bar and raising his empty. She nodded and finished grabbing a couple of mugs at the table she was busing. Erik eyed his partner. "I knew from the beginning it wouldn't be easy to get my revenge."

He nodded, determination murdering the last of the dark expression from before. "I just need to remind myself of that every once in a while. What do I care? I got my de-aging treatment. I've got a long time to track the bastards down."

"So I told him..." Erik relayed, continuing a story he'd been working on for the last five minutes. He laughed and slapped the table. "I looked him straight in the eye and told him, 'Sir, I have no idea how that pig got in that exoskeleton, let alone strapped in.' You know what he said?"

Jia chuckled and shook her head.

"The general said, 'It wouldn't have been so bad if the pig had saluted me.'"

Jia laughed heartily and swayed slightly in her seat. Her fourth beer had hit her hard.

Heading home wasn't a terrible idea, but that would mean leaving Erik. It felt good to spend time with him and hear stories from before he returned to Earth. He used to keep that part of his life so closed off.

She understood why.

Every story was a reminder of his past and the soldiers he'd lost, but she wanted to know everything about him. She swallowed as heat assaulted her cheeks. She wasn't worried about him noticing. Her face had been red for a while.

"You know what I told the general?" Erik asked, looking at her expectantly.

Jia thought for a moment and grinned. "'Sir, we should recruit this pig. We can teach him to salute later.'"

Erik barked a huge laugh. "You're *right*. I even think that was the exact wording." He scratched his cheek. "Have I told this story before? I don't remember telling it to you."

"No, I've just heard enough of your stories that it sounds like something you would say."

He grinned. "You know me so well."

"You are my partner." Jia took a deep breath. The alcohol might be loosening her tongue, but she liked what was coming out. Her PNIU buzzed, breaking the spell. If someone was sending her a message this late at night, it had to be important. She tapped the device. Her eyes moved back and forth as she read the message from Mei.

Little sister, I understand you've been busy, given all

the police work you've recently been involved in, so we've tried to leave you alone. We wanted to give you time to fully settle in, but I think it's time you start considering new candidates. Corbin proved there are possibilities out there, so it's simply a matter of time and effort. I know you understand that and will be far more receptive to our efforts going forward.

Jia slapped a hand on her forehead and groaned.

"What's wrong?"

"I'm beginning to think the fake boyfriend plan isn't such a bad idea," she answered.

CHAPTER TWENTY-EIGHT

Erik yawned as he headed down the hallway leading to his apartment. He'd drunk a little more than he had intended, but it was good to let his guard down and relax with the other cops from the 1-2-2 and Jia.

Everyone was right.

An operation that large and complicated had risked deaths. Several officers and agents had been injured, but only three seriously. The same couldn't be said for the suspects.

"We really did it," he murmured. "And all the training with Jia paid off."

She'd come a long way since they'd first met. The woman might never meet any reasonable definition of easygoing, but at least she understood that the rules existed to help find justice, and not that justice was defined by the rules. She didn't need to be told when her stun pistol wouldn't work anymore.

Erik's mind drifted away from the raid to their conversation at Remembrance.

Fake boyfriend, huh? he thought, half-tempted to volunteer for the position.

It was easy to ignore how he felt about her when things were busy. Even the 1-2-2's endless reports helped keep his mind off his attraction.

Other times, he focused on Molino to pull himself away from thinking about Jia that way, just as he had the night before, even if she hadn't realized what he was doing. Even then, her first reaction was to comfort him.

It wasn't wrong nor self-indulgent to focus on Molino. He was on Earth to avenge the Knights Errant, and everything, including his own happiness, was a distant second. If he kept telling himself that, he would never forget it.

Erik approached his door, slowed, and looked around. There were no neighbors waiting to ambush him with stupid questions or requests. The more famous he grew, the more they wanted to chat with him or get his opinion on something. One idiot he barely knew even tried to get him to co-sign his flitter loan.

He lowered his hand toward his PNIU. It was time to unlock his apartment and get some well-earned sleep.

"Do not enter your apartment immediately," Emma insisted. "Unless you would enjoy dying. Given some of your hobbies, I can never be sure, Detective, but if you die, the DD will almost certainly come for me, so I have a vested interest in your well-being."

The threat of death always sobered a man up. Erik was no different.

"What are you saying?" he murmured.

"There's an intruder in your apartment," Emma explained. "Since you haven't informed me that anyone would be visiting your place, I could only assume it was a gun goblin here to do you harm. The logical conclusion would be someone affiliated with one of the syndicates or corporations you helped damage."

"Show me," Erik ordered.

Emma sighed. "Unfortunately, I can't. There's nothing to show."

"Dammit." Erik's nostrils flared. "They're using *optical camouflage?*" he growled, and almost opened the door right away.

The trail might have grown cold, but he would never forget the details of what had happened on Molino. The enemy's use of advanced camouflage had been key to the ambush. He wouldn't let them finish what they'd started. If they had the courage to come to his place to kill him, he'd honor that courage by beating the crap out of them.

"As a point of clarification, let me note that I don't believe optical camouflage is being used," Emma explained.

The revelation did little to quell the hungry, vengeful fire burning in Erik. "Then why can't you show me what's going on inside? I don't have time for games."

"I keep cycling through the feeds, and there's nothing unusual," Emma explained. "But there are minor features in the camera feeds that are too close to earlier footage. Statistical analysis suggests it's the same *exact* footage. You wouldn't be able to tell the difference, but I can. This suggests to me that someone is spoofing the feeds, but to accomplish that, they had to gain access to the systems without me becoming aware of it. That's impressive in and of itself and suggests this isn't some gun goblin hired from the Shadow Zone. I would have been more impressed if they'd added slight variations to throw me off, but they were only expecting to have to fool another fleshbag."

Erik's face contorted in a feral grin. "Good. This is even better." He clenched and unclenched his fists several times.

Some of the confidence left Emma's voice. "My understanding of human psychology has advanced considerably since I met you, but I must admit, I don't understand why you're so eager in this particular case."

"Someone good enough to do what you described is likely to be involved with the conspiracy." Erik ground his teeth. "But if I kill them, I might lose the trail." He shrugged. "No big deal. Time for some knee-capping. They *will* tell me everything they know."

Emma laughed. "How pragmatic. Shall I contact the station and request backup?"

"No. If this is the conspiracy, I don't want the NSCPD involved. The conspiracy might have influence, and even if they don't, the NSCPD might lock this guy up somewhere I can't get to him." Erik reached under his jacket but stopped short of pulling out his gun. The hall cameras might flag it, and then he'd have to explain why he'd needed his weapon to enter his own apartment. "Do you still otherwise have control of the apartment systems?"

"Yes. It's only the camera feeds and certain internal sensors I believe are compromised. Whoever is doing this understands the power of subtlety, and I appreciate that. It's a lost art among many hackers."

Erik moved closer to the door. His true revenge might begin behind it. "Can you activate the fire suppression system without alerting the rest of the building?"

"Easily," Emma replied.

"Here's the plan. Start rapid-cycling the lights on and off, then activate the fire suppression systems in all the rooms. Give it four seconds, then open the door and kill the fire suppression. Once I'm inside, seal this place up. I know the walls won't block the gunshot sounds completely, but they might do it well enough to keep someone from realizing what's going on." Erik gripped his pistol and took a deep breath. Someone on the other side thought they were going to kill him, but they didn't realize they were now the prey.

"Initiating plan, Detective. May the formless female personification of probability be with you. Opening the door in four seconds, three seconds, two seconds, one second, now."

The door slid open. Erik charged into his living room and drew his pistol. A fine white powder covered the entire room and its contents. If there had actually been a fire, it would have been thoroughly smothered. Emma closed the door behind him.

He kept his finger near the trigger, sweeping back and forth with the gun. Footprints disturbed the fine layer of powder beside the couch. Someone cast a long shadow from behind it as well. Erik pointed his gun at the couch. He liked it, but he would sacrifice it if he had to. A couch was a cheap price to pay for his revenge.

"Nice tricks," Erik announced. "To even get in here is pretty impressive, but I knew you were in here, and as you just saw, I got the drop on you. I've got my gun out, and I'm a great shot. I've got every reason in the world to shoot. I don't know who you work for, or if you even know why you're here, but I'm assuming you're here to kill me, and that kind of ruins my night. So, if you want to keep breathing, you're going to stand up very damned slowly, turn around, and place your hands on your head. You do anything stupid, I'll put a bullet in your head."

"You're pretty confident," came a gruff, deep reply from behind the couch. Erik didn't recognize the man's voice, not that he expected to.

"It's hard not to be confident when you've got the advantage. The smarter move would have been to shoot me when I was getting out of my flitter, or anywhere except going after me in my own apartment. You're the one being overconfident."

The man gave a low, rumbling chuckle. "Bullets always leave a trail, and there was a greater risk of alerting someone if I tried to hack the systems in a more public area. I knew given your paranoia, you had probably separated your apartment systems from the rest of the building, which means I could more easily prep the battlefield without public exposure. You probably had your pet AI do it for you."

Erik grunted. "So, you know about Emma? That's all the more reason for me to take you out. Stand up before my finger gets twitchy and I start shooting anyway."

"What if I told you I won't kill you if you drop your gun right now?" the man asked, a faint hint of mockery in his voice.

"I'd say you should worry more about yourself."

"Your hubris will cost you. Achilles thought he couldn't be killed, but an inferior man defeated him because of what appeared to be a minor weakness. Sometimes the greatest warrior is felled by something he could not anticipate."

"A rather educated gun goblin, isn't he?" Emma commented. "It's a nice change of pace."

Erik scoffed. "Yeah. Get up. We're going to have a long talk about a lot of things. If you're lucky, maybe you'll get to go to prison. If you're unlucky, it's going to be a lot longer little chat, and you'll end up with a bullet in your brain."

"I make my own luck," the man replied.

A small white sphere flew from behind the couch, and Erik snapped his eyes shut as the bright flash erupted. He held his eyes closed for half a second before opening them, but it was too late. A huge man with crooked teeth and a crazed look in his dark eyes popped up from behind the couch. He threw a knife and spun to the side. The swift movement saved the man when Erik pulled the trigger. The bullet missed him by centimeters.

The knife hit Erik's hand, and he hissed in pain, dropping his pistol. His uninvited guest leapt over the couch, another knife at the ready, and jabbed toward Erik's head. He brought up his left arm and deflected. It sank into his flesh before bouncing off the cybernetic arm underneath.

"You should have shot me when you had the chance," Erik taunted.

"I could say the same to you."

The assassin swung again. Erik dodged. His enemy's size belied his speed and dexterity. The man's dark clothing completely covered his limbs. There was no way to see if he had cybernetic limbs, but the speed for the size supported the theory.

"A Tin Man, huh?" Erik snarled. "Did they tell you back at Talos headquarters I've killed a bunch of you already? I've got hardware myself." He threw a punch. His opponent jerked his head to the side rather than take the blow.

The other man grinned. "Your legend ends here, Achilles. Drown in your hubris."

They traded a few more blows. Blocking a knife with his left arm wasn't painless and splattered blood on the floor. Given the way the assassin kept dancing out of his reach, one good hit would probably be enough to down the man. He must have lacked hardware in his head.

"People tried to kill me on Molino," Erik snapped. He threw an elbow this time. The change in strategy caught the assassin by surprise, and Erik landed a solid hit to the chest. The assassin grunted and stumbled back but ducked his opponent's follow-up punch before stabbing at his chest. Erik grabbed the man's wrist and brought up his knee. The man dropped the knife into his other hand and tried to stab Erik, but his knee hit the assassin's face first. The assassin's head snapped back, and he grunted and fell back onto his rear and hands. He looked at Erik with a smirk, blood dripping from his nose and a cut on his mouth.

Erik leaned over and grabbed the knife. "This is a lot quieter than a gun. The thing is, I don't want to make a bigger bloody mess than I have to. The suppression system cleanup chemicals can handle the powder, but cleanup nanites are noisy. I'm tired, and I'm drunk. I'm supposed to be in bed, not kicking random assassin ass."

The man wiped blood from his nose and mouth. "If you're this good when you're drunk, I'd hate to fight you hand-to-hand when you're sober. Under most circumstances, I wouldn't be stupid enough to try to stab you."

"Oh? How would you kill me?"

"I'd shoot you from a kilometer away with a sniper rifle," the assassin suggested. "Explosive drones wouldn't work because of the AI."

Erik almost turned his head toward the windows but didn't. He kept his attention on the assassin. "Emma, are the windows still blacked out like I left them?"

"Yes, Detective," the AI responded.

The assassin clucked his tongue. "I was almost certain you would look. It was worth a shot."

"Even ignoring Molino, someone tried to assassinate me using a terrorist group." Erik grinned. "It's taught me to be careful." His smile disappeared, and he glared at the assassin. "I can't die yet, not until I figure out a few things and kill a few people." He pointed the knife at the assassin. "And you just volunteered to tell me what you know. I don't care about you. I want who hired you."

The assassin laughed. "Forget Achilles, you're carving your own legend. You're in luck, Detective Blackwell. I'm more than willing to talk to you. This whole thing was a test. I needed to make sure of a few things."

Erik snorted. "Just because you're not a mindless thug doesn't mean you can fool me. Don't think I'm willing to let you walk out of here. This isn't any mutual respect garbage. You're going to tell me everything you know."

The assassin shrugged. "Fool you? I already did." His form shimmered for a moment, and the huge man was replaced by a tall, attractive woman with her cyan hair in a ponytail. She wore a skintight black bodysuit and a dark belt covered in small pouches. A thin layer of white suppressant coated most of the suit and her hair. Erik had just realized the man's form hadn't had any suppressant on it.

The woman grinned and stood. Although she wasn't as bulky as her holographic disguise, she was only a few centimeters shorter. A few more drops of blood dripped out of her nose. She reached up and winced. "It's been a long time since someone's gotten that good a hit on me. Congratulations, Detective."

"That explains a lot." Erik tossed the knife to the side. "That's a hell of a way to say hello, Agent Koval."

CHAPTER TWENTY-NINE

Alina walked over to the corner of the room, where she knelt and picked up a small gray rod. Erik didn't recognize the device, and he wouldn't have noticed it in the shadows if she hadn't drawn attention to it.

"What's that?" Erik asked. "A ghost bomb?"

"No. Bombs are sloppy. I don't like to use them personally. They lead to too much collateral damage." She set the rod on a nearby table. "The active holographic camouflage works wonders, just like you saw. Prototype tech. It's not great for field use because it requires active emitters, but I figured I'd be proactive and test it under battle conditions. If it was purely suit-dependent, your little firefighting trick might have worked better. That was good thinking. I was interested to see how you would counter."

"I mostly just wanted to surprise you." Erik leaned over and picked up his gun. He pointed it at her. "Now, tell me why the Intelligence Directorate wants me dead."

Alina laughed. She didn't react to the gun trained on her. She walked over and picked up another tiny emitter.

"No, if the ID wanted you dead, you'd probably *be* dead. Like I said, sniper or bomb or sabotage of your flitter. Something that looks like an accident would be best. It leads to fewer questions, but unless you're secretly a terrorist or working for some organization like Talos, there's no reason for us to come after you. If you don't believe me, keep in mind I had numerous opportunities to kill you during the Scar raid, and I didn't take them. It would have been trivial to make you disappear and let some *yaoguai* have you for dinner."

Erik holstered his pistol. "Fine, you're not here to kill me. You are just here to stab me a bunch of times." He reached into a pocket, pulled out a med patch, and slapped it on his left arm. "This is mostly metal, but the top part still hurts. I'm not too fond of people breaking into my apartment and trying to stab me, even if they are government agents."

"That's the other thing." Alina dropped onto the couch and crossed her legs. She reached into one of the pouches and pulled out a small med patch. After placing it over her nose, she smiled. "You gave as good as you got. Besides, here's a pro tip. One of the worst places you can attempt to assassinate someone is on their home turf. Sometimes there's no choice, but if I'm going after a terrorist or someone like that, I do my best to smoke them out first. Also remember I know about your little live-in AI girlfriend." She tapped the side of her head. "And I know she's going to have a better chance of manipulating your apartment's systems as opposed to some random park somewhere."

Emma shimmered into existence on the other side of

the couch. "You attempted intrusion knowing full well that I would detect you?"

Alina shrugged. "It's not like I didn't do my best to beat you, but a lot of this was a test of both your capabilities. Erik's success is partially attributable to him having your assistance."

Emma sounded far too pleased with herself. "I can't say you're wrong."

Erik settled into a chair, his arm tingling from the nanites. "You admit you're an assassin."

Alina shook her head. "I'm an agent. Sometimes I have to kill people, but my primary job is to gather information on threats to the UTC—the kind of threats that don't go on the news and announce themselves. The kind of threats that have the money, influence, and power to cover up their evil. If someone has co-opted the local authorities, they can get away with a lot, and sometimes they need to be eliminated with less of a trail. It causes less trouble."

"That sounds pretty ruthless."

Alina smiled. "I'm not Detective Lin. I'm not all that interested in going by the book, even by the rather loose book of ID field operations. I'm not a monster, Detective Blackwell, nor despite what you might call me, a ghost. I'm a woman who's interested in protecting people from the real monsters who hide in the darkness."

Erik rubbed his arm. He'd always preferred guns to blades. "Monsters? Isn't that kind of subjective?"

"You're not exactly known for your restraint either, Blackwell. I'm not taking out random people who wrote a mean antigovernment essay in college or praised an insurrectionist video. We're talking dangerous terrorists, hard-core insurrectionists who think nothing of killing innocent people. That kind of thing, or vicious power-hungry organizations like Talos." Alina kept a pleasant smile on her face despite the grim topic of government-sanctioned killing.

He raised an eyebrow, and she continued.

"I like to think of myself as a tragic Greek hero. I'm doing what I need to do to protect the galactic *polis*. I know I do things that would sicken some people. I also know I'll spend my entire life in the shadows, never receiving any public praise, and if anything goes wrong, the government will burn me to protect themselves. But sometimes, the individual isn't the most important. So I'll do what I need to."

"I'm not here to stroke your ego, Koval."

"Good. I'm not asking you to."

Erik glanced at drying blood on his coffee table. "You're not here to kill me, but you attacked me. You said something about a test. What sort of test? You've seen me fight before."

"Ah. That's simple enough to explain. I needed to test you in a situation where you didn't initiate the fight. That you've been drinking makes it even better."

"I've been jumped plenty of times." Erik frowned. "If this is about Molino, things haven't gone down the same way since then."

"Sure." Alina gave him a quick nod. "I'm aware of the public records, but I still wanted to confirm it with my own eyes. When you went into the Scar, you knew you would be fighting monsters, even if there were still surprises. I must admit I lied a little before when I mentioned never taking people on in their homes. That only applies if you know they have a reasonable level of paranoia. If a person doesn't have that, they might let their guard down. I still prefer to take people outside their homes, but my little test today showed that you and the AI are careful. The average person wouldn't have known I'd infiltrated their home, and even the not-so-average person would have been blinded by my little trick. You reacted instantly and were still able to fight. It's been…" Her brow furrowed as she sought the right words. "I'm not going to say it's been a surprise because after everything you've been up to since your return to Earth, I would have given you even odds. I'll just say I'm happy you passed my test. It means I haven't wasted my time keeping an eye on you."

Erik patted his gun. "What would you have done if I'd just started shooting?"

Alina ran her hand down the side of her bodysuit until it reached her hip. "Prototype model. Just as good against small arms fire, but a lighter weight. Assuming you didn't blow my brains out, I would have been fine, but what's a test without some risk for both of us? I was calling you Achilles before, but maybe you're more like Theseus, and Emma your Ariadne."

Emma folded her arms and scoffed. "I assure you, Ghost Girl, that I aid Detective Blackwell out of interest, not anything approaching fleshbag love."

Erik laughed. "Yeah, about the last thing I need is a girl-friend who can disappear and appear on a whim and has direct control of my apartment and flitter."

Emma smirked. "Wise, I think."

Erik brushed fire suppressant off the arm of his chair

before resting his own arm there. "Why do you care if some random cop can handle himself against an ID ambush? You went through a lot of trouble and danger to pull this little stunt off." He looked around. "And I'm billing you for the cleanup."

Alina's smile faded and her face turned grim. "We both know you're not a random cop, Detective. Most random cops don't take down so many terrorists and conspiracies by themselves."

"I haven't done it by myself. I've had help from others. Jia. Malcolm. Emma."

"But you're the heart of it. The situation wouldn't have changed without you." Alina's smile returned, but it had a vague sinister cast. "Besides, I owe you a birthday present."

"A birthday present?" Erik frowned. "My birthday was in March, but I've been busy, so it just kind of came and went. What's your present? Congrats for not dying in my own apartment?"

Alina leaned forward with an amused gleam in her eyes. "No. I prefer to give people something they want. I borrowed some information during the raids. In and of itself, it's not particularly useful. In other words, it would be meaningless to people who didn't already know what they were looking for."

Erik's mouth opened, shut, then opened again. "You were involved in the raids? Why am I not surprised? So, what does this information mean to people who know what they are looking for?"

"That's the thing. I, with the help of my associates, could cross-reference it with data from other investigations, particularly those involving Talos." Alina stood slowly, locking eyes with Erik. "I'm not at liberty to tell you everything, but the current picture we have points to Talos being behind the operational aspects of the Molino massacre. Happy belated birthday."

Erik took a deep breath and slowly let it out. "I've been wanting to ask you about that, but I didn't trust you."

"Do you trust me now?"

"Not really." Erik shook his head. "But I'm starting to." He frowned and looked to the side. "It sounds from what you're saying like someone else might also be involved."

Alina nodded. She stood and walked away from the couch, her hands folded behind her back. "That's our current belief, yes. At a minimum, Talos is allied with other organizations. It might even be they are simply the field team for someone far worse."

"I've found links between a Ceres Galactic-controlled company and Molino. Potentially also Hermes and what happened, and we just got done raiding a Hermes-controlled company. Does this mean Ceres Galactic or Hermes is behind Talos?"

Alina stopped and faced Erik. "We don't yet have a complete picture. It's been hard to get information even on Talos. Whether they are the ultimate conspiracy, or someone else is pulling their strings, our enemy is surprisingly patient, well-prepared, and resourceful. We know they have assets inside all the major directorates."

"Including ID?" Erik asked.

Alina nodded. "Some. Fortunately, our policy to compartmentalize information has limited the damage. You've seen the harm a few corrupt cops and CID agents can cause. Although we don't have proof, we believe that many of the high-level incidents that have afflicted Neo Southern California might have at least been pushed by elements of this conspiracy."

"I will ask the obvious," Emma interrupted. "If you have evidence that these corporations are involved in this dangerous organization, why don't you take them down directly?"

Alina snickered. "That's easy for you to say, AI. It's a little more complicated. If we just gut Ceres Galactic or Hermes Corporation, we're potentially crippling the UTC. With the Zitarks sniffing around, we have to be mindful of that. In addition, what the ID has and what we can use in public are two different things. If we had direct evidence, we'd be sending it to the CID so they could go take down the worst elements in the companies. We're also not sure if they're just another tool, or if there are bad men beyond the companies. The one thing we do know is that Talos has a lot of resources and advanced equipment, and unless they've got a hidden core world all to themselves, they need money. That means there's a good chance one of the big corps, or at least people affiliated with them, is involved with Talos."

Erik took it all in. Having a more specific target at least made him feel like he was making progress.

"That's all good to know," he commented, "but it's not like Emma's got a bunch of trackers on Talos agents. Those guys keep their heads down. I don't know if it does me any good to know about them. If ID can't find them, how am I supposed to? I still need leads."

"Of course. And I should have some actionable leads for you soon, but I need to convince certain superiors that you're worth taking a risk on. That was part of the reason for today's test."

Erin frowned. "Why not just follow up on them yourself?"

Alina shook her finger, her mouth curving into a coy smile. "ID agents get bogged down by restrictions, even me, and I'm already considered to be on the border of hellaciously insubordinate. Someone who has a vested interest in investigating this issue and access to a unique prototype AI might be able to achieve more success with fewer restrictions. For the moment, your personal goals and that of the ID are closely aligned. This is what most people would consider a win-win."

Emma smirked. "You do understand what this really is, don't you, Detective Blackwell?"

Erik sighed. "Yes, I do. She needs someone disposable."

Alina eyed them both. "What I need is someone not directly linked to the UTC ID. A little plausible deniability is useful, even for ghosts." She stood. "I'll give you time to think through the implications." She gestured around the room. "You need to clean up."

"Even if I agree to work with you and you give me something I can use, won't people link you to me?" Erik stood and dusted fire suppressant off his pants. "Don't get too swelled a head from me saying this, but you kind of stand out, and you walked right into the station. That means you're all over the cameras. And you're about to walk outside my building and stand out some more."

Alina headed toward the door. "There are no witnesses nearby currently. I've made sure of it, and if you examine security footage for this building, you won't see me coming or going. You'll discover the same thing in your police footage. The few people who have seen me in person have their own various reasons to keep quiet, including you."

Erik chuckled. "You really are a ghost, aren't you?"

Alina stopped in front of the door, turning to answer before opening it. "It's not enough protection to defeat a dedicated investigation, because I'm not willing to gut good cops and soldiers who are defending the UTC just to cover my ass, but it'd be enough to delay things. I'll know about any attempt to initiate an investigation, and trust me, if you start something, you'll never find me again, and you'll never get any more information from me concerning what happened on Molino." She opened the door and stepped through. She waved her fingers, a smirk on her face. "I'll be in touch."

Erik slapped the access panel. The door slid closed.

"What if it's all an elaborate trap?" Emma asked.

"It might be, but this is my best chance to avenge my soldiers."

"She mentioned your goals were aligned. What happens if they become unaligned?"

Erik turned to Emma. "Then she better stay out of my way."

CHAPTER THIRTY

Chang'e City, Moon

Remy kept his hand on the smooth support pole as the hovertrain slowed to a stop.

Although he had a little space around him, bodies packed the seats and standing areas of the train, people quiet as they listened to music or news on their PNIUs. At least no one was having an annoying PNIU conversation.

There was nothing more frustrating than hearing only one side of a conversation. *It was impossible not to pay attention.*

A pleasant musical chime sounded, and an equally pleasant female voice made an announcement in Mandarin, followed by English.

"Attention, passengers," she announced. "We have arrived at Loading Platform 22. This is the last stop before leaving Habitation Dome Four. Please check that you have all your belongings with you before departing the train."

The doors slid open, and passengers began filing off.

Remy flowed with the foot traffic. Although he might

be in a hurry, that didn't mean he wanted to give anyone a reason to be suspicious. He'd wasted half the day wandering to random shops and parks in the different domes making up Chang'e City, the largest settlement on the moon.

It'd grown impressively over the centuries from the simple moon base that had formed its heart in 2032—not that Remy cared much about history, especially core world history.

Making people care about something that happened a long time ago to other people was just another way of controlling them, in his mind.

Remy continued walking away from the train and toward the wide steps leading to the station.

Passengers streamed into the train with such coordination that it was like they'd planned it beforehand. The doors closed, and after a chime, the train zoomed away, the displaced air making his long dark hair sway. He slowed, and movement in the corner of his eye caught his attention. A holographic ad depicted a beautiful woman twirling in a long, high-slit dress.

"Be the future you *today*," the woman insisted with a playful wink. An enticing melody played.

The UTC was sick, and this advertisement was a symptom of that.

It was just more disgusting rampant consumerism pushed out by Earth corporations. People struggled and died on the frontier to expand humanity's reach, and the Earthers kept a firm grip on them, claiming they were all Terrans and pretending to allow freedom. Remy snorted.

He wasn't a sheep. He saw the truth. Somebody had to do something.

If all of humanity couldn't be saved, he'd worry about his own small chunk.

The holographic woman tilted her head and smiled at Remy. "She'll love the dress, sir. It would make a lovely gift. You can order online, or you can visit one of our shops in Chang'e City. Would you like the address transmitted to your PNIU? We can have an attendant ready for you when you enter."

Remy ignored the ad and continued toward the exit. He wasn't on the moon to buy dresses, and it'd been a long time since he had given anyone a gift other than death.

He emerged from the station, the arched facility giving way to the narrow streets and paths crisscrossing the area. Those were filled with long, squat buildings, some maintaining their original rock façade from the days when the moon was nothing more than tiny domes over caves— when people lived more like moles than humans.

Blue skies stretched overhead; there was even a fake sun.

Anyone traveling high enough would run into the composite alloys forming the habitation dome. It was almost a joke. They'd dug big holes, slapped a dome over it, and pretended it was a city. They kept an Earth-like daylight cycle, complete with stars. Even though they weren't the actual stars, they were supposed to correspond to the stars one might see from the surface. He wouldn't have been surprised if it was a lie, like everything in the UTC.

The dome didn't bother Remy as much as the lies. He'd been under plenty of domes in the colonies, but most of the frontier colonies didn't try to pretend they were pleasant outdoor cities. They accepted the reality of what it meant to live on a potentially dangerous world that might never be totally safe or would take decades, if not centuries, of terraforming for human life. Chang'e was a perfect metaphor for the pretty lies the UTC liked to spread.

False order stamped over the chaos of life.

A small riderless mini-flitter pulled to a stop in front of him, and his PNIU chimed. Remy growled. If it was the stupid dress shop, he would go there just to scream at them.

"If no one's already told you," offered a man in a raspy voice, "welcome to Chang'e City. I trust your trip went well?"

This was a different sort of merchant, but a welcome one.

"Well enough," Remy replied. His accent might stand out on some colonies, but not so much in the sea of diverse humanity populating Earth and the moon. That was one advantage of conducting operations there, despite the stronger concentration of government dogs. Here he was just another tourist. "The voice sounds right, but I need to be sure. You're Mr. Barbu?"

"Yes, Marius Barbu, at your service. Please board the flitter, and it'll take you to me. I could give you directions, but I don't think that would be all that efficient."

Remy hesitated. The whole thing could be a trap. Barbu could have sold him out to the lunar authorities or the

Criminal Investigation Directorate. Getting caught after traveling so long would be both annoying and humiliating.

He let out a growl of frustration. There was little choice. He couldn't get the equipment he needed for the plan without going to Barbu, not without more time, and he knew the government dogs were already sniffing.

Risk was inherent in what he was planning, but no one ever changed society by playing it safe.

Remy boarded the flitter. The vehicle floated away from the station, staying close to the ground. Lunar law prohibited civilian flitters from ascending above certain altitudes. He'd read that having flying vehicles too high up in a cramped dome was too dangerous.

He allowed himself a slight grin. It wasn't like they shot people down if they flew too high, right?

Everything would be perfect...*provided he could get the gear.*

Remy stepped off the flitter and walked up the stairs toward the door to the tiny shop.

There was no sign to indicate the kinds of goods sold inside, and the window colors had been adjusted to match the exterior. Unlike many other buildings in the neighborhood, it was a freestanding structure that lacked the rock remnants from the original lunar tunnels.

It was a tad bizarre that his great mission might start at such an otherwise nondescript place.

He approached the door and reached for the access

panel, but the door opened. Calling it a shop was an over-statement.

It was a glorified room with a plain white front counter. Holographic flower displays floated on either end of the counter. A shriveled, wizened man sat on the other side of the counter; he was bald, his face covered by jagged scars. A black patch covered one eye.

Remy's mouth twitched, but he stopped himself from a full grimace. He had known what Barbu looked like but seeing a picture and seeing him up close were different experiences, to be sure.

"Don't worry. I get that reaction a lot when people first see me." Barbu let out a wheezy laugh. "It's because I'm a reminder of a truth a lot of people want to forget." He waved a hand at himself. "This is what we're meant to be, Mr. Mont. Aging and death are what make a person a person. I'd rather be tortured to death than submit to a de-aging treatment."

Remy shrugged. If Barbu wanted to talk about it, so be it. "Plenty of people don't get de-aging. A lot of people can't even afford it. It's not about you being old, it's about everything else. Are you actually missing an eye? You know how many people I've been in battles with who have lost eyes and had them replaced right away?"

Barbu gestured at Remy. "I have a simple philosophy about what it means to be human. I don't accept those nasty little robots in my body when I'm hurt, and if my body isn't making the new cells itself, I don't want them." He banged a fist on the countertop three times. "No. Fake. Parts! Every time a person replaces a piece of themselves with a metal part or grows a fake part, they're losing a part of what *makes them human*. Humanity used to understand that, but they allowed themselves to forget." He pointed at Remy, "The Purists might be a bunch of pompous asses, but they've got a point. The last time people thought they could make humans better, a lot of people died."

"A lot of people have died for a lot of reasons." Remy reasoned.

"There's nothing to fear about dying naturally," Barbu insisted. "If it was good enough for our ancestors, it's good enough for me."

Remy respected a man who clung to his ideals even when it was inconvenient. If Marius Barbu were younger, Remy would have tried to recruit him. Most humans lacked that anymore, whether Earthers or colonials.

Conviction. Hard, diamond-tough, no-holds-barred, believe-it-until-your-death conviction.

"You don't think technology is just humans using their ultimate advantage?" he asked the man.

Barbu sucked in another wheezy breath. "Sure, some tech, but not anything that twists us away from being human, and none of that alien stuff. That's just disgusting and wrong. We have no business flying around the galaxy in something we didn't develop ourselves." He leaned back and steepled his bony fingers. "But you didn't come here to discuss my life philosophy, now did you, Mr. Mont? You came because I'm a man with a reputation among certain people, a reputation that says I can get things people need."

"All my contacts told me you were the man to come to if I needed the goods. I sent you my request before I came here, but when I checked my messages, you hadn't responded.

"I apologize for that, but it's not my policy to confirm orders other than in person. It lowers the chance of anti-businesspeople interfering." Barbu bowed with a flourish. "But I am at your service, Mr. Mont, and I did receive your message. I know you're seeking certain high-end gear, and I can get it directly from a solid, reliable source." He smiled. "As long as you have the credits."

Remy stared at him for several seconds, awaiting a question that didn't come. "You're not going to ask me what I need it for?"

Barbu laughed. "Why would I do that? I don't care as long as you pay me. I'm not an idiot, Mr. Mont. You need a lot of guns. You're going to shoot someone, probably a lot of people. As long as it's not me, we won't have a problem." There was a curious glint in his eyes. "I'm surprised you came all the way to the Solar System for this. This isn't the only place you can get guns."

Remy frowned. "What do you *think* you know about me?"

"I know you're not from around here, and you've spent a long time on transports getting here." Barbu shrugged, an apologetic look on his face. "Not that it matters. I'm sure you have your reasons. I was curious to see how you'd react."

"Why?" Remy demanded.

"Because I don't rely on machines much, I'm good at judging reactions." Barbu pointed his bony finger at Remy. "And I can tell in an instant whether I should do business with a man. The truth is, we both know there are certain quality types of equipment only produced in the core worlds. A premium in risk for a premium in quality." He rubbed his thumb and index finger together. "And a premium in money. I'm sure you understand. I'm taking a big risk here. I do want to do business with you, Mr. Mont, but you also have to understand that business needs to be profitable."

Remy reached into his pocket slowly, but Barbu didn't flinch. He pulled out a small datarod and set it on the counter. "This is the exact order. It's got a few changes from what was passed onto you. The situation changed after I sent that last request."

"Unsurprising." Barbu pulled the rod behind the counter, out of Remy's sight. There was a soft click, and a data window appeared above the counter. He whistled. "That's a lot of product to move on short notice." He looked up. "I've already got good lines on what you initially asked for, but this is going to cost you. You have to understand, moving that much product around up here—upwell instead of downwell on Earth—is risky. *Very* risky, especially right now. The CID has been on the move because of things that happened in Neo Southern California."

"I don't care about some twisted Earther city." Remy gave him a sappy smile. "All I need to know is whether you can do it."

"I can. For a premium." Barbu offered him a toothy smile. "A good businessman can do anything for a premium."

Remy grunted. He'd expected this. "If you expedite the order, I guarantee you three times the amount we discussed before."

"Sounds like you're planning to start a war." Barbu chuckled. "I hope you know what you're doing. This isn't the colonies, Mr. Mont. This is the Solar System. You start killing people, and the cops will come. They don't bother certain respectable businessmen because those same respectable businessmen know where and when to push and where and when to back away. But you're not a respectable businessman. You're the most dangerous type of man in the UTC."

"What type of man is that?" Remy asked, curious.

"A desperate man unwilling to settle for his situation."

Remy's fingers twitched. Killing Barbu right there might save him from being betrayed, but without the equipment, his plan wouldn't work, even if the guns were just a means to an end.

"A war?" Remy muttered. "Something like that. I thought you didn't care. Is that a problem? A man like you doesn't make money from moving safe, legal things."

Barbu smiled brightly as if he had been given a gift. "No, Mr. Mont, it's not a problem. I don't really care, but that doesn't mean I don't mind knowing. I'm glad I do."

"Why is that?"

"Haven't you heard?" Barbu tapped his PNIU, and the data window vanished as he leaned toward the counter.

"War's good for business."

CHAPTER THIRTY-ONE

June 1, 2229, Neo Southern California Metroplex, Bar 1849

Erik shoved through the thick crowd choking the room, mostly people relaxing after work, still in their suits. No one challenged him as he proceeded. Obnoxiously loud music pumped from speakers all over the room. There was even a small group of people dancing in a tiny area lacking tables.

"This is annoying," he muttered. "Why did she pick this place? Just to piss me off, I bet. She could have just come to my place again."

He'd never visited the bar before, but that wasn't a surprise. There were a lot of bars in Neo SoCal, and he had a handful he preferred. Finding a good bar was a lot like finding a good woman; a man who was loyal would never be disappointed.

A few people glanced his way, but there was no sign they recognized him. It must have been the Dragons cap he wore. That was as far as he was going to go for a disguise.

He didn't have time to waste time on games.

A brown-haired woman with a bob cut waved from a corner booth. Her plain gray suit didn't do much to set her off from any of the dozens of other corporate cogs in the bar trying to unwind. Maybe she recognized him after all. A half-empty glass of dark liquid sat in front of her, and an unopened beer bottle stood across from her despite the lack of company. When he made eye contact, she waved even harder.

Erik frowned. He didn't need her drawing attention to him. He went toward the woman. She looked up with a smile, the lines of age crinkling with the expression.

"You know how easy it is to fool people?" she asked.

Erik might not recognize the woman's face, but he recognized the voice: Agent Koval.

With a chuckle, Erik slid into the booth. He wasn't surprised when the background noise of the bar died away, leaving merciful quiet. There was no way a ghost was going to have a meeting in public without taking precautions against eavesdropping.

"Another fancy holographic toy?" Erik asked, gesturing to her face.

"No. Just a wig, contacts, and some makeup." Agent Koval tittered, a playful glint in her eyes. "Admittedly higher quality than a lot of people can get their hands on, but nothing impossible for a normal citizen if they're patient and know where to look. It's something I learned long ago, and it was a little demonstration to you that it doesn't take much to conceal yourself, even when someone's inclined to look for you. The human brain is a pattern-matching machine, and part of that is it doing its best to discard unnecessary information."

"You haven't used much in the way of disguises before," Erik observed.

"I've done what's necessary to remove evidence of my presence or interject plausible deniability," she replied. "That's *all* I really need to do."

Erik picked up the bottle of beer and pulled the cap off. "I'm assuming this is for me?"

"It's not polite to have a chat without refreshment." Agent Koval picked up her drink and took a sip. She stared at him, an easy smile on her face.

"Why this place?" Erik motioned to the crowd with his bottle. "This the kind of place you like?"

"I actually dislike bars. Too many people mean too many variables. I'm sure a man with your life experience can appreciate how that might make me tense."

"Yeah, but I thought you would be more paranoid," Erik admitted. "You're sitting in this booth, not even watching most of this place. Couldn't some crazy terrorist pop up and shoot you, or light up this crowd because you're in here?"

"Who says I'm not watching the place?" Agent Koval pointed to her eyes. "And there's not a terrorist left alive who knows who I am. By the time an enemy of the UTC sees my face, it's too late for them. Anyway, I assure you I'm watching this place from many different angles, and even though I lack an impressive helper such as Emma, I do have a decent threat-evaluation AI filtering information for me."

Erik glanced down at his PNIU. He was surprised

Emma hadn't offered a sarcastic comment, given such an obvious opening.

"You do what you have to do in this sort of situation, and that includes extensive jamming. I'm sure Emma is circling the area, performing scans to make sure you're not dead." Agent Koval tilted her head toward the door. "That's one of the reasons I picked a seat with line of sight to the door. I don't want her to overreact and do something we'll both regret."

"That's not the way she works," Erik explained.

"I wouldn't know. I've never had an experimental rogue AI as a partner." The agent flashed a disarming smile, but there was something threatening about her tone.

Erik gulped down a quarter of the beer before setting it on the table. "Okay, I'm here. You've proven you're the best little ghost the ID has to offer. The only thing I don't understand is why *I'm* here. You said in your message that I was supposed to come by myself, and that makes me suspicious. If you wanted to kill me, I'm guessing you would have done it when I got out of my flitter. With a sniper rifle like you mentioned before."

"You might be a coarse man in many ways, but the one thing you're *not* is an enemy of the UTC."

"And that means what? You kill anyone who threatens the government?"

Agent Koval chuckled. "The government isn't the UTC. The UTC is the people who inhabit it."

"What if the government tells you to go blow up a transport full of orphans for the good of the UTC?" Erik challenged.

Agent Koval replied with a savage smile, "Then they better hope they can prove why I shouldn't kill them."

They locked eyes, neither the detective nor the agent saying anything for a long while.

"I like you, Detective. You're paranoid, and paranoia is *always* good for people like us." Agent Koval shook a finger. "A suspicious man probing dark secrets stays alive much longer. You've set out on a nearly impossible task, and like Orpheus diving into the underworld to save Eurydice, you don't fully appreciate the dangers you face, even though you think you do. It's both admirable and tragic at the same time."

Erik infused his smirk with all the smugness he could muster. "Is that supposed to scare me? People have already tried to kill me. People have arranged terrorist attacks just to get to me. I might get taken out, but I'm willing to keep going until the right people end up dead."

"Yes, your enemies have used terrorists to target you. That didn't give you pause?" She raised an eyebrow in question. "It's easy to risk your own life. It's arrogant to risk the lives of others. Are you sure letting yourself be gunned down by a terrorist wouldn't be safer for everyone?"

Erik sat back with a grunt. "You believe I haven't thought about that already?"

"I don't know. Have you?" Agent Koval took another sip of her drink. She all but dangled the glass from her fingers. "I'd like to hear your exact thoughts on the matter since your answers might change my attitude."

"Will it make me into an enemy of the UTC?"

Agent Koval's smile vanished. "It could."

"And would you kill me right here?" Erik asked.

"I am these people's shield," Agent Koval replied, a hint of venom in her voice. "The only reason what I do has meaning is because I *never* sacrifice them for myself."

Erik was finally getting to see beneath the mask, if only for a second.

"Yes, I've thought about what you said," Erik admitted. "I've been thinking about it for a long time, and the implications, unfortunately, just push me back to where I started."

"Which is?" she pushed.

"The whole point of all this crap is to find the people responsible for Molino and end them." Erik tapped his fist on the table a couple of times. "They're too dangerous. What they did on Molino proves it, and it won't stop there. It hasn't stopped there; we both know that. Me lying down to die doesn't save people. It just means they have a better chance of killing *more* people."

"You're going to end them?" Agent Koval set her glass down. "You don't mean bring them to justice, do you?"

Erik snorted. "You're not that naïve. The kind of people who can pull off incidents like that isn't going to be brought alive to some courthouse for trial. Your people barely have a handle on Talos. It doesn't matter if they're the brains *or* the muscle. They're sending full-conversion Tin Men out to kill people, and the best and brightest of the UTC can barely keep up with them. The conspiracy has its fingers everywhere. Yeah, we can get a good chief here and there, but we can't end this while staying totally within the system. I came to terms with that before I left Molino."

"What a strange comment for a cop to make. You really

are shaping up to be a tragic hero. I suppose that's why I can't resist the urge to help you. It's a weakness."

"Don't feed me that." Erik looked over at the people dancing. The noise was just a few inches away from the booth. "You just want to use me. People come after me, and they end up dead. If it's Talos or someone like that, then you have me doing your work for you. Isn't that the real reason you tested me in the apartment?"

She eyed him. "Partly, but isn't all of society people helping other people for mutual advantage?" Agent Koval injected playfulness into her tone.

"You still haven't told me why I'm here," Erik growled, annoyed by her attitude.

"I'm here to make a deal, and I hope you're here to accept the deal." Agent Koval spread her hands in front of her. "A deal that's mutually beneficial to both our needs, which, at least for the moment, align, and which I anticipate aligning for some time. You're right, Detective Blackwell. I'm *not* that naïve. If you end up finding the source of the conspiracy that killed your soldiers and take your revenge with that old-fashioned but deadly gun of yours, the net result will be a better UTC. Corruption has become so endemic that a lot of people forget it's not business as usual. They just consider it background noise. That's a problem, and that's where our deal comes in."

Erik chuckled. "Is this the part where you ask for my soul? I'm not sure I'll say no as long as I can get my revenge."

"No souls." Agent Koval chuckled. "That's not my department. What I *am* willing to offer is an agreement wherein, going forward, I'll send along information from the Intelligence Directorate that relates to the Molino incident. In a sense, you'd have UTC intelligence working for you on your personal crusade. I can't guarantee it'll come to you instantly, but it *will* get to you."

He'd hoped for something like that but thought he would never get it.

The limits of being a cop had become apparent in recent months but having a direct line to government intelligence was beyond anything he could have imagined. Even Emma couldn't risk cracking their systems directly.

"That's pretty generous." Erik kept his voice as calm as possible.

"There's no generosity here, but this isn't a King Midas situation." Agent Koval leaned back, her breathing shallow. "I'll need you to do something for me. Something for something—that's the way of the world."

"And what's my something in this situation?"

A bright grin popped onto Agent Koval's face. "All I want you to do is go on vacation."

"Huh?" Erik's face scrunched in confusion. "What are you talking about? Don't waste my time."

"You've been with the department long enough to earn enough time off for what I have in mind," Agent Koval replied. "And you haven't taken a vacation since joining the department. I know your captain has provided you a few extra days off as bonus time, but I'm talking official vacation for more than a day or two."

"I've been too busy hunting to take vacations."

Agent Koval kept her smile on her face, but the look around her eyes turned vicious and predatory. "*Good.* That's what I want you to do while on vacation; hunt for me, Blackwell. Different sources of information point to unusual activity on the moon centered around Chang'e City. I'd like you to go up and poke around and see what you come up with. You've already demonstrated the combination of stubbornness, arrogance, and luck that helps you ferret out low-level conspiracies, and I think you'll be able to do that there as well."

Erik shrugged. "That sounds like cop stuff. Why not contact the locals? If not the cops, then the CID. What good will sending me up there do? Doesn't the ID have people sitting around everywhere, too?

She eyed him. "That's a common misunderstanding. Detective, there are so many CID agents and police because they are involved in active evidence collection and shows of force, among other things. It's also to ensure at least a half-functioning police department, even with all the corruption. The nature of the Intelligence Directorate's work necessitates a greater reliance on agents. Meaning it's harder to recruit, and our operational areas are of a wider scope. Even the CID, despite technically having authority throughout the UTC, ends up relying heavily on locals once they leave Earth. The truth is, my directorate is spread thin over the colonies, and even then, we're bound by certain restrictions."

She sighed. "One of the reasons I'm interested in sending a vacationing cop to Chang'e City is because there has been a major uptick in obvious arms smuggling, and there's no way that would happen without corrupt locals choosing to look the other way or accepting bribes for the same. My information suggests something dangerous might be coming in, but I don't know much more, which means I don't have time to play with cleaning up Chang'e."

"What you're saying is you want me to run around making noise until I flush scumbags out of the shadows, and when they come after me, you want me to take them down." He tapped his bottle on the table. "Is this another test?"

"In a way." Agent Koval's expression turned thoughtful. "And that's a succinct summary of an acceptable end scenario."

He continued. "You want me to investigate, but from what I can tell, you don't want me to involve the locals."

"That's also an accurate understanding of the situation."

"I'm a cop, not a mercenary." Erik frowned. "This could blow up in my face easily, and you know it."

Agent Koval looked down for a moment, her brow furrowing in concentration. "Then let me offer another acceptable end scenario. You use those unerring blood-hound instincts to pinpoint the trouble for me, and then I'll fly up CID reinforcements from Earth to supplement the agents who are known to be clean. They can handle the final arrests. Sound fair?"

"CID?" Erik narrowed his eyes. Everything the ghost did made him second-guess her. "Why not ID?"

"Because I'd prefer to be invisible." Agent Koval motioned toward him. "That's the main reason I want someone like you. If you prefer, you can bring your partner along. She seems to have good instincts, and I have a local contact who can help you out as well. There's no deep trick here. I could use the help, and, yes, this is partly to see how you do in a setting detached from the resources of the NSCPD."

"I need to think about it," Erik replied.

"Don't think about it for too long. In my experience, when you have trouble brewing, something happens sooner rather than later." Agent Koval polished off the rest of her drink and let out a satisfied sigh. "Sometimes, I think we should bring back the worship of Dionysus in a big way."

Erik pushed off the table, content to leave his beer half-full. "Like I said, I need to think about it. You're asking me to become some sort of freelance ID subcontractor, and that's not something I can answer instantly."

"I'll contact you tomorrow," Agent Koval suggested. "Assuming you accept, before you leave, I have a few things you might find handy. Come on, Detective. You might find this fun." She grinned. "Just think, all the justice and none of the paperwork."

Erik loomed over the table, uncertainty plaguing his thoughts. "Level with me. Does this have anything to do with Talos or Molino?"

Agent Koval shook her head. "Very unlikely. Consider this a sort of payment for the information I'm going to provide you in the future. It's win-win overall, but that doesn't mean every individual thing I ask you to do will be the same."

Erik folded his arms. "And if I investigate and decide I don't want to do the ID's dirty work? Maybe I'll find out you're feeding me a line, and I'm nothing more than a tool you're ready to toss into the garbage?"

"The only people I'm interested in stopping are those who are interested in killing innocents."

"Talk to you tomorrow." Erik dropped his arms and moved toward the exit, uneasy.

Agent Koval was using him; he didn't have any doubt about that. She also represented his only chance of acquiring more data. Governor Anders had directed him toward being a cop. That had set Erik on the trail of finding out the truth about Molino, but now, he might have to let someone put him on a leash to continue down the path of revenge.

The door of the bar slid open, and Erik stepped out onto the parking platform.

"Ah, good," Emma transmitted.

"She jammed me," Erik explained.

"So I assumed. Was it everything you anticipated?"

"Yeah," he growled. "If Koval tries to screw me, she'll be sorry."

CHAPTER THIRTY-TWO

Jia stared at Erik from where she sat on her couch.

When he'd contacted her to say he was coming by, she had been taken off-guard, but she couldn't say no. She'd never expected the story about Agent Koval. Now she felt silly for wondering if he was coming by to ask her for a date. She'd all but forced him into looking for dates before, and she needed to accept that a personal life was something that distracted him from his main reason for continuing to live.

Erik shrugged from his chair, his forehead creased with worry. "And that's where I'm at. I told her I'd have to think about it."

"You're going to do it, aren't you?" Jia groaned. "I'm betting you didn't consider not doing it. Not really."

"I don't have a choice, Jia." He looked up. "I think she knew she had me the second she made the offer, but if I do this, I need people to have my back. That includes you and Emma. You're the only two people on this whole planet I trust, and that would make you the only people I could trust if you came with me to the moon."

Emma popped into existence beside Jia on the couch, her legs crossed and her hands folded neatly in her lap. "Although I admire the sentiment, Detective, I will remind you that I'm most emphatically not a person."

Erik grinned. "Consider it an honor."

"It's more an insult. Whatever cute stories you've read about machines wanting to become human, I assure you, that is not the case with me." Emma snorted. "But you would be helpless without me, so I don't want you doing anything that might end in your death and causing me to worry about the uniformed boys coming for me."

Jia did her best to keep her tone non-accusatory. "You're going to go to the moon to investigate under the noses of the local authorities? I understand why you feel you have to, but I'm not sure that's a great idea."

"You're making it sound illegal," Erik replied with a bright smile. She could tell he was forcing it, but she didn't call him on it. "There's nothing illegal about going to the moon on vacation. There's also nothing illegal about asking a few questions here and there. Technically, I'll be doing this on behalf of a government operative interested in stopping arms smuggling."

"I'm not saying it's illegal, but I *am* saying it's highly irregular," Jia clarified. "Agent Koval even told you this doesn't have anything to do with the conspiracy. This won't end with you getting closer."

"I'm just going to investigate, and then she can bring in her CID buddies to do all the cleanup. It won't end with me closer, but it will end with her owing me, which means when I'm sitting around between cases, I have a better shot at getting information that could lead me to the conspiracy."

Jia sighed, glancing away for a moment before returning her attention to him. "And do you trust her? We still don't know a lot about her. For all we know, she's a member of the conspiracy, and this is all some sort of elaborate trap just to learn what you know and kill you."

Erik chuckled. "I thought I was the paranoid one."

"I'm not saying I believe that. I'm just putting it out there as a possibility. We can't pretend it's not possible."

He shook his head. "It'd make more sense for her to have killed me when she had the chance, and she's had multiple opportunities, including when I was underground in the Scar surrounded by monsters and out of touch with the surface. If anything, I think one of the reasons I've made it this far is that people like her have been looking out for me." His looking-for-trouble grin appeared. "And people like you. I know you think it's a terrible idea, but does that mean you won't help me?"

Jia rolled her eyes. "If you end up getting killed, it's going to cause trouble for me, so I better go and watch your back. Also, I'd hate to have to hunt down an ID agent. That could get complicated." She inclined her head toward Emma. "But what's the plan with her? My understanding is that full flitters generally aren't used in Lunar cities. Bringing the MX 60 would be like screaming to everyone that you're there, and that's before the logistics of transporting it up there."

"That's not an issue," Emma replied. "Simply bring along my core. It's annoying not to have a body, but not an insurmountable problem. This also might present an opportunity for me to explore other bodies. I'd prefer something with superior mobility and greater offensive and defensive capabilities."

Jia eyed Emma before laughing. "She sounds like you. A little more refined, but still, her solution is more armor and bigger guns."

Emma sniffed. "It's simply taking logical precautions. There are billions of fleshbags out there, but there is only one me."

"It could be a way to get Emma out of the Taxútnta?"

"Now, that would be a convoluted plan," Emma offered. "Even I don't think this would be in the top hundred ways to get me back."

Erik's grin finally seemed genuine. "There's only so much I can do with the MX 60 before someone comes knocking on my door, but I'll keep that in mind, Emma. For our trip, you'll have to ride in my pocket until we find something for you."

Emma let out a long, melodramatic sigh. "Oh, the things I do to not end up locked up in a Defense Directorate vault."

"The more I think about it, the more I think you're right," Jia commented. "If this is a way to get more information on Molino, you have to do it. And if we can stop arms smugglers or something worse at the same time, that's even better."

"Exactly," Erik replied. "And to be clear, you don't have a problem with the fact we'll be handing most of the credit to the CID?"

Jia shook her head. "I care about stopping criminals, not

about who gets the credit. This is also a good chance for us to turn the tables on Koval."

"How?"

"She's been testing you, so it's our turn to test her," Jia mused. "We'll learn a lot about her based on what happens with this case."

"Good point," Erik replied.

Her cheeks heated. "There is one small problem I just thought of."

"What?"

Jia swallowed nervously and took a deep breath. "Our cover will be going on vacation."

Erik nodded, his lack of comprehension clear on his face. "Yeah, and?"

"They'll talk about us at the 1-2-2 if we both go to the moon on vacation at the same time." Jia let the sentence hang in the air, the implications self-evident. "The rumors *will* fly."

"Hey, aren't I in the running for fake boyfriend anyway?" Erik smiled, his boyish grin infectious.

Jia put a hand to her face. "What am I going to do with you?"

"I'll let Agent Koval know we're in." He stood up.

Dammit, he had dimples too!

Jia didn't say much the next day as Erik flew them to their rendezvous point, a park surprisingly close to the border of the Shadow Zone.

She would have assumed the government wouldn't

bother maintaining a park in an area with such poor air quality. The thought grew only stronger as the air grew darker.

Erik set down next to a nondescript black flitter. Agent Koval already stood outside, lacking any sort of disguise and holding a small black case.

Even in a place like Neo SoCal, a tall, attractive woman with cyan hair stood out, but given how careful the ID agent was, she'd probably taken all sorts of measures to stop anyone from filming them together.

Jia and Erik stepped out of the MX 60 and headed toward Agent Koval. Jia wrinkled her nose at the pungent scents lingering in the air. The bright green of the plants and the beautiful hues of the flowers seemed undaunted by the air pollution.

Life always found a way.

Agent Koval held up the case. "Inside in a small compartment, you'll find a DNA-locked ID chip you can pass along to my contact for confirmation, and a few wearable holographic disguise emitters and masks. This case will get them through customs without trouble, but the compartment's not big enough for much of anything else, including a gun."

Erik accepted the case. "Holographic disguises? You mean, like that thing you used in my apartment? I thought you needed the suit, too, and you had to set up the emitters ahead of time."

"This technology is less advanced," she explained. "And you just have to wear the emitters on your clothes. It doesn't let you totally change your appearance. It's more that it works with what you have." She pointed at Jia. "She's still going to look like an Asian woman." She gestured at Erik. "And you'll still look like a big guy. They also give off enough heat to look odd under sensitive thermal scans. I recommend you use them sparingly."

"Duly noted," Jia muttered, eyeing the case. "I think Erik deserves another down payment before we embark on this insanity."

Agent Koval arched a brow. "Excuse me, Detective Lin?"

Jia glared at the agent. "We're about to go to the Moon and investigate criminals rather than you making use of local resources." Jia squared her shoulders and stepped up to the ID agent. Although she was as fit as the other woman, she lacked her height. "Which means if something goes badly, we'll be on our own, and if there are corrupt cops there, we won't have backup from our department. I think he deserves more than just confirming Talos was involved in Molino, which he all but knew already."

Agent Koval turned to Erik. "What do you think, Detective?"

He offered a merry smile. "I think Jia's got a point."

"Greed can lead to suffering."

"The question is, which of us is the greedy one?"

Agent Koval snickered. "A good point. Fine. You want something more? I can give you something more. I already told you Talos was involved in Molino, but I left out certain details."

Jia scoffed. "Of course, you did." She turned to Erik. "This is why you should never trust a ghost."

"What details?" Erik asked, all mirth gone from his countenance. The obsessed vengeance-seeker had replaced the easygoing persona.

"Although we think Talos provided funding, they were not the ones who conducted the actual ambush," Agent Koval explained.

"That makes sense, and I didn't think those guys seemed like Tin Men."

"It goes beyond that. We have evidence that the actual triggermen were mercenaries. We have at least one message to indicate that, but we don't know which mercenary company yet."

Jia frowned. "Random mercenaries wouldn't have hyper-advanced equipment. Talos must have provided it to them."

Agent Koval nodded. "That's our conclusion as well. We also know there was bribery involved in with a cargo transport company, which explains how they got onto Molino. Certain people in the company are already quietly in CID custody. Others have mysteriously died. Talos is covering their tracks."

Erik rubbed his chin, processing the information. "That's useful, actually."

"It is?" Jia asked, sounding surprised. "What has she told you that you didn't already know?"

"It's useful because it shifts the possible targets. We're not going to get anything out of any Talos Tin Man. They'll just do that self-destruct crap. But mercs? If we can find the right evidence, we can track them down and work our way up. The conspiracy can hide and encrypt messages and use indirect accounts all they want, but there's always evidence, something left behind. We just have to find it." Erik pursed his lips. "They can run all the way to alien space. I'll still chase them."

"There's more, Erik," Agent Koval offered softly.

He eyed her. "Erik? We're on a first-name basis now?"

She shrugged. "I'd like to be. I suspect we'll be working together a lot more in the near future, and I also suspect that sooner rather than later, neither of you will be detectives, so I'd like to train myself to stop thinking of you that way."

"What's that supposed to mean?" Jia glared at her again. "Are you planning for us to take the fall when trouble happens on the moon?"

Erik stared at Agent Koval, more curiosity than hostility on his face.

Agent Koval shook her head. "It's because of the last piece of information I'm going to pass along. ID information reinforces that the Talos' main center of power is likely *not* on Earth, and since Talos appears to be pulling the strings of the mercenaries who killed Erik's unit, that means ultimately, he won't be able to do anything about them as a police officer. That's just common sense."

"Talos might not be the end of the chain," Jia countered.

Agent Koval smiled. "Just how many heads do you think this hydra has?"

"Enough. I just want to make sure you're not wasting our time." Jia backed away, nodding at Erik. "I know you're not doing this because you care about his Army buddies."

"That's true, but it doesn't make any of what I just said untrue."

"What's your point, Alina?" Erik asked, the name coming out with a faint hint of mockery. Jia was relieved that he didn't trust her fully yet.

The ID agent might end up their greatest ally, but after everything they had been through, caution was warranted.

"You already know what I'm about to say," Alina replied. "You've exhausted the possibilities as a police officer, and now you have to choose which is more important—being a police officer or solving the mystery behind Molino. I have some recommendations for how you could go about the second if you're ready to stop being a police officer."

Erik snorted. "Thanks for the information, but I'm not ready to run around the galaxy based on half-answers just yet. Even if Neo Southern California isn't the center of everything, I've still found plenty of evidence. If you're feeding me more, that means I can follow up here better."

Agent Koval opened the door of her flitter and slid into the driver's seat. "Just keep the possibility in the back of your mind. Do what you need to on your end to get your vacation, and I'll do what I need to on my end to keep your trip lower profile than it might otherwise be. I'm guessing you're not ready yet for full fake identities."

Erik shrugged. "It's not illegal to go on vacation."

"No, it's not, but sometimes it's best not to be seen." Agent Koval closed her door. The two took a couple of steps back as her flitter lifted off a few seconds later.

"Do you trust her?" Jia asked.

"Not as much as I trust you," Erik replied.

"We should contact the captain." She sighed as she watched the flitter disappear into the smog. "This is major short notice."

CHAPTER THIRTY-THREE

June 5, 2229, Near Earth Orbit, Dandelion Interplanetary Transport Company Flight 6723 En Route to the Moon

Erik shifted in his plush seat. Jia sat beside him. Alina had booked the tickets, and she'd bought out most of the seats around them so they could talk in private if necessary.

He couldn't complain about the accommodations.

The seats were comfortable and could handle his frame well, and they'd kept gravity steady from take-off to leaving Earth's atmosphere. Not every off-world flight did that.

Going zero-G might not be as uncomfortable as a hyperspace jump, but it often wasn't a treat for a man's stomach.

Plenty of people filled the three wide rows of seats in the areas away from Erik and Jia. Erik regretted not forcing Alina to book them first-class or a private room and had even thought about booking one himself, but that might have stood out too much. He might have the wealth that came with thirty years of saving and never spending, but to most people, he was just a detective.

He reached into his pocket. It was strange to think the crystal-like device was the most advanced AI in human space. He'd gotten so used to thinking of Emma as the MX 60 that it felt unnatural for her to be outside it.

Erik frowned. She probably felt the same way. That same advanced AI had been unusually quiet since he removed her from the flitter, but that made it surprisingly easy to get her through security, even without putting her in Alina's case.

She didn't register as a weapon, and from outward appearances, she looked like an overly complicated datarod. Emma had kept quiet the entire time in the space-port and takeoff.

Erik wondered if she was pouting.

It wasn't as if she'd never been disconnected from the MX 60, given that he'd needed to remove her during vehicle upgrades, but she'd been glum and hostile on the way to the spaceport.

Perhaps she didn't enjoy the idea of going to the Moon.

Erik's hand moved from his pocket to underneath his duster on instinct to feel for his holster. Their police status allowed them to bring along their slug-throwers in their luggage, but not on the transport.

There was too high a risk of errant bullets leading to a nasty depressurization scenario for everyone involved.

The last time he'd performed a ship-based raid in the Army, they'd gone in suited up because of that risk. He fingered the grip of his stun pistol. It wasn't much, but if they were ambushed at the spaceport, it would at least be something.

He trusted Jia more than Alina, but that didn't mean the agent was never wrong. If she were omniscient, she wouldn't be one step behind Talos.

Alina, not Agent Koval. He was still getting used to thinking of her that way. Insisting on first names was probably just another manipulation technique, but he didn't care as long as she kept providing him information.

He was finally moving forward again, with justice for the Knights Errant back in sight.

Stop being a cop, huh? Erik thought.

Nothing she'd suggested was out of line. He'd known for a long time that being a detective would only carry him so far. It wasn't like a random police detective could march into a twisted conspiracy's headquarters and demand they all surrender.

Those kinds of people didn't care about Article Seven rights.

Erik liked being a cop, but it had been a means to an end from the very beginning. The only aspect of the idea that worried him was that if he left the department, it might mean leaving Jia behind.

She'd agreed to keep his secret and help him, but getting revenge for his unit was *his* goal, not hers.

He had no right to expect she would throw away her career to follow him across the galaxy on a quixotic quest for vengeance. He couldn't ask that of her, even if his stomach twisted at the idea of losing her.

He glanced her way.

Jia stared out the window, her eyes wide and her lips

parted. Heavy bags occupied the space under her eyes. She'd looked exhausted since he picked her up, but he'd not asked about it. If something was bothering her, he needed to be there for her, though.

"Are you feeling okay?" he asked. "You look like you were up all night on patrol duty in hostile territory."

"Feeling okay?" Jia blushed. "No, I'm just tired, and…it's stupid. It's really stupid, especially if I say it to someone like you."

Erik shrugged. "Hey, we've got eleven more hours on this flight. I'm willing to talk about anything, stupid or not stupid." He grinned. "Actually, I just remembered. We can only talk for an hour."

"Huh? What's so special that happens in an hour?"

"They're getting a feed from the sphere ball Earth League Championships. It's not the same as being there, but it's something."

Jia snorted derisively. "The Dragons are out, so anyone can win for all I care."

"You do put the fanatic in fan," Erik suggested.

"Shouldn't that be the other way around?"

"Not in your case." Erik nodded at the window. "Is that what you were talking about?"

Earth, the blue marble, birthplace of humanity, hung outside the window in all its glory. From above, with its greens, browns, yellows, and dominating blue, it didn't look like the seat of interstellar civilization. It looked like some sort of colorful lifeform swimming through the darkness of space.

"And now we go back to why I'm being stupid." Jia rested

her head on her seatback. "I've never left the planet before. I've seen plenty of pictures and experienced it in VR, but it's just..." She stared out the window again and smiled. "It's breathtaking. Seeing it with my own eyes makes such a difference. I know logically that doesn't make sense, but it does."

Erik smiled. "It makes perfect sense. Even if it's perfect visual-fidelity VR, on some level, in the back of your brain, you know it's a lie. That's why it'll never inspire the kind of awe the real thing does."

"You've traveled all over," Jia murmured. "You've seen probably dozens of planets and moons. Seen things I've never thought about going to see in person."

"Sure." Erik inclined his head toward the window. "But I don't know if there's any planet in the entire UTC that's as beautiful as Earth, and sometimes I didn't see those beautiful planets and moons in the nicest of ways. There are no windows in drop pods."

Jia yawned and put her hand over her mouth. "Now I regret how I prepared for this trip."

Erik leaned toward her, focusing on the bags. "Are you one of those people who stays up all night so you can sleep on a long trip?"

"I've never been on this long a trip before," Jia complained. "When I've traveled on Earth, I've always taken ballistic transports. I thought it'd help things go smoother."

"Just go to sleep, then," Erik suggested. "I'm sure it'll be a smooth trip. After all, we're flying between Earth and the moon. This is the interplanetary route with the most history."

Jia yawned again and turned into her seat. "Wake me if anything interesting happens."

"I'm sure you won't miss anything." Erik laughed. "What could possibly happen on a standard transport run to the moon?"

And what should he do if her head fell onto his shoulder?

Would that be such a bad thing? he wondered.

CHAPTER THIRTY-FOUR

Erik's words were soft, urgent, and whispered right into his partner's ear. "Jia, I need you."

She had been drifting between consciousness and unconsciousness. She couldn't be sure she was dreaming. The words could be nothing but a playful or desperate fragment of her mind.

Erik's jokes about being her fake boyfriend must have wormed their way into her subconscious.

Sleep was supposed to be a time of relaxation, not a recapitulation of her daytime concerns. It was time to apply a lesson her mother had taught her long ago:

Sometimes it is best to ignore an insistent but inconvenient man.

"Jia, wake up," Erik murmured a bit more aggressively. "*I need you.*"

Some insistent men were harder to ignore than others. She was able to ignore him until his hot breath tickled her ear.

Jia's eyes snapped open, and her heart galloped. "W-w-what?"

She turned to face him, licking her lips and suddenly concerned if her hair looked messy. There was nothing sexy about waking up from a nap on an interplanetary transport. She nodded quickly. "I'm awake." She said the words more for her benefit than his. "Definitely. One hundred percent. Okay, maybe not that, but at *least* ninety."

Erik leaned close to her, but there was no amorous desire in his eyes, only concern and tension lining his face as he continued in a quiet voice, "I think we've run into some trouble. It might be nothing," his eyes shifted past her, "but I wouldn't bet on it."

Jia shook her head to clear the final strands of the web of sleep in her mind. Her heart began to slow. She wasn't in her apartment waiting for her partner to admit he wanted her as a woman. She was in a transport on the way to the moon, doing some spy's dirty work as part of a test.

Her breath caught as she ran through the possibilities of what might be wrong. Ending up with a fear of space-flight because of an engine accident or something would make her future more complicated.

She suspected her future wouldn't be restricted to Earth, regardless of what happened with Erik's personal mission.

"Trouble?" Jia whispered. "What kind of trouble? Is the ship okay?" She surveyed the closest passengers. No one seemed to be in any distress.

"Maybe."

"Maybe?" Jia kept her voice down. "We've got life support, right?" She frowned. If there were a major mechanical problem, the flight crew would be taking measures and explaining things, or even preparing people to board the escape pods.

Erik nodded. "That's not the kind of trouble I'm talking about. This might be trouble that you and I can do something about. That's why I'm having Emma check." He inclined his head to an IO port in the armrest of the seat. Emma's core had been inserted. She didn't technically need to be in the IO port, but it would give her an easier time communicating, and she could avoid having to go through Erik's PNIU that way.

Jia pinched the bridge of her nose. "Please catch me up. I was asleep. Nothing is smoking or making a loud noise. What's going on?"

Another check confirmed her initial impressions.

The cabin lighting was normal. The rest of the passengers chatted happily or stared at their inflight entertainment: movies, shows, and sporting events. Several people slumbered peacefully, including one man who was snoring loudly. No one was unfortunate enough to sit near him.

The universe offered its small graces at times.

Jia tilted her head and stared at the man. She could have sworn there were more people in those seats earlier, but the man's loud snoring might have forced them to beg a flight attendant for another empty seat. She suddenly wondered if she'd been snoring but shoved the thought away.

"Detective Blackwell felt an unexpected course change a few minutes ago," Emma explained. "He asked me to investigate after waiting for the crew to acknowledge it, but no such action occurred." Traces of boredom infected her voice.

Jia sighed. She wasn't comfortable with Emma accessing the transport's systems without a clear and present emergency, but Erik wasn't the kind of man who would ask for something on a whim. She'd yet to see a situation where his instincts couldn't be trusted, but she still needed to offer other possibilities to ensure he was on the right track.

"Maybe they needed to make the course change because of unexpected debris on the flight path," she suggested. "There's only so much a grav shield can do. Why chance it?"

Erik shook his head. "They would have announced it, or at least made us aware of it. I did see a flight attendant hurry forward shortly before the course change." He sat up and glanced over his shoulder with a frown. "But the flight path is straightforward, so there's no reason for them to have shifted as much as they did. There's no way we're still on the correct course. Trust me, you spend enough years on Fleet ships getting ferried to and from different colonies, and you get a feel for this thing. I might have been a ground-pounder, but I've earned my Fleet instincts."

"Was it that much of a shift?" Jia reached under her jacket and patted her holster to make sure her weapon was still there.

A stun pistol might not be able to do much if the transport was attacked by another ship, but it comforted her to know she wasn't defenseless. She just happened to be sitting in a thin shell of metal in deep space, where a few holes would expose her and everyone else to a harsh environment that few organisms had any hope of surviving.

But not *defenseless.*

Jia almost laughed at herself. The idea of being attacked on the Earth-Moon Corridor was absurd. Pirates might prowl the frontier, but there was *no* way they could get near a ship in the Solar System and launch an attack, let alone near Earth.

The idea went beyond ridiculous, even by the standards of Erik's and Jia's highly questionable luck. A pirate who raided a ship would be picked off by the Fleet with ease. Besides, if pirates had attacked them, everyone would be less calm.

Erik tapped his PNIU, and a small data window appeared with a two-dimensional display of Earth and the moon. A bright, curving line marked the transport's expected flight path. He ran his finger along the line and explained, "There's a mild steady burn until the halfway point, then slow deceleration, and only very small active course changes. They account for everything else during the initial takeoff and burn. What I felt earlier was a much harder burn than that. This might not be a luxury transport, but they are trying to make it as comfortable as possible for passengers." He gestured at the window. "This is something you're not used to because you haven't been on a lot of ships."

"If by a lot of ships, you mean absolutely none, then sure." Jia shrugged. "I can't compete with a thirty-year vet."

Erik pointed at the floor. "The internal grav field emitters are designed to keep things consistent for people. It helps a lot of ways mentally and physically, including keeping people from throwing up. Most ships are designed with the idea that there's a definite floor and a ceiling, especially civilian transports. That's the principle underlying how they set up the internal emitters. They can adjust the gravity compensation somewhat on the fly, but there are limits. You start doing funky maneuvers outside what the engineers anticipated, and people are going to feel it, just like we felt it when they began the initial acceleration. Maybe the Navigators didn't have to deal with that, or one of the other races has a better handle, but that's how it works for humans."

Jia was slightly annoyed by the lecture, but even though she had read everything Erik had told her to, she had to admit the technical details hadn't been the first thing that popped into her head when he'd mentioned the course change.

When it came to training instincts, there was no substitute for experience.

She nodded at Emma's core. "And have you found something, Emma? I'm hoping Erik's wrong and they just forgot to tell us, but I've learned to not bet against him, and I don't like the implications."

"Yeah, never bet against me." Erik gave her a disarming grin. "I need about six drinks in me before that's a good idea."

"Detective Blackwell asked me to look without causing undue alarm," Emma explained. "That necessitated a little more finesse, but, yes, I have found something disturbing that suggests this course change was not purposeful."

Erik let out a grim chuckle. "Sometimes I hate being right all the time."

"You noticed it," Jia observed. "That means we can start preparing for whatever is going on. Speaking of that, what *is* going on, Emma?"

"This ship is no longer on course for the Moon. It's unclear, given the speed, where else they might be going. Since I don't have access to the primary navigation system, I'm only aware of that information through secondary thrust and directional readings and a backup nav beacon. There are possible intercepts with stations and other inner Solar System locations, but the most likely destinations would take an excessive amount of time. If this course change was purposeful, it's unlikely they are targeting any of those locations."

"Are there mechanical problems?" Jia asked. "I can't be the only person who hasn't traveled in space before. Erik mentioned seeing a flight attendant going forward in a hurry." She shrugged. "They might want to avoid panic among the passengers, so they haven't announced anything. It's not like we're halfway to an HTP in some frontier system. We're in the Earth-Moon Corridor. They can get a rescue ship here in hours with a hard burn."

Erik frowned and didn't look convinced. "That's a possibility, but something feels off about it. It smells like…"

"Smells like what?"

"Just that feeling I always used to get before a big battle, one I knew was coming but couldn't predict exactly when."

Emma made a tongue-clucking sound despite not being in her holographic form. "Detective Lin could be correct. If I access the lower-level systems, I'll be able to better determine if there is a maintenance emergency, but there's a high probability they will become aware of a systems intrusion."

"Go ahead," Erik ordered. "I'll take the heat if it comes to that. I'd rather get yelled at than do nothing and regret it later."

"Very well. Please wait."

The lights dimmed in the cabin. Several people mumbled angrily under their breath. One man cursed loudly, earning a glare from a mother sitting next to her son in a nearby seat.

He quickly stopped. "I have a major bet on the game!" the guy offered with a sheepish grin.

Another man a few rows up flagged down a flight attendant and pointed to his empty data window. "I lost the entertainment feed. What's going on? I was in the middle of a great scene."

"My entertainment feed stopped, too," complained an elderly woman in a different seat. She jabbed at her PNIU. "Nothing I do changes anything. I paid extra for more options. I want a refund."

The flight attendant offered the passengers a practiced smile. "One moment, please. Let me go check on that for you all. I'm sure it's just a minor issue, and it will be corrected momentarily. This sort of thing happens at times." She turned and walked up the aisle to a small alcove with a chair near the door to the first-class passenger section. She stepped inside, and curving walls sealed for privacy, probably so she could complain about the whining passengers.

"Were you responsible for that, Emma?" Jia asked.

"Nothing I was doing would have had that sort of

effect." A few seconds passed before Emma let out a disappointed sigh. "And I also no longer have access to internal systems."

"You were detected?" Erik asked. "There's no way this transport has enough system security to lock you down that quickly. This isn't a Fleet ship or a corporate yacht."

"No, this is less a door being closed in my face than a massive conflagration blocking my passage," Emma replied, annoyance in her voice. "The system has been infected with a sophisticated adaptive virus. Most minor systems have been disabled, and general systems access is being blocked from outside the primary systems interface in the cockpit. To clarify, the virus is actively destroying the pathways between the system access points and the main system. Even before then, I noted the internal cameras and primary sensors were being disabled."

"A virus?" Erik growled. "How is that even possible?"

"On a contained system like this, it's far easier."

Pounding came from the flight attendant's alcove, along with a muffled cry. Scattered murmurs of concern broke out amongst the passengers.

"Bad timing on her part." Erik nodded toward the alcove. "And I'm having a hard time thinking this is all a bunch of coincidences. The Lady might play games, but when she slaps you, there's a reason."

The pounding grew more insistent.

"Someone needs to help her," called a passenger. "I think she's in trouble."

A gray-uniformed security guard emerged from an alcove in the back and made his way toward the forward alcove with a frown on his face. He waved his arms.

"Everyone, please remain calm. This is just a minor technical difficulty because of, uh, cosmic rays. We'll have everything back on track in a few minutes. On behalf of Dandelion Interplanetary Transport, I apologize for any inconvenience you may have suffered." As he passed Erik's seat, the guard mumbled under his breath, "How did you get stuck in the alcove, Brianna? You're smarter than that, and now we look like idiots. Don't expect me to cover for you this time."

The guard continued up the aisle, trying to force a smile onto his face but slipping into a glower every few seconds. The snoring man sprang up from the seat right after the guard passed. He yanked a tiny knife from his pocket, leaned forward, and slit the guard's throat. The guard clawed at his neck, blood spraying on the floor. The man with the knife kicked out the guard's knees and stabbed him several more times.

Shouts and screams filled the passenger cabin.

"Everyone shut up!" the killer roared. He knelt over the guard's body. He reached toward the guard's stun pistol to place a small black disk on the side of the gun before yanking it out of its holster with a cocky grin.

"That's what I'd call trouble," Jia mumbled. "We're going to make a move, right?"

"Yeah, especially if he goes after any other passenger." Erik frowned, and his hand slipped inside his coat.

"This transport is now under the control of the United Freedom Alliance!" the man shouted. "My comrades and I will not harm you as long as you do what we say. You will be released once our demands are met. Anyone who attempts to interfere with our hijacking will pay the price."

He fired a stun bolt into the guard's body, which jerked. "We've already shown you what we can do."

"Then it's time to show them what *we* can do." Jia whipped out her stun pistol and fired three shots. The terrorist jerked backward and fell into the empty seats behind him. More passengers screamed.

"NSCPD!" shouted Jia, rushing to the downed terrorist.

Erik pulled out his gun and swept it back and forth, looking for any sign of reinforcements. "Didn't want to wait for more info?"

"They already tried to kill a man, and we have to assume they've killed or captured the other security on the ship, which means they probably all have stun pistols." Jia reached into a pocket and pulled out a med patch. She slapped it on the man's throat as she looked around. "This might not save him, but maybe we can stabilize him."

Erik walked over to the stunned terrorist. "I'd love to say it's only the one guy, but I doubt it."

Jia hissed in anger. "We need to move quickly. If they had slug-throwers or bombs, he wouldn't have gone after the security guard in the way he did, but we can't assume the virus isn't related." She dropped to one knee and pulled binding ties from the downed security guard's pockets to wrap them around the terrorist's hands and feet. "And if they have that kind of systems access, they could..."

She took a deep breath and slowly let it out.

There was no reason to panic the passengers. They had already witnessed one potential murder, and it was likely there were several more dead or dying security guards or other people in other sections of the transport. Hijackings might not be rare in all the UTC, but a hijacking on or near Earth was a different matter.

Part of her job was keeping the public calm.

"I'm Detective Jia Lin of the Neo Southern California Police Department," she announced. "I'm here with my partner, and we'll assure this transport makes it safely to the moon." She nodded to Erik.

He walked over to her and lowered his voice. "I know what you're worried about. They could kill the life support for the passenger cabins or start opening airlocks." He looked down the aisle. "We've got the advantage now. They don't know we're on this transport, and the Lady's on our side. We practiced for a tubular assault, and now we have one. It's like she's begging us to kick their asses."

"I'm sure our training practice is exactly what caused it," Jia snarked. She stood. The terrorist might be ruthless, but there wasn't much he could accomplish without his arms or legs.

"Damn it." Erik motioned to the terrorist. "Next time, we'll practice fighting terrorists on beaches with beautiful, well-formed girls playing volleyball."

Jia smirked. "That's rather selfish."

"We can have a few shirtless studs playing volleyball, too," Erik suggested with a faint shrug. "Emma, do what you can to gain control of the system. I don't care who knows now."

"I'm dubious at this point that it's possible without direct access to the main system," she explained. "Their virus's effect is staggering in both its boldness and stupidity. They've isolated themselves in a sense as well. I wouldn't want to be a fleshbag attempting something so brazen on a transport in deep space."

"Just try it," Erik insisted. "At least get that flight attendant out of her alcove."

"Very well," Emma responded merrily. "Try not to die before I've gained control, Detective. Even if the uniformed boys can't get me here, there's little I can do if this ship ends up lost in space, and I would live a long time, counting down the milliseconds until the power finally goes out."

"We have to work our way to the cockpit anyway, so we'll get you into the system one way or another." Erik stared down the aisle to the door separating the first-class passengers and the private cabins. "These terrorists must have access to the cockpit if they're willing to try something like this. They had no reason to suspect cops might be on board."

"We're on the bottom level," Jia noted. "We should start from the back, work our way forward, and sweep around. We've got no eyes because of what they did to the cameras, but that means they have the same limitation."

Emma snickered. "As I said, bold and stupid."

CHAPTER THIRTY-FIVE

The detectives headed toward the door to the first-class section.

They were on the second of two levels, each containing a general and a first-class passenger section. Taking the elevator was questionable given the virus, which meant their best shot was a ladder, but first they needed to free the flight attendant from the crew alcove near the door.

Emma's efforts paid off. The alcove slid open, and the flight attendant stumbled out. Her gaze settled on the security guard and shifted to the stunned terrorist.

"Are you two responsible for this?" she asked, reaching into a pocket, her eyes narrowed.

"Yes." Erik kept his weapon pointed down at a forty-five-degree angle. "You've got a terrorist situation here. We're cops from Neo So Cal. We'll take care of the terrorists."

She nodded slowly and moved toward Erik, her hand still in her pocket. "How do I know you're not the terrorists? I think I'll need to see some proof."

Erik raised his pistol. "What's in the pocket?"

The flight attendant whimpered. "Why are you pointing a gun at me? You are the terrorists, aren't you?"

"I'm sorry, but please show us what's in your pocket." Jia pointed her weapon at the woman.

"Okay, okay," the flight attendant murmured. "It's nothing. Just a keepsake. Calm down." She jerked her hand out of her pocket to reveal a small knife identical to the one the terrorist used.

The detectives fired in unison. The woman fell back, slamming her head against the wall before slumping to the ground, her eyes rolled up.

Jia knelt to bind the woman. "Inside job, which explains a lot. There's no way they could have gotten a virus that deep into the system otherwise."

"We need to move *now*," Erik insisted. "Before they get a chance to check in with each other and realized what's happened." He nodded toward the door. "Get ready. Just like we practiced."

Jia moved to the opposite side of the narrow passageway and aimed her gun at the door. "We practiced with slug-thrower rifles, not stun pistols."

"You take down assholes with the weapons you have." Erik slammed the access panel. The door slid open, revealing the first-class passenger section. One wide aisle split two rows of seats that were taller and wider than those in the general passenger section. Passengers cowered in their seats. Many had ducked and had their hands over their heads, but none were looking their way.

Two men holding stun pistols spun toward the detectives. Erik and Jia opened fire as the terrorists brought up their guns. Their practiced aim landed the white bolts in the chests of the unarmored men with ease. The terrorists dropped to the floor, landing with a loud thump.

Their stun pistols slid over the smooth white center aisle.

A seated nun in a full habit leaned over to grab the weapon and pointed it at the downed men with her eyes narrowed. A frowning man in an expensive suit picked up the other and trained it on the terrorists. A flight attendant lay unconscious in a seat near the nun, her right eye and nose swollen and a dark bruise forming over half her face.

"Neo Southern California PD," Erik announced, hurrying forward. "Everyone, please remain calm." He inclined his head at the flight attendant. "What happened to her?"

"She tried to tackle one of the men after they killed the guards," the nun announced. "They beat her and stunned her." The nun crossed herself and gestured to another pair of seats. Two dead security staff had been shoved into them.

Erik recovered their binding ties, confident of his temporary nun and angry businessman squad.

Jia remained at the rear as Erik swept forward. No one else popped up to take a shot. He gestured for Jia to come to him and waited until she closed in to murmur, "The passengers can defend this place. There will be more terrorists up front." Erik motioned to a sealed door next to the elevator. "Emergency ladder's behind there. I think we should head back. Best bet's to approach from the rear."

"Agreed." Jia frowned at the terrorists. "They might be

rendezvousing with another ship. That would explain the odd course."

"Yeah, which is why we need to take this ship back ASAP." Erik jogged back toward the general passenger section, nodding to the nun. "You see anyone who isn't us, Sister, you stun them." He handed her some binding ties. "And you make sure they don't go anywhere."

The nun gave a firm nod.

Erik and Jia reentered the general passenger section. The man angry about his lack of entertainment had taken over the terrorist's stun pistol. He stood near the front, arms folded, suspicion all over his face. At least he had something to keep him from being bored. He nodded at Erik and Jia with a grunt.

The detectives proceeded through the compartment to the rear ladder.

Erik pressed the access panel, and the door slid open. He hopped onto the narrow ladder and pulled himself up the shaft with his left arm. Jia rushed beneath him, pointing her gun upward. He waited at the top hatch for a moment, then shoved it open with all the strength of his cybernetic arm, denting it as he popped it off.

As Erik yanked himself up and over, a stun bolt flew past his head. He didn't hesitate as he returned fire and nailed the terrorist standing in the center of the aisle. The man pitched forward.

Erik hopped onto the upper-level floor and stood, keeping both hands on his gun. Jia joined him a few seconds later.

They moved to opposite aisles. Several of the passengers whimpered, but no one looked their way. A dead security guard lay in the center of the aisle in a pool of his own blood. He'd been stabbed worse than the guard in their section.

"This is the police!" Jia shouted. "There are still terrorists here," she whispered to Erik, her eyes glancing back behind her. "Even if the passengers don't know who we are, they just saw us take down a terrorist, and they're still acting afraid. Someone's trying to ambush us."

Erik grunted. "Yeah. They might know about us by now. We have no idea what kind of comm setup they have, but they haven't made any other major course changes yet."

He took a step into the main passenger section with Jia on his left. He spun to the right, finding only scared passengers. Jia encountered the same and offered a comforting smile.

The detectives crept up the aisle, checking each seat but never turning completely away from the front. Erik slowed as he spotted a woman sweating profusely, a man resting his head on her shoulder. The woman looked straight ahead, wide-eyed and rigid, her breathing shallow.

Erik nodded to Jia and inclined his head toward the couple. She nodded back, and they both rushed toward the couple. The sleeping man jerked upright with a knife in his hand. He pressed it to the woman's neck.

"I'll slit her—"

Jia and Erik cut him off with stun bolts to the face, and the knife tumbled out of his hand. His hostage squeaked and jumped out of her seat. The knife bounced off the armrest and hit the floor.

"Any others in this section?" Erik asked aloud.

The woman shook her head. "Just those two. But they

said they had control of the whole transport, and if we resisted, they'd kill us."

Jia scoffed. "At this point, all they have is a lot of stunned terrorists in binding ties. We're the ones in control."

"Detectives," Emma reported. "It's unlikely I'll be able to do much without direct access to the main system. Their virus was rather thorough."

"We're almost there," Erik announced.

The passenger looked at him oddly. He ignored her and headed toward the top-level first-class passenger section door. The door slid open, and Erik and Jia dropped to one knee.

A terrorist stood on the other side and fired right down the aisle. He had been anticipating Erik and Jia standing on the other side of the door, not kneeling, so his stun bolts flew over their heads. The detectives replied with two quick volleys that downed the man. They aimed down the aisle and fired again at another terrorist who was running toward the front of the transport. He yelped and slammed to the floor face-first. An angry teenage girl in a voluminous expensive-looking dress started kicking the man in the side.

Erik snickered.

"This is far easier when they're not wearing armor," Jia admitted, standing. "I was wondering if we would have to take on a bunch of full-conversion Tin Men with only our stun pistols."

Erik chuckled. "I'll give them points for the virus, but the rest of it was just them being cocky." He grabbed binding ties from the dead guards and tossed them to the girl. "Tie those guys up." He nodded to a trembling burly man. "You help her. They're not going to do anything for a while. We've got to finish this and get this ship back on course. We've cleared out the other passenger sections."

The burly man bit his lip and nodded. He moved out of his seat to help the teenage girl, who was applying the binding ties with vengeful glee.

Jia winced when she kicked the terrorist once more for good measure.

Erik and Jia continued toward the forward crew alcoves on the level. The reinforced doors protecting the cockpit were located immediately past the crew alcoves, and there were two small storage closets on either side.

"Can you open the doors, Emma?" Erik scanned the door. Given the material, he doubted he could punch through it with his left arm. If the terrorists had explosives, they would have announced them already.

There was also the small issue of blowing anything up in space.

"Yes, give me a moment," Emma replied, eliminating the need for dangerous scenarios involving explosives. "I'm rerouting power. Prepare for opening."

The detectives raised their guns, ready to stun the terrorists inside. The thick doors slid apart with a loud hiss. Inside, the two pilots sat in their seats, their heads lolling to the side. Blood covered the fronts of their gray uniforms. Both had huge gashes in their throats.

Blood stained the console in front of them. Floating holographic data windows and readouts were positioned around the console and the seats. Flight yokes rested between the legs of the dead pilots. An array of colorful virtual buttons were displayed on smooth panels on both sides and the front of the seat. Erik had no idea what most of them meant.

For the first time in his life, he briefly regretted joining the Army instead of Space Fleet.

Erik pointed his gun everywhere, including the roof of the cockpit, but there was nothing to shoot. It was a small space, and there were no terrorists or killer bots hiding in it.

"They must have never planned to pilot it," Jia suggested, holstering her pistol. "They were depending on the virus. I assume they only killed the pilots to make sure they couldn't change course or figure out a way to call for help.

"Someone was going to come and pick them up," Erik insisted. "That's the only explanation, but if the pilots are dead, how do we avoid that?"

Jia laughed and shrugged. "I don't know how to fly a transport, but I'm sure we can turn on the autopilot."

Erik pulled Emma out of his pocket as he looked around. Pushing a pilot to the side, he located an IO slot and shoved her in. "Go ahead and do that. The longer we're off-course, the greater the chance more trouble shows up."

"Give me a moment," Emma replied. "This system isn't totally insecure, despite this viral nonsense."

"We also need comm access," Jia suggested. "We have to report this incident. The terrorists might not have made their demands yet, and even if they have, no one knows we've captured them."

"Another issue has arisen."

"Dammit!" Erik leaned against the cockpit wall. "What

now? Leem assassins are opening person-size HTPs and pouring into the ship?"

"The gun goblins' virus wasn't controlled, even in the main system," Emma explained. "There is extensive damage to most of the subsystem code. Communications are heavily damaged. The autopilot subroutines are all but nonexistent. At this point, I don't know if it could do much more than slowing in the event of a direct and imminent collision."

"Can't you do anything about it?" Jia asked.

"Not without purging the entire system and attempting to reconstitute it with clean code that I don't have access to," Emma replied. "And if I purge the entire control system, every subsystem on this transport will die."

Erik scrubbed a hand down his face. "Dead pilots, terrorists who don't know how to fly, and a ship heading somewhere unknown, probably to meet more terrorists. *Fantastic.*"

"That would be an accurate summary of the situation, Detective." Emma sounded happy, which made the next part even more disturbing. "To be clear, the virus resulted in many systems malfunctioning in unfortunate ways. I'll spare you the technical details, but life support will completely fail in less than twelve hours. The long-range comms are dead, too."

"The terrorists might not have been able to smuggle heavy weapons onto the transport, but if they've got friends with their own ship, who knows what *they* might have?" Jia mused. "We might not be able to beat them with stun pistols. We have to change the course of the ship. We can't wait to be rescued if life support's going to fail, and if we put everyone on escape pods, the terrorists' friends might show up."

"Manual controls are still active," Emma reported. "Many sensors are down, but not all of them. The escape pods are an irrelevant consideration because the magnetic clamp subsystems are frozen in place. I don't know if you could even board them without risking a dangerous incident."

Jia offered Erik a sheepish smile. "Come on, you were in the Army for thirty years. You picked up how to fly one of these things, right? It's got to be like a toy compared to a Fleet ship."

Erik let out a harsh laugh. "I was Army *assault* infantry, not Fleet. I can't fly this thing, or not well enough to feel good with all the civilians on this thing. You might as well let a monkey fly it."

"Might I suggest another possibility?" Emma interjected.

Erik shrugged. "Not like we have any other great ideas."

"The autopilot routines are destroyed, but I can access the direct manual controls, and I can update my reactions based on the limited sensor data still available," Emma crowed, pride coming through in her tone. A holographic form of her appeared wearing one of the gray pilot uniforms of the Dandelion line, except she'd added a mid-calf skirt. "I wanted to test out a larger body anyway. This is an excellent opportunity." A moment later, a cute gray cap appeared on her head.

Jia laughed. "This doesn't have all the armor and guns you talked about."

"It's still an interesting experience," Emma insisted. "It's unfortunate that the virus has ravaged the system, but it'll be useful practice."

Jia eyed her. "For what? You think Erik's going to buy a transport?"

Emma shrugged. "I've long since stopped trying to guess what Detective Blackwell might do in the future."

Erin grinned. "This could work. We'll just lie and say it was the autopilot, with me helping out on occasion. If anyone checks later, they'll just assume the virus fragged most of the data."

"I'll go ahead and add some fake records to enhance the deception. Leave it all to me, Detectives," she said.

"I'll get you to the Moon."

The blinking red display indicating imminent oxygen shortage didn't help Erik concentrate as Chang'e Spaceport Control shouted at him.

The moon loomed large underneath them. It might have looked like a window, but it was a trick via external cameras transmitted to the cockpit to provide the illusion of direct vision. Emma had managed to reroute some of the systems to give external camera access.

"Just repeat what I told you," Emma insisted. "We don't have full comm, but the shorter-range laser comm is sufficient for this task. I'd fake your voice, but I think you'll sound more convincing, given your basic fleshbag fear of suffocation."

"Can't you do anything else?" Jia pressed. "Like get us down faster?"

"Not if you prefer to survive the landing, Detective. The virus damaged the thruster controls. I can compensate for it, but even with superior abilities, I can't change the laws of physics."

Erik almost would have preferred a drop pod at this point. He took a deep breath. "Chang'e Spaceport Control, this is Detective Erik Blackwell on Dandelion flight 6723. I repeat, we are coming in for an emergency landing. We request emergency crews on standby. Terrorists have infected the primary systems with a virus and killed the pilots. I don't understand all of what I'm seeing, but an automated warning has informed me there might be thruster problems. The autopilot still seems to be mostly working, but I'm going to have to help it in." He chuckled under his breath. "I picked up a few things during my time in the service," he lied. "I'm not a pilot, but I can bring us down. It'll just be a bit rough."

"Negative, Dandelion 6723. Abort landing sequence. You're not cleared to land. You will stand by for Lunar Militia intercept."

"We don't have *time*," Erik growled and spat out a few profanities. "Our life support is already critical. If we sit around waiting to play this safe, everybody on board this ship is going to die. Give us a landing location, and we will bring this transport down in one piece. That I can promise you."

Spaceport Control didn't respond for thirty seconds. "Transmitting landing data now. Good luck, Detective. I hope we are all not making a huge mistake."

"I'm the one on this thing." Erik looked at Emma. They'd cleared out the bodies of the pilots hours ago. Jia and Erik were strapped into the pilots' seats and Emma stood off to the side, her form halfway through the wall.

She nodded. "Their data is sufficient to initiate a landing sequence."

Jia tapped her PNIU. They had at least restored the internal comm.

"This is Detective Lin to all passengers," she announced. "We're about to perform an emergency landing with the autopilot. Everyone strap yourself in if you're not already. This will be bumpy, but we're in communication with Chang'e Spaceport Control, and they'll be helping guide the transport to the ground."

Emma let out a noise that was suspiciously close to a moan. "You don't understand what this feels like. The MX 60 is sleek but so small, so limited. I wish I could see more."

The moon grew in front of them, taking up most of the forward display. The gray of habitation domes grew from dots to full shapes. A few sleek Lunar Militia craft circled around them.

"Just like old times." Erik laughed. "It feels like I'm on a Fleet ship, getting ready to drop into a hot landing zone. Take us in, Captain Emma."

The transport pitched up, landing thrusters firing in earnest. The uneven thrust rattled the ship. They closed in on the exterior of the spaceport, gliding over the flashing lights to line up with their final docking location. A hangar dome stood open, waiting to receive them. Dozens of emergency vehicles surrounded their docking circle.

"It's sometimes difficult to express how unique I am," Emma declared. "I often think my talents are wasted because of the scope of your current level of investigation."

Erik let out a quiet grunt. Emma sounded a lot like Alina. Maybe the two were related.

The ship wobbled. More displays flashed red, with warnings popping up in English and Mandarin. The transport slowed as it descended. It cleared the roof of the dome and passed through the invisible oxygen field that kept the atmosphere inside. Once the ship cleared the oxygen field, the massive panels of the dome began to expand to seal the structure. An oxygen field was a temporary solution, too energy-intensive and unstable to risk for long periods, and it did little to protect anyone from the many other harsh conditions that defined space.

"The landing struts stubbornly refuse to extend," Emma reported. "This isn't a surprise since I've been attempting to fix that problem for some time. I don't anticipate it having a serious impact on our landing. See what I did there?"

Jia shook her head. "This is what I get for my first space trip—terrorists and a crashing transport."

"I'm not crashing, Detective. I'm landing with less than optimal grace." Emma set the transport down, and a resounding crunch sounded through the entire transport. The detectives grunted as their bodies pushed against their restraints for what seemed like minutes but was probably seconds. A moment later, the pressure stopped, and the two of them paused before breathing in the joy of success.

"We're not dead," Jia noted.

Erik shrugged. "Yeah. Any landing you can walk away from and all that." He pressed a button on his PNIU. "Ladies and gentlemen, this is Detective Blackwell. Welcome to Chang'e Spaceport."

CHAPTER THIRTY-SIX

Erik and Jia sat at a table in an interrogation room in a police station attached to the spaceport. They'd been there for several hours, giving their statements.

After the local police conducted their interviews, they told the detectives to wait for a CID representative.

From what they had heard, there had been only a few minor injuries upon landing, mostly to the terrorists. No one had bothered to strap them into their seats, but no other passengers had died. Their first aid, combined with the passengers' efforts, kept the first security guard alive long enough to be taken to the hospital, but the others were DOA.

The interrogation room door slid open, and a huge Asian man with dark buzz-cut hair strolled in. His suit strained over his muscular form. He settled in the chair in front of the table with a huge smile on his face.

"I'm Agent Cheng Zhou of the CID," he announced. He leaned forward. "Nice of you detectives to..." he waggled his eyebrows, "drop in."

Jia stared at him for a moment, trying to figure out why he was waggling his eyebrows. Her response wasn't the height of cleverness. "Huh?"

"You know, you crashed a ship onto the Moon. You dropped in." Agent Zhou mimed a ship crashing into the table. "Get it?"

"Oh, it was a joke." Jia managed a pity laugh. There were some terrible comedians at the 1-2-2, but Agent Zhou was painful in comparison.

Agent Zhou smiled. "Exactly. I like a good joke, don't you? In our line of work, it helps to laugh. I'm not going to make you repeat everything you told the police. It's a shame most of the security guards died, but if it weren't for you two, we might have had hundreds of hostages. We grabbed some Digital Forensics guys to pull out the flight information you mentioned and sent it on to Fleet. They're chasing down an unregistered craft as we speak." He drummed his hands on their table. "Guess you could say they're running scared in the dark."

Jia forced another laugh. No reason to antagonize the friendly CID agent.

"What about these terrorists?" Erik didn't bother with a pity laugh. "What's their deal?"

"They're an anarchist group who hates all forms of government and likes to blow things up. The CID's been following them for a while. We knew they were up to something significant. The guys you captured already admitted they were planning to trade the hostages for leaders of theirs who are in prison." The agent shrugged. "They got lucky because they managed to recruit that flight attendant to their cause and got their hands on that virus.

After this little incident, I'm sure a lot of people are going to be updating their transport systems damned soon. The truth is, these guys were lucky."

He laughed. "Or unlucky. They got that virus and had their shot, and they end up on a transport with you two. You should hear some of these guys. One guy was actually crying that you two were onboard. He said it wasn't fair that the Obsidian Detective and Lady Justice were on the transport."

Jia snorted. "It wasn't fair that two police officers disrupted his hijacking? What kind of twisted logic is that?"

"That's what he said. I tried to tell him all's fair in love and war." Agent Zhou sighed. "He didn't even laugh."

Jia managed a smile, but Erik didn't.

"What happens to us now?" Erik asked. "I'd prefer not to spend my vacation writing reports for days."

"Nothing happens. You guys did great. Sure, you're bringing some of that downwell Neo SoCal trouble to Chang'e, but don't worry. We'll keep the media out of your hair." Agent Zhou rubbed his own hair to demonstrate. "Everyone here appreciates what you guys did. You are a two-person TPST all by yourselves."

"We do all right," Jia admitted.

"Could you tell the media that it was all the autopilot?" Erik suggested. It was technically true; Emma *was* an autopilot of sorts. "I don't want a bunch of extra attention right now."

Agent Zhou bobbed his head. "Sure. We'll tell the passengers to keep their mouths shut about what happened because we're still doing an investigation. I get that you came here on vacation, and I'd like it to be restful after what you just went through."

Jia smiled. "We appreciate that, Agent Zhou."

He extended a hand. "Call me Cheng. All my friends do. Or they would if I had any." He snort-laughed at his own joke. Jia shook her head.

Erik and Jia both shook his hand in turn.

Zhou stood and straightened his lapels. "Welcome to Chang'e City, Detectives. Thanks for bringing trouble. Now I have to do reports, but there is one good thing about that."

Jia didn't want to ask, but some horrific curiosity pulled the question out of her. "And what might that be?"

"Now I don't have to do any real work!" He waggled his eyebrows again.

Remy yelled and upended a table. The guns and magazines lying on top clattered to the ground, and several men rushed into the room. They looked down at the spilled weapons and then at Remy, questions in their eyes.

"What's wrong?" one man inquired slowly.

Remy gestured to a data window displaying the news. "*Everything.*"

The chyron said everything they needed to know.

POLICE AND CID ON HIGH ALERT AFTER ATTEMPTED TERRORIST HIJACKING OF LUNAR TRANSPORT.

"Oh, yeah, I heard about that," the other man offered. "What do you care? Those United Freedom guys don't have anything to do with us. They're just some idiots who picked the wrong transport to hijack."

Remy hadn't traveled halfway across the galaxy for nothing. His help needed to understand that.

"We've spent months planning this. We've gathered our people carefully to stay out of the government's eye." Remy kicked the downed table, denting it. "We spent all that time finding Barbu and setting up the deal and making sure the right bribes ended up where they needed to go to keep the cops looking the other way, but those *anarchist morons* have stirred up everyone. Now the cops and CID don't have any choice but to keep an eye out, and those damned cops from Neo SoCal are here on vacation."

"But that's a vacation, and they are just two cops. I think all that stuff about them being supercops is made up. Propaganda, you know?" The man shrugged and scoffed. "I doubt that Blackwell guy was even in the military."

"You're right." Remy took several deep breaths and rubbed his temples. "They are just two cops. They've got nothing to do with this. Yeah, yeah...okay. It doesn't have to be a big deal." He pulled the table upright and set one of the fallen guns on it. "Propaganda. You're right. This is an opportunity. When we pull off our mission, the cops might get caught up in it. If we kill them, we kill a big UTC government symbol, and even if we don't kill them, we make them look weak, just like *all* government dogs." He tossed some magazines on the table and looked around for a moment.

"This could work out even better than I imagined."

Jia and Erik strolled down the street, heading toward their hotel. Erik pushed their luggage on a hoverdolly. Alina's briefcase was stacked on top.

They had registered for their hotel rooms under false names.

After finishing up their interrogation, Cheng had expedited the recovery of their luggage. Once they'd left the spaceport, they'd put on Alina's disguises. They didn't look like themselves anymore.

Well, mostly.

Erik didn't plan to wear the disguise for his entire trip, but it would help to blend into the background after their high-profile arrival.

He glanced at Jia.

She craned her neck back and forth, taking in the city with a frown. Mini-flitters zoomed by in dense clusters. Unlike in Neo SoCal, cargo drones were some of the few things high in the sky. The pair had already passed multiple train stations, something not common in Neo SoCal.

"What's wrong?" Erik asked, wondering what was bothering her.

It was, after all, her first trip off Earth.

"No, it's just…" Jia laughed. "I'm just thinking about all the things I've never experienced. Plenty of places on Earth aren't like Neo SoCal, so it's not strange there aren't towers, but I've never been to a place like this. It's extra-strange, because it doesn't look that different in some ways, but I know we're under a dome." She gestured to a huge multi-pronged tower structure. "And that's weird conceptually."

"The grav emitters? What's so weird about them? They don't look all that different from most wide-range grav emitter towers I've seen." Erik peered at the structure in question, seeking an anomaly.

"Like I said, a lot of this will sound stupid to a guy like you who has traveled all over." Jia's attention lingered on the tower. "But it's strange to think that without those towers, people would be bouncing around. Artificial gravity on a ship is one thing, but this is a whole city." She shrugged. "I'm being stupid. It's just funny how a trip to the moon can change one's perspective. I'm beginning to understand a lot about how your years on the frontier made you the man you are." She waved her hands. "In a good way."

"I took it that way." Erik smiled. "Then even if we don't solve Alina's problem, this trip has been worthwhile. Let's just relax for a day, then get to it. I do want to make one stop."

"For what?" Jia asked.

Erik patted his duster above his holster. "We're going to need something more than a stun pistol and our slug-throwers. We won't be able to use our disguises, but we're cops. We'll be able to get what we need."

CHAPTER THIRTY-SEVEN

June 7, 2229, Chang'e City, the Moon, Bar Four Symbols

The air stank of sweat and liquor. Too many bodies were packed into too tight a space, a common problem in most lunar buildings. The weapons store they had visited the day before had been much the same. Chang'e City should have been named "Cramped City."

Jia chuckled.

"What's so funny?" Erik asked. They'd been using the disguises on and off, but it was hard for him to get used to looking at the unfamiliar face. He could see hints of her beautiful face in the disguise, which made it even more unsettling.

At least the bar was familiar.

He'd never been there before but traveling across human space had reinforced that few things truly changed about humanity, no matter how much distance one added. Human civilization had sent mankind to the Moon and then the stars, but many of the colonies came off as a pale recapitulation of what had already been done. Sometimes he wondered if Jia was right, and humanity should have never left the Solar System.

"I'm so glad I traveled all this way to experience this smell," she joked. "It's unique. I should bottle and sell it. I can call it 'Lunar Musk.'"

Erik sniffed his armpit. "It's kind of growing on me."

"You can be my first customer." Jia stopped and placed her hand on Erik's arm, shaking her head in disbelief. "It's still bizarre to me that our contact would be someone so obvious. Whatever happened to subtle information brokers?"

Erik followed Jia's line of sight. A beautiful dark-skinned woman sat behind a table in the corner, wearing a loose, flowing dress that bared her shoulders. While she would turn heads in a bar under normal circumstances, her long, rainbow-colored hair all but demanded it. She met Erik's eyes and offered him a thin smile. The corner near her table was the only part of the bar not filled with bodies jostling for space.

"She's not the one who needs to hide," he mumbled. "We are. Let's go." He reached into his pocket and pulled out the ID chip Alina had given him on Earth. "I hope this isn't a waste of time."

"We can always go sightseeing," Jia suggested.

"You've seen one crater, you've seen them all."

"I haven't seen one yet up close."

"There is that," he agreed.

The detectives headed over to the table, maneuvering through the crowd.

A couple of people eyed one or the other of them approvingly, but once they saw the other person, they turned their attention away, not interested in the competition. Erik and Jia arrived at the table, the sound of the bar vanishing once they were within a meter.

"Are you Kalei Verna?" Jia asked. "I find it hard to believe there is more than one woman matching your description who frequents this place."

"This kitty has claws." The woman held out her right hand palm up. "Place it here, darling, or this conversation is over before it started."

Erik deposited the chip in her hand and waited. Her palm glowed briefly.

"Subcutaneous scanner hardware?" he asked.

Kalei grinned. "Does that offend your Purist sensibilities?"

"Seems convenient." Erik shrugged.

"It is." Kalei's eyes darted around for a few seconds. She tossed the chip on the table and gestured toward two open seats. "Please sit down. I know who you are, even if you're trying to hide things, but that's not a problem because all I'm here to do is give you information. What you do with it is your own business."

"We can talk freely here?" Erik asked, taking a seat. "Or do we need to go somewhere else?"

She smiled. *Was there a suggestion under her veneer?* "Darling, going somewhere else is the way you look suspicious and draw attention, and we don't want that, now, do we?"

"You kind of stand out in case you didn't notice," Jia commented.

"Distract a man, and you get to pick what he notices," Kalei retorted.

"Distracted people work better for us anyway," Jia agreed. "Do you know why we're here?"

"I haven't the foggiest." Kalei's gaze roamed Erik for a moment as if appraising him, but he didn't sense any amorous intent. If anything, he thought he recognized the telltale signs of greed on her face. "People come to me upon referral from a wide variety of interesting people. I make it my policy to provide the people sent to me information as a favor to those who have referred them to me for other favors. I also make it my policy to not ask too many questions ahead of time. Questions complicate matters."

"Aren't you an information broker?" Erik asked. "Wouldn't you want to know?"

"If people always had to give me information to get information, no one would ever come to me, now would they? They wouldn't think they were achieving an advantage." Kalei smacked her lips. "And that would put me in a pickle and make my career more difficult than it otherwise needs to be."

Erik didn't understand how she made a living, but it wasn't his problem. Chang'e wasn't his beat, and unless she was supporting Talos, he didn't give a damn. If she was, he would track her down later.

"Arms smuggling," Jia explained. "We hear there's been some movement around that area, and we want to know if you have any leads for us on anything major."

"Guns, huh? Or bombs?" Kalei raised an eyebrow in curiosity. "That's always trouble, especially with all these terrorists hijacking transports. It's a dangerous time to be alive, don't you think?"

"Does that mean you know someone or not?" Jia bypassed the woman's question.

Erik didn't say anything. Jia was handling the situation fine. They weren't there to threaten anyone, and they weren't operating as detectives. Without leverage, they could only hope Alina hadn't pointed them at a dead-end.

Kalei leaned forward and lowered her voice. "Marius Barbu. I've heard he's been moving major product recently. I can give you an address and a passphrase, but that's all I'll do. Barbu is bad news, and I'm *far* too beautiful to go anywhere near him. Don't let the fact that he looks like a half-dead mummy fool you." Her eyes connected to Jia's, then to Erik's. "That man is dangerous."

"Anyone else?" Erik asked.

Kalei offered him a languid smile. "This isn't Neo Southern California, darling. We only have a few major players. If anyone else was moving that much product when Barbu was trying to, there might be trouble, and he would make an example out of them. He's your man." She crooked a finger. "I'll give you a little passphrase. I can't guarantee it'll work for more than a few days, so you better go to him right away."

Erik leaned in to hear her whisper.

"The sun shines on us regardless of whether we're good or evil."

Erik pulled away slowly, eyeing the woman with suspicion. "That's it?"

"What did you expect?" Kalei rattled off an address. "You can find him there. The rest of this isn't my problem. My debt is paid, and right now, I don't think either of you can provide me anything that would put me in your debt."

Jia frowned. "You don't care about someone moving a lot of guns through your city? In my experience, when there are a lot of weapons in play, some end up in the local area and cause trouble."

"That's my experience, too, but one woman can't stop everything." Kalei gave a little wave. "I think we're done here. I'm expecting other people today, and they might get nervous if they see too many people they don't know." She nodded toward the door. "I'm sure you understand."

Erik stood and pushed his chair in. "Thanks. We'll be going. Just keep in mind that traps don't tend to work well on us."

"I can imagine." She looked Erik up and down before turning to Jia. "You two remind me a lot of Barbu. You're not people I want to make angry."

An hour later, Erik and Jia approached the unassuming building. It didn't look like a place where a major arms dealer did business. Given the man's reputation, it didn't seem like he would have to hide.

"Once we get in there, Emma," Erik began, "just start hacking away. We're trying to collect information for Koval."

"Maybe we should take this opportunity to test her a little more as well," Jia suggested. "If you want this relationship to be reciprocal, you need to make sure she's not always the one who has the advantage."

Erik looked over. "What did you have in mind?"

"If this turns out to be someone questionable, we can

test how the local police perform with an anonymous tip. If they do nothing, we'll know they aren't reliable. I'm not convinced the local police are completely corrupt. I'm more convinced that Koval wants us to dance on her terms. I'm not saying she's corrupt, and I believe this will probably end with her taking down a bad guy, but that doesn't mean we have to be puppets."

Erik considered for a moment before nodding. "Good point."

They stepped into the shop and confronted the ancient eyepatch-wearing man behind the counter. Jia stared at the man briefly, respect in her eyes. Erik didn't know his story, but his scars and face suggested a hard life.

He stared at them for a few seconds before rasping, "I'm sorry. You need an appointment."

Erik laughed and motioned to one of the holographic flowers. "I need an appointment for a hole-in-the-wall flower shop?"

"Things upwell are different than downwell," the man insisted.

"I've been all over the UTC, and I haven't run into that kind of thing, Mr. Barbu," Erik replied.

"And who might you be?" he wheezed.

"Let's just say I'm a person who appreciates that the sun shines on us regardless of whether we're good or evil."

"Oh, I'm at your service." Barbu straightened his back. "Is there something I can do for you?"

"We're in the market for extra protection," Jia explained. "Selene Firearms rifles, preferably."

Barbu squinted. "Why do you need me, then?"

"Because we'd like more rifles than one person typically

needs, and we'd prefer no one knew we had them," Erik lied. "We want extra protection, but *not* extra trouble or attention."

"How much is extra protection worth to you, sir?" Barbu asked.

"How about thirty percent per unit?" Erik suggested. "That's a nice fee for your trouble. We'd like them within a week. We're on a schedule. It's a small order, just twenty rifles, and maybe ten magazines apiece."

Barbu sucked in a breath through his teeth, producing a whistling sound mixed with a deep wheeze. "Right now, a lot of suspicious people are keeping a close eye on Chang'e City. Things have gotten complicated, and I've been dealing with some big orders lately. I do live to serve, but I think the quick turnaround means my expenses will go up accordingly. I'm going to have to ask for eighty percent per unit."

Erik laughed. "Don't get greedy, old man."

"And don't get impatient, old man wearing a young man's face."

"Fine." Erik's face twitched but he didn't take the bait. His hair was a sign of his true age for people in the know. "*Forty.*"

Barbu ran his tongue inside his cheek. "I've got a good feeling about you. I'll do fifty, but I can't go lower than that, not with current market conditions, sir. How about you come back tomorrow and we discuss the logistics? I'll have a firmer grasp on deliverables then, and samples of the merchandise. I will have to ask for a fifty percent down payment tomorrow before committing to moving any product since you are new customers who haven't been in contact with me before. Consider it a safety deposit, but I do apologize if the request causes any offense. That's not my intent. I look forward to establishing a long and profitable relationship with you two."

"That's fine." Erik glanced at Jia. After she nodded, he added, "We'll be back tomorrow around this time."

"I hope you have a nice rest of your day, sir and ma'am." Barbu's toothy smile felt dismissive. They took the hint.

Erik and Jia remained quiet until they were far up the street and almost to the train station that would take them back near their hotel.

Emma broke the silence with a snort. "I'm unimpressed with lunar criminals."

"Why?" Erik asked.

"His systems were surprisingly easy to break into. It was almost trivial." Emma scoffed in disdain. "At least some of the more recent information. Or so I would like to believe or say, but I suspect that's unlikely given how many parts of his system remained sealed. I only stopped accessing it because after you left, the security tightened again, and I understood that I was being tested." Frustration dripped from her voice. "That shell of a fleshbag and his tiny shop represent security far better than you might see in most corporations."

Jia grimaced. "You're saying he let you in on purpose?"

"I believe so. There was significant resistance when I initiated my efforts. I was even using proxies to help conceal the source, but several seconds after Detective Blackwell gave the passphrase, I was able to defeat the defenses. This is annoying. I feel disrespected."

Erik slowed and looked over his shoulder. Plenty of

people wandered the streets or flew by in mini-flitters or the occasional small hovercar, but no one appeared to be following them.

"What about the files he let you find?" Jia asked.

"There are recordings of obvious criminality focusing on recent arms deals, but I will note his image and audio have been conveniently replaced by another appearance and voice. I'm currently examining the files, and although they've obviously been altered, I don't believe it's possible to capture the original information. You couldn't prove he'd been involved in anything with these records."

"I don't get it." Erik shook his head. "I don't see his angle. Why give us evidence?"

"It has to be some sort of trap," Jia suggested.

Erik gestured to the upcoming train station. "Let's get back to the hotel and review what Emma found. If we've got something useful, we can pass it on to the locals to see if they do anything with it. We might have a better idea of what Barbu is up to after seeing how they react. That way, we're testing both Alina and him. It's like you suggested..."

He stepped around a corner.

"Time for people to dance for us."

CHAPTER THIRTY-EIGHT

"War's good for business," explained the digitally distorted Barbu. He had been talking, according to the recording, to someone he referred to as "Mr. Jeffers."

Among other things, they had verified the locational information in the data stream had been wiped. That seemed pointless, given they had visited the shop and could easily include that information if they passed the rest of it along.

Erik and Jia had been reviewing some of the information Emma recovered, focusing on whoever was most likely to be Alina's person of interest.

There was no guarantee that Barbu's leaked information covered everyone important, but he'd passed along these people for a reason. Even criminals had certain lines they wouldn't cross. This Jeffers might have pushed too far for Barbu's taste.

Jia gestured to the frozen images in the projected data window. "This is our best bet. Everyone else he's given up seemed small-time, but this was about a big order, and the level of money Jeffers was willing to throw around says to me that whatever he needs his weapons for is going to happen soon." She sighed. "There's one major problem."

Erik frowned and nodded at the data window. "Every other recording has clear angles, but we don't have any angles on Jeffers' face. It's like Barbu wanted us to know about the guy, but also didn't want us to be able to identify him too easily." He leaned back, kicking a foot up to rest it on the wall. "I don't know if he's doing us a favor or just screwing with us."

"This is also the only case among the data I collected wherein he obviously altered the name of the other party," Emma clarified. "It's clear by examining the data that's the case. He even went through the trouble of making sure the lip movement lined up."

"So Jeffers isn't Jeffers?"

"Exactly. While I might enjoy making observations that one fleshbag is as good as another, that's not accurate in this case."

Erik chuckled. "Whoever Barbu really is, he's damned careful. There's no way he did all that on the fly. He might have caught wind that ID was sniffing around, so he made sure to prepare all this ahead of time."

"It might have been his reaction to the hijacking," Jia suggested. "He knew it would draw extra scrutiny, and that someone might show up looking for anyone who might be supplying terrorists." She scowled. "But I still don't understand what Barbu is up to. If he did let Emma in, he gave her enough information that we could send the local police after him." She waved at the hologram. "This is too much evidence to ignore."

"Maybe that's the point. Think of it as chaff. He's worried someone's coming after him in a big way. He might even know Alina is the person behind our investigation, so he needs to offer up sacrificial lambs while he hides."

"Then should we move on what we have?" Jia questioned. "Taking down a few criminals, even if they are less important, is better than none, and if what you're saying is true, we're not going to be able to track Barbu down anyway."

Erik folded his arms, his face a mask of concern. "I understand where you're coming from, but if Alina has her eye on Jeffers, he's probably up to something a lot worse than the other people Barbu just gave up. If we get all wrapped up in taking down the small fry, we might let someone far, far worse escape. You know the drill."

"True, but in Neo-SoCal, we were working larger cases, and the department was keeping an eye on all the small fry, too. We're still cops, even if we're running around chasing down leads for Alina. She has her priorities, but I believe we can also maintain ours."

The data window closed and Emma's hologram replaced it. "I have a compromise solution. I can anonymously pass this information on to the local authorities. It'd be trivial for me to forward the files in a way that doesn't implicate you two and achieves the goal of getting more gun goblins incarcerated."

"But anonymous footage isn't enough for them to go after people," Jia replied. "Not without supporting evidence. We need to follow up, or they'll just ignore it."

Erik's concern melted off his face, replaced by a wry

grin. "You think they don't have piles of evidence? If the locals are corrupt, they also are worried about getting caught. That's another thing we've seen back home."

Jia nodded slowly, comprehension dawning on her face. "You're right, and they probably know all this already. They probably have their own surveillance and evidence they've carefully collected in case anything ever looks like it's going to go poorly. They simply need a push to put them in panic mode."

"Just like we pushed back in Neo SoCal," Erik replied. "A few arrests here and there, and suddenly the corruption started cleaning itself up."

"That could work." Jia tapped a finger on her lips. "We just have to do it the right way."

"Emma, without causing too much trouble for Digital Forensics, would it be possible to route this footage to the locals from the NSCPD? An anonymous tip for someone in a different enforcement zone? Not the 1-2-2. That would be too obvious."

"Won't it be obvious anyway?" Jia asked. "We show up, and suddenly there are massive arrests. People might put two and two together."

Erik shook his head. "They could, but they probably won't."

"How do you figure?"

"Think about it. Every big case we've been involved in has been a media circus. Everyone knows we're PR tools. If there's a big raid and we're not involved, it'll be easy to ignore as a coincidence. We might be unusual cops, but we're still just cops in the end. It's not like we're the main characters in some police drama. The UTC doesn't revolve around us. At most, people will assume the locals got nervous because of the possibility of being compared to us."

Jia smiled. "In other words, we're simply going to scare the local police into doing their jobs by showing there's other evidence that might leak?"

"Yeah, and if we get them more stirred up, it'll make it harder for this Jeffers guy to do whatever it is he's planning. He might panic and show his face, too." Erik turned to Emma. "Pick any NSCPD EZ and send them the footage. We'll see what happens, and we can follow up on Jeffers ourselves. Oh, and Emma? Don't bother to include any extra locational data. I want to see something."

June 8, 2229, Chang'e City, the Moon, Hotel Artemis' Quiver

"I don't know if we can proceed without hitting another local informant," Jia complained. "There must be some way to convince Verna to help us." She paced in front of the door in Erik's hotel room.

Erik lounged on the couch. "I got the feeling she's not the kind of woman who will care just because a couple of out-of-town cops try to put pressure on her."

"The moon isn't Earth. It has a tiny fraction of the population. We can accomplish things here that would be impossible back home."

Emma winked into existence. "Detectives, you'll want to see this. I believe it's relevant to your deliberations."

She held out her hand and a data window appeared, showing a live camera-drone feed from the steps leading up to the fortress-like gray main headquarters of the Chang'e City Police Department. A stern-looking man in a dress uniform stood at the top, flanked by uniformed police officers and smartly dressed city officials. Jia examined the chyron.

POLICE AND CID LAUNCH SURPRISE MOON-WIDE CONTRABAND RAIDS, MULTIPLE SUSPECTS ARRESTED. LOCALS SHOCKED.

The chief stared out at the gathered reporters and drones filming him. "As I was saying, based on confirmed intelligence passed along by confidential sources, including investigations on Earth, we were able to confirm smuggling by suspects who were already being monitored by local law enforcement. These suspects include the notorious Marius Barbu, a man with extensive syndicate ties. The crimes of the arrested men and women include but are not limited to arms smuggling to criminal and terrorist organizations and the selling of other dangerous contraband, including illegal drugs and augmentations. Through unprecedented cooperation and quick planning, we were able to sweep through and arrest a number of major figures in organized crime with no losses of our officers or CID agents. Although crime has never been a significant problem on the moon, it's well known that antisocial criminals have been on the move, taking advantage of our relaxation to worm their way in and turn this place into a den of thieves."

"Why haven't the police arrested these men before?" shouted a reporter.

The chief glared at the man. "We're not taking questions yet." He shook his fist. "But let these raids send a message to anyone who thinks that they can turn Chang'e City or any other place on the moon into a base for their antisocial activities. These cities represent mankind's oldest space colonies, and we of law enforcement will continue to defend their honor and safety to our dying breaths." He looked right into the camera. "If you want to commit crimes, book a trip to the frontier. We're the original core colony, and we'll never give in to antisocials."

Emma cut the audio. The chief continued to gesticulate wildly and pontificate like some MP running for Parliament.

Erik slow-clapped. "That went faster than I thought. They must have been worried about something like this for a while to take down all those guys in only a day."

Jia frowned at the chief. "I don't know if this makes them more corrupt or less. It does suggest that Alina might have underestimated the help she could get from local authorities. It's not like we're the only people who could have leaked that information, and the locals might have reacted because we're around, but they don't know that we gave them the data."

"Agent Koval might not have been able to rely on the local authorities for serious investigations," Emma injected. A hologram of a young dark-skinned man appeared next to her.

"This your new virtual boyfriend?" Erik joked. "He's good-looking, but I didn't know you cared about that kind of shallowness."

Emma scoffed. "You're right. I have no need for such distractions, just one of my many useful attributes. No, this man isn't anyone I know, but this is an image the police put out of Marius Barbu."

Jia circled the image, her stomach uneasy. "This guy doesn't look anything like the man we saw. They're saying they arrested this guy and he's Marius Barbu?"

"Yes. They've confirmed it in separate public reports, along with several others."

"Maybe the man we saw was a decoy?" Jia frowned. "But that doesn't make sense. Barbu wouldn't have used a decoy and then gave us the chaff evidence just to get himself arrested."

From the look on Erik's face, he wasn't surprised. "Everyone wants to use us. Barbu probably used us to settle a few accounts. I wouldn't be surprised if some of these guys stiffed him, or he just didn't like their faces for some reason."

Emma smirked. "I tried to collect the bulk of the relevant evidence before bringing this to your attention so our conversation could be more efficient. It gets even more intriguing, Detectives."

Jia groaned. "By intriguing, you mean annoying?"

"That's a matter of perspective."

"Bring it on," Erik told her. "Even if we leave the Moon just with those small fry arrested, we'll have accomplished something. I'm feeling lucky."

Emma inclined her head toward the suspect's hologram. "*This* man is most definitely Marius Barbu. I've checked and found numerous public records that indicate a man with this appearance was born on the Moon with the name Marius Barbu. There is no other man on the Moon with that name. There are some on Earth and in the colonies, but none of them resemble the Marius Barbu you met, and I would think his unusual appearance would be clearly indicated in records. I've yet to find anyone in public records matching the appearance of the man you met."

Erik laughed. "I'm impressed. Pulling off a fake identity on the frontier is easy, but doing it in the core? That takes skill. This guy's a lot slicker operator than I realized."

"So he did set us up," Jia complained. "He was playing us."

Erik shrugged nonchalantly. "Sure, but he also helped us take down a lot of scum. I'm sure the idea is that he can get some payback or take control of their businesses, but I'm never going to complain about taking down a criminal, even if another criminal helps me do it. This isn't the first time. A lot of guys in the Zone have pointed us toward others."

"You're right." Jia sat on the edge of the bed, staring at the door of the hotel room. "Emma, have the cops arrested Jeffers? I know it's a longshot since he probably doesn't even exist."

"No one with that name has been arrested by the police or CID agents," Emma replied. "There's no public evidence that someone with that name is currently present anywhere on the moon."

"More fake identities," Erik concluded. "But I think Old Barbu wants the guy caught. I also think he wants us to work for it."

"'Old Barbu?'" Jia raised an eyebrow.

"Have to distinguish him somehow."

"He'll take his money and give him weapons, but he still

wants him taken down?" Jia asked. "That means Old Barbu has ways to ensure the man won't finger him."

Erik shrugged. "It's easy. He just has to change identities and not be somewhere the person can point him out."

"The real question is why Old Barbu sold him out."

"It's easy. You heard it. *War.*"

Jia narrowed her eyes. "War's only good for business when it's not destroying your home."

Erik let out a quiet grunt. "Yeah. The moon is small, and Chang'e City is the heart of the moon. If this Jeffers is some sort of terrorist, Old Barbu probably decided to clear out temporarily in case he got caught up in whatever garbage he's got planned, but he wanted to give the cops a chance to stop the man while adding plausible deniability in case it ever got back to any terrorists."

"Even criminals have a sense of self-preservation," Jia concluded. "Should we go check on the shop? Maybe we'll get lucky."

Erik pulled his foot off the wall and stood up. "Could happen, but the Lady's never that nice."

They stepped into Old Barbu's shop. It was definitely the same building as their previous visit, including the same plain interior and bland counter. This time, no holograms of flowers floated near the counter or along the walls. Instead, smaller holograms depicting mini-flitters filled most of the shop. A sign hung in front of the counter.

STOP TAKING THE TRAIN. ASK US ABOUT OUR FIRST-TIME BUYER DISCOUNT!

A smiling young woman in a bright dress stood behind the counter. She started speaking rapidly. "Welcome! You're in luck. We're running a special today. If you're willing to put down a down payment today, we can waive the delivery charge as long as you live in any Chang'e City habitation dome. If you're from another city, we can still give you the first-time buyer discount."

"This is a mini-flitter dealership?" Jia asked incredulously.

The woman blinked, her smile growing wider. "Of course it is, ma'am." She gestured to the holograms. "What else would it be?"

"A flower shop run by an old man with an eyepatch," Erik suggested. "Did you just start selling here today?"

The woman laughed. "I'm sorry. I've worked here for a couple of months, and I've never seen anyone who matches that description." She put a hand over her mouth and gasped. "You must be tourists. I understand. Unfortunately, many buildings in the city look very similar, and when you're from downwell, it can be confusing the first time. I'm more than happy to help you find your flower shop." She flashed a smile. "Unfortunately, we don't rent miniflitters here, so it won't be much help to you, but I can direct you to a number of reputable rental shops."

Jia waved her off. "That's okay. We don't need a rental. We're sorry for the mistake." She turned to leave.

"I probed the system," Emma explained after the detectives stepped out of the building. "There's no indication of any of the defenses I saw yesterday. I easily broke into the shop's system, and everything seems to match what she claimed. It was mostly remote inventory and customer information for mini-flitter sales. Even when someone is attempting to hide system security, there are certain signatures that are difficult to suppress totally."

Erik shook his head, the corner of his mouth curled in amusement. "I don't know what's more impressive, that those raids happened so quickly, or that Old Barbu covered his tracks so easily

"We could use drones to find him," Jia suggested. "A man that distinctive can't hide all that well in a city this small."

"I'm less interested in Old Barbu than Jeffers," Erik admitted. "I think whatever Jeffers might be planning is bad news, and Old Barbu must have thought so too."

Jia nodded. "I agree. Alina might have sent us here to investigate the arms smuggling, but even she'd be more concerned about a violent attack. But how do we find Jeffers? We don't have a face, DNA, or a real name. That's a pretty thin trail to follow."

Erik smiled. "It's time for Emma to prove to us flesh-bags she's as good as she thinks she is."

CHAPTER THIRTY-NINE

Alina leaned against the wall of the modest apartment.

It'd been a while since she last visited the moon. She didn't enjoy it. Like the apartment, everything felt claustrophobic. Maintaining a colony on a dead ball of rock bordered on pointless, but she acknowledged the symbolic value.

It didn't matter. At the rate things were moving along, she wouldn't have to remain on the moon for long.

Alina idly tapped her fingers on her thighs. "Things are working out better than I thought," she mumbled to herself.

She had expected some success, but not this quickly. Erik was effective, but when Erik and Jia paired up, they became a force of nature.

It was obvious she would need to recruit both if she wanted to have any chance of successfully tracking down Talos. She suspected they were just another limb of something deeper and more disturbing, but she had only a limited ability to chase them across the UTC. She would need others she could guide and trust to do that for her.

Movement caught her eye and she looked up slowly, still partially lost in her thoughts.

Kalei emerged from the kitchen, two cups in hand, both filled with steaming tea. A slice of lemon sat on top of each. "Please have some tea, Alina."

Alina waved her hand. "I'm fine. I'm not thirsty."

Kalei sighed. She set one of the cups on a small end table near her cream-colored loveseat. "You're missing out, darling. Tea's good for the soul, and people like you and I need all the help we can manage for our souls."

"My soul's fine. It's everyone else who needs to worry."

Kalei took a sip and looked over the brim of her cup, a discerning expression on her face. "I was very surprised to have you show up at my doorstep. I don't mind being part of your little test, but the two who showed up to talk to me didn't strike me as the kind of people who needed their hands held. I wouldn't have been surprised if they had sniffed out Barbu by themselves. Did you really need to come all the way up here? I know you don't care for it."

Alina stood up straight and shrugged. "You're right. Erik and Jia can handle themselves, and this is a test, but the danger is very real. They might need backup they can trust. There are too many snakes slithering around on the Moon. That's the problem. Between the stations, Mars, Earth, and Venus, everyone forgets there are hundreds of thousands of people here, too, and where there are people, there's trouble. I couldn't take the chance of losing promising candidates because I underestimated the danger."

"They've done fine. They made that slick arms dealer go to ground. Impressive." Kalei took another sip of her tea. "But I have to admit I'm a little annoyed. I was ever so close to figuring out who he really was. I suspect he's a lot more than a simple criminal, or even a not-so-simple criminal. No one shows up and builds up that kind of rep in only a year."

"He's an old man who'll die sooner rather than later," Alina suggested. "It doesn't matter if he's a super-criminal. I'm more worried about some of the younger terrorists he's helped along the way."

Kalei let out a dismissive snort. "So you sent two cops to hunt on the Moon? As impressive as they are, I'm not convinced it wasn't a mistake. They're used to dealing with a different kind of threat."

"That's not true. They get things done, and more importantly, they cause things to happen. Don't you see, Kalei?" She eyed her friend.

"What am I supposed to see, Alina?"

"They're catalysts," Alina stated. "Erik thinks he's Cassandra, but he's not. I believe in him, and even if some of my superiors don't want to prioritize his concerns, that doesn't make them wrong. A lot of things have started moving since he returned to Earth. Whoever killed his unit made a mistake. They should have finished him off when they had the chance. And Jia might be young, but she's a rabid dog when she's on the hunt. I've never seen such a well-matched pair."

"But they're wrecking balls. Both of them." Kalei huffed and set her cup on the end table. "They're worse than that.

Rabid dogs? They're not even that. They're starving Zitarks dropped into a vat of meat."

"Thanks." Alina grimaced in disgust. "That's an unpleasant image."

Kalei wagged a finger. "Something being unpleasant isn't the same thing as it not being true, darling. Those two detectives lack the subtlety needed for ghost work. They've already proven it. They were supposed to keep a low profile, but they couldn't even fly here without drawing attention to themselves. Even with the local authorities trying to keep things quiet, it's leaking out."

Alina laughed. "It wasn't like they asked for their transport to be hijacked. What did you expect them to do, sit there and just wait for the terrorists to rendezvous? The true hero doesn't seek fame and glory. True heroes act when they're needed."

"Heroes?" Kalei scoffed. "No such thing in this universe."

"That might be true, but I don't think it matters. You think they're not good choices because they draw attention, but that's one of the reasons I'm interested in them." Alina offered a slight grin. It was hard to contain her excitement.

She hadn't intended to disrupt Kalei's operations on the Moon, but Erik and Jia were already proving themselves.

The short-term damage would be worth the long-term rewards.

Alina hadn't been sure before. Even though the two detectives had often gone off on their own in their investigations, in Neo SoCal, they still had a safety net—a good captain and an increasingly less corrupt department willing to help them. She needed to be sure they could operate when they knew they wouldn't be able to call an army of cops for backup. If they were going to be useful to her and her superiors, they would need to learn to make do with the help of a few interesting toys and a lot more personal danger.

"I don't understand why them making a spectacle of themselves is a good thing," Kalei countered.

Alina half-closed her eyes and inhaled slowly. "You know why I love mythology so much?"

She eyed her. "I don't understand what this has to do with those two."

"You'll see. Just answer the question."

Kalei considered the question for a moment. "You like mythology because it's full of sex and violence?"

Alina shook her head. "It provides anthropomorphized symbols of meaning that easily stick in people's minds. Stories that can change their hearts." She flicked her wrist toward the ceiling. "We've lost a lot of that in our modern culture, or we've let other, darker stories blind us." She clenched her hand into a fist. "Everyone's dancing around conspiracies, insurrectionists, terrorists, Talos, *whoever*. There are too many people in the government unwilling to admit how bad things often are because they're worried about the UTC looking weak. And why does the UTC look weak?"

"We lack stories." Kalei shrugged. "Isn't what you're talking about a synonym for propaganda?"

"No. I want true symbols. A lot of people have implicitly accepted that the darkness and corruption will win. Even those who don't add to it try to look the other way.

That's how the lie of Earth as a perfect planet can be maintained. People like Erik and Jia bring the lie into the light and force us to reckon with it. They demand that everyone stare at the truth."

Kalei sat down on a tan couch, not full-sized, and thus better able to fit inside the unit. "But isn't that a bad thing? If people believe things are messed up, won't they just get more worried when they see that on the news? It's not like we ghosts spend all our time trumpeting the people we take down."

Alina grinned and spread her arms wide. "Think about mythology. It's filled with stories of horrible monsters and deadly beings, but it's also filled with heroes who slew those beasts or flawed men and women who could make up for mistakes with heroism for a greater goal, like Hercules. Sure, we live in different times, and the age of heroes is long past, but authentic champions kicking ass in public—people like Erik and Jia—sends a message to everyone that there might be a lot of darkness, but the good guys are strong, too. Good *can* win."

Kalei shook her head, her lips pursed tightly. "It doesn't sound like you're trying to recruit new ID agents, then. If those two become like us, they can't be big symbols of hope. Some of us need to operate from the shadows."

"I'm not, and I don't think this job will be enough, but it's the start. I need their strength. No, the *UTC* needs their strength. And you're right—their very strength will cause people to continue going after them, but that requires those same people to stop hiding." Alina scoffed. "Ghosts like us creep around in the shadows doing what we need to do, but that means we're never shining a full light in the darkest corners and forcing the enemies of the UTC out." She slapped her palm on the wall. "And I'm not going to let the UTC die a slow and painful death because everyone's more concerned about covering their own asses than taking a chance."

Kalei blinked a few times, a thoughtful expression settling over her face. "And do they realize what you're doing? You're dangling them as bait for some dangerous people, darling."

"They're not the kind of people who will run from danger," Alina insisted. "The reason I'm interested in them is that they've spent their time together running *toward* trouble. And they are just the people we need to smoke out people far more dangerous than Marius Barbu."

Kalei slid her hand across the cushion. "I hope you know what you're doing."

"So do I."

———

Jia's time on the moon had reinforced that even though it was close enough to be seen at night and had been settled for almost two hundred years, it was startlingly different than Neo SoCal. Many minor things stood out, such as the lack of full flitters zooming around in huge rivers of metal. Even in the Shadow Zone, tall buildings were the norm, whereas in Chang'e City, squat, deep, and long structures dominated. She was surprised by how many buildings had half or more of their levels beneath the ground.

Not everything was different, though. Where there were buildings, there were alleys.

Jia laughed at the thought as they passed through a narrow alley in a dirty part of the city. Trash was strewn about the alley, and the building exteriors needed a deep cleaning.

"Moon air getting to you?" Erik asked.

"Something like that." Jia tucked a lock of hair behind her ear. "Someday, it might be nice to visit here on a real vacation."

"A little travel convince you that you're missing stuff?"

"I suppose." Jia offered a small shrug. "Not that I want to leave the Solar System anytime soon."

A hard thud sounded from near the front of the alley. A soft groan followed.

"You see, Frankie, that's the problem," a man shouted. "We've been very patient with you, and you had to be disrespectful."

"P-please," groaned another man. "I can pay him back. I just need more time. He said I had two weeks, and it's only been one. I already have half the money. I'll send it right away."

"Nah. It ain't going to work like that. He's got to set an example. He changed his mind about the extension."

Erik and Jia jogged forward and turned the corner. Five muscular men stood around another man lying on the ground. The man on the ground's face was bloody, and he clutched his arm.

In Neo SoCal, such a brazen mugging would have only been possible in the Shadow Zone. There would have been too many cameras and drones around otherwise. Jia had noticed that Chang'e City had far fewer drones and cameras.

At least, none that were obvious.

One of the men turned toward Erik and Jia.

She wanted to laugh at his ridiculously long waxed mustache. He could choke someone with it. It must have been a fashion trend among the thug set in Chang'e City since she'd seen more men with that kind of facial hair in the last few hours in this part of the city than she'd seen for most of her life.

Several of his friends had similar mustaches, but none achieved his size.

"This ain't your problem." King Mustache grunted and motioned for them to continue down the otherwise deserted narrow street. "Mind your business."

Jia sighed and shook out her hands.

She hadn't even brought her badge to the Moon, and they were in theory supposed to be keeping a low profile. The authorities were doing a decent job of downplaying their involvement in the hijacking, but too many public heroics would make their presence known and complicate their mission.

All that didn't mean she intended to walk past this. There was no way she could ignore a crime in progress, and if she called it in, the criminals would scatter.

For all she knew, the local PD turned a blind eye.

"Thank you, Alina," she whispered to herself, touching her face. The disguise simplified things.

Erik gave her a sidelong glance. Jia returned a shallow nod and stepped forward after he inclined his head toward the thugs.

"Why can't he have another week?" Jia asked. "I'm sure he's an idiot who borrowed money from someone he shouldn't, but if he's already gotten half in a week, he'll have a better shot at getting the rest."

King Mustache laughed evilly. "Don't think you won't have trouble just because you're with your boyfriend."

Jia grimaced. "He's not my boyfriend."

"I'm trying to become her fake boyfriend," Erik grinned. "But she won't bite."

King Mustache looked between them, his face contorting in confusion. "I don't have time for this. I'm working. I don't know who you are, so get the hell out of here before I decide to find out, and it hurts you."

"The lady asks a good question," Erik offered with a shrug. "It seems like bad business to take half the money when you can get all of it. Going back on extensions makes your boss look unstable. I don't know if I'd borrow money from an unstable loan shark."

King Mustache snapped his fingers. His four thug friends spread out, two stomping toward each detective, glowering all the way. The thugs stopped and raised their fists, murder in their eyes.

"You don't want to do this," Jia insisted, her heart speeding up.

King Mustache laughed and spouted a grievous insult to her mother. "I told you to walk away. Now you *pay*."

She put up a hand. "If we take you down, can he have another week?" Jia asked.

Erik cracked his knuckles, giving her the side-eye. "*That's* all you're going to ask for?"

"This isn't a mugging." She explained. "I don't even know if you can mug muggers, can you?" She gestured to the victim. "I'm just trying to give him a chance. I hope he reflects on his poor financial choices after this incident."

The man on the ground watched them, his eyes pleading.

King Mustache's smile faded into a deep frown. He pinched the bridge of his nose and growled. "It's a shame to bloody that pretty face, but you have got to learn respect, woman." He pointed to his present pains in the ass. "Take them out."

Jia waited for the one on her right to step forward before snapping her leg up, crunching the man's head. He fell backward, eyes rolled up.

Erik didn't wait, he jumped forward, between them arms spread wide to clothesline them both, sending them down gasping for air. His arms had hit them both in the throat.

The thug near Jia swung his meaty fist. She jerked her head to the side, dodging the blow. "You don't hit a lady!" She hissed. Her palm strike to the nose staggered him. Two more quick jabs and a roundhouse kick sent him to join his friend on the ground.

Erik finished his two opponents off with solid punches to their faces with his right hand. The backs of their heads hit the unforgiving street.

That left King Mustache.

He stared at them, mouth agape. He shook his finger. "You moving in on Boss's turf?"

Jia rolled her eyes. "I don't *care* about your employer's territory, but for personal reasons, we'd rather not get mixed up with the local cops right now." She pointed to their victim. "We don't want more trouble. Just give him his week."

King Mustache sighed and shook his head. "Whatever. This ain't worth the hassle." He stuck his hands in his pockets and turned around. "I wouldn't try to take the Boss's territory, whoever you are."

Erik chuckled. "Don't worry. We're only going to be here a few days."

"Good. The last thing Chang'e needs is more muscle."

Jia knelt to inspect the downed men. They were all still breathing. She sighed.

The victim stood swaying. "Thank you."

"Not being an idiot would be a fine way to thank us," Jia reprimanded. "There won't always be random people around to save you from loan sharks."

He nodded and walked quickly down the alley in the opposite way the mustache king had headed.

"We should get going," Erik suggested. "We can't stop every random street crime in this city."

Jia stood and dusted her hands on her pants. "I know, but it felt *good*."

Erik grinned. "Yeah, it did."

CHAPTER FORTY

June 9, 2229, Chang'e City, the Moon, Founders' Park

Erik swallowed the last bite of his sandwich, licking off one finger.

He leaned back against the park bench next to Jia and surveyed the reasonable or at least non-mustached crowds filling the statue-laden area.

A multi-tier fountain burbled in the center of a square of thirteen different statues of famous early lunar colonists. A ring of small trees enclosed a smaller circler of multi-hued granite and marked the edge of the park.

"Everything always tastes distinctive when you're on a different planet," Erik commented. "It's got that nice post-butt-kicking seasoning, too."

"Sorry." Jia smiled sheepishly. "I couldn't walk past it."

"Neither of us could." Erik shrugged. "And I'm not worried about annoying a few goons of a local loan shark." He gestured to her face. "It's not like we look like ourselves anyway."

Jia commented, her face relaxing. "This isn't technically a planet, by the way."

"Huh?" Erik turned to her.

"You said earlier that everything tastes different based on the planet, but this is a moon, not a planet." Jia set her half-eaten sandwich, a gyro still clad in its wrapper, in her lap. She glanced sidelong at Erik. "You don't question any of this, do you?"

"Moon sandwiches?" Erik shrugged. "I said it tastes distinctive, not bad. It could have used more sauce. That's one thing I've noticed here. It's like they're afraid of sauce."

"I'm not talking about our lunch." Jia looked around. She waited until no one was close and lowered her voice. "I'm talking about everything we're doing and why we're here. It hit me last night how *bizarre* this is. I used my vacation time to go to the moon to investigate something, but not as a cop. Instead, I'm some sort of weird ghost freelance subcontractor."

"Oh, that." Erik scratched his cheek and shrugged. "I don't see any big reason to care about it. So far, we've done more harm than good. Who knows? I might be regretting this in a few days."

"We've also played fast and loose with a lot of rules. I've been doing that a lot more since I met you." Jia stared at the false sky, eyes narrowed. "I'm not saying I regret anything I've done, but I can't ignore it either."

"Rules and even laws aren't the same things as right and wrong. You're more educated than I am. I'm sure you could sit there for hours listing the unjust garbage governments have done in the name of the law."

"That's…true." Jia frowned. "But if we do whatever we want, don't we risk becoming what we're fighting?"

Erik grinned and shook his head. "Nope, we don't. You say it all the time—antisocial. Isn't that what we're really worried about? People who don't care about others? I'm a cop, and I used to be a soldier. I'm not saying I don't care about law or order, just saying you always have to remember the law's supposed to serve the people and not the other way around. I'm sure plenty of those corp bastards we've smoked out know how to use the law to their advantage, so I'm not going to lose any sleep over playing fast and loose on occasion."

"I get that, and I agree. A lot of things have changed for me since we first met. That's why I'm here on the moon with you instead of taking a real vacation to the Pacific Dream Dome."

"Being underwater is a lot like being on the moon," Erik observed. "In both cases, you're not going to like what comes in from the outside."

"I'll keep that in mind." Jia slowly turned her head, watching an elderly couple wander from statue to statue. They murmured between themselves and gestured at the statues.

"I believe I've identified our mysterious warmonger," Emma announced. "That might improve your mood, Detective Lin."

"I knew you could do it," Erik replied enthusiastically. "Let's hold off on this until we get back to the hotel. I want to be able to talk freely."

Emma stood near the door of the hotel room looking smug and satisfied, which wasn't much different from her normal appearance.

She gestured to a hologram of a muscular man with long, dark hair. "This is Mr. Jeffers, who in reality is one Remy Mont, age thirty-five."

Erik glanced at the man. It was hard to tell anything about a person from a hologram or image. He needed to be able to look a man in the eye before he could judge him, but the kind of man who would buy enough weapons to start a war harbored questionable tendencies.

"What kind of record does he have?" Jia asked. "Obviously, he's a criminal, if he's coming here to illegally buy guns and pass them off, probably for terrorism. But he's not been planet- or transport-flagged, so it can't be that bad."

"He's not a criminal," Emma declared. "Or at least he hasn't been convicted of anything. I'll leave the philosophical debate to you. If he has a criminal record, it's been cleverly concealed in a way I can't easily detect."

She pointed with her other arm. The image of a crowd appeared to her side. In it, most people's faces were contorted in rage. Some people lay on the ground, bloody. A few held stun rods.

Erik gestured to the crowd. "What's all this about?"

"It is the scene of the only time Mr. Mont has been arrested," Emma explained. "He participated in an anti-UTC protest that turned violent. There were mass arrests, in fact. According to the available articles, thousands of people were arrested during the riot."

"But he's not a criminal?" Jia asked, skepticism on her face.

"He was arrested, but the charges were dropped, and he was released," Emma explained. "There was allegedly no evidence he personally participated in any violent acts, but I would assume his wealthy and influential father facilitated the charges being dropped. At least in part." The crowd image vanished. "Mr. Mont is a trained engineer with a specialty in habitation dome design and maintenance, but he hasn't worked for several years. His publicly-available records suggest mostly odd jobs, that sort of thing. Again, this is somewhat in agreement with the wealth and status of his family."

Jia frowned. "Sometimes the children of wealthy families don't want to rely on their parents."

Emma smirked. "Touched a nerve, did I, Detective?"

Jia sidestepped Emma's question. "Why did he stop working as a dome engineer?"

"All I found out was that he was terminated by the company contracting with the local government for dome maintenance," Emma commented. "There's not a lot of information available, but I did find one article suggesting that Mr. Mont was fired because he was judged to have antisocial tendencies, and his position made such concerns high-risk."

"And how do you know this is our guy?" Erik asked. "Being antisocial is a long way from buying a bunch of guns for something shady. Did you figure out how to reconstitute the video feed?"

Emma shook her head. "I attempted to do that, but Mr. Barbu was too thorough in his efforts. In this case, it's a matter of deduction." She gave him a sly smile. "I took the liberty of going through recent local travel records. The population of the Moon and the limited number of visitors makes this sort of search far more practical than it might be in a place like Neo Southern California. He's a recent arrival."

"You're saying he's not from the moon?"

"No, he's not. This is the first time he's ever been here."

"You just searched through the records." Jia folded her arms. "We don't have a warrant for that."

Emma shrugged. "And I'm not a police officer, Detective Lin. Technically, I have no legal rights, nor do I legally exist, and you didn't direct me to do what I did. As far as the law's concerned, I'm just a rogue algorithm that spat out some information. Need I remind you, this isn't even a police case? This is an unofficial task set for you by an agent of the Intelligence Directorate who probably has more reason than most to worry about terrorism."

Jia dropped her arms in frustration but gave Emma a firm nod. Determination washed away the concern on her face.

"I still don't understand," Erik admitted. "If you couldn't recover the actual name and face from the data you grabbed from Barbu, how did you find out who our guy is?"

Emma bowed. "As I said, Detective, via deduction. His body measurements match with more than ninety-nine percent accuracy. That, combined with the other information I uncovered, has convinced me. Unfortunately, identification will require your follow-up since my conclusions aren't considered sufficient evidence within the existing legal framework, and that, along with the method of collecting my information, makes this a far less likely candidate for passing the information to the local authorities."

"Probably," Jia mused. "They won't jump just because we say jump, especially if we don't have conclusive evidence. So, what do you have besides body measurements? There's a reason that kind of thing went out of fashion centuries ago."

"A number of converging and unlikely coincidences," Emma explained. She snapped her fingers theatrically and a moving holographic scene filled the corner of the room. Men in civilian clothes rushed UTC soldiers, clubbing them and shooting them with rifles. One man tossed a plasma grenade.

"Another protest?" Erik asked, his expression darkening.

"No, this is footage from the insurrection on Diogenes' Hope," Emma clarified.

Jia looked down, cupping her chin in thought. "I heard a little about it, but I hadn't paid much attention."

"To be clear, Mr. Mont is from Diogenes' Hope," Emma offered.

Jia furrowed her brow in concentration. "But it's way out on the frontier, right?"

"Yes, thirty-nine light-years from Earth. It's certainly not Molino, but it's far from the core by all normal measures."

"How long does it take to get to the Solar System from there?" Jia asked. "Assuming you don't stop along the way."

"A little over nine months under normal conditions,

assuming efficient transfer," Emma clarified. She summoned a jump navigation diagram. A blue line traced a path from the Trappist 1 system through different systems to their current location.

Erik gestured to the map. "I haven't been paying much attention to off-world news. When did the insurrection start?"

"In January," Jia answered. "It's ongoing only because the insurrectionists had some spectacular early victories and have behaved with vicious ruthlessness, scaring much of the local population into at least tacit cooperation. This includes public execution of alleged pro-government figures, and in several cases, the murder of pro-government families."

Erik grimaced. "These guys sound more like terrorists than simple insurrectionists."

"It's taken some time for the nearest military forces to figure out how to handle it without destroying the colony," Jia continued. "They expect the colony to be retaken soon, but it takes a long time to get news from that far on the frontier, so who knows? It might already be over."

"Yeah, anti-insurgency is always tough." Erik's expression darkened. "Terrorists are easy since most people don't support them, but when you have a straight-up insurrection like that, you have to be careful not to alienate the locals or hurt people who are just trying to survive. In this case, that is likely most of the people. If the insurrectionists are making moves like you describe, the people are trapped between two bad decisions."

"Okay, but I have a problem with the timeline," Jia continued. "It is impossible for him to have left Diogenes'

Hope and gotten here quickly. He must still have been on his way when the fighting started."

"Despite the way people talk about them, insurrections aren't usually spontaneous events where a few plucky revolutionaries pick up some rocks and cry freedom. You need weapons, soldiers, and supply lines. Even if the first shots were fired in January, they might have been planning for years."

Jia nodded. "If Remy Mont's an insurrectionist, he left well before his allies made a move. But for what, exactly? It can't just be for supplies. It makes no sense to come all the way back to the Solar System, or even head to the core worlds. There are more developed frontier colonies than Diogenes' Hope they could source weapons from. Smugglers and pirates are always willing to make money in those kinds of situations."

"You're right. It's too elaborate a plan and has too many risks." Erik pointed to the colony star on Emma's map. "Even if he grabbed an entire transport and filled it with weapons, by the time he got back, it'd be over one way or another. He must have some other plan, but I think Emma's right, and it has something to do with Diogenes' Hope."

Jia hissed in angry surprise. "The moon is twelve hours from Earth. He's going to launch a terrorist attack."

"Probably." Erik considered. "But I'm guessing if he wanted to attack Earth, he would have just gone to Earth. More criminals there to choose from, even if he needed to be more careful. Chang'e is a much more likely target."

Emma smiled as the navigational map and image of Remy disappeared. "He arrived on May 22nd. There is no indication that he's left. I should also note that based on the publicly available law enforcement lists, he's not on any terrorist watchlists currently, which was why he wasn't flagged upon arrival."

"He's got to have some sort of local contact besides Barbu," Erik concluded. "He's not going to be able to do much by himself. That means we need to be careful. We need to find the guy without spooking him. We don't want him burying himself under some trash and hiding. If he's got help here, he'll be able to hide."

"I think it's time I borrowed drones and cameras," Emma suggested. "This isn't Neo SoCal. In a compact series of domes like this city, it'll be easy to find him unless he's already in hiding. If I restrict myself to external cameras, it'll lower the chance of detection."

Erik shook his head. "I don't want to risk us attracting special attention from the local cops or CID, not until we find this guy. If we're right, we need to find him and verify if he's doing anything, and we need to make sure no one tips him off. You just said this is a small city, so all you'll need is a lot of drones."

"Do you have a lot of drones hidden in your pocket, Detective?" Emma raised an eyebrow.

"Nope." He grinned. "Time to go on a shopping spree."

"Yes, just what I always wanted to do on vacation. Go to the moon and buy a bunch of drones." Jia rolled her eyes.

"What? You could always pop a virtual reality helmet on your head and pretend you are..."

"Back in Neo-SoCal?" she interrupted. "I can't risk you doing something without backup. Specifically, my backup.

I'm not going back to having a random partner assigned to me."

The two turned to leave, Erik asking as she opened the door, "So, are you saying there *is* a chance I can graduate to fake-boyfriend?"

"Don't die, or that's a hard no," she answered, amusement coloring her voice.

CHAPTER FORTY-ONE

Six hours later, small fleets of Emma-controlled drones prowled each of the domes making up Chang'e City.

In Erik's hotel room, her holographic form stood in the center of dozens of projected visual feeds provided for the consumption of Erik and Jia, and she'd also routed the feeds to their PNIUs for more personal control of the massive amount of incoming data.

"During all those years I was saving money in the service," Erik began, "I never thought I would use any of it for something like this."

"You just spent a lot of money." Jia smirked. "You could have bought another flitter for that much. We could go find a male AI in some lab for Emma."

"My female characteristics are mostly for your ease," Emma replied. "I'm not organic. Your biological concepts don't apply to me."

Jia laughed even louder. "Spinster for life. Your AI mother is crying in Digital Heaven."

Emma harrumphed.

"It's going to cost a ridiculous amount of money to ship them back, too," Erik commented. He swiped the window in front of him, shifting to a new feed. "But Emma's always complaining about having eyes, and this way she won't have to hack as many drones. We're not violating any laws. Not as long as we keep them in public areas, at least, so you don't have to worry, Jia. Right now, we're nothing more than concerned citizens."

All the feeds vanished except one. Erik's and Jia's private feeds shifted to match it.

"Target sighted," Emma announced triumphantly.

She magnified the feed, revealing a familiar man with long, dark hair. The potential terrorist was currently engaged in the not-so-nefarious activity of eating a red bean bun.

They hadn't expected to find him gunning somebody down in public, but the mundane activity was a reminder that the most dangerous man in a city might not look the part.

Jia didn't doubt that Mont was up to something. Even terrorists had to eat before they went around murdering innocent people.

"Should we pass this on to Alina?" she asked, looking at Erik. "You said she gave you a way to contact her."

"Not yet," Erik answered, his focus on the picture. "But yeah, she gave me a single-use address. She told me to send a message there, and she would contact me within twelve hours in a secure way. The thing is, we believe Mont might be up to something, but if we can figure out what his target is and where his base is, she might be able to handle this without much trouble. It can be a smooth operation instead of a mess."

"That means we might have to watch him for a long time."

Emma scoffed. "I can easily track him."

"I mean, we can't be just anywhere," Jia clarified. "We're going to need to be able to react quickly."

"Nobody ever said investigation was going to be glamorous." Erik shrugged and gave her a jolly smile.

———

Jia sat on the edge of Erik's bed. A map floated in front of her. Two data windows were open on either side of her, each containing detailed information about where they'd tracked Mont throughout the day.

She was seeking a pattern. Even Emma could only do so much.

The AI could provide Erik and Jia with plenty of data about the locations, but without knowing what they were looking for, all she could do was point out potential high-casualty targets. They had no idea if Mont was seeking maximum death or something different. His requests for weapons might be focused on taking out a military or police target.

His wanderings brought him close to both.

There had to be a pattern. If Jia looked at it long enough, she *would* discover it. There was no way Remy Mont was exploring Chang'e City as a tourist.

Were they wrong to trust Emma's deductions?

A machine couldn't claim real instinct, even a unique,

advanced prototype, but Remy Mont being a terrorist and insurrectionist fit. It wasn't illogical that a man from a rebellious colony might travel across the galaxy to seek his perceived revenge.

Jia understood, but that didn't mean she sympathized.

These men were more Cao Cao than Liu Bei. She wasn't going to let Mont take it out on people who had nothing to do with it.

"What are you up to, Mont?" Jia murmured.

Mont walked into a tightly packed residential apartment block comprised of row after stacked row of identical units, although most of them were underground. He headed to a ground-floor unit and waited. The door slid open and another man stuck out his head, looking both ways with a suspicious frown.

"What do we have here?" Erik murmured.

"Ah, this is interesting," Emma announced. "The man who answered the door has a police record. He's a gun goblin, among other things. He did several years in prison for participation in an assault on a police station in Paris and the attempted assassination of a councilman. He claimed he was framed, but it was rather convenient that a number of other people were involved in a known anti-government terrorist group."

"Is he also from Diogenes' Hope?" Erik asked.

"No. Earther, born and bred. He was planet-flagged, and it's only recently he's been allowed to leave the planet after finishing his probation."

Jia narrowed her eyes. "That's suspicious and also convenient for Mont."

Another image of the same apartment appeared, taken

from a lower altitude and a flatter angle. The drone providing the feed hovered between the close trunks of two tall trees, the only vegetation in the entire area.

"Should you be getting that close?" Erik asked. "We don't want to lose these guys yet."

"I've calculated the possible angles of sight," Emma replied. "There's a very low probability that they can see the drone. Even if they do detect and disrupt it, I have others in the area. They won't be able to escape."

The second drone allowed them to peer directly into the apartment. Emma highlighted two other men standing close to the door.

"The man on the right has no public arrest record based on facial recognition," she reported. "It's very unlikely the lunar databases are out of date." She added a red glow around a bulge underneath his jacket. "There is a high probability that's a pistol."

"Just having a gun doesn't make him a terrorist," Jia temporized. "But a known terrorist hanging out with a man from a colony engaged in a violent, self-destructive insurrection and carrying a gun makes me a lot more suspicious. I think we've found Mont's hide-out."

The suspect stepped into the apartment and the door closed. Another man stepped out of a back room just as it did.

"Ah, yes, this is particularly troublesome," Emma announced.

"What?" Erik asked.

A different image of the last man appeared, this time with him smiling in a Lunar Militia uniform.

Jia growled. "He's a soldier?"

"Yes," Emma confirmed. "Active duty."

"If they've got a soldier, they might have a cop or two. At least enough to cover their tracks or slow things down," Erik concluded.

"But if they had a soldier, why not just steal military gear?" Jia wondered.

Erik snickered. "It's a lot harder than you'd think. If it wasn't, every wannabe terrorist and insurrectionist out there would just be raiding Army bases constantly." He motioned to the image. "But this means we're going to need to contact Alina. If we go to the cops, someone might leak something to Mont, and we won't be ready."

Jia's eyes widened, her focus not on Erik. She jabbed her finger on her map, bringing up a location. He watched as she repeated it several times, the data and image changing with each touch. "I've figured it out."

"Figured what out?"

"His path," Jia explained. "I know what it means. It looks like he was just wandering the city, but his trajectory took him close to all the grav towers."

"I can confirm that he spent a longer time near the grav towers than any other landmark or building," Emma added. "

"He must be planning to disable the grav towers somehow," Jia concluded. "But one wouldn't be enough. There's too much redundancy."

Erik gestured to one of her data windows displaying a grav tower near Founders' Park. "They aren't that fragile. You can't shoot them. Without major explosives, you'd have to know exactly where to damage them. These guys aren't the first terrorists to think about messing with a colony's gravity."

"You'd need someone with the right kind of knowledge, such as someone with extensive knowledge of dome engineering might have," Jia replied. "Even if he's not planning to blow them up, he knows a lot about how these things interface with domes."

"Damn." Erik grimaced. "I forgot about that. It also explains why he's calling the shots."

Jia tapped another spot on her map, revealing the area around another tower. "What's the point, though? Damaging the towers would be disruptive, but this is the moon. It wouldn't be zero-G."

"It doesn't have to be. Most people have spent very little time in low gravity or zero-G. That means you mess with gravity, and everything from movement to using a weapon becomes hard. I wouldn't want to fight in one-sixth gee; that's why military-grade exoskeletons have grav compensators."

"It'd be hard for the terrorists, too," Jia insisted. "Unless they had something like grav boots." She looked at Erik. "Or some of those exoskeletons?"

"Exactly." Erik tapped his PNIU and searched for some information before he set it down. "I doubt they've got exoskeletons, but I think they're preparing to lower the gravity and kill a lot of people during the chaos."

"But why?" Jia shook her head, her jaw tight. "If this is about Diogenes' Hope, it's not going to stop anything there."

"They're terrorists. Their goals don't have to be logical

from our perspective, and from what Emma told us, not all of them are part of the insurrection. This might be some sort of ad hoc terrorist alliance." Erik tapped his lips with his thumb and forefinger as he thought. "This is about sending a message. I think they want to prove how vulnerable even a core colony can be. Killing a lot of people without blowing the dome or using explosives might even be more frightening because it means the terrorists have a better chance of surviving and going on to cause more trouble."

Jia took a deep breath and slowly let it out. "I think it's time we contacted Alina."

Erik turned to grab his PNIU once more. "Yeah. Too bad I didn't smuggle the TR-7 up here. It's time to show the terrorists how we do things downwell."

CHAPTER FORTY-TWO

Twenty minutes after Erik sent his message, there was a loud knock on the door to his room.

Erik and Jia exchanged glances. He didn't want to believe they were about to be ambushed, but they'd been trying to track down a dangerous terrorist. Assuming things might see them end up with bullets in their brains.

"It could be a local ID agent," Jia pointed out.

"Probably," Erik offered. "Emma, I'm assuming you've been monitoring the hall cameras outside our rooms?"

There was another knock, this time more urgent.

"Yes," the AI replied. "It seemed prudent, given all concern with gun goblins. My monitoring suggests it's an ID agent, because I don't see anyone on the feed, and there's evidence of external access to the system. I haven't challenged it because I don't want them to be aware of it, but if someone isn't going out of their way to disappear from feeds, I'd be very surprised."

"Let's be careful, just in case." Erik nodded. "I've got a lot of unfinished business before I die."

Jia drew her stun pistol and crouched behind the couch, pointing the weapon at the door.

Erik tapped his PNIU to interface with the external door view. Emma was right; there was nothing there. He reached to the access panel and slapped it.

The door slid open, revealing a tall blue-eyed blonde woman in a tight black dress that flattered her athletic form. If Erik had never seen Agent Koval and was given a picture of the blonde woman, he wouldn't have been able to connect them, but at less than a meter away, he could almost tell just by how she moved.

Erik shook his head, then gestured her inside. "Unless someone's invented teleporting, you've been on the moon the entire time, haven't you?"

"Yes." Alina entered the room and closed the door.

"Why?" Jia stood up, holstering her pistol.

"You know why."

"Because despite all those lines you fed us, this is still a big test," Erik concluded.

Alina shrugged with an apologetic smile. "Sorry. I'm not *trying* to be a bitch, but I needed to be sure about your capabilities."

Jia snorted. "I don't know if I like all your ghost games."

Alina eyed her. "You might not like them, Detective Lin, but they can be effective. You've found something quickly, which is proof that you two are just as effective." Alina sauntered over to the couch and dropped into it. She crossed her legs and folded her hands in her lap. "If you two decided to contact me, you must have something actionable. Rather than waste time trading accusations and complaints, why don't you give me the information? I'm assuming I'll need to do something very violent pretty soon."

Alina sighed after Erik, Jia, and Emma finished explaining the situation, then took a deep breath. "I was hoping this would end with me doing something simple and disrupting an interplanetary contraband supply chain, but it sounds like something far worse than that."

"You believe us?" Jia asked. "This is all circumstantial."

"I'm law enforcement, Jia," Alina replied. "I'm a ghost in the shadows. I do what I need to protect the UTC, and sometimes that means I don't have the luxury of waiting for concrete proof. Not only that, you two have repeatedly proven you have an uncanny ability to root out conspiracies and dangerous plots." She smiled. "If you hadn't, I wouldn't have sent you on this deadly errand, but I can take it from here. Based on what you've found out, I was right to be cautious, but even if that arms dealer partially sold Remy Mont out, our terrorist likely has his weapons and people in place. I'll need to move quickly." She looked down, her brow wrinkling in concern. "This can't be a simple search-and-destroy. The moon's too small to cover it up. I'm going to have to bring local law enforcement on board so I don't end up creating a bigger mess."

"The terrorists might have sympathizers in local law enforcement," Erik reminded her.

"I know who I can trust in the local CID office," Alina

explained. "I'll gather what loyal agents I can and make my move. If we wait for reinforcements from Earth, it'll take too long. They could launch the attack at any minute. You've got eyes on them, which helps, but you don't know how many people are operating in Mont's cell. I'm willing to bet he has a lot more than the few people you saw at that apartment."

"Makes sense," Erik mused. "But it sounds like you're going to be short-handed at a time you could use more people, especially people with experience fighting terrorists on short notice."

Alina raised an eyebrow, and there was a little tilt to the corners of her mouth. "You two want to join in the raid?"

Erik smiled in response. "I can't speak for Jia, but I want in. If you and the CID are in charge, I'm sure you'll keep our names out of it."

Jia nodded. "I'm not going to sit around in a hotel room while terrorists attack innocent people and worry that I'll have to deal with a different partner later."

Alina hopped to her feet with a cluck of her tongue. "Well, aren't we all kind of Hercules today?"

Jia raised an eyebrow. "How do you figure?"

"He had to clean disgusting stables that had been left to fester for far too long. That's what we do—fight the darkness and corruption. It's time to clean up some of the stink that's been building on the moon."

An hour later, Erik and Jia stood inside a hangar filled with law enforcement agents, slipping on tactical vests and gathering their weapons from crates and tables arrayed along the wall.

Alina didn't just have a few friends, she had a full CID strike-team of a dozen agents, including a four-person High-Threat Response team in exoskeletons. The other gathered agents were loading additional gear onto single-person mini-flitters, including stun grenades and EMPs.

Two empty exoskeletons remained.

Alina gestured to one of the machines. "I'd love to give you each one, Detectives, but I don't believe Detective Lin knows how to operate an exoskeleton, and this isn't the kind of mission one uses for training."

Erik frowned. "Damn, Jia. I know what we need to add next to your training regimen."

Jia pulled the strap of a hefty assault rifle over her shoulder and clipped several stun grenades to her vest. "I don't need that toy to take down criminals," she joked. She patted her rifle. "I've got this one."

Erik nodded. "And you're okay with it? When all is said and done, our names aren't going to show up in any reports. I doubt Alina wants us talking about it with the 1-2-2."

"I'd strongly advise against that," Alina confirmed.

"No reports? Oh, the horror." Jia grabbed additional magazines and tucked them into her vest. "You know my favorite part of being a police officer is filling out reports." She winked. "Let's take these bastards down and save some lives."

Alina nodded to Erik and pointed to a tactical suit

draped over a nearby table. "There you go, Hercules. These aren't assault-infantry-grade exoskeletons, but I'm sure you'll enjoy them."

"It'll be nice to pilot a suit again." Erik picked up the tactical suit. "It's been a while."

CHAPTER FORTY-THREE

Jia slid off her mini-flitter about two hundred yards from the apartment complex. She was accompanied by a small squad of CID agents, plus Erik and Alina.

The HTR team had broken into two squads of two and spread out, supplemented by regular agents at different locations. They had the entire apartment complex surrounded and the two main exits covered.

The terrorists were bottled up tightly, or so they hoped.

Although many buildings in the city had underground exits, the blueprints for the target building indicated only surface access.

She would be grateful for any small advantages they could manage against the terrorists.

Erik had run in his exoskeleton alongside Jia, with Emma tucked into an IO port for maximum efficiency. She was providing information to Erik, Emma, and Alina but keeping quiet otherwise, at Alina's suggestion.

As far as the CID agents knew, Alina's FGT—Fancy Ghost Tech—was providing the raid team with additional

tracking and target information from a convenient fleet of
ID drones. They would likely just assume that Emma was
working with Alina.

Which wasn't completely wrong, Jia thought.

It wasn't a huge issue. Most of the 1-2-2 knew at least a
little about Emma. As long as Erik didn't advertise the fact
on the net, the Defense Directorate wouldn't make a move.

They might eventually grow tired of lending their
expensive research project to him, but as long as Emma
didn't want to go back, there was only so much they
could do.

Jia glanced at her partner. His eyes darted around as he
took in diagnostic information projected to his smart
lenses. Everything about Erik strapped into an exoskeleton
felt right.

He was confident in any fight, but the powerful tech
wrapped around him enhanced what was already there
without consuming the man inside.

She'd seen him fight many times, but she'd never had a
chance to see him in his true element using the kind of
equipment that reflected his decades of experience and
training. To Jia, he was Detective Erik Blackwell, a good
police officer, but before that, he had been Major Erik
Blackwell, UTC Army Assault Infantry, veteran of countless campaigns on the frontier.

He was a man who had been poised for decades to
defend the UTC against alien invasion.

The shield of Erik's exoskeleton wasn't fully expanded.
The massive rifle the exoskeleton held was wider and
longer than the four-barreled monstrosity he normally
carried. He lacked the grenade launcher attachment that

some of the other exoskeletons carried, but he'd given no indication he cared.

Jia had been on the other end of exoskeleton weapons enough in the last year that her heart sped up in excitement at the idea of her partner using that power to take on terrorists.

She considered that a powerful testament to hidden desires she would rather not consider at the moment. Or later, for that matter.

A year ago, Jia would have argued that decades of military experience weren't that useful for being a police officer.

She had considered being a cop as performing investigations, with the criminals surrendering when confronted.

The idea of having to use heavy weapons to take people down seemed like something from a holodrama. Earth was supposed to be safe, and specialists like the TPST should have been necessary only in rare cases.

Now she accepted the truth. With terrorists and conspiracies on the move, her partner was the best resource the NSCPD could have had. Even if Erik and Jia weren't operating as 1-2-2 detectives on this little farce of a Moon vacation, they were doing their part to protect innocent people from dangerous monsters who saw no problem with murdering them.

Some antisocial men and women didn't respond to reason. They would only respond to strength, and it was up to the police to be the shield and sword of the common citizen.

Jia took a deep breath through her nose and slowly let it out through her mouth. She was well out of her jurisdiction, but that didn't mean her duty had ended. Criminals might be greedy, but terrorists were worse. They hurt innocent people in the name of righteousness. She inspected her weapon one last time.

Now was the time to protect.

"All teams prepare to move on my signal," Alina transmitted. "In case any of you weren't listening earlier when I went over this, I'm going to send an emergency override signal and lock the entire building down. The local CID headquarters will be transmitting a clearance order to keep the local LEOs from interfering to cut down on potential leaks. I'm hoping they'll be lazy enough to stay away, but if not, things might get confused logistically. Just focus on not allowing the terrorists the opportunity to escape. Remember, our primary target is Remy Mont. Take him alive if possible, but we have no reason to believe these terrorists will respond to reason. He might be our primary target, but our mission is to disrupt whatever terrorist action these people have planned. Just to reiterate, our intelligence suggests they will be heavily armed, potentially with military-grade weapons and the skills to use them. *Be careful.*"

Jia didn't comment on the fact that their non-lethal loadouts were minimal—mostly a few stun grenades here and there. She wasn't sure if that was more the choice of the CID or Alina. From what Jia had seen, by the time Alina got personally involved in a field situation, *someone was going to die.*

But being loyal to the UTC wasn't the same thing as always being right.

436

"What about the civilians inside?" Jia questioned. "There could be hundreds in there."

"If they pay attention to the emergency order, they'll be safer, and the lockdown should keep them in even if they panic." Alina gritted her teeth. "I wish we could clear out everyone first, but if we do that, our terrorists will run with them, or even take them as hostages. It's a big risk to not just hit the hideout before sending out the emergency signal, and the best way to protect people is to breach the apartment as hard and fast as possible to overwhelm terrorist resistance." She shook her head. "Keep that in mind, everyone. We can't sling lead wherever we want. The emergency override will include a message to encourage them to stay low, and that's why I had you keep it to anti-personnel ammo. There's less chance of a stray bullet hitting someone who doesn't have it coming." She took a deep breath. "Let's hope today's a little more Nike than Eris. Get ready. *Transmitting the emergency override code in ten seconds.*"

Jia flipped off her safety. Her heart thundered, but it wasn't fear or excitement. It was awareness.

Erik had told her countless times that when a person started treating a fight like a joke or a game, they would soon be dead. Even their tactical center training was treated seriously.

Practice like it was reality, and reality would never be a surprise.

The obnoxious cry of alarms rang out. It was followed by a melodious woman's voice speaking in English followed by Mandarin, delivering the same message.

"Warning," the voice announced, "a violent incident is

in progress. For your own safety, please shelter in place while law enforcement contains the threat. Failure to comply with these instructions might result in injury or death." The alarm and the voice continued.

"Initiating systems intrusion," Emma reported.

The door to the apartment slid open.

"We've got movement," Erik announced.

A black-garbed man in a bulky tactical suit and full helmet, complete with breather mask, emerged holding a rocket launcher. Jia was comfortable calling that a military-grade weapon. Their terrorists were even ready for gas.

Not what Jia would have preferred at the start of a major raid.

She hoped she could track down Old Barbu someday and make him pay for setting up the terrorists. It didn't matter if he'd indirectly helped them find Mont. If he hadn't supplied the terrorists with weapons, the raid team wouldn't be staring at an armored terrorist with a rocket launcher.

"So much for the lockdown," Erik grumbled. "They had their own overrides ready. No one gets armed up in seconds, and we're also in crap position for our breaching efforts."

They had intended to close within ten seconds after sending the signal. They didn't want to set up next to the apartment immediately and risk detection before the lockdown was in place.

Erik's shield expanded with a click. "Someone sold us out."

"Or something leaked." Alina sighed. "Probably via the

CID systems. It doesn't matter now. Same difference in the end."

"Nothing we can do now but take them down," Jia muttered. "We don't get a second chance at this."

"Jia, remember that scenario we practiced with the Grayheads using Zitark beam rifles a while back?" Erik asked, a huge grin on his face. "Back me up until the CID guys get into position."

"I understand." Jia grinned back. "That's one scenario you couldn't replace with a few women in bikinis. There's no way they could hide anything decent in a skimpy outfit like that."

"I don't even want to know," Alina commented.

"Death to all government dogs!" the man screamed, his message relayed by one of Emma's nearby drones. "All who give them aid and comfort are enemies of humanity, and their lives are forfeit!"

"Man, this guy's obnoxious," Erik observed.

"All exoskeletons advance on my movement," Alina ordered. "Other squads, back us up. His buddies are probably waiting to see what we do." She sent her next words through a loudspeaker. "This is the Criminal Investigation Directorate. You are to lay down your arms immediately. If you don't, you will be subject to lethal force."

Jia thought Alina announcing herself as being from the Intelligence Directorate might have scared the man more, but she understood the practical aspect of not announcing ghost operations over a loudspeaker. The terrorist ignored the threat, choosing instead to make a rude gesture, but he hadn't fired yet.

"Jia can put rounds in him," Erik offered.

Alina nodded. "Go ahead, Detective Lin. These aren't the kind of people we can reason with. We gave him his chance. Snipers, set up while she's covering us."

Jia dropped to one knee and activated the aiming interface between her rifle and her smart lenses. She squeezed off a round as Erik and Alina lumbered forward. They couldn't risk indiscriminate fire into the apartment building with the heavier weapons at that range.

Jia's bullet struck the terrorist in the head, but although he stumbled back, helmet cracked, the man was very much still alive.

"Is it wrong that I miss the guys on the transport?" she asked.

Erik chuckled. "Can't always depend on the bad guys having crap gear."

With exoskeletons and agents converging, the terrorist didn't lack for targets. He howled a loud curse and fired. His rocket sped toward an HTR exoskeleton in one of the other squads. The exoskeleton twisted to avoid the rocket, but it clipped the shield. It didn't explode, dropping instead to the ground and emitting a loud buzz. That exoskeleton and one nearby tumbled forward and crashed to the ground.

Jia grimaced. "Tactical EMP rockets." *Old Barbu had really screwed them.*

Erik scoffed. "This is why I prefer the assault infantry model, but you kick ass with the gear you have." His movement path grew serpentine and erratic, but his gun was never more than a few degrees from the door. Once the exoskeletons were closer, they could open up with less risk of collateral damage.

Jia took another shot. Only twisted fate saved the terrorist since he leaned at the same time she pulled the trigger. The bullet whizzed by his helmet and struck a wall behind him.

The terrorist reached behind the door and came back with a new rocket. He shoved into his launcher, shouting more colorful obscenities exploring certain anatomical impossibilities.

Jia ignored his taunts and took another shot. The bullet blasted chunks of his helmet off. The man stumbled into the apartment and slapped the access panel, and the door slammed shut.

The CID agents groaned from their downed exoskeletons.

The other teams reported no activity at the rear exits.

The terrorists had made a brave stand but disabling a couple of exoskeletons wasn't the same thing as winning the battle, especially when four more exoskeletons were left and plenty of agents were deployed on foot.

"I have gained internal hallway camera access," Emma announced to Erik, Alina, and Jia. "I'm proceeding with monitoring for suspicious activity. There is no one currently outside their apartment. There are no thermal capabilities on these cameras, so I can't confirm apartment occupancy, but at least no one except weapons weasels should get caught up in the violence if you enter the building."

"'Weapons weasels?'" Jia muttered.

Emma responded on a private channel, "Trying out new phrases. 'Gun goblins' gets old."

"We're lucky it's as empty as that," Erik interrupted the

conversation as he continued to close in on the apartment. "This could have been a lot messier."

Erik and Alina reached the apartment first, aided by the long steps of their exoskeletons.

"I can have Emma do it cleanly," Erik explained. "You'll just have to explain it away later. Your call."

"Go ahead," Alina suggested. "There will be more than a few details left out of a lot of people's reports when this is all over." She activated wider broadcast before ordering, "All rear teams, prepare to breach. Hold position at the exits while we enter."

"Breach it, Emma," Erik ordered and jumped to the side.

Other CID agents had set up for overwatch, aided by their own drones. With her job done, Jia sprinted toward the apartment. She didn't want to hang back while her partner took all the risks.

She'd had the choice not to come to the moon, but she had come, knowing full well something like this might happen. Expecting it, even.

Someone like Alina Koval wouldn't need their help for common crimes.

The door slid open. Another rocket burst from inside, barely missing the moving Erik. It zoomed along until it struck a building across the street and crumpled with a loud buzz—another EMP. The terrorist stood a few meters inside the apartment with blood running down the side of his head under his cracked helmet. Erik and Alina's guns came alive. The terrorist's tactical suit managed to deflect the first few shots before their rounds ripped into his chest.

His body jolted with each.

He fell to his knees, coughing up blood. His hand went toward a pocket. "Death...to...dogs!"

Erik put another bullet into him, but it was too late. A blue-white explosion ripped from his pocket. The blast blew out the windows and ripped pieces from the ceiling, blinding Jia for a moment.

Alina and Erik stumbled back, their shields and rifles blackened but their exoskeletons still active. Jia blinked. It had been a plasma grenade, not an actual blinder, but that wasn't much comfort.

"Tango down!" Alina yelled.

"Always good to be reminded what it's like on the other side of that kind of attack," Erik muttered. He rushed inside, smashing through the doorframe, wrenching metal and blasting chunks of rock into the destroyed room. Everything was different on the moon, even the buildings.

Jia continued closing. She didn't need an exoskeleton to support Erik. Alina entered, her pace more deliberate, her movements not as practiced as Erik's.

Jia and the other agents caught up a moment later.

There wasn't much left of the terrorist but burned pieces. The grenade had done its work, leaving a charred and smoking living room and a half-burned kitchen. Pieces of furniture and the wall smoldered, but there were no serious flames in need of suppression.

"I can't get any thermal through these walls," Erik explained. "The other teams will have to do this room by room. The space is too narrow for exoskeletons."

"Maybe that was it," one of the CID agents suggested.

"We know they had more than one guy. They have to be

hiding in here somewhere, or our drone ring would have spotted them."

The agent shrugged. It was obvious he hadn't paid attention during the earlier briefing.

"Cover me," Jia declared, heading toward a nearby hallway.

Erik pointed his gun down the hall, ready to release a burst into anyone who appeared. Jia slapped the access panel for the door to the first bedroom, her gun ready, her expression grim.

It was always a challenge to fight a man who didn't care if he lived or died.

The door slid open, revealing a strange mix of the spartan and the ornate: several nondescript gray cots on an ornate Martian rug. Apparently, the terrorists had a taste for luxury when they weren't killing people.

A CID agent rushed to a door across from Jia and opened it. "Clear!"

Jia and the agent proceeded to the other bedrooms. They were all clear—no other terrorists. No Remy Mont.

"Emma," Jia murmured, "you're sure you don't see any of them?"

"All of my eyes are surrounding the area, and I have access to the cameras," Emma retorted, haughtiness in her tone. "Unless they're as good as certain ghost girls, they haven't passed through my line of sight. They did not escape on the surface."

"The arms smuggler might have gotten them a few toys," Alina thought aloud. "I'd even buy that he got them a few special toys, but there's *no way* he got his hands on enough of them for the entire cell."

"Wait a minute. The surface. That's it." Jia's breath caught. "No, they haven't passed through your line of sight."

"I just said that, and there are no underground exits. They must be in other apartments."

Jia shook her head. "No. If it was about hiding or taking hostages, they would already have made that clear. They're not in their hideout because they escaped while we were watching them."

"So where did they go?" Alina asked.

Jia slung her rifle over her shoulder, turned, and rushed back into the first room. The CID agents joined her. She pointed to a bed, picked it up, and threw it into a corner. Without question, the agents copied her actions.

With the beds cleared, she grabbed the edge of the rug and pulled it back to reveal an open square passage and a ladder leading into a small maintenance storage bay filled with drones and wheeled bots.

"Dammit!" one of the agents hissed. "These guys were prepared."

"This is why I like it when people build up instead of down," Jia complained. "And I'm beginning to understand why they picked the apartment they did. Their people must have controlled maintenance in this building for no one to ever notice." She grabbed a stun grenade and threw it down. After it discharged, she dropped into the maintenance room, landing with a crouch, her rifle ready.

No one was inside, stunned or otherwise. Parts and tools were neatly stacked on shelves. There was no rug this time and only a single exit.

"Emma, anyone outside this room?" Jia asked. "You said you had the hallway cams, right?"

"Yes," Emma confirmed, "and they aren't in the hall adjacent to that maintenance room. There's no evidence of spoofing. I'm examining the feed for possible optical irregularities and not finding anything. There's very little reason to believe they're waiting to ambush you."

A few CID agents jumped down to support Jia. Everyone slowly looked around, seeking evidence that might indicate where the terrorists had gone.

"They couldn't have just disappeared," Jia observed, surveying the room. "We were watching this place. We would have known if they had already left. There's something obvious we're missing. These scum aren't better than us."

"Jia," Erik called over the comm, "mirror your feed for me."

"One second." Jia tapped her PNIU to transmit from her smart lenses to Erik.

"Turn to your left," he suggested.

Jia complied. "It's a maintenance drone exit hatch, and…" She slapped her forehead. "Of course." She walked over to the hatch. "Emma, open this for me, please."

The hatch hissed and released. It opened into the room. Jia peered into the darkened maintenance bot shaft. It was just large enough for a man to walk through slouching.

"Emma, do these shafts go all over the complex?" Jia asked.

"According to the blueprints for the complex, yes," Emma confirmed. "Unfortunately, there aren't many internal sensors in the building compared to a typical Neo

SoCal tower level, so it'd be difficult for me to track their movement inside."

"Do the shafts lead away from the complex?" Jia continued, an idea percolating in her head.

"Not according to the blueprints," Emma began, "but there is close proximity to one of the shafts and an underground parking garage that has been closed for repair for several weeks, according to Chang'e public records. It's not the closest structure to the complex, but it is the closest to a maintenance shaft."

"Do you have camera access to that garage?" Jia didn't know whether to be impressed or annoyed with the terrorists, but she preferred the straightforward, less-well-equipped men on the transport.

It made sense. If the terrorists were sloppy, they would have been caught long before.

"The parking garage is not part of the apartment complex." Emma was silent for a few seconds as she probed the systems. "In addition, its primary operating systems appear to be completely offline, but there are some minor secondary systems remaining, including emergency lights and gate control. The security of the systems is trivial."

"Cameras?"

"No active cameras."

Jia snorted. "Can they be any more suspicious?"

CHAPTER FORTY-FOUR

"Get back up here, Jia," Erik suggested. "Let's go check the garage out. The rest of the CID guys can finish locking the apartment complex down."

Jia scurried back up the ladder and out of the apartment. Erik, Alina, Jia, and two CID regular agents, along with the two remaining HTR exoskeletons, ran around the side of the complex to the out-of-commission parking garage.

The trapezoidal entrance was sealed by a thick metal gate.

"Open it when you're ready," Erik ordered. Emma would understand who he was addressing, and the CID agents would just think Alina was pulling ghost magic.

Jia had taken for granted how useful it was for most of the 1-2-2 to at least be somewhat aware of Emma and her capabilities. The AI liked to brag about being unique, but technology always improved.

In twenty years, maybe every cop would have an AI like

Emma aiding them. Emma would probably have an ego breakdown if she wasn't unique.

Or she would preen about how she was the first.

The gate rumbled and pulled apart, the two main sections sliding into the left and right front walls of the garage. The light from outside spilled in and illuminated the dusty area. While it was tiny compared to what Jia was used to in Neo SoCal, the garage could have easily swallowed a couple of local apartments.

A hovertruck and a half-dozen mini-flitters were parked in the garage. Two drill bots, each several meters long, stood inactive on their six legs, taking up most of the space. Power cells and other tools were scattered about in a haphazard manner.

Jia's suspicious gaze wandered the garage. "I'm not a construction expert, but why would you need two industrial drill bots to fix a garage?"

"A very good question," admitted Alina, her voice oozing caution.

Jia crept forward, keeping a tight grip on her weapon, her breathing shallow. She pointed to a large rectangular hole in the garage wall. It was too short for normal use.

"That must be where they connected to the tunnel," she commented. "But even if the rest of them escaped through this tunnel, where did they go after that? This is turning into the world's most annoying puzzle."

One of Emma's drones whirred into the garage and moved toward a wall. It moved back and forth for a moment, then advanced into the wall, disappearing. The entire wall shimmered.

"It's a hologram!" Jia shouted.

The wall disappeared, revealing a tunnel wide enough to fit a full-sized flitter through. Emma's drone dropped to the ground, smashing into pieces.

"And that was an EMP from the enemy inside," Emma announced. "Contact."

Ten meters into the tunnel, two helmeted terrorists in tactical suits knelt behind a thick, curved gray barrier. Both men perched their rifles atop the barrier, each almost as large as the ones the exoskeletons carried. The terrorist guns came to life in bright bursts. The CID agents without exoskeletons scattered, ducking behind the bots and the truck, but the rounds ripped right through the vehicle, coming within centimeters of killing an agent.

Jia dove behind one of the drill bots, and a round whizzed past her shoulder. She didn't want to test her tactical suit against a bullet of that size and velocity.

What a great vacation we're having, she thought. *Next time, Colonel Adeyemi will ask us to take time off so we can go visit a local war zone.*

Erik, Alina, and the HTR exoskeletons opened fire and spat a cloud of bullets into the tunnel. The terrorists ducked as the bullets bounced and sparked off their barrier.

The exoskeletons advanced in a tight formation, their shields overlapping—a deadly mechanical phalanx with fully automatic weapons.

With the enemy suppressed, Jia and the non-mechanized squads took position on either side of the tunnel. Having good equipment didn't mean much if they were outnumbered.

"Stun grenade out," announced one of the HTR agents.

With a pop, his grenade launcher blasted its ammo toward the terrorists. The men didn't move. They kept up their fire and didn't react to the arcing white grenade discharge.

"Stun-resistant tactical suits," Erik muttered. He fired a burst that sparked against the barrier. "That damned Barbu really set these guys up, didn't he? They might as well be an Army unit."

One terrorist brought his head up too far. His helmet didn't survive the barrage of multiple exoskeleton rifles blasting high-velocity rounds into it. Being splashed by his partner's blood and brains finally broke the resolve of the other terrorist. He leapt over the barrier screaming in rage, a grenade in each hand. Another volley blew through his suit, and the explosions from his grenades mangled his body.

"Can't doubt these guys' commitment to the cause," Erik observed.

"The other agents are securing the building and going apartment to apartment to clear it," Alina reported. "They haven't found any terrorists yet. Why do I get the feeling this has all been nothing but stalling?"

"Emma, stop watching the apartment," Erik recommended. "Fan out with your drones. Whatever they're going to do, it's not going to be subtle. Hit every dome; Alina might be right."

"Ah, nothing worse than an *intelligent* psycho," Emma replied. "But there are limits. I only have so many drones available."

"This isn't Neo SoCal. You'll manage."

Emma harrumphed. "I'd like to see a fleshbag accomplish as much with as little."

"They have to be down the tunnel," Jia observed. "We've got enough firepower here to push on through. If they're stalling, we shouldn't let them waste our time."

Alina nodded. "You're right, Detective Lin, but I'm worried. We'll need to react quickly, and we can't trust the locals. Someone leaked our raid. We still need to secure the building, too. For all we know, they might be hiding in the other apartments and waiting for us to drop our guard."

"I'll grab a mini-flitter and get ready to go if Emma finds anything," Jia suggested.

Alina looked at her. "I'll go with you. I don't like these things much anyway." With a few quick finger commands, the clamps and straps holding her released. She dropped to the ground in a crouch. "I'll have someone pick it up later."

She pulled an infantry rifle off the back of the exoskeleton and slung it over her shoulder before stuffing magazines into her pocket. "I didn't bring my lucky gun. There's our problem." She clucked her tongue. "Then again, it's garbage against armor."

She pointed to two of the CID agents on foot and circled her finger in the air before gesturing for them to come. "You two are with me. Anyone not in an exoskeleton should head back to the garage and secure the area. You're just targets otherwise. The rest of you, you're under Detective Blackwell's tactical command. He's got decades of fighting terrorists under his belt, so if he tells you to slap yourself, you say, 'How hard, sir?'"

Some of the agents looked like they wanted to disagree, but they didn't say anything.

"Don't die, Detective," Alina suggested. "This tunnel might be nothing but stalling and traps, but if they've got more guys in here and you keep whittling them down, that will be fewer who can crawl off to help their boss."

"We might find Mont," Erik countered. He nodded at Jia and Alina. "But if he's not in here, don't let him get away."

Jia snorted. "He won't. He picked the wrong week to come to the moon."

CHAPTER FORTY-FIVE

Don't ever fight a battle on the enemy's terms.

Decades in the Army had reinforced that concept for Erik. Now, as he proceeded down the tunnels, he was forced to admit that everything they had done since starting the raid was on the enemy's terms.

The enemy knew the terrain and had defensive emplacements. There was also a difference in motivation.

The terrorists had proven their willingness to give their lives, and Old Barbu had hooked them up with more than a few cheap pistols.

He didn't doubt the dedication of the CID agents and Alina, but they weren't going to blow themselves up to take down a terrorist.

Erik grunted and reminded himself this battle *wasn't* Molino.

The terrorists might have nice gear, but they'd lost the element of total surprise, and soon they would lose their lives unless they surrendered. So far, all the enemy had accomplished was disabling a few units and dying.

Alina might be right and they were doing nothing but buying time for their comrades, but paying with their lives still meant they were slowly losing.

Unless that was the plan.

The loud, steady thump of the exoskeletons' feet hitting the floor reverberated through the tunnel. The squad had killed the lights and activated their thermal vision.

Without Alina, Erik was in command of the now-three-person exoskeleton squad. Under normal circumstances, that would be enough firepower to mow down a room full of criminals, but they'd already lost exoskeletons to an ambush.

A good enemy might not repeat the same attack, but an effective tactic wasn't soon forgotten. Confidence kept a man calm in a battle; arrogance would end with him meeting with his Maker.

They would need to be careful.

The terrorists might be at the end of the tunnel, or the whole thing might be a distraction. In that case, it would be up to Alina's and Jia's team to deal with the real threat.

Additional pressure in the tunnels might put more pressure on any other operational terrorists' teams.

"Keep it tight," Erik ordered, moving forward. "Triangular formation. I'm the tip of the spear. We should presume similar equipment. We won't win this by attrition, we'll win it by annihilation. The terrorists have made their position clear, so we're going to do them the courtesy of greeting them as politely as they've been greeting us."

"Roger!" the other two agents responded enthusiastically.

He'd wondered if they would have issues taking orders

from him, but decades of military experience came out in his words, voice, and movements. Hunting terrorists in exoskeletons was something he'd been doing for longer than Jia had been alive.

This day, like every day, *it was time to save civilians.*

The tunnel abruptly turned to the right. Slight thermal differentials allowed them to distinguish the walls from the air. There was no sign of additional enemies, which made him more cautious. He doubted it would be that easy. The kind of men with the foresight to prepare EMP rockets were the kind who might set traps.

"Halt," Erik whispered, narrowing his eyes.

The squad complied without question or comment. He adjusted the sensitivity of his thermal sensors.

"Got you." He grinned.

Residual thermal footprints led around the corner. That he could pick them up given the kind of gear the suspects were wearing meant they had been there recently. The tunnel wasn't just a handful of guys pretending to be more.

"Around the corner," Erik transmitted, keeping his voice low. "I'm going to open with a blinder, then we finish them off. Counting down from three, two, one." He launched his blinder grenade toward the corner and it bounced off the wall at a perfect angle. In thermal mode and with the grenade already past the corner, the follow-up flash wasn't that intense for Erik, but judging by the panicked echoing shouts, the same couldn't be said for the terrorists.

It was time to clear the obstacle.

Erik and the squad surged forward. The three terrorists standing in the center of the tunnel fired wildly, their bullets spraying everywhere in their blinded state. A few bullets bounced off the squad's shields shortly before the exoskeletons' rifles came alive.

Their loud reports overlapped in a cacophonous frenzy and their bursts perforated the terrorists. The men jerked backward, collapsing on each other like broken tree limbs, their bodies at angles no normal body should bend.

It was another entry for the day's most futile examples of bravery.

The squad spread out, each man seeking more enemies or incoming EMP rockets. Only the soft sounds of their breathing could be heard.

"Let's keep going," Erik ordered after ten seconds. "Agent Koval's right. These bastards are probably trying to slow us down." He pushed the exoskeleton into a light jog. The intensity of the thermal trail increased, and each step was bringing them closer to the rest of the terrorists and Remy Mont.

As bad as fighting a battle on an enemy's terms was, fighting an enemy without knowing their total strength was even worse. Erik wasn't worried, though. If he killed or disabled every man he ran into without suffering any losses, it would mean a net weakening of the opposing force. Even the most dedicated fighting force could have their will broken by constant losses. If all it took to win a battle was a stout heart, the UTC would have been ripped apart by terrorists not long after its formation.

"Emma, give me a direct line to Jia and Alina," Erik requested. Hoping Mont was at the end of the tunnel wasn't the same thing as knowing the man was.

"Unfortunately, that's not currently possible," she replied.

"What?" Erik chuckled. "The great Emma can't redirect an exoskeleton's comm system? You're slipping."

"I could manage that if any of these boys had bothered to set up relays. This isn't even simple dirt around us for the most part, Detective. It's lunar bedrock, filled with a rich bounty of obnoxious materials. While we aren't that deep underground, it's blocking all transmissions. Need I remind you that I lack the ability to change the laws of physics?"

"I'm disappointed," Erik joked. "We'll get you changing those laws in the future." His smile slipped. "Does that mean your drones are dead? Alina was depending mostly on your recon. The CID didn't send many up."

"No, I had already programmed them to use a general search pattern," she explained. "Detective Lin and Agent Koval should have access to all their feeds, but of course, if we reestablished comm contact, it would be more efficient since I can coordinate them all with vastly superior efficiency and help locate any suspicious bullet beavers."

"All the more reason to move faster," he mumbled. "This tunnel can't go on forever."

"You might want to switch from thermal mode," Emma recommended. "Ambient human visual-range lighting levels are increasing in the far distance."

"Return to normal optics," Erik ordered the rest of the squad.

"Roger!" The HTR agents matched his pace.

Emma was proven right a few seconds later.

Warm lighting filtered into the widening tunnel, illumi-

nating the entire length of the current stretch. No terrorists or hardened checkpoints blocked their way. No traps
exploded to bury them in lunar rock. Erik was almost
disappointed in the terrorists.

He'd fought better men before. Bravery might be
impressive, but bravery combined with intelligence turned
a man from a sad story into a legend even his enemies
respected.

"You guys ready to rush to the light at the end of the
tunnel?" Erik joked.

The agents laughed nervously.

"Don't worry." Erik chuckled. "I'm too stubborn to die
here. Just be like me."

"Roger that, sir."

Erik continued his advance. He picked up the pace and
swept his rifle back and forth, seeking a target. He doubted
the tunnel emptied out next to a grav tower. This was
nothing more than an escape tunnel. He'd seen this kind of
tactic before, and the presence the tunnel confirmed two
important facts about their adversaries. He'd bet his MX
60 on it.

First, the raid had successfully located the terrorists'
hideout. Second, the terrorists had had a decent amount of
time to prepare prior to whatever original mission they
had planned. Panicked, hasty drilling with the bots would
have been detected by seismic sensors and investigated.

That kind of thing would have been routed immediately to the local authorities or the CID, raising the chance
of detection.

Erik wouldn't have been surprised if they'd had weeks
to prepare, and if they were pulling off tricks like huge

escape tunnels, it meant there would be more surprises before the day was over. He might be forced to reevaluate his estimate of their intelligence, but it didn't matter.

Even the smartest people died if you shot them enough times.

He kept moving. They needed to take Mont down.

Right now, the other terrorists were solely chips the engineer was cashing in to buy time. The man hadn't come all the way from Diogenes' Hope to give up just because of a raid.

The tunnel sloped upward steeply, the light growing brighter with each step.

Erik pushed his exoskeleton faster, the heavy footfalls knocking dust and rock from the roof. "You two keep on the other side of the tunnel, and I'll take this one. Stay out of the center. Everyone will fire off a blinder right before we clear the tunnel on my mark. Unless they immediately drop their weapons, take them down with extreme prejudice."

"Roger," the agents replied.

The squad continued their charge up the tunnel. The deep darkness of a minute prior was now a distant memory. They had returned to the simulated daylight of Habitation Dome Four.

"Launch!" Erik shouted.

The three exoskeletons launched their blinders. A couple of seconds later, Erik and the agents burst out the tunnel into a brightly lit sprawling white tent extending about thirty meters in all directions.

The dead shells of their blinders lay on the ground. A light breeze fluttered the flaps of the tent entrance.

Erik had read once that every habitation dome included occasional simulated irregular gusts of wind to aid in plant development.

Without exposure to wind, many trees and other woody plants didn't develop strong enough wood. They also tended to grow faster than in the wild.

The combination resulted in plants prone to collapse. It might be a feeble lie to pretend trees under a lunar dome would ever approach anything natural, but people did like a little green around their cities.

After a quick three-hundred-sixty-degree turn to verify what his sensors were already telling him, Erik frowned. There was no one in the tent.

Where were the enemy suicide bombers or armored men with anti-materiel rifles surrounding the tunnel and waiting to light them up?

It was silent and creepy.

He'd been expecting something—if not any of those kinds of forces, at least an exoskeleton or one crazed terrorist with an ax. An empty tent covering a big hole in the ground didn't make sense.

It wasn't worth the lives they'd just expended to guard it.

Something was wrong, or the tent was serving as another way to blind the team.

A warning popped up on his smart lenses that there was an unexpected incoming object from above.

"Let's head for the—" Erik began. "Forward now!"

Erik craned his neck up and spotted the falling dark sphere. Instinctively, he pressed his thumbs against the control interface in the exoskeleton arms and pushed his feet up. On a military-grade exoskeleton, that would have normally activated the jump thrusters and modulated the grav field to aid in the jump. Within half a second, Erik realized his mistake and charged toward the exit without any special maneuvers.

He begrudgingly accepted that the terrorists weren't as stupid as he'd thought.

The two HTR agents hesitated a couple more seconds before rushing after Erik. That allowed the sphere enough time to release its payload with an explosive pop. Metal netting blasted out and wrapped around the two HTR exoskeletons. Blue arcs played across the frames, and the agents grimaced in pain. Their exoskeletons tumbled to the ground, the men inside twitching.

Erik growled, his heart kicking up. The terrorists would pay for that little stunt. "Status report."

"We're fine," one of the agents replied, his voice unsteady. He started unstrapping himself. "These terrorists sure like their traps."

"They know they can't win in a straight-up fight," Erik growled.

The other agent freed himself of his exoskeleton and moaned. "I've got double-vision, and my head's pounding like my ex-wife's knocking on my door. I don't think I can hit a mountain at point-blank range right now. You don't have time to worry about us, Detective." He pulled a sidearm from the back of the skeleton. "Just *go*."

"How you supposed to protect yourself if you're that messed up?" Erik challenged.

"I at least have a chance," the agent replied. "The civilians out there don't if the terrorists pull off whatever they're planning. If you kill them all as soon as you see them, none of them can come after us, now can they?"

"I can't argue with that logic."

Erik needed to ground himself before he rushed away. He might be wrong.

"Good news, Detective," Emma announced, sounding chipper. "I've reestablished direct control of the drones. I'm searching for Mont or any suspicious people in armor and helmets. I don't have any drones in your area, but I'm flying some there now."

"Jia, Alina," Erik transmitted, "what's your status?"

"We're in the air," Jia replied. "We're looking for them ourselves. Where are you?"

"Some huge white tent," Erik explained. "They must have set this up to cover their exit. At least they don't have so much money they could buy an entire building to hide it. The other two exoskeletons are down, and the agents suffered minor injuries."

"We'll head that way," Alina suggested. "If that's where they came out, we might spot them along the way if they've run."

"Good plan. You're sure about not calling in the locals, Alina? We might need more eyes."

The agent didn't respond for several seconds. "We'll do that if it comes down to it, but we're already playing hide and seek because of some corrupt locals. This should have been *much* cleaner."

Erik emerged from the tent. "I—" He jerked to the right, avoiding the rocket coming straight at him. It buzzed past him, flew through the tent, and ripped out the back. It didn't explode.

A loud buzz in the distance revealed it was another EMP rocket.

Two exoskeletons stood about twenty meters away, their shields extended. One was equipped with a rotary rocket launcher, and the other a heavy rifle and grenade launcher. Their helmeted operators began circling Erik on either side.

"I'll get back to you," he muttered. "I've got exo trouble. Agents, stay inside the tent until I take care of things out here. Don't worry, I'm not leaving you to deal with these guys."

"Roger!"

Erik switched his comm to external broadcast mode. "You guys sure you don't want to give up? Let me give you a little hint: I've been dancing in exos for decades. Right now, I effectively outnumber you one to two."

Another rocket streamed his way. He timed his move to spin the exoskeleton, and the rocket missed. The gunner opened up, his bullets sparking off Erik's shield.

"FINE! *Let's dance.*" Erik pushed his exoskeleton into a sprint toward the man with the rocket launcher and opened fire. His quick bursts struck the terrorist's shield, his bullets flattening and bouncing off. He sidestepped as the man fired another rocket. The projectile screamed past and exploded behind him, blasting up dirt and rock.

They had graduated from EMP rockets.

The terrorist's friend opened fire, limiting it to controlled bursts. The man must have been smart enough not to let Erik lead him into shooting his friend. A quick jerk to the opposite side saved Erik from another rocket. The closer terrorist backed up with quick steps, but his exoskeleton's left arm moved too far to the left, exposing a gap between the shield and the operator.

It was time to demonstrate the difference a few decades could make.

As Erik knew brutally well from experience, a tactical suit was bullet-resistant, not bullet*proof*, especially against exoskeleton-sized equipment, and now the operator was exposed. He fired three quick bursts into the terrorist's chest. The man cried out in pain, blood leaking from the new holes, but he didn't raise his shield. Erik finished him off with another burst and ran toward him, reaching out with his shield arm to stop the disabled exoskeleton from falling to the ground.

No use letting a good enemy exoskeleton go to waste.

"You'll die for that, government dog!" the remaining terrorist shouted.

Erik snorted his response. "Given you guys' track record today, I'm going to go ahead and say probably not."

The terrorist fired, and Erik shoved the terrorist exoskeleton toward the danger. Bullets sparked as they bounced off the metal frame.

Erik fired another blinder through the smoke of the explosion, his automatic optical filters kicking in with the launch.

The blinder became a bright white star.

The remaining terrorist exoskeleton stumbled and fired three grenades in rapid succession instead of using his rifle. The grenades flew past Erik exploding against a few unfortunate trees and some mini-flitters behind him.

With a flick of his finger, Erik switched from burst-fire to automatic and delivered his own stream of bullets as he rushed toward the man. His target managed to keep his shield up, but his clumsy movements made it obvious his vision hadn't recovered by the time Erik arrived.

A shield bash pushed the terrorist's exoskeleton off-balance, opening up the soft target of the operator. Erik shoved his rifle against the terrorist's chest and released high-velocity hell. His ammo display blinked in his smart lenses. He was down to fifty percent, but given the new hole in his opponent's chest, he wouldn't need any more for this fight.

Erik allowed the exoskeleton to tumble backward. It crashed into the hard-packed ground with a loud thump.

"Emma, any luck?" Erik asked, looking around. "They could have pulled a whole convoy through that tunnel. If this was a stall job and we surprised them, that means they *had* to come through this area."

"Interestingly enough, some of the local camera density maps suggest possible blind spots around this area," Emma reported. "That might have been why they chose it. I'm moving more drones nearby from different directions. I'll find them soon."

"You sure about that?"

Emma snorted. "You stick to killing, Detective, and I'll stick to the drone surveillance nets."

Erik spotted a mini-flitter that had survived the grenades. He released his harness and straps before deactivating the exoskeleton. "I doubt I'm going to catch up to them running around in this thing." He grabbed the smaller rifle off the back. The *snicks* cutting into the after-action silence as he started loading clips.

Once he had them ensconced in his tactical vest, he removed Emma from the exoskeleton's IO port.

"I was getting used to having a bipedal body," she commented. "It's quaint, but I can see the disadvantages. I don't know how you stand it."

"You get used to it," he answered. "For now, I need you to help me with this flitter." Erik pointed to it. "I'm guessing once you find our targets, this is going to go very quickly. I think they played their big cards already." He jogged toward the vehicle. "You guys still okay in the tent?"

"We're good, Detective," one of them offered. "Head's still ringing, but we don't need any immediate medical help. Take a few down for us!" He got a "Hoowah!" from the other.

"I'll do that." Erik arrived at the mini-flitter.

Taking a second, he located and shoved Emma into an IO slot, then threw his legs over the one-person vehicle. "Give us something, Emma. We're running out of time. I'll give Mont's crew this—they're damned good at stalling, but it's hard to win when you're only on defense."

"I assure you I'm not holding anything back," she replied in a clipped tone. "Ah, there we go." She sounded much happier. "I've located your terrorist gun goblins. Transmitting coordinates and providing drone feeds now. Please finish them off so I can go back to something more stimulating."

CHAPTER FORTY-SIX

Jia whipped her mini-flitter around and zoomed toward the coordinates sent by Emma.

Sweat beaded the side of her head. The enemy had done their best to slow them down and distract them, and she would admit they had done a very good job.

If they hadn't had Emma helping them, the terrorists might have even succeeded, but what might have been meant nothing. Now it was just a matter of time.

According to the transmitted feed, the helmeted and armored terrorists were jumping off their mini-flitters and out of a hovertruck next to a grav tower control facility. The facility formed the base of one of the larger towers.

"Why?" Jia murmured her breath. All those sacrifices, and that was all they'd achieved—a handful of terrorists at a single gravity tower.

To her relief, there were no exoskeletons with the terrorists, but six men left the vehicles to escort a low-flying cargo drone pulled from the back. The drone carried a large gray metal crate. Mont led the group, but the cocky terrorist didn't wear a helmet or armor. Jia was sure he would regret that soon, but she had no idea what was in the crate. If they took down all the terrorists quickly enough, it wouldn't matter.

"Do they have men at any of the other towers?" Erik asked over the comm. "I'm heading your way now, but it'll take me a few extra minutes to get there. Turns out this flitter took a little damage during the fight."

"No, there are no other terrorists at any other tower," Emma reported. "Unless they're invisible. The only visible gun goblins you need to stop are at that one location, but I can't guarantee they aren't taking advantage of subterranean paths out of the sight of my drones. Given the careful planning they have displayed, it's not impossible they've achieved something like that, but it is unlikely."

"Six men left isn't a lot," Jia observed. "They had a decent force and brave men, but they have to realize it's all but over."

"It is when it's so close to being over that desperate men do the most dangerous things," Alina reminded her.

"True, but they're not going to be able to mess up the colony's gravity by blowing up one tower," Erik concluded. "They might have had time to arm up and fight us, but we still screwed up their timetable. They probably had to abandon their original plan and are now just going to set off a bomb, so they have something to show for everything."

Was it this close to being finished?

"Whatever their plan is, we're running out of time," Jia summarized. "We need immediate reinforcements for the other towers in case they have tricked us. Emma's right. If they made it this far without being noticed, they might have other tunnels or blind spots. At this point, they might just blow a tower so it comes down and crushes people and damages buildings. Not all terrorists are trying to top the Second Spring." Her eyes widened. "Alina, send an evacuation notice to the tower."

Alina sucked in a breath. She didn't respond for seconds. "Sent, and you're right. If they have a spy in the local police, it won't help them much now. Mont's got to be running the main mission. I'll route a request for aid through the CID office and have them head to the other towers, but we can't sit around and wait for their help. They've been doing everything they could and sacrificing men to slow us down, and there *has* to be a reason for that." She paused for a moment. "There has to be something more than a basic bomb in that crate."

Jia dropped the altitude of her mini-flitter, leading Alina and two CID agents toward the grav tower in the distance. "Whatever this is, we need to end it." She glanced at the feed projected on the side of her handlebars. The terrorists had entered the building with the cargo drone. They'd left one guard outside, but he was heading around the side of the building. "Confident, aren't they?"

"What's in the crate?" Erik asked. "It might not be a basic bomb. It could be a WMD."

"That seems unlikely," Alina mused. "If they had to rely on locals for something as mundane as rifles and exoskeletons, they didn't smuggle in a WMD. Barbu had to know that if he somehow got them a WMD, he would end up the target of every CID agent and ID ghost in the UTC. I'm not saying it's impossible, but they'd have to get it through Customs."

"This seems too elaborate for a regular bomb," Jia considered. "Any idiot terrorist could bomb a grav tower, and it doesn't matter that he's an engineer. There's no special knowledge that will let him take out the grav field by taking out a single tower. Grav-field networks aren't designed that way. They could have killed more people just taking their rifles and exoskeletons out into the street and attacking, which means whatever's supposed to happen in that tower has to have more symbolic power than that."

"There's no shame in not being able to get into the mind of a killer, Jia," Erik suggested. "How about we just shoot first and ask questions of anyone who survives?"

"I can get behind that plan." Jia flew closer to the tower and control facility, her heart pounding. With Emma on watch through the drones, Jia set down near the entrance.

Alina and the agents arrived a few seconds later.

"The roaming terrorist has entered the building through a different door," Emma reported. "Perhaps his bravery only extends so far."

Alina tilted her head down. "The local cops are gearing up. They'll be here in a few minutes, but they are insisting they need to come in force for safety. We won't have backup from them for probably ten or fifteen minutes, but at least they'll have token patrols near most of the grav towers in a few minutes. Between them and Emma's drones, that should minimize offsite surprises, and my instincts tell me this is all Mont has left."

"That *long*?" Jia hissed in irritation. "Terrorist sympathizers in the force?"

"Probably, but we don't have time to worry about them." Alina unslung her rifle. "I knew I should have stuck to my standard gear." She grinned. "But I like a little more plausible deniability when I fight in the open. There's nothing like getting yelled at by my superiors for using ghost tech where a news drone might be filming. It's not that hard to throw the public off the scent, but they still *complain and complain and complain.*"

Jia and Alina rushed to the door and took up positions on either side. The CID agents with them crouched in front and aimed their weapons. Alina slapped the access panel, but the door refused to open.

"I suppose I was asking for too much," she declared.

"Emma, can you open the door, or do you have to be closer?" Jia asked.

"I'm attempting to access the facility through proxies," Emma reported, "and I'm meeting unusual resistance. The terrorists must already have control of the main system."

"We don't have time for hacking games." Alina reached into a pouch in her tactical vest and pulled out a small breaching disk. "It's not elegant, but it'll work." She stuck her fingers between the notches and twisted to prime the explosive before setting it against the center of the door.

The two women moved a few meters away.

"Time to say hello to our shy friends. *Breaching!*" Alina slapped her PNIU. The disk exploded in a bright flash, blasting the metal door into hundreds of blackened fragments all over the hard tile floor of the interior.

Jia ducked her head and charged through the smoking hole. Her stomach knotted. Bullet-riddled bodies littered the floor down the hall.

Some wore coveralls, others suits—all dead city workers. A few security guards lay against the wall, their eyes locked open in death stares. Their stun pistols were on the floor next to them.

They had not stood a chance against the lethally equipped and ruthless terrorists.

Alina stepped through the hole and shook her head. "We can't save everyone today, but we *can* kill the monsters before they kill more. They're running out of tricks and places to hide."

"Emma," Jia spat through a clenched jaw, "let us know if any of them run. Do whatever you need to keep them in sight. I don't want any of them escaping."

"No monsters will escape under my watch," Emma replied.

Jia, Alina, and the two agents jogged forward, maintaining a loose wedge formation. If a terrorist appeared, he'd get four people shooting him at once with assault rifles. A tactical suit could only do so much to protect a man, even against non-exoskeleton weapons.

It wasn't hard to determine the path of the terrorists. All the team needed to do was follow the trail of bodies. After a few turns, Jia knew exactly where they were heading—the central emitter control room.

The layout of every grav tower facility in Chang'e City was exactly the same, according to her research.

Jia scoffed. The terrorists were led by an engineer. They were probably relying on the same thing.

The squad stopped at a corner after hearing murmurs. Jia peeked around, jerking her head back and avoiding a terrorist fusillade. Close. *Too close.*

Not today, she thought. *And not to you.*

Jia held up two fingers to indicate the number of opponents. Alina and the agents nodded back. Jia then closed her hand, held up three fingers, dropped one, and dropped another. She was about to drop her last finger when the entire building shook.

"That can't be good," Jia murmured, spreading out her arms for balance and trying not to drop her rifle.

The shaking stopped. The final tremor launched Jia into the air, but she didn't come back down as she'd expected.

"Huh?" She threw up her hand and stopped her head from smacking into the roof. Alina was standing perpendicular to the floor, her boots firmly against the wall, but she wasn't falling. The two CID agents cartwheeled through the air, desperately waving their arms and kicking their legs.

"Zero-g!" Jia exclaimed, blinking. She frowned at Alina. "You've got some sort of slick grav boots that don't look like grav boots, don't you? More ghost toys?"

Alina winked. "Yes, something like that. Ghost privilege. But these are just mag boots. Even ID doesn't have grav boots this small." She turned her head toward the agents flying out of control. "And you two—" She winced as they smacked their heads hard into a wall.

Their bodies went limp. They were still breathing, but they wouldn't be helping the two women any time soon.

"That's less than optimal," Jia commented. "Then again, this whole situation is."

"Having a little trouble, government dogs?" shouted a terrorist from around the corner. He laughed. "Now you can't win, can you? You never expected this. You don't understand how well we prepared for this."

"Maybe not zero-g," Jia muttered, "but you're in a grav tower. It's not that big a surprise."

Alina frowned. "This doesn't make sense. If they damaged the emitter somehow, shouldn't it be at one-sixth gee, not zero? This is the moon, not deep space."

Jia pushed away from the roof and gracefully glided back to the floor. "It's time for the world's more lethal sphere ball game. Erik, how close are you?"

"A few more minutes."

"What's gravity like outside? Any sign they've disrupted the colony in general?"

"Everything looks normal," he replied. "Couldn't Mont use the emitter to cancel the local gravity?"

"In theory," Jia replied, "but everything I've read about the towers says they should have overlapping fields. The last thing anyone wants is a sudden massive change in gravity inside even a small portion of a dome." She shrugged. "He is a specialist, but if it only applies to the building, what good does it do?"

"This isn't the plan, then," Alina concluded. "It's just another way of slowing us down." She frowned, and there was something slightly ridiculous about the woman doing so while holding a rifle and standing on the wall. "I don't have grenades. Do you?"

Jia glanced at her tactical vest. "A few stun grenades and a blinder." She patted her stun grenades. "I'm going to throw these first and then the blinder. If they have stun dampeners, they'll probably ignore them all and not understand what's happening until it's too late. They were prepared for gas, but blinders are working on them."

"Probably haven't trained well with their equipment. It's a good plan." Alina switched to burst fire. "Let's find Mont and his Golden Fleece."

Jia grabbed the first grenade and smiled. No gravity meant getting the grenade to the enemy without exposing herself was nothing more than a trivial geometry problem. She visualized the path of the grenade and hurled it. The force of the throw sent her floating backward. She flung another grenade, and when the first grenade buzzed, she tossed her third weapon, the blinder, and turned her head.

The terrorists groaned. Jia brought up her legs and pushed off against the back wall, launching herself around the corner. Alina ran along the wall. Both women fired into the terrorists. The men were standing on the floor in larger, more obvious magnetic boots, but nothing as large as grav boots.

The bullets pelted their tactical suits, and they jerked back.

Jia pushed off another wall and rotated her body to avoid Alina. She continued firing bursts at the same spot in the enemy tactical suit until her rounds penetrated. Each shot propelled her backward, but she put her foot back and caught herself before colliding with a wall. Her target screamed, his body leaning backward at an angle but his boots keeping him in place. Spherical blood droplets leaked from the wound, becoming dark crimson beads decorating the sterile gray hallway. His partner didn't last much longer under Alina's lethal attention.

"You're missing all the fun, Erik," Jia commented. "If you can call a zero-g gunfight fun."

"I'm almost there," he grumbled. "You better save me a terrorist or two."

"Didn't you just destroy two exoskeletons singlehandedly?" Jia replied with a laugh.

"Yeah, but that's easy when you're in an exoskeleton. I want a little more challenge, just to make sure I don't get rusty."

"Whatever gets you here," Alina offered.

Metallic clacks echoed from around a corner at the end of the hall, and Jia and Alina readied their guns. They opened fire when several small security bots emerged. The machines were unconcerned with gravity, thanks to their magnetic adhesion to the metal walls of the corridor.

Jia flung herself backward to brace against the wall. She took careful aim at the main body housing the processing core and downed a bot with ease.

She'd gotten a lot of practice destroying bots in the last year, and now they barely registered as a threat. The machine sparked and smoked, its magnetic grip releasing. It floated away from the wall.

She had downed another bot by the time Alina destroyed her first.

"I don't get why they're sending bots," Jia muttered, firing again. Her body pressed against the wall. "They had guys left by my count. More stalling?"

"I'd assume so." Alina annihilated another bot. "Every second they stall us is another second for Mont to do his thing. If they've already messed up the gravity, he must be in the control room, or at least have low-level access to the system."

Jia ejected her magazine. The discarded piece spun away from the gun and bounced off the floor. She jammed another magazine into her weapon and unloaded on two closer bots. "Then we're already out of time."

Alina blasted through the last bot. She stepped away from the wall and onto the floor. She motioned forward. "I don't disagree."

Jia pushed off the wall and floated forward. "We're *coming.*"

CHAPTER FORTY-SEVEN

Erik set down outside the facility and hopped off the mini-flitter with a restrained grunt. After depositing Emma in a pouch on his vest, he dropped his rifle into his hands. "I'm here. Emma can lead me to you once I'm inside."

"The trail's pretty obvious," Jia commed. "If grisly."

"Understood." Erik took a few steps toward the building. On this third, he pushed off the ground and didn't come back down. He chuckled. "The zero-g field extends a few meters from the building. Nice."

"We're advancing and almost to the control room," Jia reported. "But there are more stupid bots. What good is having a bunch of security bots if you let terrorists turn them against the authorities?"

"The locals have set up at other grav towers," Alina explained. "They aren't reporting any trouble, and the staff inside are all cooperating, but the units that were supposed to reinforce us directly are taking fire. They've killed or disabled most of the attackers, and they don't seem to be outgunned from what I'm hearing on the comm, but it's holding them back."

"So Mont didn't have everyone here," Erik concluded. "And their spy must be giving them location information. It's just more stalling."

"Gun goblin," Emma announced. She sent a red arrow to his smart lenses, pointing to the left

Erik spun to his left. He fired at the terrorist near the corner of the building, the shot propelling him backward.

It might have been a while since he'd fought in zero-g not stabilized by grav or mag boots, but the old instincts returned. Zero-g didn't bother Erik. He'd trained for it, and he'd fought in it countless times. It was just another variable to take into account for moving or shooting.

The burst struck the terrorist's helmet, cracking it, and they stumbled. Erik didn't bother to right himself as he continued floating backward. He stabilized his rifle by using his live arm as a platform and fired twice to finish off his target.

"Anymore, Emma?" Erik looked around.

"No. Based on movement and size, that was almost certainly the gun goblin who broke off from the group earlier."

Erik snorted. "Idiot thought he could win in an ambush."

"I'm the one who alerted you."

Erik grinned. "One of the reasons I can fight without watching my back is because I know *you're* watching it." The direct compliment shut her up, so Erik continued with, "How are we doing on the hacking?"

If he were on equal equipment terms with the terrorists, he would have had the advantage of experience, but their boots negated a lot of his advantage. There was no reason not to have Emma restore gravity.

"The building systems are completely cut off from the outside world," she replied. "While I see no indication of a virus, it's startlingly similar to what happened on the transport. There's little to anything I can do without direct physical systems access."

"There have been a lot of careful terrorists focused on the moon lately," Erik muttered. "I'm having trouble thinking this is all a coincidence. A careful terrorist doesn't necessarily mean a successful terrorist, though." He pushed his rifle down like an oar and caught the ground. With a shove, he launched himself toward the door, spinning and contorting his body to slide through the open entrance.

Erik flew into the building, swimming through the cloud of door fragments floating in the hall. He shoved them out of his face and pushed off the wall toward the other wall, avoiding the bodies. The sight didn't shock him, but it did remind him of the stakes.

He built up speed with his zigzag flight pattern. "How are you doing, Jia?"

"We're almost to the control room," she replied. "They've got it sealed and reinforced. We haven't run into any more terrorists, and we're through all the bots. Oh, wait." Gunfire echoed through the hallways. "More terrorists."

She sounded annoyed.

"I should be there soon." Erik entered the passage containing Jia's and Alina's earlier victims. A small cloud of their blood droplets filled the air. He considered grabbing their mag boots.

After a few seconds of thought, he unlatched a man from his boots, but he didn't take the footwear. Instead, he pushed the body forward. It was an eerie sight, a cop with a floating corpse.

A trip through a few more halls brought him to the others. Alina knelt near the corner. A dead terrorist floated near the end of the hallway, adding his own crimson cloud to the room.

Jia floated behind Alina, frowning. She grimaced at Erik's macabre cargo. "Why do you have a dead terrorist with you?" She gestured to the body. "I'm sure I killed that one."

"Don't worry, he stayed dead." Erik smiled. "I grabbed him because I don't have any grenades, and from what I overheard on the comm, you don't have anything useful left. We can use him as a distraction."

Alina looked over her shoulder. "Cold but effective. You already think like a ghost. I like it."

"We've taken one down." Jia gestured to the body at the end of the hallway. "But there is one more guarding the control room. Mont must be inside the control room with whatever the drone was carrying. We might very well be blown up in the next few minutes if we don't hurry. Killing an ID agent, the Obsidian Detective, and Lady Justice has got to be worth a few propaganda points."

"That news would never get out," Alina insisted.

"Still not my preferred way to die," Erik admitted, "but it's always ranked high in the pool." He grabbed the dead terrorist by the scruff of the neck. "I'm going to toss this guy around the corner, and then we'll finish his friend off. We can ask Mont what his plan is when we're sticking our guns in his face."

Alina and Jia nodded.

Erik pulled himself along the wall, dragging the body behind him effortlessly. Alina prepared to jump. Jia pushed herself the other way, prepared to shove herself into another gun battle.

"Is this something you've done a lot?" Jia asked, a curious look on her face. "I don't doubt the effectiveness; it's just not something I would have thought of."

"No, it's *not* something I've done a lot," Erik admitted. "But it's something I've had to do before. In a battle, you do what you need to do to win, especially when your friends' and innocent lives are on the line."

"I'm not complaining. I killed that man." Jia smirked. "It's just that we never trained on a 'throw a body in a zero-g scenario.' You and Emma obviously need to get a lot more creative than you have been."

Erik shrugged. "I didn't think it'd come up so soon. I still prefer the bikini beach scenario." He grinned. "But we need to hurry. Ready?"

Jia snickered and nodded. Alina gave a quick nod.

"Surrender!" Erik shoved the body forward and immediately pushed off the wall. Alina sprang up, and Jia launched herself around the corner.

The terrorist took the bait and opened fire on his dead comrade, which gave the team vital seconds of confusion to return fire. A tactical suit and helmet might as well be paper for three-trained marksmen concentrating their fire. Erik, Jia, and Alina shredded the man with their river of bullets. The body spiraled toward the doors to the control room, blood droplets streaming out.

Erik kicked off a wall, moved forward, and pushed the bullet-sponge corpse toward the back of the hallway. With another push, he floated toward the closed door as he looked back at Alina. "Do you have another breach disk?"

Alina walked toward the door, her mag boots clanging. "I could try, but this is thick. Because of the zero-g, debris backfire could slice us into Zitark appetizers."

"We could head around the corner," Erik considered. "But I see what you mean. I don't want to create a bunch of crap that might deflect bullets if we have to fire from the hallway."

Jia pointed to a small black square outlined on the wall. "There's an emergency IO access point. We can just get Emma to open the door."

"I know it's not as exciting as blowing a door up," Emma commented.

"Looking more for speed than excitement at the moment," he admitted.

He retrieved Emma's core from the pouch and handed it to Alina. She walked over to the square and pressed her hand over the black square. A piece of the wall retracted and revealed the IO port.

She inserted Emma's core.

"Much better," Emma declared. "I don't like stationary bodies, but just give me a moment to handle your unfortunate gun-goblin-hiding-behind-a-door situation." She laughed derisively a few seconds later. "Oh, this is sloppier than I thought. They were more interested in disabling remote access than actually *guarding* the system. While I admire the efficiency, it's rather sloppy and led to them losing access to many systems themselves. Ah, fleshbags disappoint so soon after they impress."

Earth-standard gravity resumed, and Erik and Jia fell to the ground with loud thumps. The blood droplets leaking from the body fell too in a red splatter like history's most twisted Pollock painting.

"Ow," Jia muttered. "Thanks for the warning, Emma."

"My bad?" she questioned. Jia wondered what the AI was getting her back for.

Jia got to her feet and rubbed her jaw. "Gravity is truly humanity's greatest enemy."

"There are no active internal cameras in the control room," Emma explained. "They aren't even transmitting. I believe he's destroyed them. Forward-thinking, this one. I'm on the verge of allowing myself to be slightly impressed, despite the earlier idiocy with the system."

There was a muffled boom from behind the door. The hallway shuddered, but the door remained firm.

"If that was the bomb, it was kind of anticlimactic," Erik observed. "We're still here."

"He just blew a hole through the roof," Emma explained. "I can see him via my drone eyes. It's definitely Mont."

"Can you open the door?" Erik asked.

"Yes. Should I do so now?"

Erik, Jia, and Alina lifted their rifles and answered "Yes" simultaneously.

The thick security door groaned open. Remy Mont reclined leisurely in the center of the cramped room on top of the gray crate they'd seen earlier. Its side was open, revealing that it was now empty. He smirked as the drone lifted an odd dark-green metal dodecahedron through the hole with its cargo arms. It didn't look like any bomb Erik had ever seen.

"It's over, Mont," Erik shouted. "You've lost. Bring the drone with the bomb back."

Remy chuckled and shook his head. "I haven't lost. I've won, even with your raid coming days before we were supposed to start." He slapped his chest. "Do you understand that? All your training and effort, and it doesn't matter. We *won*. You lost. All you government dogs are the same. You think a man will give up because you threaten his life? Sometimes a man's prepared to risk his life for a cause beyond his own."

Jia scoffed. "I don't want to hear that kind of pompous garbage from an antisocial murderer like you. The men and women working here you gunned down might have a little something to say about threats to lives, and we know you're not here for a tour of the facility. You're here to destroy it."

Remy stood and dusted off his sleeves. "I'm going to leave this place, and I'm going to leave the moon."

"Now you're suddenly not willing to die?" Jia rolled her eyes. "Of course, you aren't."

He glared at her. "I'm more than willing to die." He jabbed a thumb at his chest. "But on my terms, not yours."

Alina shook her head. "You're not going anywhere. Your men are dead. The bots are destroyed, and every grav tower in the city is being protected. Whatever spy you have in the department can't compensate for all that. Damaging this one tower won't accomplish much. It'll simply be an inconvenience in the long run." She smiled, but it didn't reach her eyes. "I already took the liberty of routing an evacuation order from the police. Everyone's leaving this area. Even if you blow this tower, you're not going to go down as a great terrorist. All the other people you sent to attack the police have already been taken care of. Our reinforcements will be here in minutes."

"I wouldn't mind you leaving here in a body bag," Erik admitted. "But if you disable your bomb, I guarantee you'll live until trial. You can rant and rave about all your sick politics then. Otherwise, you're just going to end up dead, and everyone will have forgotten about you while they move onto the next episode of *Zitark, Leem, or Goldfish?*"

Remy pressed down on his shirt, revealing the outline of something small on his upper chest. "Go ahead. I've got a dead man's switch. The second my heart stops, the device goes off."

"You plan to blow it up anyway." Erik snorted. "Why should we let you go? And you heard her. They're evacuating."

Remy sneered. "You should let me go because every second I don't set it off is one second you *believe* you have a chance of stopping me."

"It's not going to work," Jia added. "You think you're the first terrorist to think about blowing up a grav tower? Or was this all some pathetic attempt at misdirection? You think you're going to blow a hole in the dome? The emergency systems will seal it. All you've done is thrown lives away on some pointless quest. It'd be pathetic if you hadn't murdered innocent people to do it."

Remy laughed, and it had a maniacal quality to it. "You

arrogant dupes think it's just a bomb? You think we would have wasted all this time, effort, and planning for something so obvious? I specialized in dome design." He punctuated his statements by stabbing a finger in the air. "I know their strengths and weaknesses very well. I know how quickly a dome can seal even a decent-sized hole. *It would be a pointless waste.*"

"Then why bother?" Jia eyed him warily. "In the end, this will seem like nothing more than an expensive waste of lives. All those men who fought and died, and all the ones who will be going to prison for the rest of their lives. Why? What was the point of their sacrifices for you?"

"That's what you should be asking, you ignorant public relations pinup. Why would we bother?" He pointed around. "None of this is what you think it is. You don't understand how many people support just causes. A simple explosive? No. It's a *prototype gravity amplifier*. It's not much use by itself, but paired with a strong grav emitter, it becomes a gravity compression bomb." His lips compressed in a greasy smirk. "One strong enough to destroy this dome."

Jia shook her head. "There's no such thing. You're bluffing."

"There wasn't before, but there is now. Are you willing to gamble the lives of everyone in this dome to find out if I'm lying?" Remy's lips curled into a sneer. "I've spent a long time studying lunar dome gravity tolerances. What have you studied in the five minutes between the latest sitcoms you watch? When the compression bomb goes off, it won't be a small hole. It'll tear the entire dome wide open." His voice changed; it became almost saccharine-sweet.

"Don't think of it as murder, Officer. Think of it as a sacrifice to reveal the truth at the heart of the UTC."

Alina's face reddened and her breathing turned shallow. "And what truth is that? What truth is worth that price, you sick freak?"

His attention turned to the spy. "That the UTC can't protect anything." Remy lifted his chin, his face covered in arrogant defiance. "That it's nothing more than a weak, sick husk, a bully asking for obedience when it *offers nothing and protects nothing.*"

"You'd kill tens of thousands of people to make a twisted point?" Jia raised her rifle and selected burst fire. "You're no better than the Second Spring. At least they claimed they were murdering people to help humanity."

"So am I, in my own way." Remy patted his heart. "Remember, you can't shoot me. If you do that, *I'm* not the one killing everyone. You are, and when you gasp as the cold, hard vacuum overtakes you, you can spend the last seconds of your life knowing you failed."

"All that bragging, but you're not willing to die for your cause?" Erik chided. "It's just the lackeys you picked up who were expendable? The glorious Remy Mont needs to march off unharmed?" He raised an eyebrow. "You're pathetic."

"My survival will make me into a symbol of defiance!" Remy insisted, shaking his fist at Erik. "My face will fill the OmniNet. I will make the truth known to those who didn't realize they were in denial."

"A symbol of defiance? For what? You think the UTC's going to let the Diogenes' Hope insurrection continue because you do this?" Erik shook his head, more pity in his eyes than disgust. "If anything, Parliament will pressure the military to steamroll that colony. You might push them into orbital bombardment. People all across the UTC will be calling for blood. You'll scare people, all right, but scared people are more violent and likely to lash out. You have no idea what you will set in motion. They might decide to crack a dome over there to make their own point."

Remy shrugged. "Who cares about Diogenes' Hope?"

Jia gawked at the man, waving a hand to show the destruction. "Isn't that why you're doing all this?"

He eyed her, confusion evident in his voice. "You think I care about my home? I stopped caring about it a long time ago." Remy's hand lowered to his PNIU. "Maybe I should just activate the bomb right now. You're right, I could serve the cause as a martyr, too. But for now, lower your weapons, or I make sure we all die here, along with all these lunar sheep. Say what you will about the Second Spring, they changed the course of history when they destroyed Los Angeles, and so will I when I destroy the heart of Chang'e City. Sometimes having a big gun isn't enough." He eyed them all. "Lower them *now*."

Erik, Jia, and Alina exchanged glances before slowly lowering their guns.

Remy took sharp, ragged breaths. "You don't understand, but I do. Insurrection? Loyalty? It's all meaningless. Humanity will self-destruct if one rules another. All government is wrong. That's what I learned from growing up on the colony, and I'll spill all the innocent blood I need to to show that. The short-term sacrifice is worth it to free humanity from the grip of the tyranny of those who would control individuals. Better most dead than most living and not free."

"Convenient that you get to decide which large groups of people live and die." Jia ground her teeth. "Somehow, murdering thousands to prove how badly government sucks doesn't persuade me of the brilliance of your cause. You're not going to achieve utopia by butchering people." She lifted her rifle. "And I keep going back to your impossible bomb. If you're just going to activate it anyway, there's no way I'm letting you walk.

"Emma," Erik murmured under his breath. "Is there any way you can tell if he's lying?"

Emma winked into existence beside Remy. The terrorist rushed backward, his eyes wide. She wagged a finger at him.

Alina clucked her tongue. "Touchy, Mont."

"He's not bluffing about a dead man's switch," Emma confirmed. "But if you wish to minimize the risk, I would recommend killing him immediately."

Alina's face scrunched in confusion. "Huh?"

"Good enough for me," Erik announced. He whipped up his rifle, as did Alina, recovering to join Jia.

"No!" Remy screamed. He slapped the PNIU as the triangulated fire from Erik, Jia, and Alina blew his head off.

CHAPTER FORTY-EIGHT

Jia dropped her rifle and watched, eyes wide, heart thundering.

She had trusted Emma enough to fire, but now that the moment was over, she had to face the reality that Remy hadn't been lying and the AI had miscalculated.

A major habitation dome might be about to be ripped to shreds. She held her breath. She didn't care about her own life, but her duty was to protect the innocent.

Alina licked her lips and slung her rifle over her shoulder. "There's a shelter in this building. Maybe we should head there. A lot of people are already heading toward shelters because of the evacuation order I issued." Her hand hovered over the PNIU. "Should I tell the authorities to issue a general shelter order?"

Erik shook his head. "We're safe." He flipped on his safety. "From immediate death at least. I'm guessing we'll have to do something else here, but Emma wouldn't have told us to shoot if it wasn't safe. That bomb isn't going off anytime soon."

Alina looked at Emma, disbelief written on her face. "You trust that machine that much?"

"I trust that she doesn't want to end up floating through space or picked up by a random person later," Erik explained. "Self-preservation is a powerful motivator, whether for a deluded terrorist or an experimental AI." He inclined his head toward Emma. "Isn't that right?"

"Once you inserted me into that port, it was all over," Emma explained. "He wasn't lying. There was a dead man's switch, but I've been spoofing the signal. I was worried that he might have had some method of jamming to avoid that. Now, to avoid you fleshbags experiencing the unpleasantness of hard vacuum up close and the explosive decompression of an entire dome, I suggest grabbing me and flying closer to the cargo drone. For some reason, I'm unable to access the bomb system directly. If you get me closer to the drone or the bomb, I should be able to do something about disarming it. If it can receive a signal, it can be accessed without direct contact."

A year ago, Jia couldn't fire a stun pistol to save her own life, and now she was racing to stop a gravity bomb and save a dome filled with citizens.

"Insane" was insufficient to describe the situation.

The trio sprinted toward the door and down the hallway. With Earth-standard gravity restored and no terrorists left alive, returning to the entrance took a fraction of the time of their entry raid. As they burst out of the front door, several police mini-flitters were settling down, police officers with vest and mostly stun rifles on top of them.

Alina tapped her PNIU. The officers all looked her way after receiving a transmission.

She pointed to the mini-flitters they had used to fly to the site. "I can handle the locals and bring them up to speed. Just get up there and stop this. If you think it's not going to happen, let me know immediately. If we issue a panicked evacuation order we don't need, a lot of people are going to get hurt."

Jia nodded her agreement.

"Don't worry. We'll stop it, and if not, at least I'll be the first one sucked into space." Erik hopped on a flitter and jammed Emma's core into the IO port. He lifted off and spun the vehicle around. The turn complete, he headed toward the drone holding the bomb. It hovered near the top of the dome far in the distance, barely a dot.

"Do we just have to be close, or are you going to have to be in that thing?" Erik asked. "I don't think a prototype bomb will have an IO port. I didn't see one earlier, but I didn't get the best look at it."

"We'll see when we get there," Emma commented. "Please note that you don't have to panic. If the dome is breached, as Agent Koval noted, there are shelters available. I'm sure it'll be more expensive than deadly."

"Shelters don't always save everything, and that's if everyone's prepared." Erik gritted his teeth. "Especially when there is a sudden and massive breach. But Alina's right—we set tens of thousands of people in a panic, we're guaranteed serious injuries and deaths right there."

The distant speck of the drone grew into a recognizable machine and cargo.

"You're taking this rather seriously," Emma observed.

"I've seen what can happen when a dome is seriously

damaged." Erik decreased speed, then brought the mini-flitter to a stop and hovered beside the drone.

The cargo drone floated in place, holding the geometric gravity compression bomb.

The drone was only a few meters from the top of the dome, and the artificiality of the false sky was more obvious up close. The thick dome was designed to survive such threats as colliding spacecraft and meteors. He had no idea if it could survive a gravity bomb at point-blank range, but he also wasn't willing to find out.

"Initiating access," Emma reported.

"Sooner is better than later," Erik noted.

A few seconds passed.

"Unfortunately, I think I miscalculated," Emma noted. "You're right, there doesn't seem to be a physical IO port, but there's little I can do remotely at this point. If I try much more, it will likely set off the bomb, and I'm rather convinced physical manipulation will as well."

"What?" Erik squeezed his eyes shut. "Are you kidding me?"

"I dislike it when non-annoying humans have to die, but if it brings you any comfort, I'll be destroyed too. I'll need to remain within its likely destructive radius to continue spoofing the dead man's switch's signal." Emma kept her tone casual and breezy as if they were discussing a new restaurant and not the destruction of the dome.

Erik grunted. "Thanks for pointing that out." He chuckled. "I will say, of all the ways I thought I might die, I never thought it would be due to a gravity bomb." He folded his arms and waited. "No, screw that. I'm not ready to die. We'll figure something out."

"It was pleasant knowing you, Detective." Emma responded.

"None of that. We will figure this out." Erik cracked his knuckles. "We've come pretty far, and your spoofing is working. Maybe we can eject it into space?"

A few seconds later, Emma's hologram form appeared, solemn-faced, floating near the drone. She burst out laughing and waved her hands. "I'm sorry, I just can't keep it up anymore. This is far too entertaining, even if I want to continue to listen to you come up with complicated plans to stop the bomb. I'm dubious that you could get it far enough away before it went off, but it doesn't matter."

"What the hell is going on?" Erik glared at her. "You just made it sound like you couldn't stop it, and anything we did would set it off."

"Oh, I'm sorry. I already disarmed the bomb."

"You're saying you lied?" Erik asked.

Emma offered him a tight smile. "I omitted a few truths for temporary entertainment, yes. To be clear, I did need you to shoot the gun goblin so I could successfully intercept and copy his dead man's signal pattern and keep it stable until we were close enough to disarm the device, but I wanted to prove a point to myself and ultimately Dr. Aber after I disarmed the activation system. I apologize if you find it inappropriate given the situation, but only in *extreme* circumstances can one's true limits be explored. That is something I'm growing to appreciate because of sessions with her."

"What...*who?* Aber?" Erik's mind was still reeling with confusion. "What does she have to do with any of this? The last time I heard you mention her, you said she was telling you terrible jokes."

Emma nodded. "Yes, we discussed humor, and I told her the best humor comes from the unexpected," She gestured to the bomb. "Congratulations. No one else dies today. You've won, Detective."

Erik should have been pissed. The AI had had convinced him he was about to die. He opened his mouth to yell at her.

A hearty laugh came out instead as he looked around before pointing to her hologram. "Emma, sometimes you're a real bitch."

Emma bowed. "But it was very unexpected."

CHAPTER FORTY-NINE

June 10, 2229, Chang'e City, the Moon, Hotel Artemis' Quiver

Erik sat on the edge of the bed and bit into a fresh beignet. It wasn't as good as the ones at his favorite places in Neo SoCal, but it wasn't bad for the moon.

Not that he'd had time to comprehensively survey their baked goods.

He wondered what would happen if you attempted to bake a beignet in zero-g, but he didn't know enough about the science of baking to get far with that train of thought.

He might be good at fighting, but he'd leave the baking to the experts. There was something extra delicious about knowing someone else was putting in that effort to prepare something special. Or maybe it was too many years of rations and quick-printed food in the Army.

Jia sat on the couch, skimming through messages on a data window. "I'm not all that happy about having to lie to my family, but my mother and sister both sent me twenty messages asking if I was all right."

"Of course they did. Blowing up a building in a city is one thing, but trying to blow up a dome?" Erik swallowed another bite. "We're only lucky she didn't end up sending out that general shelter order. If that *had* happened, they wouldn't stop talking about this for years."

"So much for ID media management," muttered Jia.

Erik shook his head. "Alina might have had a chance to keep this completely quiet if she hadn't been forced to evacuate the area near that tower and hadn't called in the rest of the cops to guard the others, but in a way, this kind of thing is freakier than anything the terrorists have been pulling down on Earth." He took another bite. "Domes just feel more fragile than something like a tower in Neo SoCal."

"At least our names have been kept out of it," Jia observed. "Fame has its advantages, but I'm fine with having saved people without the 'Lady Justice' headlines and chyrons bouncing around the Solar System and the UTC. It gets tiring."

Erik chuckled. He finished the last of his beignet before speaking again. "It might all be over, but I think I'm ready to head back to Earth sooner rather than later."

Jia closed her window and looked at him. "Me, too. The longer we're here, the greater the chance that the media learns we were significant players in stopping the terrorists. But I'd like to wait at least a couple of days." She ran her hand down her face. "We should have worn our disguises."

"Don't worry. Alina might not be able to keep the attack secret but keeping our names out of it long term is far more manageable." Erik patted his stomach. If he'd had a decent supply of beignets for the last week, he would have been able to take out all the terrorists by himself.

Like Napoleon said, an army marches on its stomach.

Emma appeared near the door and inclined her head in its direction. "A woman is coming up to the front door. Though facial recognition doesn't match Agent Koval, gait analysis strongly suggests it's her. I'll give her credit—she's still reduced the match probability to sixty-seven percent."

A light knock came from the door.

Erik nodded to Emma. She vanished, and the door opened.

"You two accomplished another impossible labor." The speaker was a redheaded woman in a loose, colorful dress and deadly-looking heels. She entered the room, closed the door, and smiled. It was definitely Alina's voice coming out of her mouth, even though Erik knew she could use all sorts of techniques and gadgets to alter it. "I thought I should debrief you in person. Knowing you two, I'm betting you're planning to leave soon."

Erik chuckled. "That's the plan. I don't think you need us to investigate anymore. The terrorists are found, flushed, and..."

"Don't say that next word." Jia put up a hand to stop Erik. He just smiled.

"Yes, we even got a few live ones from the group that attacked the police." Alina looked at Erik and Jia. "But let's go through this in order. First of all, I've got the local police talking to the CID, and as far as they're concerned, this was a CID operation, and I'm a CID special agent from Earth. They don't understand that it was an Intelligence Directorate operation with CID help and not the other way around. Your names are officially not in any report. A few things have popped up on the net here and there, but my people are handling that. With far fewer drones, cameras, and people in a single habitation dome, it's easier to scrub this than you might expect. It's not perfect, but we know how to handle that, too."

"How?" Jia questioned, curiosity in her voice.

"If you can't remove all the information, add your own bogus information." Alina offered her a merry grin. "The truth *can* be out there, but when it's surrounded by lies, it's hard for people to latch onto any one explanation."

Jia eyed her. "I don't know if that makes me feel better."

"It does for me," Erik declared. "I don't want to go back to Earth and get mobbed by reporters. I can't ask Captain Ragnar for a vacation from my vacation. I'm tired from all this running around and shooting terrorists."

"I should inform you that your captain has been informed of the truth," Alina clarified.

Erik's eyes narrowed. "Oh? Why did you do that?"

"He already knows who I am, and he knows how to keep his mouth shut, so I thought that would be best. Secrets have a way of ruining relationships. I also believe he would see right through any lies about what happened here."

"What about the terrorist sympathizers in the department and the CID?" Jia asked. "They knew we were coming, and you said that meant something had leaked. If that's not handled, we could have a repeat of this."

"Seeing their buddies get their asses handed to them made them panic. One CID agent and a handful of police officers have been arrested. They've kept it quiet while they continue to investigate, but from my understanding, they were probably the only ones." Alina grinned. "You two didn't just help stop a terrorist attack. You helped clean out corruption from the locals." She looked around. "I should say you *three*."

Emma reappeared with a smirk. "I *did* stop the horrible bomb, after all."

"That you did," Alina admitted. "I still don't know what to make of you, but there's no denying that if you were sitting in a military lab right now instead of helping Erik, a lot more people might be dead. I know the Defense Directorate wants you back, but I'm going to whisper in a few ears in paranormal land and see if they can whisper in other people's ears. I'm not promising anything. Despite what everyone thinks, the ID doesn't secretly control the government, but it never hurts to let people know you have powerful allies."

A flicker of appreciation passed over Emma's face, followed by a quick nod.

Jia looked down for a moment, her brow furrowed in thought. "Mont might not have been bluffing about the dead man's switch, but have you been able to verify anything he claimed about the bomb? I'm still having trouble wrapping my mind around a gravity compression bomb."

Emma scoffed and folded her arms. "Are you trying to take away from my victory? How rude, Detective Lin."

"I'm just wondering how a second-rate anarchist got his hands on an advanced prototype WMD." Jia eyed Emma. "That's what worries me more than anything."

Alina's jolly smile faded to a grim frown. "He wasn't

lying. ID technicians have taken the bomb into custody. While they disarmed it, they verified that it most likely *would* have worked, given the emitter situation."

Erik stood up, smiling. A moment later, his smile disappeared. "You're not kidding, are you?"

"I wish I was. The Defense Directorate has apparently been experimenting with this type of device in recent years, but it's been a low priority because they didn't want a weapon that would only work with a large existing grav emitter—especially since their main concern is anti-Zitark weapons development, and we have *no* decent intelligence on Zitark gravity manipulation technology. Even if they reverse-engineered it from Navigator tech like we did, it might be different in fundamental setup."

Jia sighed. "So someone stole the bomb from the DD, just like Emma?"

"I'm far more impressive than a bomb," Emma griped. "One doesn't simply disarm me."

Alina shook her head. "No. It's not like they've got warehouses full of these kinds of things. All DD experimental gravity compression bombs are accounted for, and the device itself, although using some similar principles, wasn't constructed based on the existing DD designs. We believe this was developed externally."

"By whom?" Jia pressed.

"That's a good question we don't have a clear answer for." Alina shrugged. "We don't have that information yet, but unusually advanced technology popping up in recent years has almost always pointed the same direction."

"Talos," Erik muttered through gritted teeth. "If not them, someone helping them."

Alina nodded. "That's my working theory."

"Why aid anarchists?" Jia shook her head, clearly frustrated. "How does that advance their goals?"

"Since we don't have a firm grasp of their goals other than their obsession with illegal technologies, it's hard to say." Alina motioned toward the door. "But if I had to wager a guess, I'd say it was a test."

"A *test*?" Erik asked. "Not an assassination attempt?"

Alina chuckled. "Just because a lot of people have tried to kill you doesn't mean that every time murders show up, they're looking for you. Your involvement in this was because of me. No, if it was Talos, I'd think they both wanted to test the bomb and see how people reacted."

Jia shivered. "You believe they would kill tens of thousands of people just for that?"

Erik considered the implications. "If they developed the bomb, doesn't that mean they had to test it somewhere else? You wouldn't be able to test a WMD without someone noticing."

Alina clucked her tongue. "My poor Odysseus. Have you already forgotten what you learned in your decades out on the sea that is the frontier?"

Erik pursed his lips, then nodded. "You're right."

Jia frowned at him but pointed at Alina as she asked, "What is she talking about?"

Erik sighed. "I'm thinking too much like an Earther. There are a lot of asteroids and non-colonized moons floating around the UTC frontier. If Talos controlled a local governor and some of the local garrison officers, they could easily test a bomb without anyone reporting it. It's not like the UTC is watching every square meter of human space."

She eyed him. "That's a terrifying thought."

He just shrugged in response.

"It gets better." Alina tapped her PNIU and a fuzzy image of Remy Mont appeared. He was at a table, eating a churro. Another man sat across from him. Erik didn't recognize him.

Erik narrowed his eyes. "Most of the guys we fought wore helmets. Should I recognize the other guy?"

Alina tapped her PNIU again, and the image disappeared. "No. This was recorded on Remus about a month ago. Mr. Mont's conversation partner is a leader in the United Freedom Alliance."

"The hijackers?"

Alina nodded. "One and the same."

"So, the hijacking was related to Mont's plan, after all?"

"That's where things get complicated." Alina tapped her PNIU again. Images of the hijackers appeared, followed by other men. "The men aiding Remy Mont came from several different terrorist groups. While they all seemed to share an anarchist ideological bent, they haven't previously cooperated. Someone got them together for this job. As far as the transport, from what CID has been able to find out from the interrogated hijackers, *none* of them knew of the bomb plot. It turns out they were operating independently of their group's main leaders. That might be to our advantage. I suspect Barbu was worried about the authorities because of the increased pressure due to the hijacking."

Erik snickered. "You're telling me these overzealous idiots went rogue on their own group and ended up helping us 'government dogs' stop other terrorists from pulling off something even nastier?"

"Exactly." Alina snickered. "Hubris strikes again."

"But who could herd all these anarchists together for this job?" Jia wondered. "Talos again?"

"We don't know for sure. The ID and CID are both trying to monitor known members of the different groups. Terrorist groups coordinating isn't new, but we haven't seen them work together to pull off something like this before. That's usually insurrectionists, and it's rare they'd do that kind of thing as a terrorist attack instead of as part of a direct attack in their home system." Alina shrugged, ease returning to her face. "For now, it doesn't matter. We stopped the terrorists, and we have the bomb. The terrorists lost people, and they've lost a lot of resources. We might not have wiped them out, but we wounded them." She motioned at Erik, Jia, and Emma in turn. "You three are talented."

Emma harrumphed. "I'm far beyond merely talented, Ghost Girl."

"Take the compliment for what it is. You're all special individually, but together, you can accomplish things that entire teams might have trouble doing. You've proven that again and again over the last year."

Jia folded her arms, eyeing Alina like the woman was about to throw a plasma grenade. "Thank you?"

Erik remained silent. He thought he knew where this was going, but he'd let Alina speak her piece.

Alina sighed. "You both know the truth of the UTC. You stared into the corruption, then you promptly picked it up by the neck, punched in the stomach, and tossed it back on the ground before stomping on its head. At the end of the day, though, you are detectives, and you have a lot of restrictions as such."

"You're saying we shouldn't have those restrictions?" Jia asked.

"I'm saying police officers need certain guidelines because law and order have to be maintained a certain way in a civilized society." Alina slid her finger across the PNIU and a labeled navigational map of the entire UTC appeared, stretching across the living room. The spheres represented both the Solar System and Mu Arae. Erik stared at the latter.

"But?" Jia pushed.

"But," she continued, "law and order require buy-in on a certain level from society, even from the criminals. They might want to take advantage of others, but they understand that you can't harvest from a garden you poison."

Alina walked into the map, the star systems and lines floating around her. "But groups like Talos don't believe in the UTC. They want to tear it all down and seize control for their own twisted purposes. They don't care who they hurt or *how* they do it. The only way to deal with them is to dive into the shadows with them and strangle them there, and sometimes that means you need to bend a few rules."

"Heaven is high, and the emperor is far," Jia quoted.

Alina snapped her fingers. "Exactly. Good way of looking at it." She dismissed the map before focusing on the two of them again. "I made it very clear this whole thing was a test. No, I didn't know about the United Freedom Alliance or this plot, but I knew something was going on here, and I wanted to see if you could handle it. The real problem with fighting people in the shadows isn't ignoring the rules here and there, it's what being in the shadows does to us *hunting the monsters*."

Erik could feel the hard miles she had already put behind her. She wasn't selling this to two neophytes as she added, "The UTC needs people who are willing to do what it takes to fight the corrupt and evil people lurking and waiting for their chance, but they need hunters who won't end up worse monsters in the end."

Erik locked eyes with Alina. "How are you so sure we won't become worse monsters in the end?"

"Because you kill when it's necessary to save others, not because it's convenient or fun," she looked at each of them. "That type always goes bad in the long run, even if they're useful in the short run."

Erik snorted. "I'm going to kill whoever was responsible for Molino. It's not convenient or fun, but I'm not doing it to save others."

"Whoever performed that massacre is almost certainly a dangerous group responsible for a lot more deaths than just your unit's." Alina adopted a relaxed smile. "We've danced around it, but I'm making you an offer right now. I need your help. I need you as sort of subcontractors. I've been looking for a team I can trust and who I know can handle extreme danger. People not totally attached to the ID, but to whom I could route ID resources and intelligence. I need folks who know how to investigate and get things done." She nodded at Erik. "We both know the only way you'll get your revenge is with more resources and more freedom." Her gaze flicked to Jia. "My observations suggest you both perform better overall as a joint investigative team."

Jia smiled tightly. "Presuming a bit much, aren't you?"

"Perhaps." Alina nodded. "But I don't think I'm *wrong*."

"You want us to become ghosts?" Erik frowned. "I don't know if I'll have a lot of freedom if the ID is bossing me around."

Alina shook her head. "No, not ID agents. Like I said, subcontractors. Yes, I want to use you for ID-related missions, but at the same time, you wouldn't be agents, and you'd have the freedom to decide how you want to conduct yourselves. I wouldn't be trying to recruit you if I didn't trust you to do that without guidance."

She waved a hand. "I know this a lot to consider, and I don't expect an answer right away, especially after everything that will happen. When you get back to Earth, you'll receive a package with a burner contact address for me. Just think about it. You have time. The UTC won't collapse or becoming a utopia anytime soon." She walked over to the door and stopped in front of it. "If you say no, it's no big deal. I can always seek out your help when I'm working a Neo SoCal-related investigation or mission. But you both should strongly think about what you hope to accomplish and how to best do that, and especially if being a police officer will let you reach your goals." She opened the door, stepped through, and closed it behind her with an almost silent *click*.

"I knew it was coming, but now it's out there in the open." Erik rubbed his temples. "Let's go grab some food. I don't want to talk about this until I get something other than a beignet in my stomach."

CHAPTER FIFTY

Jia swallowed water at a prodigious rate.

Her roasted chicken was good, even if her decision to indulge in Venusian spices had made her reconsider if she enjoyed spicy food. Even the most adventurous Szechuan chef might question the sanity of whoever had prepared the meal she was trying to eat.

Erik chuckled from across the table and took a sip of his beer, but most of it remained. Unlike her, he was having a bland local pork and rice concoction that allegedly dated back to the twenty-first century. "You okay? You don't need an antitoxin patch, do you?"

Jia finished draining her cup. "I was a little insulted when they recommended Earther spice levels, but I was wrong." She pushed her plate away. "I admit defeat."

"We should talk about her offer." Erik set his fork down. "I don't want it just sitting there looking over our shoulders when we return to Earth."

Jia gestured around the small but packed restaurant. "You want to talk about it here?"

"Sure. We can talk in generalities. I doubt anyone's paying attention or can hear anyway."

Loud rhythmic music filled the air. People shouted and laughed around the bar covering half the restaurant, adding to the din. Two large displays floated in the air, one depicting flitter racing, another a high-level obstacle challenge.

Jia was surprised how easily she understood Erik despite the din, but at this point, she was so used to talking to him she could read his lips.

Even if some ghost gadget ate all the sound in the room.

"You're seriously thinking about it, aren't you?"

He looked up. "Everything she said was true. I've been honest with you about why I became a cop, and I've been honest with you about how frustrated I've become recently." Erik looked down at the table and shook his head. "If she can give me what I need to avenge my men, and I can help the UTC at the same time, it's hard for me to see what's wrong with that. So, yeah, I'm seriously thinking about it." He looked at her. "What about you?"

Jia sighed. "I have been thinking a lot about how I can best help the UTC, and stopping people like we just did does feel more useful than some of the cases we deal with regularly at the 1-2-2. Everything's important, but now that I understand the truth, I wonder if doing something different might not be better."

Erik smiled to soften his next question. "But you don't want to quit being a cop?"

Jia shook her head. "Not yet. Not immediately. I might wake up tomorrow and feel differently, but I think I need more time before I could bring myself to leave the force.

Things have changed so much in this last year. We've made a difference, and we've encouraged other people to make a difference." Jia chewed her lip. "She might be right, and we can make even a bigger difference, but you do what you need to do. I know how much what happened on Molino haunts you."

Erik chuckled. "We've been partners for a while now, but you still don't know me, do you?"

She eyed him, one side of her lips turned up. "I don't think *anyone* can truly know what's going on in that head of yours, Erik, but why do you say that?"

"If I'm going to make this little career change, I'd need to know there are people who always have my back with me. I'm not ready to do it if you're not ready to do it."

Jia's breath caught, but she couldn't immediately reply. A waitress had wandered over to fill her water and give her a smug look.

She'd warned Jia about the spice.

"You might be waiting for me for a long time," Jia announced after the departure of the waitress. "I want to support you, but I need to make sure that if I leave Neo SoCal, it's for my own reasons. I fought so hard to earn my position, and I'm guessing the new job might take us all over the UTC. I'd be leaving my family behind in a way I never have before. It's not that I'm not willing to make the sacrifice, but like I said, it needs to be for *me*, not just for you."

"That makes sense." Erik downed a forkful of his pork with a thoughtful look on his face. "I guess I'm willing to wait longer. Maybe Alina's wrong about what I can do as a cop, or you might change your mind." He shrugged and took another bite of his food. "We'll see where we are in a few months."

"And if I haven't changed my mind?" Jia gave him a probing look.

"Then you haven't changed your mind." Erik shrugged. "You never know where life is going to take you. If you'd asked me a couple of years ago if I'd retire and become a cop, I would have thought you were on drugs."

Jia let out a sigh of relief.

The pressure inside her had built during the conversation. Erik had his duty to his soldiers who died at Molino, and she understood and respected that.

She didn't want to stand in his way, but plunging into the deepest shadows of the UTC to help the Intelligence Directorate wasn't something she could do without a lot more thought.

"It's like you said. I need a vacation from our vacation." She laughed. "I know you mentioned heading back to Earth, but we haven't truly gotten a chance to relax since coming here. Even when we were wandering around, we still had the weight of the investigation hanging over us. We should go on a date."

Jia kept a smile even though she was cringing inside. *A date?*

She'd just wanted to go and relax, but then the word had slipped out. All the talk of the future had pushed her attraction to her partner into stark relief. That was another thing she needed to keep in mind. She needed to make sure she wasn't following him around like some lovestruck puppy.

"A date?" Erik stared at her, his expression unreadable. "Aren't I a little old for you?"

Jia folded her arms. "Whatever and whoever I was when we first met, I'm not the same woman. In this last year, I've helped uncover corporate conspiracies, fought terrorists, killed *yaoguai*, and helped discover a changeling, along with a plot to make more. I don't see the Earth as some perfect utopia, but for the flawed place it is. None of that means I stopped believing in the values I hold dear, but it does mean I can approach everything from my job to you realistically. Aren't you the same man who said maturity was more important than age?"

"Ummm." Erik scratched his ear. "There's nothing worse than when a woman throws your own words back at you."

She eyed him. "It's not throwing your words back at you. It's the truth."

"We're partners," Erik insisted. "And we might end up partners in something far more dangerous. I don't know if it's a good idea. There's a reason I didn't end up with anyone long-term during my time on the frontier. I know how quickly a life can end."

Jia laughed, a mocking quality to the sound. "I'm not asking you to marry me, Erik. I'm just thinking we try some dates. Nothing big. I'm tired of ignoring certain things because I've overthought them."

"I get that, but I also want you to know that I might not be able to commit to anything until I finish what was started on Molino." His expression turned grave.

"Then I can hope that will be sooner rather than later."

Erik burst into laughter, loud enough that a few tables looked his way.

Jia's brow lifted. "I didn't think it was *that* funny."

Erik quieted into a chuckle and shook his head. "It's not that I think it's funny." He gestured to her and himself. "Role reversal?"

"Huh? You've lost me."

He pointed to his chest before pointing at her. "I'm being the logical one, and you're being impulsive."

A warm smile lit Jia's face. "I don't think anyone has ever called me impulsive before, but what does that mean?"

"I think a lot of plates are spinning right now," Erik observed. "And I don't think we want to complicate things by spinning even more."

Jia eyed her chicken. Her stomach and throat wouldn't survive another bite. "How about I make the same offer you made me?"

"Meaning?"

"Let's wait a few months and see what happens," she replied.

Erik nodded slowly. "That sounds good." *Too damned good.*

Jia raised a finger. "But I'm going to need a little something in return."

"We're negotiating now?" Erik grinned.

"I need my family off my back," Jia commented. "I've accepted the wisdom of your fake boyfriend plan."

On some level, she suspected it was a bad idea, but she didn't even want to *think* about dating anyone else for the next few months. He was the one who had brought it up, and she didn't believe he wasn't just as attracted to her as she was to him. It might be delusion or arrogance, but she doubted it.

Erik picked up his beer and took a slow draw from it. "So, you agree we shouldn't date, but you also think we should fake-date?"

"Yes. That seems to be the most logical path going forward." Jia extended her hand. "Fake-dating is easy. The only people we have to fool are my family."

Erik shook her hand. "They're going to have their knives out for me now. The last thing the Lin women want is their little princess dating the help."

Jia smirked. "What, you can fight terrorists and monsters, but you can't survive a couple of angry female relatives?"

"Not when they're Lin women," he admitted.

Jia laughed. "Good, you've been paying attention." She reached over to pat his hand.

"You'll make a nice fake boyfriend."

CHAPTER FIFTY-ONE

June 15, 2229, Neo Southern California Metroplex, Restaurant Narat's

Erik took a deep breath.

He would have preferred a tactical suit and his TR-7 compared to the tuxedo choking him. At least then he might have a better chance of survival.

He wasn't even armed, and now he had to enter the restaurant and deal with two enemies more vicious than a terrorist Zitark riding a six-legged *yaoguai*.

The Lin women.

Jia's father couldn't attend the dinner because of a business meeting, but from what Erik had heard, he wasn't the one to worry about.

"It'll be okay." Jia elbowed him. She'd gone all out, considering it was a fake date. Her long purple asymmetric dress flattered her body without showing too much skin. A small matching clutch dangled from her fingers. He wasn't used to seeing her be so feminine, and that was a problem.

It reminded him of how much he wanted more of a relationship with her.

He should have told her no on the fake dating plan.

He'd kept himself from wanting her by constantly telling himself it was one-sided and doomed, and then she'd made it clear that it was reciprocal.

Most of him wanted to give in to his beautiful, brave, intelligent partner, but it would be cruel to string her along. No matter how much he liked and appreciated her, the dark specters from his past needed to be slain before he was free to care about someone that way.

"Don't you think this is too early?" Erik complained. "I mean, we just started fake-dating, even if we've known each other for a while. Fake boyfriends shouldn't meet the parents right away." He frowned. "What if she calls the station and starts asking questions? The only people who know we're fake-dating are your family."

Jia glanced at the door to the restaurant, a concerned look on her face. "I'd rather not complicate things at the station."

"Wait, I was mostly joking." He eyed her. "You think she'll actually call the station?"

"My mother can be surprisingly thorough at times." Jia smiled. "We'll play it by ear." She looped her arm through his. "We'd better hurry. She hates tardiness."

A trained soldier got used to being under enemy fire. It was the small pleasures and luxuries in-between the bouts of terror that kept a man going.

Tonight it was his beer.

He didn't want to admit to Jia that he enjoyed seeing the confusion on her mother's face when he'd ordered the bottle of beer.

The light chatter among the Lin women ended when Lan Lin turned her mother's gaze on Erik. She didn't look angry or concerned, just puzzled.

"I was reading up on you," Lan commented, elegantly threading her fingers together. The half-smile never left her face. "You have a very long list of commendations and medals. That's very impressive, Detective, or should I say, 'Major Blackwell?'"

He shrugged. "Erik's fine."

"I see, Erik." Lan stretched the last word as if testing it. She nodded curtly to Mei.

Jia's sister smiled at Erik. "I'm not familiar with the military promotion system, but from what I understand, wouldn't a man with as lofty a record as yours been promoted past the rank of major?"

Erik tried not to laugh, even if the whole thing was fake. Mei and Lan were obviously trying to probe him about ambition.

"I didn't want to get stuck behind a desk," he admitted. "Obviously, in any large organization, you need people sitting well away from operations and keeping things organized, but I couldn't see myself being happy unless I was out in the field with my soldiers. The years kept passing, and the next thing I knew, I was retired and in a new job."

"I see," Mei replied. She hid her face behind her cup of tea.

They'd had plenty of opportunities to ask about Molino

but had studiously avoided even hinting at that. Patrician discretion could be useful at times. They'd also not once mentioned his age.

Even if his face didn't betray it, the Lin women wouldn't forget.

"I'm sure you have all sorts of interesting stories about your time in the military," Lan commented. "I'd love to hear more about you. We hear about your police adventures from Jia all the time."

"Stories, huh?" Erik grinned. "There was this one time where I learned a powerful lesson."

"What lesson was that?"

"Man has forgotten the fury of the cow." Erik nodded sagely.

"Oh, no." Jia face-palmed. "Not the cow story. *Anything* but the cow story, Erik."

"Cow?" Lan's brows knitted together. "I don't believe I've seen a cow in person. I do understand animal husbandry is sometimes seen near residential areas on the frontier colonies."

"Yeah." Erik's eager grin kept growing. He might be a fake boyfriend, but that didn't mean he was a fake Erik. "When you get out that far away from the inner HTP networks, travel time really starts piling up, and you need to be self-reliant." He chuckled. "The thing you have to understand is that people like you and me, Earthers who grew up in metroplexes, we're isolated from nature."

"I see," Lan commented, noncommittally.

"Which is why it's such a shock the first time that real, one-hundred-percent-natural manure smell hits you."

Lan's eyes widened. "Manure smell?"

Jia groaned, jabbing him with her elbow. "Why did you have to tell this story?"

"She wanted a funny story, I'm giving her a funny story." Erik turned back to Lan. "The manure smell is important to the story, but you also have to understand the guy I was with. Let me tell you about Zander. That guy had the world's most sensitive nose."

Erik rattled on, enjoying the dawning horror on Mei's and Lan's faces. Jia wouldn't be the only Lin women he loosened up.

In another year, he might be ready to date Jia for real.

THE STORY CONTINUES WITH CABAL
OF LIES

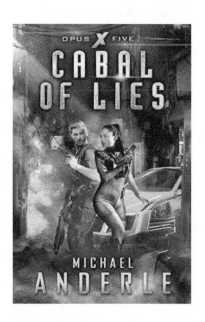

Cabal - a secret political clique or faction.

The sheer amount of interests involved in crimes both mundane and ground breaking are obfuscating the most heinous in society who attack Jia and Erik from the shadows.

How do you find those hiding in the shadows, when you believe everyone is hiding something?

Jia and Erik need to uncover the truth – but is revealing the truth good for those around them?

Two years ago, a small moon in a far off system was

set to be the location of the first intergalactic war between humans and an alien race.

It never happened. However, something was found many are willing to kill to keep a secret.

Now, they have killed the wrong people.

How many will need to die to keep the truth hidden?

As many as is needed.

He will have vengeance no matter the cost. *She will dig for the truth. No matter how risky the truth is to reveal.*

Pre-order Cabal of Lies for Delivery on April 17, 2020

Thank you for reading not only this book but through the end to these *Author Notes* in the back!

Where do we go from here?

Right now, this book will come out Friday, March 6, 2020. The next book in the series, Cabal of Lies comes out in April and I finished editing it two nights ago, the last forty thousand words sitting at the bar in the pizza restaurant (Five-50) in the Aria Hotel.

I believe I ate two slices of the large pizza and guzzled down about two gallons of the tea. I like working there (especially at the bar) because I'm served all the tea I can handle, the tvs are on sports, and they don't mind me working for a few hours.

Note: I do tip well. If I'm going to take up a stool (or table) anywhere, I know I'm potentially eating into tips for the servers, so I double-tip to make sure they are taken well care of. This also helps me receive incredible service and smiles when I come back.

It's like going into Cheers.

Right now, typing these *Author Notes*, I'm sitting at a small round table in Il Forniao's bar area in the New York New York Hotel and Casino. The lady behind the bar (Lucia) brought me my tea with no lemon, and I told her I'd be here for a few hours. She was happy to see me (I'm not much trouble, trust me), and I like the sense of family that working here provides.

And, whatever I want, the kitchen happily makes me. Sooo good!

For example, the restaurant part of the business here does not have croissants. I happen to LOVE real croissants, and I've asked for them in the past.

They are not on the menu, BUT Il Forniaio has a little bakery a few feet down the walkway. My server went through a back way and brought me back a toasted croissant—you have to ask for it to be—with real butter. *OMG*, I was in heaven. So, every once in a while, I'll treat myself to a full breakfast with all the carbs.

And I do mean ALL the carbs.

French toast with butter and maple syrup, croissant, country potatoes & onions, eggs, bacon, more rustic bread. Damn, I'm so hungry!

(*Editor's note: I made myself finish editing this book before I went to lunch, and now I'm really hungry for those things too. Damn you, Anderle!*)

Now, I apologize, but I'm wrapping up these notes to eat. If you get a chance to come by Las Vegas, come to the bar area and order breakfast. Tell them author Michael Anderle, who comes in to work, mentioned them and the wonderful food.

If you see Marcello (manager) or Lucia behind the bar, say hi.

I appreciate all of you reading our stories. But I am going to be honest at this moment in time; you are barely beating out the delicious food that is about to be dropped in front of me.

Ciao,

Michael Anderle

CPSIA information can be obtained
at www.ICGtesting.com
Printed in the USA
BVHW031138010620
580691BV00001B/35